A MOTHER'S VENGEANCE

The man writhed on the ground in pain and held his shoulder with his right hand, his eyes closed tightly. Yvonne stepped to the pistol, picked it up and looked down at him. His wounded horse screamed again, frantically flailing its legs in a losing effort to get to its feet. Yvonne cocked the pistol as she walked toward the horse, and, taking careful aim, shot it through the head. The dying animal fell onto its side, quivering, and the other horse lumbered away, retreating awkwardly with the hobbles on its front legs.

Yvonne turned and walked back to the man. His eyes were open and glazed with terror as he looked up at her. She smiled down at him.

The blood of her Cherokee mother pulsed strongly within her, demanding vengeance. And with her knowledge of the human body, she could devise tortures that would make him welcome death . . .

The Making of America Series

THE FRONTIER HEALERS

Lee Davis Willoughby

A DELL/BRYANS BOOK

Published by
Dell Publishing Co., Inc.
1 Dag Hammarskjold Plaza
New York, New York 10017

Dell ® TM 681510, Dell Publishing Co., Inc.

ISBN: 0-440-02608-3

Printed in the United States of America

First printing—May 1981

PART ONE

THE RIVER COUNTRY

1

THE RUMBLE of the wagon wheels on the dirt road and the rattle of the chains made a loud blur of sound that muffled other noises, almost smothering the stamp of the horse's hoofs in the trees and brush beside the road. But Yvonne heard it, and she stiffened, starting to react.

A man sprang out of the brush. The oxen's halter ropes were jerked out of her hand as his powerful arms wrapped around her in a crushing grip. She glimpsed his face and his exultant, triumphant smile. His eyes gleamed, and his teeth shone between his thick, black mustache and beard. Then her face was pressed into his rough tweed coat. He dragged her to the ground, a tall, brawny man whose massive strength effortlessly overpowered her resistance. Rocks ground into her back through her clothes as his shoulder pressed against her face, the odor of his coat and the stench of masculine sweat filling her nostrils.

Heavy boots clambered onto the wagon. Tangeree, Yvonne's daughter of fourteen, screamed shrilly in panic. The raw terror gripping Yvonne changed to seething, raging fury and fierce maternal protective-

6

ness, and she clawed at the man holding her, struggling to get free.

Concern for Tangeree was an urgent, clamoring imperative, slicing through her own fear, and Yvonne tried to lift her head to talk, to beg him and the other man to take her and leave Tangeree alone. The man lifted his head and glared down at her, his teeth clenched and his face flushed in animal passion. He held her down roughly, and stinging, blinding tears filled her eyes as she realized her helplessness. His shoulder pressed against her face again as his crushing weight pinned her to the ground, rocks jabbing into her back. She struggled to breathe as he tugged at her skirt, gathering it up around her waist.

Feet scuffled on the road a few yards away, and Yvonne heard Tangeree make small, subvocal sounds of panic as she struggled with the other man. Then Tangeree screamed again, the man laughed harshly, and there was the solid, meaty sound of a fist striking flesh as he hit her. Yvonne reacted automatically, digging at the face of the man who held her with her fingernails and trying to get free to go to Tangeree. The man slapped her, then gripped her hair and beat the back of her head against the road. She went limp, wavering on the edge of unconsciousness.

Tangeree wailed in a begging, pleading tone. The man laughed again, and fabric ripped as he tore at her clothes. The man on top of Yvonne had her skirt up around her waist, his knees pressing her thighs apart, and he gripped the front of her pantaloons and jerked at them in impatient haste, tearing them away from her. He slid his hands under her and dug his fingers into her as his full weight descended onto her, and he began thrusting rapidly.

Yvonne lay in a numb daze, unmoving and unresisting. His fingers gripped her flesh as he panted hoarsely and moved more rapidly, then he surged convulsively and finished. He lay on her for a moment, panting, then he rose and moved away, adjusting his clothes as he exchanged comments with the other man and laughed coarsely. Yvonne lay motionless with her eyes closed, feigning unconsciousness. The two men climbed into the wagon, and she could hear them prowling through the herb chests, bottles of dried herbs, and other things.

They talked, their tones disgusted at having found nothing of value to them, and they climbed back out of the wagon. Footsteps approached Yvonne, and she looked through a slitted eyelid. It was the other man, wearing tall boots instead of shoes. He kicked her legs wider with his toe, then lowered himself to his knees between her legs, opening his clothes and manipulating himself into an erection.

Tangeree moaned and whimpered. Yvonne almost opened her eyes and moved, but she controlled herself through an extreme effort of will. The man lowered himself onto Yvonne, then thrust into her. She heard Tangeree on the wagon cry out, and the man on her laughed with a humorless snarl. Yvonne controlled herself again, forcing herself to remain limp as the man lifted and pulled at her, driving into her.

Time slowly dragged by. Finally the men stood a few yards away and talked, but their words were unintelligible. Then one of them took the halter ropes on the oxen and led them off the road. The wagon wheels bumped over ruts, then crushed through brush and weeds, the sound becoming fainter. The other man moved around Tangeree for a moment, then walked toward Yvonne, dragging the girl. He put his toe under Yvonne's shoulder and flipped her over, tied her wrists with a piece of rope, then grasped the collar of her dress and dragged her and Tangeree across the road and through the brush the wagon had crushed down.

The man released Yvonne's collar, and she flopped limply in the deep grass, Tangeree rolling against her. As he moved away, Yvonne cautiously opened one eyelid. They were in a small clearing several yards off the road. The wagon was on the other side of the clearing, with the oxen standing patiently in their yoke. The man crossed the clearing and disappeared into the trees and brush. A moment later, the other man led two saddle horses into the clearing, tied them to a tree, and began taking the packs and weapons off the saddles. The one who had gone into the trees emerged with an armload of firewood and began building a fire.

They were both large men, dirty, ragged, and bearded, and the horses identified them positively. Other than the military forces, the only ones with horses or mules were renegades, those who ravaged the war-torn countryside in the backwash of the clashes between Union and Confederate forces, burning, raping, and murdering. Renegades were the danger Yvonne had feared most. Months before, when Union warships had come up the Mississippi and shelled Natchez, she and Tangeree had narrowly avoided meeting renegades several times during their flight along the heavily traveled roads north to Vicksburg. When the Confederate armies had begun massing at Vicksburg, she had remembered the experience. She had chosen the river road to continue their trip, a way that few traveled because the road was frequently inundated by spring floods. They had gone slowly along the road for three days and seen no one. The scattered houses along the road had been deserted, and there had been no recent tracks on the road. The peaceful days had brought a false sense of security.

Self-recrimination over the situation in which she had placed Tangeree was a gnawing agony in her mind. Yvonne pushed the thought away. Death was a certainty unless she and Tangeree could escape. The two men had unsaddled the horses, apparently intending to stay for at least a few hours. A double-barrel shotgun and a Henry rifle were leaning against a tree near the fire, and both of the men wore long, heavy Colt revolvers in holsters. They were arguing as they sat by the fire and cooked bacon and beans, and snatches of what they said were intelligible. It sounded as if one of them wanted to kill her and Tangeree when they left, and the other wanted to keep them for a few days.

Yvonne twisted her hands, pulling at the rope around her wrists. It was tied tightly and expertly, cutting off the circulation in her hands, and she couldn't loosen it. Tangeree was lying against her back. She felt for Tangeree's arm and tugged at it. There was no response. Yvonne tried to reach the knots on the ropes, steeling herself against the pain as the ropes cut into her skin and she groped blindly with her fingers, but she couldn't reach them. She relaxed, dull pain throbbing in her head, and tried to think of something to do.

Then she remembered the penknife Tangeree's father had given her before he left for the war. The girl kept it razor-sharp and used it for gathering herbs, and she carried it in her dress pocket. But it might have dropped out during her struggle with the men, or while they were being dragged to the clearing. Yvonne reached back and felt for Tangeree's skirt. She pulled it toward her and began gathering it in, feeling up and down it for the pocket. Tangeree was lying on folds of it, and it became taut. Yvonne tugged on it to pull it from under her. Tangeree moved, murmuring something in a soft whisper. Yvonne looked at the men. They were eating, and they hadn't heard. Yvonne tugged on Tangeree's skirt again, and it became slack, the folds sliding from under the girl. Her arms ached and her hands became clumsy from straining and reaching back in the awkward position as she continued gathering in the skirt. Then she felt the seam at the bottom of the pocket. There was a long, heavy lump in the pocket.

The top of the pocket was higher than she could reach, and she watched the men as she dug her heels in the ground and pushed herself along. One of the men put down his tin plate and rose, and Yvonne froze. He took a whiskey bottle from one of the packs and pulled the cork from it as he sat back down. Yvonne dug her heels in the ground again, pushing. Her fingers brushed the top of the pocket, and she wormed a hand down into it and took out the knife. She pulled at the blade with her thumbnail, opening it.

The men passed the whiskey bottle back and forth and talked quietly as Yvonne slashed at the rope with the knife. The point of the blade was like a needle, and it kept jabbing into her wrist and making her involuntarily drop the knife. Her hands became numb and unresponsive as the rope twisted tighter from her movements. She wriggled her hands until feeling returned, then continued sawing at the rope. Suddenly it went slack. Yvonne unwound the rope from around her wrists and flexed her fingers to restore the circulation in her hands.

One of the men lay back by the fire and rested his head on his saddle, tilting his hat over his eyes. The other man pushed the cork back into the bottle and put it aside as he lay back on his saddle.

There was a choice between two courses of action. Yvonne rubbed her wrists and looked at the men, pondering. She could free Tangeree and arouse her so they could escape, or she could attack. Raw, raging hate and a raving need for revenge seethed within her. She tried to force it out of her mind, to decide on the basis of what would be best for Tangeree. If they escaped, the men would search and might find them. If the men didn't find them, they would be far from any source of help and without the essentials for survival.

The shotgun was sixty feet away, the man nearest it was fifteen feet from it, and both of the men appeared to be asleep. The hobbled horses grazing a few yards from the men were a danger because they might stamp and snort if she frightened them. Yvonne decided. She picked up the knife, cut the rope from Tangeree's wrists, and pinched the girl's arm, whispering softly.

"Tangi! Tangi!"

The girl stirred and made a soft, querulous sound. Yvonne took the girl's arm and shook her.

"Tangeree! Answer me if you can hear me!"

Tangeree stiffened, then slowly relaxed. She replied in a quiet murmur, her voice sounding thick and groggy. "Yes, Ma . . ."

"Tangi, I want you to lie there and don't make a move unless I shout for you to run. And if I shout at you to run, I want you to run like you never have before, regardless of what's happening. Just run and hide, do you understand?"

"Yes, Ma. . . ."

Yvonne squeezed Tangeree's hand and patted her arm, and looked at the two men. They hadn't moved for several minutes. One was snoring. Yvonne gathered herself, pushing herself to her feet.

Penetrating pains stabbed through her head, and the trees seemed to spin around her as her vision dimmed. She shook her head to clear it as she forced her muscles to respond. Her legs were weak and rubbery. She ground her teeth together and in short, quick paces sprinted toward the shotgun.

The shotgun was forty feet away, then thirty. The horses looked at her, their ears cocked and their nostrils flared. One snorted and stamped nervously. The man with the hat over his eyes, the one nearest the shotgun, shifted and moved his feet. The shotgun was twenty feet away. The man lifted his hand, reaching for his hat. Yvonne strained to run faster, her dress whipping and her hair streaming back. The shotgun was ten feet away, and she slowed as she reached for it. The man knocked his hat off and leaped to his feet, his eyes wild with alarm. He shouted, pulling at his pistol. Yvonne slid into the tree and bounced off it as she snatched up the shotgun and leveled it at the man. As she pulled one of the hammers back, his pistol came out of the holster. Yvonne pulled a trigger, and nothing happened. She jerked the other trigger back.

The shotgun thundered and belched smoke, almost leaping out of her hands with the force of the shot. Leaves in the tree limb behind the man shredded and rained down as he was smacked backwards, obviously dead. Yvonne thumbed the other hammer back, swinging the shotgun toward the other man. He was clambering to his feet with a sleepy, astonished expression and reaching for his pistol. Yvonne pulled the trigger. The shotgun roared again and bucked in her hands.

Part of the hail of buckshot ripped into the man's left shoulder, and he reeled to one side and floundered to the ground as he dropped the pistol. The horse in the line of fire screamed and reared up as large red spots appeared on its flank and red streaks slashed across its stomach. Its rear quarters folded and it fell to the ground.

The man writhed on the ground in pain and held his shoulder with his right hand, his eyes closed tightly. Yvonne stepped to the pistol, picked it up and dropped the shotgun, looking at him. Then she cocked the pistol as she walked toward the horse and shot it through the head. The horse fell onto its side, quivering, and the other horse lumbered away, running awkwardly with the hobbles on its front legs.

Yvonne turned and walked back to the man. His eyes were open and glazed with terror as he looked up at her. She smiled down at him.

The blood of her Cherokee mother pulsed strongly within her, demanding vengeance. And with her knowledge of the human body, she could devise tortures that would make him welcome death. But he was bleeding to death and would be unconscious within minutes, and there was little time. She lifted the pistol. His feet scrabbled at the ground as he tried to move to one side, whimpering in protest. Yvonne squeezed the trigger. The pistol boomed and leaped, and the man's body arched upward as the bullet plowed through his genitals. He screamed hoarsely, his mouth gaping wide and his tongue thrust out. She shot once more, and he lay still.

Tangeree sat on the grass where they had been lying, her thin, girlish body slumped. Her disheveled hair was scattered over her face, her lips were swollen and caked with dried blood, and the skin around her left eye was puffy and discolored. And her eyes were empty.

Yvonne knelt in front of her and put her hands on the girl's shoulders. Tangeree looked at her numbly for a long moment, her features expressionless, a lost, hollow look in her eyes. Then her face twisted and her slender shoulders shook as she began sobbing. Yvonne gathered her in her arms and held her tightly, rocking back and forth with her. Tangeree wept bitterly, racking sobs shaking her, and tears trickled down Yvonne's face as she held the girl, patting her and murmuring soothingly.

2

THE HOBBLED HORSE was standing at the edge of the trees. Yvonne cut its hobbles, got a kettle out of the wagon, walked through the trees to a brook and filled it. She built up the fire, and heated the water, then carefully washed Tangeree and examined her. The physical injury was more painful than dangerous. Yvonne made a pad of soft linen, soaked it in an infusion of sanicle root and tied it on the girl, then crushed dried winterberries in a mortar and mixed the powder into a thin salve with mutton tallow to put on the bruises on Tangeree's face. Then she washed and doctored herself, put everything back into the wagon, and helped Tangeree in.

She was reluctant to take along any object that would remind her of the men, but the Colt revolvers were far more effective weapons than the old cap and ball pistol she had in the wagon. The shotgun and Henry rifle were deadly, and being well-armed would make a great difference in the event of another attack.

She put the pistol belts, shotgun, and rifle in a pile, then looked through the saddlebags and packs for ammunition. The packs contained foodstuffs that hadn't been available in Vicksburg, cans of tomatoes, flour,

16

salt bacon, beans, rice, and peas. And there was even coffee, sugar, and pepper, things she hadn't seen for months. A leather wallet in one of the saddlebags contained sheafs of Confederate and Union currency, one of little value and the other dangerous to possess. A pocket on the side of the wallet contained three double eagles, a universal medium of exchange and a substantial amount of money.

Yvonne took the coins, put the foodstuffs and boxes of ammunition into bags, and carried the weapons and bags to the wagon. She made an extra hole in one of the pistol belts so it would fit around her waist, and put on a thin linen dust coat from the wagon to conceal the pistol and bowie knife. Then she gathered up the ropes on the oxen's halters and led them out of the clearing. Her hat, an old hat her husband had left behind, was on the road. She picked it up, dusted it off and pushed it into shape, and put it on as she led the oxen along the road.

The road was a thin, dim track lined with dense foliage that grew in luxuriant profusion in the deep, rich topsoil that had been deposited during centuries of intermittent floods by the Mississippi. Thickets of willows, birches, and swamp oaks were interspersed with openings covered with thick brush and lush grass, where autumn forest fires had burned the trees. The clearings were dotted with gray, weathered skeletons of trees that had been killed by fires. They still stood, their bare, jutting limbs covered with clusters of mistletoe and curtains of Spanish moss as they slowly rotted and crumbled.

A westerly breeze stirred the tops of the trees, carrying with it the smell and feel of the Mississippi, and the gleaming surface of the river was occasionally visible through openings in the foliage on the left.

Birds chirped and sang as they flew through the trees, small animals rustled the grass and brush by the road as they fled from the noise of the wagon, and snakes wriggled across the road ahead of Yvonne as she led the plodding oxen slowly along it.

The light took on warm, golden tones as the sun dipped toward the west. The bottoms of the fleecy clouds drifting across the sky turned a faint, ruddy color that deepened into crimson. The pain in Yvonne's head had turned into a dull, throbbing ache that would keep her awake if she tried to sleep, and she felt a need for physical activity. When the light began failing, she stopped the oxen and climbed into the wagon. Tangeree was lying on her pallet with her face to the side of the wagon, either asleep or pretending to be. Yvonne took a handful of parched corn from a bag, drank from a water bottle, climbed out of the wagon and began leading the oxen along the road again.

Gnats and mosquitoes whined around Yvonne's face. The thin chirping of crickets blended with the deep, ringing bellows of bullfrogs and the higher croaking of smaller frogs. The moon rose, shining its pale, ghostly light down on the road and making deep shadows under the shapeless masses of the trees. The breeze gusted and blew the gnats and mosquitoes away from the road. Yvonne walked ahead of the oxen at the full length of the ropes, getting as far as possible from the noise of the wagon to listen for any indication of danger. The sounds around her were the normal night noises of the swampy forest, the droning of insects and croaking of frogs, the hooting of owls and mournful cry of night birds, and the scream of rabbits and chatter of raccoons caught by predators.

The trees closed together over the road, turning it

into a black, featureless tunnel. Gnats and mosquitoes hovered around Yvonne's face again in the still air as she felt her way along the road. Mud pulled at her shoes and made sucking noises under the oxen's heavy feet, and the croaking of the frogs was a loud clamor that died away as the wagon passed and resumed behind it. There was a stretch of running water across the road, a wide, shallow stream flowing lazily toward the Mississippi. Then the foliage opened out again, and the moonlight was bright after the darkness. The road went up a slow incline, going up a few inches for every hundred yards of distance. It was barely perceptible to Yvonne, but it was enough of a grade for the weary oxen to tell the difference. They dragged on the ropes and slowed even more, and Yvonne stopped every few minutes to let them rest.

The moon set, and the constellations moved slowly across the sky. After an hour of thicker darkness, the morning star became a gleaming beacon in the eastern sky as the gray, flat, first light of dawn spread along the road. A swamp buck with a large spread of antlers stood in the road ahead of the wagon, his body rigid and his ears cocked as he looked; then he bounded away with long, silent leaps. The oxen began dragging heavily on the ropes, and Yvonne stopped again to let them rest. The morning breeze was cool against her face, and the morning quiet was soothing. She felt more at peace with herself than she had the afternoon before, as her dragging fatigue dulled her throbbing headache and blurred her memory of the attack so she would be able to sleep.

A rooster crowed in the forest on the right side of the road, and Yvonne put her hand on the pistol, craning her neck and looking. Grass and brush stretched back from the side of the road for a few yards, then there was dense forest. The dirt berm at the side of the road was worn down in a place a few feet wide, an indication that a road had once led off into the forest. Yvonne gathered up the ropes and led the oxen off the road. The wagon bumped and jarred as it turned off the road, the high canvas top swaying from side to side as the deep grass and brush dragged against the bottom of the bed and sprang back up behind it. Yvonne tied the ropes to a sapling and walked toward the thicket ahead of her. The rooster crowed again, and she turned toward the sound. Then she saw the avenue through the trees where a road had been and new growth had sprung up.

The road led through the trees and around a boggy opening covered with cattails, and through another thicket. The trees opened out in front of a deserted farmstead—a small house, a barn and other outbuildings, and crop fields, a pasture, and pens fenced with split rails. The crop fields had gone to seed, with young corn springing up among the weeds and dried, weathered stalks that remained ungathered from the previous year. Vegetables were struggling to grow through the weeds and against the inroads of rabbits and other animals.

Roses that had been planted in front of the house had overrun their trellis, and chickens were roosting in a tree by the house. Rusty tools hung in a shed and utensils hung on the kitchen wall inside the sagging door. Bedding that was visible through a gaping window had been chewed and scattered by rodents. It appeared that the occupants had simply walked away from the farm. Then Yvonne saw the two graves by the house, that of a woman and a young girl. The dates of death on the crude headstones were within a few days of each other the previous summer, mute and enigmatic testimony to some catastrophe. Yvonne walked back toward the road to get the wagon.

The interior of the barn was clean. Yvonne led the oxen into it, parked the wagon, then unyoked the oxen and led them to the corn field. They were sluggish with fatigue, but they crowded eagerly through the gate into the field and began cropping the young corn. Tangeree was taking things out of the wagon when Yvonne returned to the barn. Her lips were swollen and her left eye was almost swollen closed, the skin around it a dark purple, and she was listless and withdrawn. She silently helped Yvonne carry water from the spring and build a fire in the clearing behind the barn, and helped her prepare breakfast.

After they ate Yvonne examined Tangeree again, made a fresh pad soaked in sanicle root infusion, and put it on her. She mixed more winterberry salve and spread it on the bruises on the girl's face. Then she looked at her teeth to see if any of them had been loosened. Tangeree winced as Yvonne pulled at her lips, then she made an impatient sound in her throat and turned away.

"It doesn't make any difference whether or not I have nice teeth, Ma. After what happened to me, no decent man will ever look at me."

"Tangi, once you have your growth, any man who doesn't look at you will squat when he pees, regardless of what's happened to you. And you'll need your teeth to eat, regardless of whether anybody looks at you or not."

Tangeree looked away, shaking her head. "It isn't funny, Ma."

Yvonne sighed heavily, putting her arms around Tangeree and pulling the girl to her. "No, it isn't funny, Tangi. What happened to you is the worst thing that can happen to a woman. The body can be healed, but I know of no herb to heal the soul. And it's twice as bad for a young girl. It's also twice as bad for me, because I'm the one who got you into it."

"No, you didn't, Ma," Tangeree said, pulling away. "We talked about what to do, and we agreed that the best thing for us to—"

"We talked, and we agreed, Tangi. But I'm still your mother and I decide what we're going to do."

"Regardless of that, I don't want you blaming yourself, Ma. We did the only thing we could do. Who knows what might have happened to us if we'd tried to stay around Vicksburg?"

"Tangi, a mother feels blame when something happens to her child, and there's no explaining it away."

Tangeree shrugged and looked away, and Yvonne took her hand and held it, looking at her. With her large blue eyes, blond hair, and softly modeled features, her strong resemblance to her father stirred agonizingly poignant memories.

Even though Tangeree was still a girl, she had the bearing and poise of an adult. From the age of ten, she had been assisting Yvonne in attending the ill. She had acquired a wide knowledge of herbal remedies and of illnesses, and she had the healer's gift, an instinctive empathy with the ill that gave her an intuitive grasp of their condition.

She knew life, because she had assisted in the delivery of dozens of babies. And she knew death. She had met him many times in the still, silent hours of the night while sitting and holding a feeble hand, soothing the terror and providing companionship and comfort to one passing across the threshold into eternity. Her blue eyes were wise and ageless, out of place in her young face. She had been robbed of her childhood, the healer's familiarity with human frailties, with life, and with death forcing her into an early maturity.

But she was still little more than a child, with a young girl's emotions, and she was shattered by what had happened to her. Aching sorrow gnawed at Yvonne as she looked at Tangeree's bruised face. She patted the girl's hand and released it as she rose. "It'll pass, Tangi. You won't forget it, but you'll get over it."

Tangeree nodded noncommittally, looking into the fire. Yvonne went into the barn, climbed into the wagon for her pallet, and carried it back out. She unrolled it by the rear of the barn, where the overhang of the roof would shade her when the sun rose higher, then lay down.

"I believe we're safe enough here, Tangi, but keep your eyes open. And wake me up at about noon."

The girl silently nodded, sitting with her shoulders slumped and looking into the fire, her back to Yvonne. Yvonne lay down and settled herself comfortably. Tangeree made a soft sound a moment later, and Yvonne turned her head and looked at her. The girl was weeping quietly, her shoulders trembling. Yvonne turned her head back, drawing in a deep breath and releasing it in a heavy sigh, and composed herself to go to sleep.

It was afternoon when she woke, the atmosphere that of a tranquil and placid spring afternoon in the wilderness, far from others and their conflicts. Birds and insects were dozing through the warmth of the day. The breeze stirred the trees and the tall weeds climbing the rail fences around the crop fields, and the sun beamed down on the grassy expanse behind the barn with a hint of the torrid, miasmic heat that would come to the swampy Mississippi lowlands with summer.

A half dozen hens were pecking at a pan of corn in a slat coop by the corner of the barn, and a large, fire-blackened washpot was on the smoldering coals of another fire Tangeree had built a few yards away. An old wooden washtub was on the ground by it. Tangeree had washed the dirty clothes and hung them on a rope between the corner of the barn and a shed. A kettle was simmering on the fire, with an appetizing odor of stewing chicken coming from it, and the coffeepot was on a flat stone in the edge of the coals.

Tangeree was sitting on a block of wood by the fire, wearing a clean dress. Her hair was damp and her face shone from being washed. The brown and purple splotches of the bruises stood out in sharp contrast to her fair skin.

Yvonne's headache had died away to a dull throbbing, but it intensified to a sudden stab of pain as she sat up. She winced, touching the tender, swollen spot on the side of her head, and Tangeree turned and looked at her.

"Would you like some coffee, Ma?"

Yvonne nodded, pushing back her hair. "Yes, I would, Tangi. How did you manage to catch those chickens?"

"I propped a coop on a stick and tied a string to the stick, and used corn for bait. When several of them got under the coop, I just jerked the stick out." She knelt by the fire and filled a tin cup with coffee, then stepped to Yvonne and handed it to her. "There's quite a bit of corn in the crib around there that the mice didn't eat, and I found a hand mill in the tool shed and ground us about fifty pounds of meal."

"That'll come in handy, and that chicken you have cooking there smells good."

"That's the rooster," Tangeree said as she stepped

back to the fire and sat down. "I didn't want anyone passing along the road hearing him crowing his head off. The oxen were getting bloated on that new corn, so I drove them over into that pasture. They had already eaten most of the corn, so they'll probably need drenching with checkerberry infusion or something."

Vvonne nodded, smothering a yawn, taking a drink of coffee. "Yes, they might. We'll see how they are in the morning. And you did all the washing, didn't you? You've been busy."

"I wanted to do something. That washpot is full of clean hot water, and there's cold water in the tub to mix it with if you want to take a bath."

"I won't miss a chance at a hot bath. You look like you've already had one."

Tangeree's expression changed, becoming withdrawn, and she looked away. "I took two, and I still feel nasty. And I'd feel nasty if I bathed until my skin came off."

Yvonne sighed, pushing at her hair, and took a drink from her cup. "Tangi, I know it doesn't seem like it now, but you'll get to where it won't seem that the world has come to an end. You'll get over it, honey."

Tangeree continued looking away, not replying. The silence was raw and grating to Yvonne as she looked at Tangeree and tried to think of something to say that would be comforting. They were more like sisters and companions than mother and daughter, with Yvonne barely thirty, Tangeree a precociously mature girl at fourteen. Their experiences in administering to the ill provided a close bond between them. But Tangeree was withdrawing into herself as a result of the attack by the two men, and for the first time they had less than complete understanding and communication. Yvonne finished the coffee and glanced at Tangeree as she stepped to the fire and put the cup with the other utensils. Tears were standing in the girl's eyes, and she averted her face as Yvonne looked at her.

Yvonne bathed and put on clean clothes, then took her leather working tools and the other pistol belt out of the wagon. The pistol belt had been an unfamiliar, uncomfortable weight around her waist and the long, heavy pistol had been bulky under the linen dust coat. A shoulder holster would be more comfortable, with the pistol hanging under her left arm and the bowie knife under the right, and it would be less noticeable under the dust coat. There was more than enough leather in the two belts to make a shoulder harness, and she began cutting them apart.

When the chicken was cooked, they ate, and Yvonne continued working on the shoulder harness as Tangeree washed the dishes. Tangeree finished the dishes and stacked them, then walked about restlessly, wandering out to the pasture to look at the oxen, and prowling through the crop fields. She returned to the fire with a dozen small, green tomatoes, and put them in a pan by the fire.

"Those will be good fried in the meal you made for us, won't they?"

"Yes, and they're about all there is out there. Birds or rabbits have ruined just about everything that the weeds haven't choked out."

"Crops take a lot of looking after. . . . It's been a couple of days since you've had a chance to look at your books, hasn't it, honey?"

Tangeree nodded and went to the wagon in the barn. She carried out a wooden chest filled with books, sat down by the fire, and began thumbing through a book. The chest contained school texts on history, mathematics, geography, and other subjects, as well as books on anatomy and medicine that Yvonne had collected during the years. Like Tangeree, when she had reached the age of ten she had begun assisting her mother, a woman who had been known throughout the Cherokee nation for her skill and knowledge of herbal medicine.

Through her father, Yvonne's contact with the white community had been closer than with her mother's tribe, and most of the first people she had treated had been white. She had gradually broken away from some of the things she had learned from her mother. The chants and rituals that were an integral part of her mother's treatments were counterproductive with white people, because they were either frightened by or skeptical of anything that suggested the occult. And the efficacy of a treatment was always increased by the confidence of the patient.

After her marriage, she had lived with her husband in Tupelo, Mississippi, where she had met Charles Dawson, a white doctor who had been interested in herbal medicine. They had worked together for a time, exchanging information, after which Yvonne had departed even more widely from what she had learned from her mother.

Traditional herbal medicine avoided mechanical contrivances other than splints for broken bones and probes for extracting bullets and arrowheads, but white people were prone to ailments and conditions that were rare among Indians, and for which instruments were useful. Difficulty in childbirth was unusual among Indians but common among white people, and Yvonne had learned to use instruments to assist in deliveries. White people healed more slowly when wounded, and stitching with clean linen thread promoted healing, even if it occasionally caused in-

fection. Tooth decay and gum disease was more common among white people than Indians, and the doctor
had taught her how to extract teeth and treat gum
disease.

The doctor had routinely treated animals as well
as people, as most white doctors did, and many of the
medicines he used were chemical rather than organic
substances. Yvonne had begun treating farm animals
and had supplemented her herbal remedies with some
of the chemicals the doctor used, both of which would
have horrified her mother. She had learned a crude
method of vaccination against smallpox, using the
matter from a blister on an infected person and placing it in a scratch on an uninfected person. It occasionally induced a lethal case of smallpox but more
often conferred immunity after a mild infection.

She had learned other procedures, techniques, and
methods of treatment from the doctor. And she had
learned about books. Herbal medicine was based on
empirical knowledge that had been gathered and
passed down through families of healers through the
years, most of it jealously guarded against being revealed to outsiders, and with no exchange of information between those who practiced it. Medical texts
contained a large body of information that had been
obtained through dissection, observation, and free exchange of information between countless people over
a period of many years. For the first time, she had seen
diagrams of internal organs and read theories on their
functions and on the nature of disease and how it was
contracted.

A new world had been tantalizingly revealed, but
most of it had been denied her. The key to understanding was education, which was unavailable to her.
She had developed a burning ambition to provide

Tangeree with that education, to combine in her a full knowledge of herbal medicine with the vast accumulation of knowledge developed by white people. Her husband had talked about the enormous expense of a medical education and the unlikely prospect of a woman being admitted to a medical college, but he had been provisionally agreeable if the obstacles could be overcome. Since his death, however, the prospect had become far more remote. And in the chaotic upheaval caused by the War, it was even more unlikely. But Yvonne still sustained a wishful dream of being able to send Tangeree to medical college.

It was a subject they discussed often and one Tangeree enjoyed, and she frequently brought it up while looking through the books. But she remained silent as she leafed uninterestedly through one, then closed it and sat with it on her lap, looking blankly into space.

Yvonne joined two leather straps together, punching holes in them with the awl and lacing them with rawhide, and looked at Tangeree as she knotted the rawhide. "Don't you feel like reading yours books, Tangi?"

Tangeree drew in a deep breath and released it in a heavy sigh, shaking her head. "No, I don't, Ma. And I don't feel like doing anything else. I feel like there's nothing left in me and no point in doing anything."

"You'll feel different in time, honey. You remember how I was when I first heard about your pa, don't you? It took me awhile to collect myself, but I did. And you will, too."

Tangeree shrugged doubtfully as she put the book back in the chest and closed it. Then she rose and walked away from the fire. "I'll go make sure the oxen have plenty of water."

"All right, Tangi. Watch for snakes."

Tangeree went to the pasture fence, dropped a rail

to step through the fence, then disappeared into the
pasture. Yvonne continued sewing the straps together
and trying the shoulder harness on herself as it began
taking form. The sun set and the light began to fade
as she finished the harness and fastened the holster
and knife sheath to it, and Tangeree returned from the
pasture. Her shoulders were slumped, and she walked
with slow, dragging footsteps. Yvonne looked up at
her as she approached the fire.

"Are the oxen all right, Tangi?"

"Yes."

Her voice was tense and strained; she had been
crying again. She took the chest of books in to the
wagon, came back out with her pallet, and lay down
on it a few yards away, her back to Yvonne and her
attitude not inviting conversation. The light had faded
into soft twilight, and Yvonne tossed a handful of
wood on the fire. She looked at the harness in the light
of the fire as she put it on and put the pistol and knife
in the holster and sheath. They hung comfortably,
resting snugly against her sides and within quick,
easy reach. The heavy, deadly weight of the long
pistol felt reassuring. She put on the linen dust coat
and looked down at herself. It concealed the pistol
and knife completely. Satisfied, she took off the coat
and shoulder harness and lay down on her pallet,
placing the pistol beside her.

Full darkness fell, and the stars were bright in the
purple velvet of the clear sky. Crickets chirped and
frogs chorused in the swampy spot between the farmstead and the road. A quiet, rhythmic sound of weeping came from Tangeree's pallet, her soft sobs barely
audible over the night sounds. Yvonne listened to
the girl's weeping, and slowly drifted off to sleep.

* * *

The winterberry salve had started taking effect on the bruises on Tangeree's face the next morning. The swelling was diminishing, and the edges of the discoloration were beginning to turn brownish-yellow and fade. Yvonne looked at her face in the mirror on the wagon. The bruises had been less evident on her darker skin.

The physical evidence of the attack was disappearing rapidly by the following morning, but Tangeree showed little indication of recovery from the deeper effects. In contrast to her energetic, spirited, and cheerful disposition of before, she continued to be lifeless and indifferent, rarely beginning a conversation and silently going about her chores, wanting solitude and frequently weeping at night.

One of the rear wagon wheels had been squeaking loudly. Yvonne looked through the tool shed and found a bucket of axle grease. She and Tangeree greased all of the axles in preparation for leaving, using a long pole to lever the corners of the wagon up, sliding large blocks of wood under the axles to hold the wheels off the ground, and taking off the large, heavy wheels. Tangeree helped Yvonne grudgingly, reluctant to leave the farmstead.

"I don't see why we can't just stay here, Ma. We have plenty of food, and we don't have to worry about anyone bothering us. You can't say that about anywhere else."

"No, but I'm not so sure that you can say it about this place, either. A bunch of renegades could always roam through here. And if the Confederates push the bluebellies north out of Vicksburg, they might come right up through here and we might find ourselves in the middle of it."

"Do you think they might?"

"I don't know, Tangi. I do know that I don't want to take any more of a chance than I have to, though. Maybe we can get on up to Memphis, or maybe we'll run into some people we can trust."

"I can't imagine any group of people without men among them, and I don't see how you'd be able to trust any man after what happened to us."

"All men aren't like those two, Tangi, and you know that as well as I do. There're men a body can trust."

"If there are, then there're probably frogs that have wings so they won't bust their ass when they hop. But I don't know that I'd go looking to find one."

Yvonne smiled, looking at Tangeree. The girl's face was unsmiling, her eyes cold and her lips in a thin, bitter line as she stood waiting for Yvonne to finish greasing the axle. Yvonne's smile faded, and she put another daub of grease on the axle with the wooden paddle. They lifted the heavy wheel and slid it back onto the axle, and Yvonne put on the axle nut and tightened it down with the wrench.

When they finished greasing the axles on the wagon, Yvonne found a box of split links in the tool shed and dragged the yoke chains to the shed to replace all the worn links. Tangeree had caught most of the chickens roosting in the tree by the house and had them in two coops, and she shelled the rest of the corn in the crib and put it in bags to feed the chickens along the way. Yvonne thought about what time of day would be safest for traveling. The trek through the night from the place where they had been attacked to the farmstead had been grueling, but there were advantages to traveling at night. Others would be camped, and potential attackers wouldn't expect anyone to be traveling then. And if they were attacked, she and Tangeree might be able to flee and hide under cover of darkness.

They left during late afternoon. Yvonne had a wary, edgy feel of approaching a gauntlet of danger as she led the oxen toward the road. The wagon seemed to be making a deafening noise that announced their presence to the world. The bed squeaked and groaned, the chains rattled, and the chickens in the coops tied to the tailgate squawked and clucked as the wagon jarred heavily.

Yvonne stopped the wagon and tied the halter ropes to a sapling a few yards from the road, then walked ahead to the road, a hundred feet of which was visible in both directions before it curved and disappeared. There were no recent tracks on it, and the only sound was the clatter of birds. She turned and walked back to the wagon. Tangeree was sitting on her pallet behind the seat and looking apprehensively over it. The shotgun and rifle were leaning against the back of the seat.

"Be careful with those guns, Tangi. I don't want one of the oxen shot."

Tangeree nodded and put the shotgun and rifle on the bed of the wagon by her pallet. Yvonne untied the halter ropes and tugged on them, the oxen leaned into the yoke, and the wagon began moving forward, squeaking and rattling as the wheels ground through the deep grass and brush.

The oxen had gained some weight during the days of rest and ample food, but they were still thin and rangy. The road continued sloping upward at a slight angle, and they plodded along at a tediously slow pace. The road leveled off after a mile, passing across the wide expanse of a low hillock that rose fifty or sixty feet above the surrounding terrain, and the trees opened out on both sides of the road where a raging forest fire had cleared the top of the hillock. The breeze was brisk as it swept across the low elevation, and the flat tide plain of the Mississippi stretched out for miles and faded into the misty, distant horizon, the dark green of dense forest, the brighter green of areas of swamp, and the mottled patches of burns. The sun was setting, painting the clouds with rich tones and infusing the air with a warm glow as it gleamed on the broad, roiling belt of the Mississippi a mile away to the west.

The road started downward at the same gradual angle at which it had climbed. The breeze died away, and the air was warmer, the swampy lowland retaining the steaming heat of the spring day. Birds swarmed through the trees, finding their roosts for the night. Then darkness fell and the resounding croak of frogs filled the air. Mosquitoes hovered around Yvonne's face as she felt her way along the road in the thick darkness between last light and moonrise; then the air began cooling as the moon rose, and a breeze moved along the road and swept the mosquitoes away.

The hours dragged by. The road wound through the thick forest, mud pulling at Yvonne's feet as it passed swamps and streams, and the trees occasionally closed together overhead and blocked the moonlight for short stretches. Yvonne sank into a reverie, one part of her mind remaining aware of her surroundings and automatically monitoring and classifying the sounds around her as she mused about other, happier times and thought about the future prospects for herself and Tangeree.

Then she became fully alert as she approached a narrow opening in the trees that lined the road on the right. It was an intersection with a road leading in from the east, and there were wagon and oxen tracks on the road. It was difficult to tell the direction in which they went, because the road was relatively dry and the oxen tracks were only dim marks in the dirt on each side of the grass in the center of the road. Yvonne walked on to examine the tracks at the next muddy spot. The wagons had gone north along the road ahead of her, a few hours before.

As the moon set, Yvonne led the oxen along the road in the faint light of the stars, straining her eyes and listening for any noise that clashed with the night sounds of the forest. The trees closed together overhead again, and Yvonne walked slowly in the thick, impenetrable darkness. Something large moved in the darkness ahead of her. She stopped the oxen and stood and listened. The croaking of frogs made a loud blur of noise around her, and she heard the sound of a movement over it, possibly a swamp buck or possibly a mounted man who had heard the wagon and stopped in the darkness. She stepped quietly to the side of the road and tied the halter ropes to a low branch of a tree, and took out her pistol as she walked forward.

Tree branches rustled and the brush crackled at the side of the road. Yvonne crept toward the noise, lifting the pistol. The noise stopped, and Yvonne stopped. Then there was a loud snort of a startled swamp buck and the pattering thud of its hoofs drumming against the ground as it ran away. But as Yvonne turned and started back toward the wagon, she heard other sounds—a light scuffle of footsteps on the road. A chill raced up her spine. She lifted the pistol again, her thumb on the hammer.

"Ma?"

Yvonne sighed in exasperation as she put the pistol

back in the holster and walked toward Tangeree.
"Tangeree, you ninny! I almost blew your head off!"

"Well, I didn't know what you were doing, Ma," the
girl said querulously. "I woke up and the wagon was
stopped, and I didn't know where you'd gone."

"All right, come on, honey. And from now on, you
stay in that wagon until I tell you to get out."

Yvonne took Tangeree's arm and helped her into
the wagon, then untied the halter ropes and led the
oxen along the road again. The trees opened out,
making the road dimly visible in the starlight, and
Yvonne tugged on the rope to urge the oxen to a
faster pace.

The trees on the right became silhouettes against
the sky as it paled with the first light of dawn. The
stars dimmed as the light spread across the sky, and
the road and nearby trees became visible in the weak,
gray light. Yvonne smelled woodsmoke. She stopped
the oxen and stood for a moment, sniffing. Though it
had been a slight whiff, carried along the road by the
eddying breeze, she smelled it again after a moment.
She walked along the road again, glancing ahead for
someplace to get the wagon off the road.

The light gradually brightened, and a stretch of
brush and grass dotted with dead trees and saplings
extended along the right side of the road. Yvonne
led the oxen off the road and across the opening into
the edge of the trees, and tied the halter ropes to a
tree.

"Tangi, I smell smoke, so I'm going to walk ahead
and take a look."

Tangeree's eyes were wide and apprehensive as
she looked over the seat, holding the rifle. "Do you
want me to come with you, Ma?"

"No, just stay in the wagon. And don't start shooting

at anything that moves. It might be me coming back."

"Yes, all right, Ma."

Yvonne walked back to the road, then along it. The sky in the east was bright with the first flush of sunrise, but the light under the trees was still subdued, gray and flat. The road had curved toward the river, and it made a soft background of noise, a low vibration in the air that was more felt than heard, a murmur that hinted of the awesome size and gigantic force of the volume of water rushing past. The scent of woodsmoke became stronger as Yvonne walked along the road. Then she heard a faint sound of pigs grunting and chickens clucking.

The trees on the left side of the road opened out into a level clearing, and Yvonne slowed as she glimpsed wagons. Then she relaxed. There were four wagons. Plows and fruit tree saplings with their roots in burlap were tied to tailgates, and crates of pigs and chickens were on the ground and ready to be tied in place on the sides. The people were farmers. A large tent was pitched in the center of the clearing, and a fire had burned down to ashes a few yards from it. A man was sitting by the fire, and others were rolled in blankets around the fire, the small forms of children and the larger ones of adults.

A dog tethered to a wheel of one of the wagons began barking, and the man sitting by the fire picked up a crutch and rifle and pulled himself erect. His right leg had been amputated above the knee. He was young, in his late teens. He looked around, then saw Yvonne walking along the road.

"Halt!"

Yvonne stopped, and he stumped toward her on his crutch. The others around the fire stirred, pushing their blankets aside and scrambling to their feet. The adults were all men, two middle-aged, one old, and one in his early teens. The man on the crutch stopped as he saw Yvonne clearly. He looked at her uncertainly and glanced back at the other men. Yvonne walked forward again. The dog barked and snarled viciously as it leaped against its rope. Yvonne heard a familiar sound in the tent over the noise of the dog's barking. It was a woman in labor.

The children looked at Yvonne sleepily, sitting with their blankets around their shoulders, as the men walked forward. One of the middle-aged men nodded and spoke.

"Howdy, ma'm. My name's Horace Dowd."

"I'm pleased to meet you. My name is Yvonne Beaunais."

"I'm mighty pleased to meet you, ma'm." He nodded toward the man on the crutch. "This is my boy Jason, and that's my boy Calvin. That's Jacob Whittacker, and this is my dad. Are you lost, or do you need some help or something?"

His attitude was one of concern and willingness to help, and they all looked cordial, their faces friendly and honest. Yvonne exchanged nods as he introduced them, and shook her head in reply. "No, I smelled your fire, and I left my wagon and walked up to see who it was. Is there a woman in the tent having a baby?"

"Yes, that's my wife, Abby," Jason replied quickly, leaning forward on his crutch and interrupting Dowd as he started to reply. "It's her first one, and my ma and the rest of the women here don't know much about helping her. Would you happen to know anything about it?"

Yvonne smiled faintly and nodded, turning back toward the road. "Yes, I do. I'll go get my wagon."

3

ABIGAIL'S FACE twisted and flushed as the first of the hard, racking pains gripped her, overriding the narcotic effect of the hemp flowers. She pressed her lips together and tried to smother the scream, but it forced its way out as the contraction intensified. A keening sound built up in her throat, rising higher and becoming louder behind her clenched teeth. Then it burst from her lips in a ragged, shrill shriek. Yvonne knelt by the pallet with a hand on Abigail's stomach, ignoring the painful volume of sound battering her ears as she felt the tension and movements in the woman's body. The instinct to thrust and eject was taking command of her body, signaling the beginning of the final stage of labor.

Tangeree was kneeling by Abigail's head and leaning over to rest the tips of her fingers on the woman's stomach. Her lips were pursed in concentration, and her shoulders slumped with weariness and the torrid heat inside the tent. The scream died away, and Tangeree sat up and took a rag from a water basin. She wrung it out and leaned over Abigail, wiping her face and murmuring quietly.

"You'll want to push now, Abby. When it comes

again, breathe deeply and push, like Ma told you."

Abigail nodded and tried to smile as she looked up at Tangeree, her face pale and tense and her lips trembling. Yvonne looked at her and at Tangeree, feeling a deep sense of satisfaction. When Tangeree had walked into the tent, the lifeless indifference that had possessed her since the attack had disappeared, and she had reverted to her former self. She was smiling reassuringly at Abigail, and her hands communicated warmth and concern as she wiped Abigail's face. Someone needing her help produced an automatic, unthinking response to push all personal considerations aside and provide that help. She was a healer.

"That's the first good squall we've heard out of her," one of the other women commented in a disapproving tone. "I was beginning to wonder if she was going to make a sound."

Five other women were crowded into the stuffy tent, and they ranged in age from one barely out of her teens to the old man's wife, an old, toothless woman with her pink scalp showing through her thin, white hair and her bright eyes peering beadily from the maze of leathery wrinkles of her face. They were an extended family group, all related by blood or through marriage. The one who had spoken was a middle-aged woman named Melvina, Dowd's sister and a widow. She had a pale, lined face that indicated poor health and a testy disposition. She sat by the door of the tent and fanned herself with the collar of her dress as she looked at Yvonne with a dissatisfied expression. Hester Dowd, Abigail's mother-in-law sat on the other side of the pallet, looking at Melvina and back at Yvonne, frowning worriedly.

"Everything's going to be all right, ain't it?"

Yvonne silently nodded. In a tradition that couldn't be challenged, the women had seen to their chores and then filed into the tent to view the entry of new life into the world. Yvonne felt a dull, weary annoyance with them. In their ignorance and shame of natural body functions, they had allowed the months of Abigail's pregnancy to pass without fully explaining what would happen to her. When Yvonne had arrived, she had been terror-stricken as well as racked with pain.

There had been no time to prepare Abigail with infusions of feverfew and valerian, because her digestive system and other unessential bodily functions had already been inactivated by the mysterious process of nature that harnessed and directed all the body's energies to producing new life. To relax her and dull her pain, it had been necessary to use the hemp, a powerful and frequently unpredictable herb. Worse than that, there had been little time to prepare the woman mentally, to explain what was happening to her, to turn her mind away from her fear and pain and toward the magic of procreation.

"It don't seem right to me," Melvina persisted. "Every midwife I've ever talked to likes to hear plenty of squalling, and I sure squalled plenty with every one I had. It's supposed to hurt."

A heated retort rose to Yvonne's lips, but she suppressed it. "I'm a healer, not a midwife," she said quietly. "Suffering saps the strength that is needed for delivering the baby and recovering from the delivery."

Silence fell, and the women looked at each other dubiously. There had been a suggestion of uncertainty and doubt in the women's attitudes since they had entered the tent, because Yvonne's methods were different and unfamiliar to them. The silence stretched out for a moment as the women looked at each other. Then Melvina grunted and looked back at Yvonne.

"One of the men said that you said you had delivered a lot of babies. How many's a lot?"

"It's been several hundred. I don't remember exactly how many."

"Did you lose many of them?"

"No, and I've never had a woman die when she was in my care."

"What do you do when the husband tells you he wants the baby saved first, regardless of the woman?"

"I haven't had that happen but once. I told him I'd think about it if he would put his worm on the chopping block and whack it off with the axe. He changed his mind."

There was a stir of amusement among the women. Tangeree was bristling, glaring at Melvina. Her eyes met Yvonne's, and Yvonne shook her head fractionally and indicated Abigail with a movement of her eyes. Tangeree looked back down at Abigail, taking the rag from the basin and wiping her face again. Melvina continued looking at Yvonne suspiciously.

"Well, I think it's natural for it to hurt when a woman has a baby. Woman's burden is pain, and if God hadn't wanted it to hurt, He wouldn't have made it hurt."

"I don't think Abby's baby is going to be born on a horse, so it's more natural for people to walk than to ride," Yvonne replied. "But people ride when they can, and it saves their energy for more important things."

The old woman laughed boisterously, slapping her thigh. "She's got you there, Vinney," she cackled. "She's sure got you there."

The others smiled and chuckled, and Melvina glanced at the old woman and shrugged as she looked away, her thin, pale features contracted in a dark frown. The drawn look about Melvina's face and the way she sat with her shoulders bowed to take pressure off her upper stomach muscles indicated a chronic stomach complaint.

"Your stomach bothers you, doesn't it?" Yvonne said. "When Abby and her baby are comfortable, I'll prepare some medicine for you that will relieve the pain."

The women looked at each other and at Yvonne in surprise, and Melvina's frown changed to a startled expression. "How did you know that my stomach pesters me? I haven't said anything about it."

"From your appearance. As I told you, I'm a healer. I've had a lot of people come to me for medicine to cure stomach pain."

Melvina blinked and hesitated, then smiled thinly. "I'd be much obliged for some medicine. It's been pestering me a lot lately."

Yvonne nodded, looking back at Abigail. The shadow of skepticism that had been in the women's attitude was rapidly disappearing. They were silent for a moment, looking at each other and waiting for another to speak first. Finally Hester took the initiative, clearing her throat diffidently and speaking.

"My youngest boy has ulcers on his lips and tongue," she said. "Could I get you to look at him later?"

"Yes, I'll be glad to."

Martha Whittacker, Hester's sister, cleared her throat and stirred. "My girl Marcy has the itch. Do you think you could do anything for it?"

"Yes, I'll make some salve for her."

"My back is troubling me something fierce," the old woman said. "And so's Grandpa's. We'd like something for it, if you don't charge too much."

"The charge is what you can pay, and I've been paid with thanks more often than not."

The old woman grinned toothlessly and nodded. The atmosphere in the tent was distinctly more cordial than before, the women regarding Yvonne with friendliness that bordered on being ingratiating. Hester smiled at Yvonne, climbing to her feet. "The men took care of your oxen, and I'll go make sure they seen to them right. And there ought to be some coffee left out there. If there is, I'll bring you and your girl a cup."

Yvonne smiled and nodded in thanks, and Hester left, stepping around Melvina and bending to go out the low door as she pushed the flap open. Tangeree's hand was resting on Abigail's shoulder, and she inclined her head toward Abigail in a meaningful nod as Yvonne looked at her. Yvonne rested her hand on Abigail's thigh, feeling the tension in the woman's body.

Her fear was still pronounced, and it was growing as the effects of the hemp wore off. She was at about the midpoint between contractions, and she was too tense, using up energy she would need. Yvonne nodded to Tangeree, and the girl picked up the pipe on top of the herb chest and struck a lucifer match to relight it. Beads of sweat on her upper lip and forehead glistened in the wavering light of the match, and it highlighted her young, smooth face in the dimness of the tent as she cautiously puffed on the pipe, carefully avoiding inhaling the smoke. A tinge of the bruise remained around her left eye and she looked weary, but her face was alert and animated with concern for Abigail.

The pungent, grassy smell of the burning hemp hung in the air inside the tent as smoke swirled around the pipe, blending with the odor of the canvas and of the women—sweat, a sour smell of age from the old woman, and the acrid stench of the sweat of fear from Abigail. Tangeree put the pipe in Abigail's mouth to take two deep puffs on it, then put it back on the herb chest. The women watched curiously as Abigail puffed on the pipe, then they talked quietly among themselves and the old woman dozed off, her lower lip drooping and saliva drooling from it. Yvonne kept her hand on Abigail's thigh, feeling the tension leaving her body. Then she sat back and moved to a more comfortable position, smothering a yawn.

The Dowds ate well, and breakfast had been ample portions of salt bacon and hominy grits, an egg, and cups of strong chicory coffee thickened with molasses. Yvonne felt drowsy from the large meal, and fatigue from the long night of walking and the soporific heat inside the tent bore down on her like a crushing weight. It was becoming hotter inside the tent as the sun rose toward its zenith, and sounds filtered through the canvas from outside. Jason Dowd stumped around the tent on his crutch, replying in a worried voice when one of the other men tried to call him away. The children laughed and played, the crated pigs grunted and occasionally squealed, cicadas whirred and birds called, and the Mississippi made its deep, whispering rumble as it rushed past, a hundred feet away. Yvonne smothered another yawn, and looked at Tangeree as the girl moved her hand to attract her attention. Another contraction was beginning, and Yvonne sat forward.

The contraction built in intensity, and Abigail writhed and screamed as the pangs gripped her. Yvonne rested her hand on Abigail's stomach to feel the rhythm of the spasms and bent over her, telling her when to breathe and push. Then the contraction passed, and Abigail collapsed limply, gasping for breath and trembling. Tangeree took the rag from the basin and wiped Abigail's face as she leaned over and talked to her in a cheerful, encouraging tone, and Yvonne lifted the loose shift covering Abigail and gently probed with the tip of a finger. The baby had entered the birth canal, and she could feel its head under the spongy, yielding cushion of the bag of waters.

The door flap opened, and Hester came back in with two steaming cups of coffee. She carefully balanced the cups as she moved around the other women and toward Yvonne, looking down at her. "It sounded like she had a pretty good one that time."

"Yes, it shouldn't be too long now."

Hester leaned over and handed the cups to Yvonne and Tangeree, and held her back and groaned with effort as she lowered herself and sat down. "The men parked your wagon over on the other side of the clearing, and they put you a stack of firewood over there. And they watered and fed your chickens, and put your oxen with ours to graze."

Yvonne nodded, taking a sip of coffee. "I'm much obliged."

"Well, it's us that's obliged to you, and I don't know how little Abby here would have done if you hadn't come along. Did I take it right that you and your girl traveled through the night?"

"Yes, that's right."

"You must be plumb tuckered out, then. Would you

like me to bring in another pallet so you can take turns laying down for a rest?"

Yvonne smiled and shook her head as she took another drink of coffee. "We're accustomed to sleeping when we can. Illness doesn't keep regular hours."

"No, I guess not," Hester chuckled. "I was just talking to Horace, and he mentioned that your oxen look like they've been doing some traveling. Are you on your way to meet your husband or something?"

"No, my husband was killed at Fredericksburg. We're on our way to Memphis."

Hester sighed heavily and shook her head. "The War's took its toll, ain't it? Our oldest boy was killed at Antietam, and our boy Jase out there lost his leg at Mechanicsville. But at least he's alive, and he's going to be a daddy here directly, ain't he?" She smiled down at Abigail, patting her leg, and looked back at Yvonne. "I guess you all are from Memphis, then, and you're going to your folks there or something?"

"No, I don't have any living relatives, and my husband's are in Tupelo. It would be too dangerous to try to get to Tupelo, and we were going to Memphis to get away from the fighting and the renegades."

"Them renegades is the worst part of it, ain't they? The things I've heard they've done has made my blood run cold. We took this river road in hopes of staying away from them, and the men keep their guns close at hand. We've been trying to make the best time we could, but we've been slowed down a little because we have an ox with a yoke gall that won't heal and one with a wen on its leg where the chain rubs it." She cleared her throat, her voice becoming hesitant. "Horace mentioned that you might could look at them, but I told him that you might not fool with animals . . . ."

"Yes, we treat animals, and we'll see to them."

"Well, we'll sure see you right on everything," Hester said, smiling and nodding in satisfaction. "Horace mentioned that you might like to travel with us, seeing as how we're going in the same direction. I know you must have had plenty of sleepless nights traveling by yourselves, and it would sure be handy for us to have somebody who can do doctoring."

Although Yvonne had been expecting to be asked to join them, it still brought a feeling of relief. She nodded. "Yes, I'd be more than glad to. Are you going to Memphis?"

"No, we're going up as far as Prior's Point and see if we can get a boat up to Missouri. We're going to California."

Yvonne blinked in surprise. "California?"

"Yes, that's about the safest place a body can be now. We've been talking about going there for a while, and our boy Jase got home at about the same time that we heard boats were running upriver again. We'd be more than proud to have you go to California with us."

Yvonne shook her head doubtfully. "I don't know, Hester. I'd have to think about it."

"Well, while you're thinking about it, you might remember that the Union's holding Memphis now. And they're treating people like dogs, too. Anyhow, you'll be going as far as Prior's Point with us, won't you?" She gathered herself and climbed to her feet with a sigh of effort. "I'd better get out there and start dinner. All the men are sitting around with their mouths gaping open like a nest full of birds, and they'd starve before they'd think of putting a hand on a pan. Charlene, you come on and give me a hand."

Charlene, the young widow of the Dowds' oldest

son, rose and followed Hester out. Yvonne sipped her coffee, thinking about the conversation. Among the Dowds, she felt secure for the first time in months, and Tangeree's safety wasn't a nagging worry in the back of her mind. She wanted to remain with the Dowds, but she had never considered going to the West. An immediate drawback was that the medical colleges were in the East, and going to the West would place an additional barrier between Tangeree and her life-long ambition, along with the other already formidable obstacles. Tangeree moved her hand to attract Yvonne's attention. Yvonne put her cup aside and sat forward again as Abigail became tense, another contraction beginning.

There was no perceptible progress during the contraction, and none during the next two. When the following contraction began Yvonne lifted Abigail so she could grasp her legs and pull them back against her abdomen to push more forcefully with the next contraction. And still there was no progress, the baby remaining in approximately the same position in the birth canal and the bag of waters remaining unbroken. The bag of waters usually ruptured at the onset of final labor and when the baby entered the birth canal, but it sometimes happened before or after. And while no two deliveries were the same, the way the delivery had progressed smoothly into final labor and then all progress had stopped was bothersome.

Childbirth was unpredictable. Abigail was a young, healthy woman with a wide pelvis and strong body, and Jason Dowd was a strapping youth with a muscular, brawny body. There was no reason why Abigail shouldn't have a sturdy, healthy baby and deliver it without undue difficulty. But at times, frail, fragile-looking women would deliver easily and a baby would

have to be forcibly extracted to save the life of a
strong, healthy woman. At times, sickly-looking people produced healthy babies and vibrantly healthy
people produced thin, puny babies that withered
away. At times, everything would seem perfect, a
young, healthy woman progressing methodically
through labor and delivered a sturdy, beautifully-
formed baby. And then the baby simply wouldn't
breathe.

Yvonne looked at Tangeree in silent communication, asking and receiving her opinion. Intuition was
a key element in determining the severity of illnesses
and the dosages to administer, and in dealing with
confusing and misleading symptoms. And while
Yvonne had far more experience and a wider knowledge of herbs than Tangeree, she had found that
Tangeree's intuition was often more accurate than
her own. A purge corrected bowel congestion, but in
instances of a condition with similar symptoms—
weakness, fever, nausea, and lower stomach pains—a
purge would bring severe abdominal pains, swelling,
and death within hours. The symptoms were frequently so similar that Yvonne occasionally had difficulty
distinguishing between the two. But Tangeree could
always tell. The girl had an uncanny degree of empathy, a contact with the ill at some mysterious level
that had nothing to do with the physical senses.

Tangeree thought the labor was too slow. Her
features were neutral, but her large blue eyes were
troubled. Yvonne looked down at Abigail, musing.
When progress was arrested during childbirth, it frequently took only a nudge for it to resume. Yvonne
looked back at Tangeree and flexed her fingers in the
signal for massage, and Tangeree rose and moved

around to the other side of the pallet, where Hester
had been sitting.

Abigail was at a stage where she was drawing into
herself and didn't want to be touched, and it took a
moment to overcome that. She was also painfully
modest, and she whimpered and tried to push her shift
back down as it gathered up around her waist. But
her modesty was overcome as the cramps eased from
the muscles in her thighs, sides, and back, and she
sank into a state of drowsy, relaxed numbness from
the gentle kneading of her body. Yvonne and Tangeree moved in unison in the Cherokee childbirth massage, hands twisting and a light pressure on the heels
of their palms as they moved up and down her thighs,
hips, and flanks.

A contraction began, and Yvonne and Tangeree
moved more rapidly, centering on Abigail's flanks and
sides and concentrating the woman's will and attention on her stomach muscles. The contraction intensified, Abigail writhed and moaned, and Yvonne and
Tangeree moved faster still, pressing and kneading.
Then the full force of the contraction gripped Abigail,
and Yvonne and Tangeree pushed their hands down
on her stomach as they leaned over her and chanted
in unison.

"Breathe . . . push! Breathe . . . push! Breathe . . .
push!"

Abigail's body began moving convulsively in rhythm
with the movements of their hands and their chanting.
Then their voices were drowned in her shrill, piercing
scream as her face flushed and her mouth opened
wide, every muscle in her body becoming rigid with
effort. She drew in a deep breath and screamed again,
shaking her head from side to side as her body arched

and tendons stood out on her neck. As the bag of waters burst in a gush and the fluid poured out onto the pallet, the contraction began subsiding.

Tangeree dabbled her hands in the fluid, and the women scrambled out of her path and away from the fluid dripping from her hands as she sprang up and darted to the door to smell and examine it in the bright light. She returned to the pallet, her expression indicating the fluid smelled normally and was clear. In deliveries where the baby was turned wrong, it was usual for the fluid to contain a brownish-green material, fecal matter that was forced from the baby by the contractions. When the baby was turned properly and the fluid contained the fecal matter, it indicated umbilical strangulation or some other serious condition that required immediate use of the smooth hardwood paddles to extract the baby. Yvonne handed Tangeree a rag to wipe her hands, and they began massaging Abigail again.

The door flap opened, and Hester looked in at Yvonne. "It sounds like we're going to have another little one here directly."

"Yes, it won't be long."

"Rubbing her legs, are you? You know, I'll bet that helps more than a body would think, because my legs always just killed me with every one I had. Grandpa caught us some nice catfish out of the river, and I have them all fried up. Do you want me to bring a plate for you and your girl?"

"No, we're going to be busy now. We'll eat later. We're about ready for the hot water, basins, and lamp."

"All right, I'll send Charlene in with them, and I'll keep your dinner hot." She looked at the other women as she backed out of the doorway. "You all can come on and eat now."

The old woman, thin and stooped with age, was already hobbling stiffly toward the door. Martha and Melvina followed her out, the flap over the door fanning and wafting a breath of fresh air into the tent. A babble of conversation rose around the fire near the tent as the men and women collected around it to eat, and dishes and silverware clattered. Charlene carried in two buckets of water, one steaming and the other cold. Then she brought in wash basins and a lamp.

The lamp cast dim, flickering shadows around the walls of the tent as Yvonne took it from her and put it between Abigail's knees to examine her. The vulval cleft was spread wide, and the top of the baby's head was barely visible. More of the baby's head became visible as the contractions seized Abigail, and it regressed slightly between contractions and moved farther forward with the next one, gradually pushing through the birth canal.

The men talked among themselves as they finished eating and moved away from the fire, and Jason Dowd began pacing around the tent again, his crutch thumping and his boot scuffling. The old woman came back into the tent, belching and sucking her gums, and the dishes and silverware rattled as the other women washed them. Then they finished the dishes and straggled back into the tent.

The crown of the baby's head protruded, stretching the vulval cleft into a round, wide opening. The soft tissue between the vulva and anus bulged massively as the baby's head pressed against the inside of it, and Abigail was in extreme discomfort, whimpering and moving her limbs. Tangeree gave her two puffs

on the pipe, then put the pipe back on the chest and
knelt again on the other side of the pallet as Yvonne
held the lamp close to look. They exchanged a glance,
and Yvonne looked down at Abigail again, musing.
Midwives and many doctors let the soft tissue between the vulva and anus tear, but Charles Dawson,
the doctor Yvonne had worked with in Tupelo, had
routinely made a small cut and stitched it with clean
linen when it was apparent that the tissue was going
to tear. The cut healed much more quickly than a
tear, infection occurred less often, and it was far less
painful for the woman.

It was a procedure that would have appalled
Yvonne's mother. Herbal medicine traditions dictated
against deliberate injury to the point that a boil was
always bound with a poltice and never lanced. But the
soft tissue rarely tore on Indian women during childbirth, and usually did on white women. And it appeared certain that it was going to tear on Abigail.
Yvonne indicated the herb chest with her chin, and
Tangeree rose and stepped back around the pallet to
it.

The powerful odor of the eucalyptus oil filled the
tent as Tangeree mixed drops of it in a tiny earthenware bowl with tincture of opium. She stepped back
around the pallet with the bowl, and handed Yvonne
the tiny, keen knife in a fold of clean linen as she knelt.
Yvonne moved the lamp closer, and Tangeree took a
small wad of rag and daubed the mixture on the taut
bulge between Abigail's vulva and anus. The women
hovered over Tangeree, watching intently and murmuring curiously. Abigail relaxed as the tissue numbed
and her discomfort diminished.

The area always bled freely, but the blood loss
could be minimized by the pressure of the baby's head

on the cut. Yvonne waited until another contraction passed and the tissue was stretched thin and near the point of tearing; then she nodded to Tangeree. Tangeree moved the lamp between Abigail's knees and held it steady, and she leaned low over Abigail's thighs to block the women's view so they wouldn't see the knife and make a comment that would frighten Abigail. Yvonne leaned down by Tangeree. She slid two fingers between the baby's head and the tight, pliant tissue to protect the baby's head from the knife as she took it out of the linen. Abigail murmured and twitched as the knife sliced cleanly through the numb tissue, and a thin stream of blood ran down. The tension that had been holding the baby's head back was relieved, and it surged forward. The entire top of the head came through the enlarged opening, and the blood flow diminished to a trickle as the baby's head pressed against the cut.

The next contraction brought the head all the way out. It was turned normally, with the face toward the mother's hips. The remainder of the fluid from the bag of waters gushed out onto the pallet as the forehead, eyes, nose, and then chin slid through. The women leaned forward and gasped excitedly as Yvonne caught the baby's head and held it, supporting it.

"Glory be, it's on its way now," Hester chuckled. "Just look at that pretty little thing."

Yvonne felt the neck to make sure the umbilical cord wasn't around it as she leaned closer to look at the baby's face. It was a normal bluish color. She looked up at Hester. "Tangi's going to need more room to move around, and we're about ready for the pan of scalding water and the fresh shift and pallet."

"That's right, let's move back and give them some

room," Hester said, spreading her arms and pushing the others back as she stepped back. "And you go get the things, Charlene. The water's boiling on the fire, and the shift and pallet are hanging on the end of the rope between the wagons over there. Hurry, and you won't miss anything."

Charlene ran out, and Tangeree moved around to the herb chest and opened and closed drawers, threading needles, cutting string, and assembling the things to make a linen pad soaked in infusion of sanicle root. Yvonne held the baby's head, waiting. Charlene returned with the scalding water, then ran back out. Tangeree dropped the threaded needles into the pan, dipped out a cupful of water to make the sanicle root infusion, then knelt on the other side of the pallet again, holding the strings to tie off the umbilical cord. The baby's head began turning, the birth process seeming to have a life and intelligence of its own as it oriented the baby so the shoulders could slip through, and Abigail moaned and twisted with the pain of the baby's movement. Charlene ran in with the pallet and shift, and puffed breathlessly as she shouldered in among the others so she could see. The head finished turning, and another contraction began.

The first shoulder slid through, hunched up against the neck, and Yvonne pushed a finger under the arm and gently pulled the small, slimy body out, automatically glancing over it as she put her other hand under the feet to support it. It was male, large and sturdy, and perfectly formed. The woman gasped and murmured, leaning closer as Yvonne and Tangeree worked in rapid, practiced coordination. Tangeree put her hands between Yvonne's arms, deftly tying the strings around the umbilical cord. She knotted the second string and slid her hands under the baby, taking it, and Yvonne picked up the knife and cut the cord. Tangeree bent over the baby, sucked the mucus out of its nose and mouth and spit it into a basin, then lifted the baby and bobbed it up and down in her hands.

The tiny arms flailed as the small face twisted and the mouth opened wide. It drew in its first breath, a deep gasp, and expelled the breath in a loud wail of protest. It drew in another breath and wailed louder, a lusty bellow that filled the tent, and its body became a flushed, healthy pink color.

Tangeree held the wriggling baby in her hands and looked at Yvonne. Her lips shone with the mucus from the baby's mouth and nose. She smiled radiantly in satisfaction. Yvonne nodded and smiled at her.

4

"IT's A BOY, Jase!" Hester bellowed, stepping to the door. "You've got a son, Jase!"

"How's Abby?" he replied worriedly, starting to come into the tent. "Is Abby all right? Is she—"

"No, you can't come in yet," Hester chuckled, pushing him away from the door. "And Abby's fine. Yvonne and her girl makes having a baby easier than losing a wart. Where's your pa? There he is. It's a boy, Horace! You've got a grandson!"

Dowd replied with a whoop, Hester went out, and the other women followed her, laughing and talking with the men as they gathered in front of the tent. Tangeree knelt by the basin, pouring warm water into it to wash the whitish, cheeselike coating off the baby, and Abigail struggled weakly to lift herself to her elbow and look at the baby. Yvonne smiled at her, pushing her back down.

"No, just lie down, Abby. We're not through yet."

"But I want to see my baby. Is he all right?"

"Yes, it's a beautiful baby, and you can see it in a few minutes. I want you to push a little more for me first." She put the heel of her hand on Abigail's Venus mound, and pulled gently on the severed umbilical cord as she slid her hand up Abigail's stomach, pressing firmly. "Push for me when I do that, Abby."

Abigail groaned and sighed tiredly, nodding. She began tensing her stomach muscles as Yvonne kneaded her stomach to expel the afterbirth. The women crowded back into the tent as Tangeree finished washing the baby and wrapped it in soft linen, and Hester took it and knelt by Abigail, showing it to her and clucking over it. The afterbirth slid out, and Yvonne examined it to make sure it was complete. She wrapped it in a rag as Tangeree washed the blood off Abigail and daubed the rest of the mixture of eucalyptus oil and tincture of opium on the edges of the cut.

Blood trickling from the cut diminished to oozing drops as Yvonne stitched it closed, gently pushing the curved needle through the edges of the cut, while Tangeree knotted the thread and cut off the trailing ends. They put the linen pad soaked in sanicle root infusion on Abigail and tied it in place, and gathered up their things as the women dressed Abigail in the clean shift and moved her to the clean pallet.

The warm sunlight of late afternoon shone down into the clearing. The fresh breeze blowing from the river was cool after the stifling heat of the tent as Yvonne and Tangeree carried their things to their wagon. Yvonne felt sleepy and weary, but deeply satisfied. The childbirth had gone smoothly, and they were safely among a large group of people they could trust. And most of all, Tangeree had largely recovered from the attack by the two men.

The experience had changed her, instilling haunted, shrinking shadows in her blue eyes that hadn't been there before, and she had lost her candid, open friendliness. One of the Dowd sons, a boy of fifteen, looked at her with an abashed grin as he walked toward the

tent to look at the baby, and Tangeree looked back
at him with a cold, hostile glance. But her despair
and despondency of before were gone, and she looked
serenely contented after the easy, uncomplicated delivery of the child.

They took a spade from the wagon and walked into
the trees behind it to find a suitable small sapling. They
dug a hole under it and buried the afterbirth among
the roots of the sapling. Charlene brought their lunch
to their wagon when they returned to it, a pan of
light, flaky catfish, a pan of crisp cornmeal balls
flavored with onions, and half a pot of the strong chicory coffee. They sat by the wagon and ate, looking at
the others. All four sides of the tent were rolled up to
let the breeze blow through it, and the men and
women were standing and sitting around the pallet
where Abigail lay with the baby. Melvina was talking
to Martha, and occasionally pressing the tips of her
fingers against her upper stomach and wincing as they
talked. Yvonne finished eating and yawned tiredly,
pushing her hair back.

"I could sleep for a week and I'm sure you feel the
same, but I see Vinney over there rubbing her stomach. And if we're going to see to her, we might as well
take care of the rest of them now."

"You wouldn't be able to go to sleep for thinking
about it," Tangeree chuckled, yawning. "But the way
that Vinney was talking at first, I was about ready to
dose her with fumic to see how high she can jump."

Yvonne laughed and shook her head as she pushed
herself to her feet. "No, that's the way some people
are, Tangi. And you have to deal with people and
things the way they are, not the way you'd like them
to be. Start a fire and put on some water to heat, and
I'll get out the things."

Tangeree nodded and yawned again as she climbed to her feet. She went to the stack of wood the men had put by the wagon and looked through it for splinters to start a fire. Yvonne let down the tailgate on the wagon to serve as a work table, and took out mixing bowls and jars of herbs.

Hester chased the children away from the tent and let down two sides on it so Abigail could rest and sleep. The people moved away from the tent, and those with complaints came over and gathered around Yvonne. Melvina's stomach complaint was a common disorder among people with her disposition, and the specific for it was a soothing burdock and peppermint infusion to be taken after meals and at night. The back pains troubling the old woman and old man seemed to be a result of their age and the hardships of traveling, rather than of any identifiable illness, and Yvonne gave them milkweed infusion to drink and sassafras oil to rub on their backs. Martha Whittacker's girl had a mild eczema infection, and Tangeree cut the hair away from the scaly spots on the girl's head as Yvonne mixed powdered jewelweed and drops of eucalyptus oil with softened wax to make a salve. Yvonne made a mouthwash and salve of alum root infusion for the ulcers on the youngest Dowd boy's mouth, and looked at the other children. They had the usual assortment of cuts, bruises, infected insect bites, and minor problems with teeth, but they were sturdy, well-fed farm children with healthy constitutions that resisted most diseases.

The people left as Yvonne and Tangeree gave them the medications, the women going to the fire near the tent and beginning preliminary preparations for dinner, and the children playing around the clearing in a noisy swarm. Dowd walked over to the wagon as

Yvonne and Tangeree were washing their mixing bowls and utensils, and he offered to pay Yvonne for what she had done. She shook her head and declined the offer. "No, we'll be traveling with you for a time, and not having to worry about renegades is worth more to me than anything I've done today."

"Well, you're more than welcome to travel with us, and we're hoping that you'll see your way clear to go on to California with us."

"I'll think about it, but I don't overly favor the idea," Yvonne replied. "California's a long way from everything that means anything to me."

"It's a good way from everything we've known as well, but it's also a long way from the War and everything that goes with it. Anyhow, you'll have several days to think about it. If you won't take pay, I'd like to make sure you have everything you need. We had a pig break its leg and there'll be fresh pork for supper, and we have plenty of food and other things in our wagons. If there's something you need and we have it, a share of it's yours for the asking."

"We have about everything we need, but it's been a long time since we've had any tobacco. If you have any extra, we could use some."

"We have more than extra," Dowd replied, nodding. "We grew a little crop of it last year and brought it along in case we could use it for trading. I'll send you some over."

"I'd be much obliged. Hester mentioned that you have a couple of oxen that need seeing to, and we'll take a look at them as soon as we're through cleaning up here."

Dowd nodded, saying as he turned away, "All right, I'll have some men over at the corral in case you need help with them."

Tangeree wiped a mixing bowl, watching him as he walked away, and looked at Yvonne. "It might be a good idea to go to California, Ma."

"You know as well as I do why I don't want to go there, Tangi," Yvonne replied. "If we get settled in the right place, we might be able to save up enough for you to go to medical college when the War's over. And California is a long way from any medical college."

"And I'm a long way from going to any medical college, Ma. I don't know where we could make money like that, because we've always just about managed to stay alive, and nobody knows when the War's going to be over."

Yvonne frowned, looking at Tangeree. "Are you losing hope, Tangi?"

"No, I'm not, Ma," Tangeree said, smiling and shaking her head. "I'm not losing hope."

Yvonne nodded as she picked up another mixing bowl and washed it. "That ox with the yoke gall will need a speckled alder bark salve, so you can go ahead and mix that and I'll finish this. And put a pinch of quinine in it."

"Quinine? What's the quinine for?"

"You wait and see, and then you'll know what to do for an ox with a yoke gall that won't heal. Just a pinch will be enough."

Tangeree chuckled and shrugged, and she climbed onto the side of the tailgate to go into the wagon for the ingredients to make the salve. One of the Dowd boys brought a large bag of tobacco, and Yvonne put it in the wagon and put away the bowls from the tailgate. Tangeree mixed the salve, and they closed the tailgate on the wagon and crossed the clearing to the rope and pole corral where the oxen were penned. As they approached the corral, Yvonne saw a large bed of ginseng in the trees beyond it, and she glanced at Tangeree. Tangeree had also seen it, and she smiled and nodded.

Dowd, Whittacker, the old man, and two of the Dowd boys were at the corral, and they brought out the ox with the yoke gall. The ox could reach the large, raw spot on its shoulder with its tongue, and it had licked off some sort of preparation they had put on the spot and continued licking it, keeping a scab from forming. It started to lick at the salve as Yvonne began spreading it on the raw spot, then it got a taste of the caustically bitter quinine on its tongue and stopped licking, foaming furiously at the mouth as it shook its head and wheezed.

The ox with the swelling on its leg was a large, aggressive animal, and it glared at Yvonne belligerently and kicked at her as she examined the swelling. It was an infection, and Yvonne sent Tangeree to the wagon for a knife and a pot of pine pitch and told the men to throw the ox. The men put a rope on the ox's wide horns, put a loop around one of its forelegs, and struggled to throw it. The ox stood with an indignant gleam in its eyes, a forefoot drawn up to its head and its head turned to one side by the pressure of the rope, and its other three feet planted firmly. The men finally pushed at it and got it off balance, and it fell heavily on its side, its legs flailing.

The children gathered around, and the other oxen in the corral moved about restlessly as the huge ox snorted angrily and squirmed on the ground, the men holding it down. Tangeree returned with the knife and a smoking pot of pitch, and Dowd and Whittacker gripped the ox's leg firmly as Yvonne leaned over it with the knife. Pus and pus-streaked blood

streamed from the swelling as Yvonne lanced it. The
ox kicked furiously, shaking Dowd and Whittacker
from side to side. Tangeree sat down on the ox's leg
and gripped it, helping the two men hold it, and
Yvonne probed for the cause of infection. It was a
large thorn, embedded deeply in the inflamed flesh.
She got it out, dipped hot pitch from the pot with a
wooden paddle, and slapped it into the wound. The
ox uttered a shrill bellow as it exploded into a frenzy
of kicking, and Tangeree and the two men clung
grimly to the ox's leg and bounced back and forth as
Yvonne dodged the heavy hoof and tied a rag around
the wound to keep the pitch in it.

Yvonne was almost exhausted when they finished
with the oxen, but ginseng was priceless, useful as an
ingredient in a wide variety of medications and in
such constant demand that it was a medium of exchange and easy to sell virtually anywhere. Others
who had harvested the bed had followed the traditions
of herb gatherers, transplanting the smaller roots in
rows so the bed would spread. Yvonne and Tangeree
carefully uprooted the plants from the soft soil and
picked through the roots, selecting the large, pithy,
three-pronged roots and putting the others aside to
transplant. They dug furrows and carried manure
from the corral to fertilize them, then planted all the
small roots and put the ones they had selected in
baskets to take them to the river and wash them.

The sun set as they finished cleaning the roots and
hung the baskets from the bows in the wagon for
the roots to dry, and Charlene brought their dinner
to their wagon in pans. There was a pan of the rich,
fresh pork, a pan of fried potatoes and onions, a pan
of collard greens flavored with bacon, and cornbread.
Sunset faded into soft twilight as they ate. Charlene

came for the pans and took them to wash. Tangeree
went into the wagon to get the bag of tobacco and the
pipes. Yvonne filled her pipe, lit it with a twig from
the fire and held the twig for Tangeree to light hers,
then tossed the twig into the fire and puffed on her
pipe contentedly. She was weary from the long day
and the lack of sleep the night before, but she felt the
pleasant anticipation of being able to go to bed and
sleep soundly and luxuriously in safety, in the knowledge that one of the men would be on guard all night.

The deep darkness before moonrise fell, insects
chirped loudly in the weeds, and the croaking of frogs
was a rising and falling wave of sound on the breeze
as it swept through the clearing, fanning the flames
and coals in the fire. The children went to bed, and
the women moved around the large fire near the tent,
washing and drying the dishes and making preliminary preparations for breakfast.

Footsteps approached: the scuffle and thump of
Jason Dowd limping along on his crutch. He stopped
and leaned on his crutch as he came into the light of
the fire, and he touched the brim of his hat and
nodded, clearing his throat self-consciously. "Well, I
just wanted to say how grateful I am for what you did
for Abby. I'm sure much obliged."

Yvonne liked the young man, because he had shown
concern for his wife. And while the loss of a limb
made many bitter and withdrawn, it didn't appear to
have affected him. She smiled and nodded. "We're
pleased that Abby did so well, and that it was a
strong, healthy baby. Is Abby sleeping?"

"Yes, ma'm. And my ma and the other women said
that it was your doing that she's done so good, so I'm
mighty grateful." He looked away into the darkness
and cleared his throat again, then looked back at

Yvonne. "My ma also said that you lost your man at Fredericksburg. And I wanted to ask you what his name was."

"It was Robert Beaunais. Why do you ask?"

"Well, me and Abby have talked about it, and we thought about naming our boy after your man. So if it's all right with you, we'll name the boy Robert Bownay Dowd."

Yvonne glanced at Tangeree, then looked back at Jason and nodded. "Yes, it's all right with us, Jase. In fact, it pleases us."

"That's what we'll call him, then," Jason said. He hesitated, then cleared his throat once more as he touched the brim of his hat and turned away. "Well, good night, ma'm."

"Good night, Jase."

He stumped away toward the tent. The moon was rising, its pale light beginning to filter through the trees on the east side of the clearing. The women were leaving the fire and moving toward the wagons to go to bed. Yvonne watched Jason as he passed the fire and went into the tent, and her eyes stung with tears. She blinked them away as she looked across the fire at Tangeree.

"It's been a good day, hasn't it, Tangi?"

Tangeree's large blue eyes were gleaming with tears. She took her pipe out of her mouth and exhaled, then wiped at her eyes with the back of her hand as she nodded. "Yes, it's been a good day, Ma."

5

THE FOUR MEN appeared without warning, riding from behind a dense thicket of willows at one side of the road. Yvonne knew what they were at first glance, without needing to see the shotguns and rifles leveled at the Dowd men at the front of the line of wagons. They were bearded, disheveled, and unwashed from months of living in the forests and swamps. Their horses were thin and rangy, and they were leading two heavily-laden pack mules. They were renegades.

Yvonne had heard Jason and his father arguing about how the armed men should be deployed. Dowd had argued that an attack would probably come at the front of the line of wagons. Jason had argued that it was impossible to stay completely alert all the time, and the only defense against surprise attack was for the men to be spread out along the line of wagons.

Both of them had been right. The attack had come at the front of the column, and the men had been caught by surprise. And the men were dropping their weapons and lifting their arms as the renegades rode to the edge of the road, snarling orders and grinning in triumphant satisfaction. Yvonne was leading her oxen behind the first wagon in line, yards from the

68

renegades as they stopped at the edge of the road. The oxen pulling the wagons behind hers straggled to a stop as the women leading them stopped, calling out in fright and shock.

"Now we don't want any trouble with you fellows," Dowd said, a quaver of fear in his voice. "And we don't want anybody to get hurt—"

"We'll sure give plenty of thought to what you want," one of the renegades replied sarcastically, and the others laughed. He was the largest among the four and appeared to be the leader. He glanced over his shoulder at one of the others. "Jake, get down and tie them up."

"No, we ain't going to be tied," Dowd said. "Now we have food and we have a little money, and we can settle with you fellows and be on our way. We don't want anybody to get hurt."

"You'll shut your goddamned mouth, or I'll shut you up with a load of buckshot!" the man barked angrily in reply. "And we'll be the ones to figure out how we're going to settle with you! We'll see what you've got to eat, and we'll see how much money you've got." He sat back on his horse, his sarcastic smile returning, and looked along the line of wagons. "And maybe we'll see what else you've got."

The other three laughed raucously in gleeful anticipation, looking along the wagons. Their avid eyes passed over Yvonne and lifted above and beyond her, looking at Tangeree in the front of the wagon. And the cold, paralyzing fear gripping Yvonne turned into seething rage. The memory of Tangeree's panic-stricken screams and the sound of a hard, heavy fist striking her flesh was still a burning agony in her mind, a raw and painful wound. The halter ropes slipped from her hand as she reached for the pistol.

The renegades had looked back at the men. The leader was barking at the men and ordering them into a line. Another one was dismounting to tie the men. One of them saw Yvonne's movement and shouted in alarm. The heavy pistol slid out of the holster, the hammer coming back with an oily click. The leader of the renegades reacted more rapidly than the others, swinging his shotgun around. Yvonne leveled the long pistol, holding it at arm's length in both hands, and put the blade sight on the end of the barrel on the man's chest. She squeezed the trigger.

The pistol leaped in her hands, smoke boiling from it as it boomed. The oxen shied to one side in a scramble of hoofs, and the man was knocked backwards from his horse. His finger squeezed both triggers on the shotgun as it pointed toward a horse two feet away. The shotgun thundered and smoke billowed from it, and the horse screamed as it pitched to one side, its right shoulder a mass of raw flesh. The man astride the horse had been leveling a rifle at Yvonne; it fired as he fell with the horse, and a geyser of dirt and grass erupted from the road ten feet in front of Yvonne.

The Henry rifle made an ear-shattering crack behind Yvonne as Tangeree fired. The thunderous noise blended with the clear, sharp sound of the heavy bullet striking one of the horses, the sound of a sledge hammer hitting a side of meat. Another horse fell floundering to the ground, screaming shrilly in fright and agony. The man astride it rolled backwards off its rump, his legs churning as the shotgun he was holding fired into the air. Then the men at the front of the wagons were scrambling for the weapons they had dropped, Jason's crutch flying through the air as he tossed it aside and leaped, the old man's white beard and his hair bright as his wide hat flew off.

The renegades and their horses were a swirling mass of motion, the wounded horses flailing and writhing on the ground, the other horses and pack mules bucking and rearing, and the men falling from them, trying to fire weapons and trying to get away. Yvonne picked out a man's face in the confusion, hatless and his hair flying, and his eyes wild with panic as he tried to mount a horse. She swung the pistol toward him. He looked directly at her as she looked down the barrel of the pistol at him. Motion seemed to slow, and noise seemed to die away. They were strangely isolated from the others and from their surroundings in an instant on the edge of eternity, Yvonne sighting down the barrel and the man looking at her with a suddenly helpless, resigned expression. Yvonne tugged the trigger gently. The pistol bounced, and he pitched backward and disappeared.

Tangeree fired the Henry again. A pack mule reared high into the air, a ragged, penetrating whinny coming from its throat as it toppled over onto its back. The front wagon slewed to the left as the frightened oxen bucked, kicked, and pulled it to one side. The men were standing, kneeling, and lying in the road with their guns. They fired a ragged volley that cut down both a man and his horse as he tried to get away.

The fourth man rode away, kicking and lashing his horse, and the men fired a hail of bullets after him. The shotguns were ineffective at their distance from the man, and the rifle and pistol bullets clipped branches and ricocheted off the trees the man was riding through. Yvonne trotted forward, cocking the pistol, and stopped near the horse that had been hit by the double charge of buckshot. A straight avenue through the trees stretched out between Yvonne and the man. She lifted the pistol.

The Henry cracked again. Its shattering noise swept over Yvonne, and the bullet hissed over her head and slammed into a tree a few feet from her. She jerked involuntarily, then gripped herself and steadied the pistol again, sighting down the barrel at the man. He was small with distance compared to the blade sight, bouncing with the horse's fast pace. She put the sight above his head and centered it over him, and squeezed the trigger. The pistol fired and bounced. The impact of the bullet knocked the man off the horse, and he spreadeagled in the air as he fell. He disappeared into the deep grass and brush, and the horse slowed to a trot, then a walk.

Yvonne's knees tremblbled violently in reaction, and she suddenly felt breathless and sick at her stomach, her lungs laboring and the sour burning in her stomach trying to work its way up to her throat. The men began talking and arguing. Whittacker walked away from them and began shooting the wounded horses and a mule, and one of the Dowd boys calmed the oxen hitched to the first wagon. The women rushed forward in a babble of voices, and Tangeree jumped down from the wagon and took the halter ropes, talking to the oxen and calming them. Yvonne put the pistol back in the holster and walked through the trees.

The horse was standing a few feet from the man. It rolled its eyes, snorted, and stamped its feet in fright. The man was on his back, still alive, and looking up at the sky. And he was hardly more than a boy, a year or two older than Tangeree. Downy beard covered his cheeks and chin. His lips were pressed tightly together as quivering shudders of pain passed through his body. It looked like a lung shot, probably but not necessarily fatal. His eyes turned toward Yvonne as she approached him, taking the bowie knife out of the sheath, and they became bright with terror as she stood over him, looking down at him.

The expression on the youthful face was much like that of a boy who feared a thrashing from his mother. He was so very young. But the boyish face had been adult with lustful desire when he smiled and laughed with the others, looking at Tangeree. And the memory of Tangeree's screams and moans still echoed in Yvonne's mind. She leaned over him. The sharp, heavy blade slashed deep. Blood spouted, and his mouth opened in a soundless scream as his face paled toward the blanched gray of death and his body jerked in spasms. Yvonne wiped the knife on his shirt and slid it back into the sheath as she walked toward the horse. The horse started to shy away from her, and she talked to it softly and moved slowly toward it until she caught one of the reins. She unfastened the saddle girth and pushed the saddle off the horse, took the bridle off it and dropped it to the ground, then walked back toward the road.

The Dowds were arguing fiercely, the sound of their angry voices carrying through the trees. The argument centered between Dowd, Hester, and Jason, and the others were staying out of it. Whittacker stood at one side and looked away, the old man and old woman silently listened, and the others listened and commented quietly among themselves. Both Jason and Hester were blaming Dowd for the near disaster, and Hester was castigating him in a loud, strident voice as Yvonne approached the road.

". . . supposed to be looking out for trouble, and you do nothing but walk along up here and pass the time of day! Now it's about time you all woke up and used your eyes more and your mouths less before a bunch of renegades robs and slaughters us, not to speak of worser!"

"They'll do it anyway, Ma!" Jason shouted. "As long as we're all in one bunch here at the front of the wagons, we're sitting ducks for any renegades who come along!"

"Then spread out!" Hester snarled, wheeling toward him. "I'm not going to try to tell you how to do your business! All I want is for you to do it!"

"It ain't up to me!" Jason barked back at her, and he pointed angrily at his father. "I told him what would happen, and it damned near did!"

"Now both of you hold your tongues!" Dowd snapped. "I'm not going to have a bunch of haggling amongst this family, and I'm—"

"No, you're going to have us all killed!" Jason stormed at him. "If they had wanted to, they could have shot us all dead in our tracks before they ever left those willows! But they didn't have to waste lead on men so stupid as to all walk in one bunch!"

"Who are you calling stupid?" Dowd roared at him. "If you don't like what we do here, there's plenty of road for you to travel by yourself!"

"By God, maybe I will!" Jason stormed. "I've got Abby and the baby to think about, and I could do a better job of protecting them by myself!"

"Now you watch your tongue, Jase!" Hester shouted. "We won't have the Lord's name taken in vain here, and we won't have no talk of nobody going their own way! And you ought to get a hold on your tongue before you say something like that to your own son, Horace!"

"Perhaps we should all be on our way," Yvonne interjected quietly. "And leave here what happened here. There'll be plenty of time to talk about what happened and learn from it when we've had time to think about it and when tempers have had time to cool."

They looked at her, and Hester sighed heavily and nodded as she wiped her face with her sleeve, her anger fading. "There's good sense talking. And from the one we've got to thank that we're all not murdered and robbed, not to speak of worser. I thought you was wearing that coat to keep the dust off your dress, Yvonne, and I'm mightly glad that you had more than your dress under it. We're all mighty grateful to you."

"Yes, we are," Dowd said as the others murmured and nodded. "We're much obliged to you for what you did, and it took as much courage as I've ever seen anybody show."

The large, brawny man's voice was gruff, and guilt, anger, and defensiveness were mixed on his red face. Yvonne silently nodded, turning toward her wagon. Tangeree was holding the halter ropes and listening wide-eyed to the argument. Yvonne took the ropes from her and motioned for her to get into the wagon. She climbed the wheel and got into the wagon, and the other women began walking back toward their wagons. Some of the children who were looking at the dead animals and men in fearful fascination ran after the women.

"Well, what are we going to do?" Jason demanded belligerently, looking at his father. "Are we all still going to walk along here in a bunch, or are we going to spread out so we'll have a chance if we meet any more?"

"You do whatever the hell you want to!" Dowd

barked in reply. "You seem to know so much about what to do, just go ahead and do it! Jacob, I'm going to walk ahead."

Whittacker nodded, tucking his shotgun under his arm as Dowd walked away. Jason glared at his father's back, seething with anger, then motioned brusquely to his brother of fifteen and stumped toward the wagons behind Yvonne's, his brother following him. One of the younger Dowd boys clucked to the oxen hitched to the first wagon, pulling on the halter ropes, and the wagon groaned into motion, Whittacker and the old man walking in front of the oxen and Dowd walking a hundred feet in front of them. Yvonne tugged on the halter ropes, and her oxen leaned into the yoke. The wagon creaked, and the wheels rumbled as they began turning. The wagons behind hers began moving, chains rattling, wagon timbers creaking, the heavy wheels rumbling along the road.

The breeze carried the scent of the forest and fields to her nostrils, a smell of life and of green growing things. The past three days had been blissful. The medications had worked well on Melvina, the children, and the old man and woman, and the Dowds had marveled at what they considered almost miraculous cures. Abigail was taking a few more steps each day and doing light tasks around the camp at night, no infection had developed, and her baby was doing well. The Dowds had enormous supplies of food, and always insisted on sharing their meals. Most of all, the heavy weight of continuous anxiety had been lifted.

And now that anxiety had returned. It was clear that the security she had felt because of the armed men and nightly guards had been false to at least a degree. The men had been caught completely unaware. If one of the renegades had been more watchful or had reacted more rapidly, she would have been shot while reaching for the pistol. The men were now spread out instead of being grouped, but that might mean only that the next attack would come in the form of sudden gunfire from a place of concealment along the road. The threat of attack had returned.

"Ma?"

Yvonne looked over her shoulder. "What is it, Tangi?" she called over the sound of the wagons.

"I think I hit one of them, Ma."

Yvonne looked at Tangeree musingly as the girl sat in the front of the wagon and looked at her over the seat, smiling brightly, and she nodded silently and noncommittally, looking ahead again.

"I was in two minds whether to use the rifle or shotgun. Then I decided that the rifle would be easier to load and shoot."

Yvonne looked over her shoulder again. "You keep your hands off that shotgun, Tangeree. I don't want you to touch it."

"Why, Ma?"

"Because I wouldn't want to be in the same county as you if you were to shoot it. You'd kill the very grass and pissants for miles in every direction. Now you keep your hands off that shotgun, do you understand?"

"All right, Ma. Don't you think I hit any of them, then?"

"No, I don't believe you did, Tangi."

Tangeree nodded, sitting back down on the pallet behind the seat in the wagon. Yvonne looked ahead again, and she smiled wryly as she thought about the girl's wild shots with the rifle.

Jason passed, swinging his crutch in long, rapid strides and carrying his rifle under his arm, and overtook the first wagon. He walked along in front of it for a few minutes with Whittacker and the old man, talking to them, then went back toward the rear of the line of wagons again. Yvonne motioned to him as he started to pass her.

"Jase, would you get Tangi to hand you down some bullets for me so I can reload my pistol?"

He nodded, hesitating and waiting for the oxen to pass, then called to Tangeree and asked her to hand him the bullets as he walked along beside the front wheel of the wagon. Tangeree rummaged around under the seat, then leaned over and handed him the bullets. He caught up with Yvonne and handed the bullets to her, smiling down at her.

"We sure want you to keep that pistol loaded. I hate to think of what would have happened if it hadn't been for you and that pistol. It looks like meeting you is the best thing that ever happened to us."

Vvonne smiled and shrugged as she tucked the ropes under her arm and took out the pistol to reload it. "I was protecting my own, Jase, and that's something most anybody will do. But it won't do us a bit of good for you and your pa to be thinking more about being mad at each other than about looking out for renegades. It would be good if you'd step up there and speak to him."

"It's up to him," Jason said curtly, his smile fading as he looked away. "He was in the wrong, not me. I told him all along what we should be doing."

"He's your pa, Jase," Yvonne replied, opening the cylinder on the pistol and dropping the spent shells out of it. "It would be expecting a lot of any man to look for him to apologize to a boy of his, and your pa's prouder than most. And I imagine he knows he was in the wrong. But if there's something that galls more than to know you're in the wrong and to have somebody tell you that you are, I don't know what it is." She pushed the bullets into the cylinder, snapped it closed, and slid the pistol back in the holster, looking up at Jason. "You're a big man, Jase. But if you were to go on up there and make up with your pa, you'd grow about two feet in my eyes. And in your own eyes, when you have time to think about it."

Jason frowned darkly and looked away, thinking, then silently shook his head as he turned away and hobbled on his crutch toward the rear of the line of wagons. Yvonne sighed, looking at Dowd a hundred feet ahead of the front wagon as the road curved and he came into sight. Then she adjusted the pistol in the holster and scanned the trees and brush on both sides of the road.

A few minutes later, Jason passed again, and he avoided Yvonne with his eyes as he trudged through the deep weeds by the road toward the first wagon. When he reached it, he slowed to the plodding pace of the oxen and walked beside the wagon for a moment, looking down at the ground and frowning in thought. Then he straightened up and took long, rapid strides with his crutch, passed Whittacker and the old man, and caught up with his father.

They walked together for several minutes, occasionally glancing toward each other and apparently exchanging terse comments. Then they began talking, motioning and nodding, and Dowd put his hand on Jason's shoulder as they laughed about something. Presently Jason turned and walked back toward the wagons, making a parting comment to his father. He grinned at Yvonne as he passed, and she smiled and nodded.

The raw feeling of conflict had faded when the wagons turned off the road and into a wide clearing behind a screen of trees an hour later, but there was still tension in the atmosphere. The children were more subdued than usual, the people were more than normally cordial and helpful with each other, and they picked their words carefully to avoid creating ill feelings. There was also an awareness of danger among the people that hadn't existed before, and everyone was more watchful. And when a mounted man suddenly appeared at one end of the clearing, men reached for their guns and Yvonne slid her hand under her linen coat to her pistol.

The man was about fifty, with white hair and a short white beard, and in a Confederate Cavalry uniform. He lifted his Henry rifle with the stock upward in the universal sign of peaceful intentions, and nudged his gaunt horse with his heels. The horse moved forward, followed by a bony pack mule. The man's uniform was faded from wear and many washings, but it was neat and clean. The wide brim of his hat was pulled low over his grizzled eyebrows and piercing, pale blue eyes. Frayed cavalry tassels hung over the edge of the brim and swayed as the horse walked forward. Yvonne took her hand away from her pistol, and the men lowered their weapons. Dowd stepped forward.

"That's far enough, mister. What do you want here?"

The man reined in his horse and rested his rifle across the horn of his saddle, touched the brim of his hat and glanced at Yvonne and the other women, then looked at Dowd. "It's been awhile since I've had a taste of coffee, so I thought I'd ride over and see if you have any extra. I can pay with gold."

"We have coffee, but we ain't in the trading business. Are you a deserter? There's no Confederate forces around here."

The man shrugged nonchalantly. "I expect that would depend on who's putting a name to me. By my lights I'm not, but there's probably some who'd say I am."

"What does that mean?"

"That means I got wounded and I had a chance to go see my daughter in Memphis. And after what I found there, I decided to appoint myself as a one-man sniper squad instead of returning to my regiment."

"A sniper?" Dowd said, frowning. "You mean you lay in ambush and shoot people in the back, don't you?"

The man nodded placidly. "I've done some of that. If it's a blue uniform, I'm not overly particular about which side of it I draw a bead on. And when there's up to a dozen of them and one of me, I don't think that's taking too much advantage."

"And you say you went to Memphis? The Union's had Memphis for several months."

A lazy smile stretched the man's lips, not reaching his hard, glassy eyes. "I did find myself some other clothes to do my visiting," he chuckled dryly.

"I don't like the sound of this," Dowd said brusquely, shaking his head. "It sounds to me like you're a deserter, whatever you say. I'm going to ask you to be on your way."

The man looked away, the slight smile still on his face, then looked back at Dowd. "I don't feel like I have to explain myself to you, mister. On the other hand, I wouldn't want to leave with the ladies thinking ill of me. So I'll say that when I went to Memphis to see my girl Nadine, I found out that she had been arrested as a vagrant and put in a house they kept for Union officers and their cronies. Nadine got some poison one way or another, and they threw her body into the lime pits they use to get rid of the twenty or thirty others they shoot and hang every day. So that's why I'd rather do my fighting in these parts."

The casual smile remained on the man's face. It had become subtly different and looked deadly, and his pale blue eyes glittered in the shadow of his hat brim. An awkward, embarrassed silence settled and stretched out. Yvonne looked at the man's rifle. The stock had a low row of notches on it.

Dowd turned and looked at one of his younger sons. "Go get a bag of coffee out of the wagon." He looked back at the man and lifted his hand as the man took off one of his long gloves and started to reach in his pocket. "We don't need your money. And we're mighty sorry to hear about what happened to your girl. Was she by herself?"

"Her husband was killed at Shiloh," the man replied, pulling his glove back on. "She was staying with an aunt of her husband's, and they were doing washing and sewing to buy food. I expect the aunt wasn't a vagrant because she didn't suit their purposes. For whatever reason, she wasn't arrested and she told me what had happened."

"Well, we're mighty sorry to hear about it. Do you think we'll run into any Union soldiers between here and Prior's Point?"

"No, there's no Union soldiers to speak of south of Paxton. And they wouldn't be any real trouble to you. Some of them might or might not sass the ladies, depending on who their officer is, but that would be all. But if you get in the Memphis District, trouble will come looking for you. There's a dark-until-dawn curfew, and anyone who brakes it is shot on sight, be they a man, woman, or child. Anyone who's caught with a gun is hanged as a renegade, be they a man, woman, or child. I was there less than a week in finding out what happened to Nadine, and they hanged and shot no less than a hundred in that length of time."

The boy ran up with the bag of coffee, puffing heavily, and Dowd took it from him and looked up at the man on the horse. "If you want to step down and have a bite of supper, you'll be welcome. It'll be ready before long."

"I'm obliged and I'd enjoy your company, but I'd better be on my way. I've just been down to Bayou Mound to get some ammunition, and I'm anxious to get back to my hunting territory."

Dowd handed the coffee up to him. "Well, we wish you good luck."

The man nodded, pushing the bag into a saddlebag, and he touched the brim of his hat and glanced at Yvonne and the other women as he reined his horse around. The horse walked toward the end of the clearing, the mule plodding wearily along behind it, and the people silently stood and watched. Then the horse and mule disappeared into the trees. The people walked toward their wagons, talking quietly. Yvonne turned and walked toward her wagon, Tangeree walking beside her, and the girl looked at her.

"From what that man said, we'd be better off out here in the woods than in Memphis, Ma."

Yvonne glanced at the girl and looked away, musing. It was a bitter choice, but it appeared that there was little choice. She sighed heavily, nodding. "Yes, it sounds that way, Tangi. And anywhere else that we could go might be the same. So it looks like we'd better stay with the Dowds and go with them to California."

PART TWO

WESTWARD

6

THE SUN BEAMED brightly down into the roofless screen of canvas around the rear of the wagon, three walls that enclosed an area for privacy while examining and treating patients. The young girl on the rough split-log bench along one of the canvas walls was feverish and weak and her face was pale with pain as she leaned on one arm and held her lower stomach. She winced and whimpered in protest as Yvonne bent over her and felt her stomach, and Yvonne stepped back and nodded Tangeree toward the girl. Tangeree sat down by her and put her hand on the girl's shoulder, smiling at her and murmuring sympathetically. Yvonne looked at the girl's mother.

"How long has she been like this?"

The woman was probably forty but looked sixty. Most of her teeth were missing and she was thin and sallow. Her shoulders slumped, her face was lined, and her hands were gnarled with toil. "Oh, it's been getting worser right along for onto three days now."

"Has she ever had this before?"

The woman sighed and pushed back a wisp of gray hair, thinking, then shrugged. "Well, kids have the bellyache so much, don't they? But it seems to me

like her stomach has pestered her more than it has
all the others."

"Has she had any tonic lately?" Tangeree asked.

"Oh, yes, she's had some not long gone," the woman
replied, then looked back at Yvonne. "You don't think
that's what did it, do you?"

"What kind of tonic did she have?" Yvonne asked.

"I usually thin out a cup of molasses and put in a
spoonful of sulfur and a drop or two of croton oil.
We ain't had no molasses around here since I don't
remember when, so I used some honey. You don't
reckon the honey did it to her, do you?"

"Has tonic ever done this to her before?" Tangeree
asked.

"Well, tonic's supposed to give you a bellyache,
ain't it?" the woman replied. "But she might have took
on a little more than the others did, now that I think
about it. It's hard to remember from one year to the
next, because a year in Prior's Point is like ten anywhere else."

Yvonne smiled and nodded to the woman, and
looked back at Tangeree. Tangeree had her arm
around the girl's shoulders and was talking to her
softly as she moved the tips of her fingers over the
girl's stomach. Then she moved away from the girl,
looking at Yvonne. The symptoms indicated bowel
congestion, but from Tangeree's questions about tonic
and the expression in her eyes, she thought it was the
condition in which a purge shouldn't be used. Yvonne
nodded and indicated the bottles and bowls on the
tailgate of the wagon. Tangeree rose and went to the
tailgate, and Yvonne touched the woman's arm and
nodded toward the flap covering the doorway in
the canvas.

The deep weeds in front of the canvas were tram-

pled down by the people from the town who had
gathered every morning to have their ailments treated.
It was afternoon, and the only one outside was the
girl's father, a male counterpart of the thin, prematurely
aged woman. He rose, glancing worriedly between
Yvonne and his wife.

"Your girl is very ill," Yvonne said quietly. "We'll
give you something that will ease her pain, but a lot
of her treatment is going to be up to you. She's going
to have to be kept quiet and in bed most of the time
during the next few days, and she mustn't do any
kind of heavy work for the next two or three weeks.
And you mustn't ever give her a tonic again."

"What's wrong with her?" the man asked.

"She has a weakness of the bowel. People who have
it suffer these attacks from time to time, and they
should never have a tonic."

"But she's going to be all right, ain't she?" the
woman asked anxiously. "Laws, everybody is talking
about what a good doctor you are. Mabel Cummings
said you're the first one who's ever give her anything
that would ease her ague, Sally Wiggins said her boy's
itch was might near cured by the time she got home,
and . . . she's going to be all right, ain't she?"

"She's young, and that makes a difference in any
illness. Give her the medicine three times a day, and
do as I said."

"We'll sure do that, ma'm," the man said, groping
in his pockets. "I think I have some money here—"

"No, there won't be any charge, because you'll be
doing most of the doctoring yourselves. Be careful
with her while you're carrying her home. Don't drop
her, and keep her lying flat as far as possible."

The man nodded, and they followed Yvonne back
through the doorway into the canvas enclosure.

Tangeree was straining the bergamot infusion into an empty whiskey bottle, and the man carefully picked up the girl and carried her out. The woman took the bottle from Tangeree, smiling worriedly and nodding in thanks, and hurried out after the man. Tangeree began washing out the bowl in which she had made the infusion, glancing over her shoulder at Yvonne.

"Are there any more out there, Ma?"

"No, that's all for right now. We didn't have too many today, did we?"

"I think we've cured everyone in town of everything they had," Tangeree chuckled, then her smile faded. "We keep finding people with that bowel condition, don't we?"

"Yes, that's right, Tangi," Yvonne replied, walking back toward the doorway. "When you've finished that, come on out and sit where it's cool."

"All right, Ma."

Yvonne went out and sat on the split-log bench outside the doorway. The wagons were parked on a low rise, a hill above the flood level of the Mississippi, and the river at the foot of it was a massive stretch of rippling, creased water that gleamed in the sunshine. It looked deceptively narrow until the eyes focused on towering trees on the opposite bank. Then the vast distance fell into a proportion that staggered the imagination. On the slope below the wagons was Prior's Point, a sprawling mass of shacks and small, flimsy houses, with a single, winding street of businesses in clapboard buildings with false fronts for second floors.

Clots of cotton littered the fields and hung in the branches of trees around the town, an omnipresent debris that marked the route followed by the huge, heavy bales from plantation to mill. It hung on build-

ings and piled up in corners where it was swept by
breezes, and in season it would cling to clothes, irri-
tate the nostrils, and permeate the lives of those along
the route, a badge of prosperity that was cheerfully
endured. But the clots in the trees were gray and
weathered and those in the fields had been pounded
into the weeds by the rains of two or three years, and
King Cotton had given way in the town to hunger,
hardship, and the desperation of those with no other
way of life and no other place to go.

War had brushed past, and the threat that it would
come again hung over the town. Patches of ashes and
fire-blackened timbers spotted the town from when
part of it had been shelled, and what had been a low
row of cotton warehouses along the edge of the high
riverbank was a tangle of burned timbers and warped
sheet metal. The wharf that had extended out over
the bank in front of the warehouses was a shambles
of broken timbers and rotting piers, and a narrow,
makeshift wharf of logs and raw timbers reached out
from the end of the main street through the town.

The road passed near the level spot where the
wagons were parked and became the main street when
it entered the town. It was gouged deep into the
ground on the slope by the iron wheels of countless
lumbering drays that had carried loads of cotton bales
into town. Overgrown and in disrepair, wheel ruts
had turned into gulleys by washing rains, and weeds
covered the ridge between the gulleys. The man and
woman who had just left the wagon were walking
along the road and nearing the outskirts of the town,
the man carefully carrying the girl in his arms and
the woman clutching the bottle to her so she wouldn't
drop it. Yvonne looked at them, thinking about what
Tangeree had said.

Two days before, a woman who had brought a child had made an offhand comment about another child who had suffered severe abdominal pains and swelling and had died after being given a tonic. Tangeree had pounced on the remark and questioned the woman closely about the symptoms and prior attacks of abdominal pain the child had suffered. She had talked about it later, comparing it with patients from years before that Yvonne had almost forgotten, and with other things she had heard. She had developed a theory that the condition of the lower abdomen that simulated bowel congestion often announced itself over a period of years. The purge that was administered as a result of the pain made the condition worse, as did tonic or any other laxative medication, but it often subsided and remained quiescent for a time, sometimes years. Eventually it became severe, and a purge would bring it to an acute condition, resulting in death.

The pattern Tangeree saw wasn't clear to Yvonne, and she was reluctant to form general theories. Many of the functions and illnesses of the abdomen remained a mystery even to doctors using the most advanced techniques. And she found the subject remotely uncomfortable to contemplate. She never took purges or tonics, believing it was better to allow the body to adjust naturally to conditions of diet and activity, but there had been two or three times when she herself had been bothered by a sharp, nagging pain in her lower abdomen.

The man and woman disappeared among the other people along the street. Most of the people were around the wharf, the center of activity in the town. A small scull from a settlement on the other side of the river had tied up at one side of the wharf, and men and women were unloading baskets of produce. Two fishermen were taking catches from rowboats, and several men were dismantling a raft of timber they had floated down the river. Old men sat in a row on a long bench by a sagging, ramshackle shed near the end of the wharf. Children and dogs ran about, and loiterers milled around.

Tangeree came out of the shed and Yvonne smiled up at her, moving over to make room for her. Tangeree sat down with a contented sigh. "It's sure a pretty day, isn't it, Ma? And this is a nice place."

"It was, and it could be again, Tangi. But there could be a battle taking place here next week. I can smell it in the air."

"Yes, I suppose you're right," Tangeree said musingly, looking down at the town. "Well, we'll probably be on our way before long."

Yvonne nodded, looking back at the wharf. The riverboats weren't following a regular schedule, but those that hadn't been commandeered by one side or the other were moving along the river again for the present, a trickle of commerce and a lifeline of contact furtively running a gauntlet of war. Two had stopped on their way downriver and one had stopped and gone on upriver since they had arrived, ancient, wheezing hulks that had been resurrected from storage or abandonment in the backwaters of river ports and pressed into service. The men had gone to talk to the captain of the one going upriver, and they had returned, shaking their heads. The boat had been enroute to Memphis. And no one knew when the boats would stop running again, a not unexpected situation at a time when life was very uncertain.

A thin, excited squeal came from the top of the slope, where the Dowd boys were taking turns watching the river from the top of a tall tree. Tangeree stood and moved away from the canvas, looking up the slope. "I'll go find out what he's seen, Ma."

She disappeared around the wagon. The other wagons were parked together a few yards away from the grassy space in front of the canvas, where the ill had been gathering and waiting their turn to be seen. There was a babble of voices among the wagons, men and boys shouting to the boy in the tree, and his voice replied faintly. Tangeree came back around the wagon, smiling excitedly.

"It's another boat, Ma. He says it's a big one, and it's just beyond the bend."

Yvonne stood and craned her neck, looking at the wide, sweeping bend in the river. The sound of voices on the other side of the wagon became louder, the men shouting to each other. Then Dowd, Whittacker, and Jason hurried down the road toward the town, a couple of the boys following them. Hester and Melvina came around the wagon and stood with Yvonne and Tangeree, watching the bend in the river. White smoke became visible above the dense foliage overhanging the near bank, then the smoke stacks and the top of the wheelhouse came into sight. The boat came around the bend, slowly forging up the river against the current as smoke billowed from its twin stacks.

It was large, two hundred feet or more long and about fifty feet wide, but it was more a barge than a riverboat, a single flat deck and no superstructure except for the smokestacks and high wheelhouse jutting up from the small cabin near the forward end of the deck. It was an old wood-burning stern-wheeler, its smokestacks canted and its gray, weathered hull and deck streaked with boards that had replaced those which had rotted through. Crates, barrels, and stacks of lumber were roped down on the deck forward of the cabin, along with a pitiful few bales of cotton that were strangely going upriver instead of down. Pens at one side of the cabin held cattle and hogs. Most of the rear deck was an empty expanse with the tiny figures of men moving about on it, carrying coils of rope.

People poured from houses and buildings in the town and flooded along the street to the wharf, and wagons inched through the throng. The boat nosed upriver from the town and edged toward the bank, then its wheel turned slowly as it drifted backwards with the current and approached the wharf. Its size dwarfed the town as it neared the bank, but the ravages that time and neglect had wrought on the boat were more evident at closer range. The smokestacks were rusty and several of their guy wires were broken, the cabin looked naked and unfinished, and there were large stumps along the rails, all that remained of the beams that had supported multiple decks. The wheel churned; the whistle tooted in a pitiful attempt at a dramatic landing; ropes snaked through the air. Then the wheel stopped turning, and the smoke coming from the stacks diminished to a thin stream.

Children climbed into trees near the bank, people stood on roofs of buildings near the wharf, and the crowd milled about in constant motion on the street at the end of the wharf. Wagons lined up on the wharf, and men untied crates and barrels lashed down on deck, opened a hatch in the deck and carried out boxes and bags, and began loading the wagons. The wagon at the head of the line moved back along the wharf and through the crowd toward the stores, and another one took its place. Men took the cattle out of the pen and drove them along the wharf, and the hogs were loaded into a wagon. Other wagons moved along the street through the crowd, and joined the line. Then the initial excitement faded, and the crowd began thinning out, people straggling back along the main street to the stores and their houses.

Two small figures weaved and darted through the scattered people, disappearing behind buildings and coming into sight again as they raced along the street toward the outskirts of the town. They were two of the smaller Dowd boys. The tallest one gradually pulled away as they ran along the street. Then as they reached the outskirts of the town and started up the slope, the smaller one caught up and pulled ahead. Their legs churned, they stumbled and fell, and they scrambled up and ran on, each of them struggling to be first with the news. The smaller one pulled several yards ahead, forging through the deep weeds in the center of the road, and their labored breathing became audible. The taller one tried to shout and deliver the news first, but his voice was drowned by the smaller one's breathless shriek.

"It's going to Missouri, Ma! Pa said to get the wagons ready for the captain to look at!"

The rest of the women, the children, and the old man had come around the wagon and gathered to look. Hester glanced at the women as she lifted her skirt above the tops of the weeds and turned to walk back around the wagon. The others followed her, and Yvonne went into the canvas enclosure and began putting the things on the tailgate in the wagon as Tangeree dismantled the canvas.

The men walked back up road with the captain of the riverboat, a short, stocky man wearing a nautical jacket and cap, with a short pipe clenched between his teeth. He touched the peak of his cap and nodded amiably to Yvonne and Tangeree, glanced over the wagon, and folded his hands behind his back as he walked toward the other wagons. The men followed him and the others watched in expectant silence as he looked at the wagons and counted the oxen in the corral, chewing his pipestem. Then he turned to Dowd.

"I'll put you on the west bank of the river at St. Joe for sixty dollars for each wagon and ten dollars for each head of oxen, Mr. Dowd. The people can go free, and I'll provide lumber for you to build a pen for your kine. And the charge is payable in gold, but I'll take Confederate money at five percent of face value and Union at ten."

Dowd winced and shook his head. "That's a lot of money, Captain."

"That's a lot of traveling, Mr. Dowd," the captain chuckled. "And I'm not charging you anything for your good luck. A lot of people are on two or three boats between here and St. Joe, and you're mighty lucky that I'm scheduled to pick up cargo going up the Missouri."

"Well, how long do I have to think about it?"

"Not very long. I'm taking on wood, then I'm casting off. If you started right now, you'd just about have time to get the pen built for your kine and load your wagons. And I'm not trying to make up your mind for you, but you'd better move while you have the chance. If the Union blockades Vicksburg, and it looks like they're going to, the boats will stop again."

"Are you going to stop at Memphis?"

"No, I'm going to stop at Paxton to unload cargo. We'll have another stop at Clinton to load wood, then we'll have a straight run to St. Louis. That's where I'll get my main cargo, goods going to Westport and St.

Joe, and supplies for the Army forts and the Indian agents up the Missouri. We'll be doing more traveling than stopping."

Dowd looked down at the ground, stroking his beard and musing, then looked at Yvonne. "Do you have the money? If you don't, we can help you out with some of it."

"No, I have enough, thank you."

Dowd nodded, and looked at the captain and nodded. "We'll go with you, then."

"I'll be glad to have you aboard. One thing I'd like to make clear is that I've been let be by both Confederate and Union forces because I go to some pains to avoid trouble. We'll be seeing a lot of blue uniforms, but a pot shot at one of them will get my boat seized and all of you put in prison. The guns go into the wagons when you get on my boat, and they stay there until we reach St. Joe. Is that agreeable to everyone?"

There were murmurs and nods as he glanced around, and he nodded. "As for the rest of it, I'll give you a fire box to do your cooking, and that'll have to be your only fire. And if we hit a storm, it'll have to be doused. You can have all the hot water you want from the engine room, but the men will have to fetch it up because the engine room isn't a fitting place for ladies. I don't hire stokers because of their manners. Now if all that's agreeable, some of your people can go back with me to get started on the pen, Mr. Dowd, and we'll get your party loaded."

"All right, Captain. Jacob, you take the boys and get started on it. Let's the rest of us get the oxen yoked and get the wagons down there."

Whittacker and the three largest boys left with the captain, and there was a bustle of noisy activity as the others sorted out the oxen and led them to the wagons, the children racing around in excitement, women calling to them, and men shouting at baulky oxen. Yvonne and Tangeree lifted the heavy yoke onto their oxen, hooked up the tongue of the wagon and the chains, and Tangeree scrambled into the wagon as Yvonne took the halter ropes and swung the oxen around toward the road. The wagon lurched through ruts and across the berm at the side of the road, turning onto it behind another wagon, and began bouncing and jolting through the ruts.

The road became smoother at the edge of town, and people stopped to stare and exchange comments with one another as the wagons trundled along the street. Many were people who had come and brought their children to be treated, and they smiled, waved, and called out as Yvonne passed. Children ran along beside the wagons and dogs barked at the wheels, and there were more people along the winding street as it approached the wharf. Then the wharf came into sight, the boat looking huge in close proximity and stretching far to each side. A few people were still standing on roofs to watch, and the wide street at the end of the wharf was crowded and seething with activity. Other wagons were moving about, and a line of men stretched along the edge of the wharf and across the boat to a hatch, passing short, thick logs of uniform size from a firewood dray too large to go on the wharf.

There was a delay when the oxen ahead baulked over the yielding footing of the wharf, and Yvonne's oxen became restive over the noise and confusion all around. Whips cracked and men bellowed, the wagon ahead lurched onto the wharf, and Yvonne led her oxen onto it. The wagon wheels thumped across cracks

between the boards, the riverbank and the edge of the
muddy water passed far below, and the smokestacks
rose high above, filling the air with a strong odor of
woodsmoke. The deck was three feet higher than the
wharf, and long, thick boards had been laid for the
wagons. Yvonne clucked to her oxen, and they leaned
into the yoke and trudged up the boards. The wagon
bumped over the edge of the boards, and the wheels
rumbled across the deck.

The deck was an enormous, flat expanse. The captain had allocated a space the full width of it at the
stern in front of the wheel housing for them. Whittacker and the boys were assembling boards into a
pen in one corner, and the wagons were swinging
around to fill in the rest of the space. Yvonne led her
oxen around in a tight turn to position her wagon.
One of the boys took the oxen and led them away as
she unhooked them, and she took her passage money
to Dowd.

The last wagon came across the deck, and the men
began chocking the wheels on the wagons and hurriedly finishing the pen for the oxen. The firewood
dray at the end of the wharf pulled away and another
took its place. The men passed the logs more hurriedly as a burly man in a peaked cap stalked along the
wharf and bellowed at them. Two of the crewmen
brought the fire box, a heavy iron box with short,
thick legs, an iron grate, and a firebrick lining. The
activity on the boat took on a feel of frenzied preparation, men running about on deck and shouting to
each other, and the dray rapidly emptying of firewood.

The last of the firewood passed along the line of
men, the line broke up, and the smoke coming from
the stacks thickened. Dense clouds of smoke began
belching from the stacks, with hot sparks shooting up

and drifting back down as cinders. The deck trembled
as the wheel jerked and began slowly turning. The
ropes fell away from the bank and men gathered
them in, and the bow of the boat turned away from
the bank. A heavy vibration shook the deck as the
wheel turned more rapidly and churned the water.
The oxen in the pen tossed their heads and moved
restlessly. A crowd had gathered again in the street
and more people were standing on roofs, and they
shouted and waved as the horn on the boat tooted as
it began making headway against the current, angling
out into the river to turn upstream.

Having an abundance of hot water was a luxury.
Yvonne and Tangeree washed their clothes and hung a
canvas screen around the rear of their wagon to wash
their hair and bathe. The sun inclined toward the
west, gleaming on the water stretching out on each
side of the boat as the distant banks crept past. The
breeze whipping across the deck made the fire in the
fire box roar, the flames leaping up through the grate.

The women stirred pots and pans on the grate and
the scent of cooking food blended with the smell of
woodsmoke. The flickering light from the leaping
flames shone on the canvas covers on the wagons as
darkness fell. There was a light, carefree atmosphere
among the people as they ate, and they laughed, joked,
and talked optimistically about the journey west from
St. Joseph. The old man went to a wagon and brought
back a harmonica, and the people sang as he played it.

Yvonne and Tangeree went to their wagon, arranged
things in it, and unrolled their pallets and lay down.
The people continued singing, and the breeze swept
away the sound of the hearty, discordant voices and
the sobbing wail of the harmonica. It sounded distant
and faint, lost in the vast open space of the river

around the boat. Yvonne lay for long minutes before sleep came, wakeful because of the unfamiliar noises and vibration of the boat, and because of the thought that each turn of the wheel represented more distance between Tangeree and medical college.

7

A ROUTINE DEVELOPED on the first day, the men taking care of the oxen and working on the wagons to prepare them for the journey west from St. Joseph, and the women doing their usual chores and looking after the children. Yvonne and Tangeree attended to the minor complaints among the group and sat with their books in a private nook between their wagon and the rail, reading, talking, and looking at the rowboats and sculls that occasionally came into sight.

The old riverboat made tediously slow progress against the current, clankings and rumbling coming from deep in its bowels as the wheel turned and the distant banks of the river crept past. It was a grim reminder of the pervasive drab shabbiness that war had brought. Other riverboats Yvonne had traveled on had been opulent, with spacious, richly-appointed dining rooms and sitting rooms, luxurious cabins, and promenades on the tier of decks where young women in their crinoline finery and bachelors in their broadcloth suits and New Orleans haberdashery had paraded and flirted. But the old stern-wheeler was only a faded shadow of its former glory, denuded of its passenger decks and converted to a cargo scow, trudging laboriously along in its old age without even a name on its bow.

The wide expanse of the deck separated the wagons and oxen pen from most of the activity on the boat. The Dowd men went to the engine room for hot water or for a firewood log to chop up for the fire box, and the captain or his assistant, a hulking, brawny man named Adams, crossed the deck once or twice a day to open doors in the wooden wheel housing and look at fittings inside. They usually stopped to talk with Dowd and the other men for a few minutes. On the third day, Dowd brought Adams to Yvonne. The man had torn off part of a fingernail a few days before and the finger had become badly infected. Yvonne cleaned out the infection and wrapped the finger in a bandage soaked in infusion of sanicle.

Adams left and returned a few minutes later with the captain, who asked Yvonne if she worked on teeth. A fireman, one of the men who supervised a crew of stokers, had a tooth that was keeping him from sleeping and eating, and the captain commented whimsically that the man couldn't keep the stokers working if he couldn't sleep and eat. Yvonne and Tangeree took the herb chest and the chest of dental instruments out of the wagon, and followed the two men across the deck to the cabin.

The captain went for the fireman, and Adams took Yvonne and Tangeree into a dingy room that had a low beam ceiling and several heavy deal tables and benches scattered about. Adams left to get a basin of hot water and a bucket, while Yvonne and Tangeree put the chests on a table, placed a bench in front of it, and opened several shutters to let light and air into the dim, stuffy room. Footsteps on the deck outside approached the door. The captain came in, leading another man by the arm.

"Here you are, Carp. Just have a seat, and the ladies will put you right soon enough."

Carp was a tall, muscular man in a greasy, sweat-stained cotton shirt and trousers, with a ragged, dirty handkerchief knotted around his neck. The left side of his upper lip and his face were swollen, and he looked at Yvonne, Tangeree, and the chests on the table with an apprehensive frown as he followed the captain with reluctant, dragging footsteps. "I ain't never had no lady knock out any of my teeth," he muttered in a muffled voice.

"Well, it's between them and Adams," the captain said and chuckled. "And his experience in knocking out teeth isn't for surgical purposes, is it? Sit down, man, and don't be such a baby."

Carp turned and looked as Adams came in with the bucket and basin, then looked back at the chests and at Yvonne again, his eyes wary and suspicious. "Have you knocked out a lot of teeth?"

"Yes, but perhaps it won't be necessary to remove it. Sometimes it's possible to ease the pain and fill the decay with gold."

The man's expression brightened, and he stepped to the bench and sat down. Tangeree put the bucket at his feet and moved around Yvonne to the instrument chest, and sorted through things in it. Adams left. The captain folded his hands behind his back and teetered up and down on his toes as he hummed cheerfully and watched. Yvonne pushed Carp back against the table behind him and placed her feet carefully as she stood between his feet to tilt his head back, lifting his upper lip. Working on men's teeth wasn't unlike treating large farm animals, and there had been a number of times when she had been knocked off her feet by a blow or shove that had been an automatic reflex to a stab of agonizing pain. And Carp was a huge man, with a barrel chest and rippling sheaths of muscles in his powerful shoulders and arms.

Tangeree put out a thick board inset with holes to hold hardwood blocks and dowels of various sizes, and Carp jerked nervously and rolled his eyes sidewards as the board clattered on the table. Yvonne lifted his chin higher and stretched his swollen lip. Several of his teeth were badly decayed, and most of them were loose in the gums. Areas on the teeth that hadn't been scoured by the action of chewing food were coated with thick matter that ranged in color from a pale yellow to brown. The tooth causing the immediate problem was the first premolar on the left side, and it took only a glance to see that the decay couldn't be scraped out and gold wire pounded into the hole. The decay had eaten deep into the tooth, making the gum around it swollen and an angry red color. Tangeree began mixing olive oil and morphine paste in an earthenware bowl, while Yvonne released Carp's lip and looked at the hardwood blocks, selecting one.

Carp swallowed, explored the tooth with the tip of his tongue, and looked up at Yvonne. "Will it have to be knocked out?"

"I haven't examined it thoroughly yet. You should clean your teeth with either a sassafras brush or bristle brush each day, and every two or three days you should take a fine linen twine, soak it in butter, and work it around the base of each tooth to clean under the edge of the gum. And once each week, you should clean your teeth and gums with a mixture of salt and woodash."

"Oh, I don't have time to bother with all of that," Carp grumbled.

"Then you'll have to find time for someone to knock them out, won't you, Carp?" the captain said.

Carp grunted, looking at the captain glumly. Yvonne lifted his chin again, opened his mouth, and put the hardwood block between his front teeth to prop his mouth open. Tangeree put the bowl of olive oil and morphine paste on the edge of the table, and put out a handful of steel picks and probes. Yvonne selected a pick with a tiny spoon on the end, dipped it into the bowl, and began cleaning the matter off the tooth and working the mixture into the cavity. Carp made choked, gagging sounds as saliva accumulated in the back of his throat, and his tongue moved as he swallowed convulsively. His fetid breath brushed Yvonne's face as she bent low over his mouth, registering in her awareness only as an indication of the condition of his teeth and gums.

The cavity in the tooth was clogged with both the thick, gummy matter that covered his other teeth and odorous particles of food from days before, and Yvonne gingerly cleaned it out and flowed the mixture into the cavity. Twinges of pain were telegraphed by Carp's movements as she held his lip up with her left hand and rested her wrist against his nose. He began relaxing, a positive sign that the mixture was penetrating to the nerve. Yvonne tossed the pick onto the table and selected a probe with a depression on the tip, and worked the mixture deep into the cavity and under the gum around the base of the tooth.

Carp relaxed completely. Yvonne tossed the pick onto the table and glanced at the tooth pliers Tangeree

had quietly laid out in a row. She pointed to the set
with narrow, serrated-edge jaws and selected a short,
thick hardwood dowel from the board. Tangeree
scooped up the pliers in her left hand and moved
closer, a mallet in her right hand and both of her
hands below Carp's line of vision, and her attitude
that of an interested spectator. Yvonne looked at the
tooth and gum closely as she placed the dowel. There
was a pressure point at which force could be exerted
with either the pliers or a blow, and the root of the
tooth would unseat without causing undue damage
to the surrounding bone. The point was a matter of
judgment, and a wrong estimate could result in the
disaster of a broken tooth and the bloody, painful digging out of roots, or loosened adjacent teeth through
shattering the bone. She seated the dowel firmly
against the gum just above the point where it met the
tooth, keeping the same pressure on Carp's lip with
her left hand to avoid telegraphing that anything different was going to happen. Then she nodded.

Tangeree lifted the mallet and struck the end of
the dowel sharply in a single quick, smooth movement. The tooth buckled inward, blood streaming
down it, and Carp's head snapped back as a loud,
gargling squeal came from his throat. Yvonne leaned
forward, gripping his lip tightly and following the
movement of his head, and she dropped the dowel
and opened her right hand. Tangeree tossed the mallet onto the table, caught the dowel as it fell, and
slapped the pliers into Yvonne's hand. Yvonne gripped
the tooth with the pliers, twisted it out, and plucked
the hardwood block from between Carp's front teeth
as she stepped back. Carp snapped his mouth closed
and froze, his head still leaning far back and his eyes
wild and glaring as he looked at Yvonne.

"By George!" the captain exploded. "If that's not the smoothest job I've seen of knocking out a tooth, I've never seen one. It's out, Carp. Go ahead and spit in the bucket, man. It's done with."

Carp slowly sat up, probing with his tongue, then leaned over and spat a mouthful of saliva and blood into the bucket. He straightened up, his lips shining with blood and stretched in a wide grin. "It's out," he mumbled in wonder.

"Indeed it is, man," the captain said heartily. "Surprised you, didn't it? It surprised me, and I was watching. If ever I need another tooth knocked out and these ladies are about, I know who I'll get to do the job. Well, go ahead and pay and get back to work, Carp. How much do you charge for knocking out a tooth, Mrs. Beaunais?"

Yvonne examined the tooth to make sure the root was complete, and tossed it into the bucket. "I charge what a person can pay. Ten cents or so will do."

"Ten cents?" the captain snorted. "No, nonsense. Carp makes good money, and a job like that calls for at least a dollar. Put a dollar on the table there, Carp, a silver dollar. It's worth it, isn't it?"

Carp spat another mouthful of saliva and blood into the bucket, and grinned and nodded as he took out his wallet. He took a silver dollar from it and put it on the table. He shuffled toward the door, feeling his swollen lip with his fingers and exploring the new gap between his teeth with his tongue. The captain chuckled and shook his head as Carp walked out, and he looked at Yvonne.

"That tooth's been bothering the man for a month or more, but somehow it stopped hurting every time we stopped where there might be someone who knocks out teeth. A doctor isn't to be seen anymore, as I'm sure you know, and I have some other men you could look at if it suits you. They have various aches and pains of one sort or another."

"Yes, we'll see to them."

The captain nodded and touched the peak of his cap as he turned toward the door. "I'll have Adams gather up those who aren't working and send them in, then."

He left, shouting for Adams, and Yvonne helped Tangeree wash and dry the instruments they had used on Carp. As they put them away, voices and footsteps came across the deck toward the door. As a few men lined up outside, Tangeree went to the door and called in the first one.

The men came at irregular intervals, two or three lining up outside the door, then a long wait until the next ones arrived. Some were amputees who had been in the War, some were oldsters who had been rejected for enlistment, and a few were those who had escaped conscription in both the North and South by one means or another. Many were foreigners the captain had collected in the port cities along the river to fill out his crew, Lascars, Chinese, Polynesians, and others whose wanderings had brought them to the Mississippi, and they pointed, gestured, and struggled with their heavy accents and few words of English to describe their symptoms. All were abashed and uncomfortable to varying degrees over being examined and treated by a woman and a young girl.

The illnesses ran the gamut of afflictions suffered by those subjected to hardship and grueling toil, and rarely given medical attention or advice. There were skin diseases, lung congestion, infected injuries, and stomach disorders, and a few showed signs of scurvy. The older ones had rheumatic pains, two of the amputees endured frequent pain because of clumsy and poorly-healed amputations, and some had heard of Carp's experiences and wanted teeth extracted. A Lascar had a skin rash Yvonne had never before seen, and she had Tangeree make a salve containing a wide range of specifics for various skin diseases. Others had confusing or vague complaints that she treated symptomatically, and several of the Chinese wanted ginseng infusion for a tonic.

The men worked on two twelve-hour shifts, and there was a full day in examining and treating the ill among the men as they finished work. There were even more men lining up outside the door the next day, when word of the efficacy of the medicines Yvonne administered spread enough to overcome the reluctance of those who mistrusted being treated by a woman, but it appeared that her being a woman still kept some from coming forward. Significantly, there were no complaints of venereal disease among a group in which it would be common.

After the second day, Yvonne and Tangeree resumed their routine, spending much of their time sitting between their wagon and the rail with their books. Clusters of houses and small hamlets on knolls were occasionally visible on the distant river banks. More rarely there were towns. The riverboat approached Paxton late one afternoon, threading its way carefully through the channel in a sand bar near the river bank. Paxton was a large town, with straight streets of houses and businesses that covered the slope overlooking the river, and scattered houses along roads that extended around the inside bend in the river in which the town was located. A complex of docks stretched along the edge of the river in front of the town, and the waterfront teemed with activity, people milling about and several small boats at the docks.

The arrival of the boat caused less excitement in the larger town than it had at Prior's Point, but a number of people crowded onto the docks as the river-boat approached, tooting its horn. Yvonne and Tangeree joined the others at the rail near the oxen pen and watched as the boat eased up to a wharf. The children ran back and forth excitedly, shouting and waving to those on shore. Men on the boat threw ropes to those on the wharf, the wheel stopped turning, and wagons began appearing through the streets and moving onto the wharf. When Dowd barked at the children angrily, they stopped running about and became quiet, and silence settled over the rest of the group by the rail. Two Union Army officers were walking along the wharf toward the boat.

Men on the boat untied cargo on the forward deck and opened a hatch to carry out cargo. The two officers walked through the men moving about on deck and went into the cabin. They emerged with the captain a moment later and talked to him as they crossed the deck to the wharf, then they walked back along the wharf. The captain walked across the rear deck to the group by the oxen pen, smiling and nodding amiably as he approached.

"Mr. Dowd, we'll be making a stop I didn't anticipate. There's some wounded soldiers here who need to get to the railhead at Beech Hill, so we'll be taking them and we should get there tomorrow morning. They'll be on the forward deck, and I trust you'll keep your people in the vicinity of your wagons. We don't want any trouble, do we?"

Dowd sighed morosely and shook his head. "No, we don't want any trouble. And none of us will start any."

"I couldn't ask for more," the captain replied cheerfully, turning away. "Thank you very much, Mr. Dowd."

Jason muttered something under his breath as the captain walked away. Dowd frowned at him darkly, and Jason glared back at his father stonily as he turned and stumped away on his crutch. Yvonne touched Tangeree's arm, and they walked back across the deck to their wagon. The people by the rail scattered, returning to what they had been doing.

The line of wagons formed on the wharf, and men from the boat and the teamsters walked back and forth, carrying the cargo and loading the wagons. A wagon left, and another took its place. The line of wagons gradually became shorter until the last one left. The men on the boat moved about, coiling ropes and putting them away, and the activity ebbed. Minutes dragged by. Then wagons rumbled along the wharf again. They came into sight, Union Army wagons drawn by mules.

Men from the boat and hospital orderlies from the wagons unloaded stretchers, carried them onto the boat, and disappeared around the cabin. The first wagon moved away, and the stream of men and orderlies unloaded the second one. The third and last wagon contained food, medical supplies, and bags of personal belongings, and two officers walked along the wharf and stood by it as the men and orderlies unloaded it. One was one of the officers who had come onto the riverboat before, and the other was a taller man.

They saluted, and the tall officer looked in the wagon and talked to the orderlies as the other officer left. The captain crossed the deck and walked along the wharf to the officer, and he and the officer talked as they walked slowly toward the boat. Yvonne looked at the officer musingly. He looked remotely familiar. His hat shaded his features and his face was averted, but there was something about the way he stood and moved that tugged at her memory.

The officer and the captain walked onto the deck, and Yvonne looked at the man, frowning with thought. Then she stiffened and slowly stood up. The man was Charles Dawson, the doctor she had worked with in Tupelo.

8

DAWSON GLANCED AROUND as he talked to the captain, his hand automatically lifting to touch the brim of his hat as his eyes passed across the women. He glanced at Yvonne and looked back at the captain, saying something. Then he broke off, and his head snapped back around. He looked at her, a beaming smile spreading across his face, and he took off his hat and walked toward her with long, rapid strides, leaving the captain standing and looking at him blankly.

Yvonne moved toward him, joyous pleasure swelling within her at seeing him again. And he almost clasped her in his arms. Then she hesitated, and he hesitated. When they had worked together, she had been fascinated by what he had to teach her, he had been interested in what she had learned from her mother, and they had been dedicated to their work. They had been warm friends, companions, and healers, and both of them had been married. Now her husband was dead, and his wife was dead. And when she had been eighteen he had seemed old, a man over thirty. But to a thirty-year-old woman a man in his early forties was virtually a contemporary. And he was a very appealing man, tall and well-built in his neat, bright uniform, with a full, thick blond mustache, smooth, bronzed cheeks and chin, and ruggedly handsome features. She put out her hand, and he took it.

"Yvonne, I cannot believe my eyes! Only this morning I was telling a friend about you, and telling him about the remedy you gave me for bed sores. And there's no need to ask how you are, because you haven't aged a day."

"And there's no need for you to dishonor yourself with a falsehood, Charles," Yvonne laughed. "But you're looking very well yourself. This is my daughter Tangeree, and she has changed a bit since you last saw her, I believe."

"Indeed she has," he chuckled. "I'm very pleased to see you again, Tangeree."

Tangeree was livid, her blue eyes enormous in her flushed face. She looked at Yvonne in disgust, then her eyes moved to Dawson's extended hand and up to his face, her lips curling in a silent sneer.

"Tangeree!" Yvonne said impatiently. "This is Doctor Dawson, and I'm not going to have you—"

"No, I understand, Yvonne," Dawson interrupted, smiling affably at Tangeree. "She's very much like Bob was, isn't she?"

"In looks and in disposition. Bob could be the most stubborn, but seeing that uniform took me by surprise, Charles. I would have recognized you right off in gray, I believe."

"Warriors choose sides, but healers are all on the same side, Yvonne," he replied, then shrugged and smiled ruefully. "And it's also a matter of circumstances. I found myself in Boston when everything began, and I had a choice of this or spending the duration on a prison hulk in the harbor. And I chose to do what I could to save lives and ease pain."

His voice faded as he looked at the Dowds. They were in a silent, intent group a few yards away, looking at him with expressions varying from dark distrust on the women's faces and frowning antipathy on the men's, to belligerent hatred on Jason's features. Dawson seemed nonchalantly indifferent to their hostility, and he pursed his lips and looked at Jason musingly, tapping his hat against his leg.

"Wasn't it Mechanicsville, son? Or was it Gaines's Mill?"

Jason blinked, his mouth dropping open as his expression changed to one of stunned shock. He lifted his hand, pointing. "You're the—"

"That's right, I'm the sawbones," Dawson laughed, walking toward him. "How's the leg? Does it ever give you any pain?"

"No, no, it don't ever hurt at all," Jason replied as they shook hands. "I sure didn't recognize you at first. Now ain't this something to run into you again this way."

"No, this is why a doctor has to be careful with his patients," Dawson chuckled. "We never know when we'll meet them again. I didn't like pulling out and leaving you fellows as we did, but as your sergeant said, it would be better than a prison camp."

"Oh, he was right, and the Georgians was in there not more than two or three hours after you all left. We was all talking about how skinny you all had cut it in getting out. And we was wondering if you had got out all right, because you had been really good to us."

"I didn't suffer anything more serious than exhaustion from trying to keep up with the Army as it was advancing to the rear," Dawson laughed. "How about the lad with the shell fragments in his eyes. Do you happen to know if he recovered his eyesight?"

"Hank Johnson? He sure did, and he swears by your name. He was sure he'd never see another thing as long as he lived. . . ."

Yvonne watched them as they talked, Jason more animated than she had seen him before, a comradely attitude between him and Dawson as he talked about experiences which were a part of him and which his family didn't share or understand. The hostility in the group had faded completely before the warm, compelling force of personality that Dawson projected, a bearing that had always made men friendly toward him as much as his appearance had always brought him a second glance from women. And the captain had walked forward and stood at one side, his beaming smile reflecting relief that the possibility had been averted that a skirmish of the Civil War would be fought back and forth across the deck of his boat.

Jason introduced the others, and the strain in the atmosphere disappeared completely as Dawson shook hands with them and they joined in the conversation. He took the baby from Abigail and held it with the easy, accustomed familiarity of a physician with babies, and he looked at it in admiration and commented on the baby's brawny size and weight as Abigail and Jason glowed with pride. Abigail talked about minor problems with the baby and what Yvonne had done for them as she took it back, and Dawson glanced at Yvonne, smiling and nodding.

"Yes, I'm well aware of Yvonne's capabilities. Sometimes I think she taught me more while we were working together than I learned in medical college."

"She's well onto having me with the healthiest crew

on any boat on the Mississippi," the captain broke in. "Surgeon Major Dawson, I'll leave you with your friends here and see about casting off. If your men need hot water or to heat food or anything, they can see the fireman in the engine room and he'll take care of them."

"Thank you very much, Captain, and my thanks again for accommodating us," Dawson replied as the captain walked away. Then he looked back at Yvonne. "I'd better have a look at my charges to see they're settled. Would you like to have a look at them with me, Yvonne?"

"Yes, if I can be of any assistance. Would you like to come, Tangi?"

Tangeree's intense animosity had changed to cold, withdrawn reserve, and she had been standing and silently glaring during the conversation. She hesitated, the conflict between aversion toward the situation and her automatic impulse to render assistance showing clearly on her features, then she nodded. Dawson shook hands with the men again and made parting comments, and Yvonne walked toward the front of the boat with him, Tangeree following.

"From what I saw when the men brought the stretchers on the boat, those are all serious cases, Charles."

"Yes, the walking wounded we had here were sent by wagon to the railhead, but I was afraid that trip would be too much for these fellows. I have one I'm particularly worried about, a man with an open abdominal wound."

"His stomach's open?" Tangeree said, catching up with a quick step.

Dawson nodded, looking down at her. "Yes, a shell

fragment passed across his stomach, and it's still very doubtful about him."

"He hasn't developed peritonitis?"

"No, so I still have hopes for him. If he can avoid inflammation for the next week or so, I believe he'll make it."

"Do you follow the practices recommended by Dr. Semmelweis in preventing inflammation?"

Dawson nodded and started to reply, then he abruptly stopped and looked down at Tangeree, blinking. He appeared to have suddenly realized he was talking to a young girl, and he looked from her to Yvonne in bemusement. Yvonne smiled at his expression, nodding.

"Tangi does her reading, Charles. I only wish I'd known as much as she does when I was her age."

"Yes, it's obvious she's done her reading. She helps you, then?"

"Tangi does more than that. She can deliver babies, and she can do a lot of other things by herself. The main thing holding her back is the fact that people won't trust anyone as young as she is."

"Well, I'm delighted that you have your mother's talent, Tangeree,' Dawson said, looking back down at her. "And needless to say, I wish you every success. As to your question, it's often impossible to do more than follow the most basic practices of cleanliness in a military field hospital, but I do happen to agree with Semmelweis's theories. . . ."

Yvonne listened and looked at them as they began walking along the deck again, Dawson talking about the techniques of hospital hygiene he practiced and Tangeree looking up at him intently, totally absorbed in what he was saying. The stern wheel turned and

the bow swung around as the boat moved away from
the dock. Tangeree stumbled and almost caught her
toe in the hem of her skirt as the deck swayed. Dawson reached for her arm to steady her on her feet,
but she pulled away from him and looked up at him
as he continued talking. She had an engrossed interest
in what he was saying, but she didn't want him to
touch her.

The sixteen stretchers were scattered around in the
shade behind the stacks of lumber and remaining
crates and barrels that were tied down on the deck.
Orderlies were moving back and forth among them,
talking to the wounded men and carrying water to
them. There was no fresh blood on any of the bandages or any indication of acute distress among them,
and Tangeree began helping the orderlies as Yvonne
walked from one stretcher to another with Dawson,
talking with the wounded men.

Dawson glanced at Tangeree occasionally as she
moved among the stretchers, and he nodded toward
her as he and Yvonne stepped from one stretcher to
another. "She does have the talent, Yvonne. A patient's
spirits make the difference, as we well know, and
every man she's talked to has improved as much as a
week's good care would do."

Yvonne looked at Tangeree. The girl was kneeling
by a young soldier, the tips of her fingers resting lightly on his hand, and she radiated encouragement and
concern as she talked to him. The drawn lines of pain
on his pale face were almost hidden by his cheerful
smile as he replied. Yvonne nodded. "I want that girl
to go to medical college more than life itself. But
everything that can has got in the way of it."

"She's young, Yvonne, and you have years to work
things out. I was far older than she when I went."

"When you were her age, you were in school learning things you'd need to know when you got to medical college. She's going with me to California to get away from the war."

Dawson looked at Tangeree musingly, and he silently nodded as he stepped to the next stretcher and looked down at the soldier on it.

The sun set, and the breeze eddying around the lumber and cargo became cool. The orderlies took blankets out of a box and spread them over the soldiers. As the light began fading, they lit lanterns. They prepared to feed the wounded soldiers, some emptying cans of food into large pots and taking the pot to the engine room to heat the food, and others taking tin plates and cups from a box. There was a light step behind Yvonne and a tug on her skirt as she stood at one side and talked with Dawson, and she turned. It was one of the small Dowd boys.

"Ma says supper is about ready, ma'm. And he's to come, too."

Yvonne smiled down at the boy and patted his head. "Thank you, Tod. Will you have dinner with us, Charles?"

"Yes, I won't miss a chance to eat something besides Army food. And I've eaten with you before, haven't I?"

Yvonne looked up at him in the darkness as they began walking along the deck, puzzled by the teasing tone of the last sentence. "Yes, you came to our house any number of times in Tupelo. . . ." Her voice faded, and she laughed as what he had referred to occurred to her. "Charles, you would remember that! Honestly, it still embarrasses me to think of it."

"The only thing wrong with the dinner was that you

were embarrassed," he laughed. "Everyone thought
the food was good."

She clicked her tongue and shook her head, chuckling. "Everyone felt sorry for me. I could have boiled
that old hen for a week and she would have still been
as tough as wet leather."

"No, the dinner was good, Yvonne," he said reminiscently. "And I really enjoyed the dinner and talking with you and Bob that evening."

Yvonne smiled, remembering the evening as he continued talking about it. Suddenly she missed Tangeree.
She glanced around and saw the girl in the darkness,
following a few feet behind them. Light from the
cabin windows fell on the girl as she passed them,
and Yvonne could see that she was frowning darkly
in annoyance.

Hester and the other women had prepared a special
meal. There was a generous part of a smoked ham that
had been thickly encrusted with cloves and broiled
until it was crisp, a pan of yams candied with molasses
and flavored with cinnamon, buttered cushaw, snap
beans and collard greens flavored with drippings from
the ham, and crackling cornbread made with the trim-
mings from the ham. The food was delicious, and the
conversation was a keen pleasure. Jason and Dawson
chatted and related stories about their experiences,
and Dawson recalled amusing incidents that made the
group roar with laughter. Others talked, and when
the plates were put aside the old man took out his
harmonica and the others sang as he played. The only
jarring note was that Tangeree sat at one side on the
edge of the light from the fire box, and she picked at
her food and looked away into the darkness in dis-
interest as the others talked and sang.

The fire burned down, and Dawson took out his watch, turned the face toward the glow of the embers in the fire box as he snapped the top open, and looked around with a regretful smile as he closed it and put it away. "Well, I've certainly enjoyed the food and company, but I'd better see if my patients are comfortable. Would you like to go for another visit with them, Yvonne? And you, Tangeree?"

"It's past my bedtime," Tangeree replied curtly.

Yvonne turned and looked at Tangeree, irritated and embarrassed by the girl's pettishness. "Tangeree, since when have we had a bedtime?"

There was a brief, strained silence as Tangeree shrugged and looked away. Then Hester chuckled and stirred the boy who had gone to sleep across her lap. "Laws, that's the God's truth. I've seen these two going for so many hours without sleep that it would put me in a grave. And I expect you're about the same, ain't you, Doctor Dawson?"

"No, I'll have to admit that I miss my sleep only when I can't avoid it," he laughed. "And while Yvonne and I were working together, I always marveled at the way she could go without sleep." He stood, extending his hand to Jason, "Jase, I understand I'll be getting off early in the morning, so I'll say goodbye now in event I don't see you then. It's been a pleasure meeting you again, and I wish you every happiness."

"Well, it was your doing that I'm here at all, and I'll always be obliged to you."

Yvonne stood and straightened her skirt as they talked and Dawson said goodbye to the others. She glanced around, looking for Tangeree. The girl was a shadow in the moonlight, walking rapidly toward the wagon. Dawson began moving away from the group and hesitated, looking at Yvonne. She caught up with him with a quick step and smiled up at him as they walked away.

The lanterns near the stretchers made eddying pools of yellow light as the flames in them weaved and danced in the breeze seeping through cracks around the globes. The sleeping orderlies and wounded soldiers bundled in their blankets were dark, shapeless forms in the glow of the lanters and weak moonlight, and several of the soldiers moaned and whimpered in their sleep, a sighing drone of pain. One orderly was awake, kneeling by a stretcher, and Dawson bent over the stretcher and looked at the soldier as Yvonne walked around the stretchers and tucked blankets into place. Dawson went to the boxes of supplies for a flask of laudanum and administered some to the soldier, then he took Yvonne's arm and they walked around the stacks of lumber to the bow of the boat.

The sky was a bowl of glittering stars, the night cloudless and the constellations obscured by the myriad pinpoints of winking light. The glowing disc of the moon was at its zenith above the river. Water gurgled under the bow as the boat forged slowly ahead against the racing current. The gleam of the moon on the river was diffused by wispy tendrils of mist that were rising from the surface of the water, and the distant river banks were dark, dim shadows at the limits of vision. The breeze was strong at the rail, tugging at Yvonne's hair. She stepped to the lumber and sat down in front of it. Dawson sat down by her and looked at her as she folded her arms.

"Is it chilly for you, Yvonne? I can get my overcoat."

"No, I'm warm enough, Charles. It'll probably be a lot cooler where I'm going."

"It certainly will, because it's still early spring in Missouri." He looked away, musing, then looked back at her. "Are you sure you're doing the right thing, Yvonne?"

"In going to California? It's the only thing I can do, Charles, if I'm going to get myself and Tangi away from the fighting, renegades, and everything else connected with this war."

"No, it isn't the only thing you could do. There are other places you could go."

"From what I've heard, I'd as soon be back in Vicksburg. I was going to Memphis until we met a man who'd been there."

He leaned back against the lumber and looked away, the moon shining in his eyes and his profile silhouetted against the night sky, and he slowly nodded. "Yes, Memphis is under martial law and General Cuttler is in command there, and he has a heavy hand. But I have friends in Memphis, and I could see that you and Tangeree have protection. Or there are other places you could go."

"Your friends wouldn't be able to help me unless they have influence with the military authorities, and I wouldn't want anything to do with them if they do. And any other place could turn into another Memphis. No, I'm lucky I met the Dowds, and I won't have to worry about the War in California. We'll make do, Charles, and in any event there's no reason for you to be concerned."

"But I am concerned, Yvonne," he said quietly, his voice vibrant with meaning as he looked down at her. "I can think of nothing that concerns me more, because I've thought of you countless times, wondering where you were and if you were safe. I've never been a great believer in fate, but it appears that our paths were meant to cross again. And I don't want us to ever lose contact with each other again. This war can't last forever, and there'll come a time when people can rebuild their lives. I can think of nothing I want more than to do that with you."

Yvonne felt breathless as she looked away into the moonlit night. There had been more than hints in his attitude toward her, in the way he had smiled and in his small courtesies and attentions, and she had kept herself from taking cognizance of them and thinking about it, fearing the cruel disappointment if he had said nothing. It seemed abrupt in its impact, and her mouth felt dry as her heart pounded.

Her hand was resting on the deck, and his large, warm hand covered it. She looked back up at him, and his eyes held hers as he lifted her hand and pressed it to his lips. He leaned over her, pulling her to him, and his lips touched hers. It was a tender, gentle kiss, building in intensity as he took her into his arms. Then his arms enfolded her and his lips covered hers, and she pressed herself to him as they kissed passionately.

A glowing warmth kindled within her, pulsing and throbbing. It became fiery and demanding, and other yearning needs came to life. An entire dimension had been missing for too long, the satisfaction of the urge to love and to be loved. And the brutal rape by the renegades had created a need for reassurance and a bitter, gnawing anger that had been suppressed and endured, but that ached to be soothed away.

A numb, burning haze enveloped her as she clung to him, crushing herself against him and pressing her open lips to his as she touched his face and hair. His fingers pressed into her back and he pulled her down to the deck with him. Then she took the initiative, opening the buttons on her dress and pulling his hands to her. His eager hands and lips made the hungry need within her become imperative, an insistent, driving force.

The damp breeze was cool against her naked body, and his hard, lean body was warm and a firm pressure on hers as they moved in a heavy, primitive rhythm. Reassurance and fulfillment came, and there was an end and no end as the thrusting urgency of his need for her remained, the contact between them surpassing a physical touch. Pleasure became mounting ecstasy that brushed the edges of pain, instants dragging out for an eternity as the gushing torrents of sensation gripped every fiber of her body.

Then he held her and kissed her, his breath warm against her face as he whispered his love against her lips. A languid contentment possessed Yvonne as she lay in his arms and explored the wonder of the love for him that she had discovered within herself, wistfully longing for the moment to last forever. Time seemed to stop, then it seemed to leap past and was gone. She stirred, reaching for her clothes. He pulled her back to him, holding her tightly.

"Yvonne, I can't lose you again. I can't bear to let you out of my sight again."

Yvonne sighed and pulled away from him, and she sat up and began dressing. "I love you, Charles, and in a way I think I always have. But we aren't children. You have to do what you must do, and I have to do what I must do. This isn't our time, but we can stay in touch—and perhaps our time will come."

He started to reply, then he drew in a deep breath and released it with a heavy sigh as he sat up and began putting on his clothes. Yvonne stood, fastening the last buttons on her dress and tugging the bodice down to a smooth fit. He finished dressing, stood up and took her in his arms, and held her to him.

"Yvonne, you could get off the boat with me in the morning, or there are any number of cities along the river where we could meet and you—"

"No, Charles. We're in the middle of a war, and we both have more than ourselves to think about."

"But I'd see that you and Tangeree have protection and everything you need. I beg you, Yvonne, at least consider it. I don't want to lose you again. Please think about it."

Yvonne hesitated, then nodded. "I'll think about it, Charles."

"We don't have much time, Yvonne. It's only a few hours before we reach Beech Hill, and I'd like to explain how I can—"

"I'll come back and talk to you before we get there."

He started to say something else, to plead and persuade further, but she put her arms around his neck and pulled his lips down to hers. His arm tightened around her and they kissed; then she pulled away from him.

The breeze pulled at her hair and dress as she walked back around the lumber and cargo. All the orderlies and wounded soldiers were asleep, their snores blending with the quiet sounds made by those moaning in their sleep. The lanterns were burning low and guttering. Yvonne passed them and walked back along the deck by the cabin, thinking of what Dawson had said. With the feel of his kisses still on her lips and her body still warm from being pressed against his, it seemed simple to do what he wanted and she wanted, merely a matter of proceeding. But an inner voice of experience spoke warningly, reminding her of other failed hopes, of other times that had seemed bright and full of promise, and that had brought disaster. She recognized the need to put a distance of clear, logical thought between herself and his embraces.

The oxen were dozing in the pen, and there was no movement around the wagons as the moonlight shone brightly down on the canvas covers. Yvonne climbed into her wagon to find absolute silence in it, not a whisper of Tangeree's breathing or her usual soft snoring when asleep. She lay down on her pallet, and reached out to make sure Tangeree was there. Her hand touched Tangeree's slender shoulder, and the girl jerked away.

"Don't touch me!" she hissed. "You think I don't know what you've been doing? It's disgusting!"

Something that was gentle, precious, and beautiful suddenly began turning sordid and ugly, and Yvonne lay back and pulled the cover around herself. "You watch your mouth, Tangeree, or I'll close it for you. And I don't have to explain myself to you."

"I don't want you to! Do you think I want to hear about it? It's disgusting, and I hope you've caught a pox. I hope you're poxed right up to your eyeballs!"

Seething anger exploded within Yvonne, and she snapped up to a sitting position, leaning toward Tangeree. "Tangeree, do you think you can talk to me that way and get away with it? I'll thrash you!"

"Go ahead and thrash me, and I'll still hope you're poxed! If you are, I'll fix it for you, and I'll fix it good! I'll fix you so you won't be able to sit on a wagon seat without the whole wagon falling up you, and then we'll see how many men you go crawling around with!"

Yvonne snarled wordlessly in fury, lashing out, and

her palm cracked loudly against Tangeree's face. Indignant wrath toward the girl blended with the burning sense of insult, the frustrated helplessness over the situation that kept her and Dawson apart, and other emotions. It exploded into a frenzied, churning maelstrom within her and found an outlet, and she knelt over the girl, smacking her viciously with both hands.

Then she realized what she was doing. And she realized that Tangeree was making no effort to move away or to protect her face. Tangeree made small, choked sobbing noises as Yvonne slumped over her, appalled by what she had done. Yvonne put her hands under Tangeree, gathering the girl into her arms.

"Tangi, I'm sorry . . . I'm sorry. . . ."

Tangeree burst into tears, wriggling away. "No, just leave me alone," she sobbed. "I know you don't love me!"

"Don't be foolish, Tangi," Yvonne said, pulling the girl closer. "I love you more than I could ever love anyone else, and I'd give my life for you."

"No, you don't love me," Tangeree murmured tearfully. "You want him!"

"You don't understand, Tangi," Yvonne sighed. "I didn't love you any less because I loved your father. It's a different love."

"He's not my pa, he's just a man. You're the only one I have and the only one I want, but you want somebody else."

Yvonne started to try again to explain, then hesitated. Tangeree's sobs faded, and she waited expectantly. Yvonne patted the girl and held her closer, rocking back and forth with her. "No, you're the only one I want, Tangi."

"Do you swear it?"

Yvonne brushed the tears off her cheek, drawing in a deep, shuddering breath and releasing it in a sigh, and she nodded. "Yes, I swear it, Tangi."

Tangeree made a sound of satisfaction in her throat, sniffling and wiping at her tears. Yvonne pulled the girl over to her pallet and lay down with her, drawing the cover over them, and Tangeree settled herself in Yvonne's arms, nestling against her. Tangeree's breath caught in her throat in the aftermath of weeping, then her breathing became slow and deep. Yvonne patted and stroked the girl's head, holding her tightly, and tears trickled from her eyes as she silently wept.

Yvonne's tears stopped. Her eyes were dry and burning as she held Tangeree, a hollow, lonely feeling of anguish within her. Tangeree snored softly, and the moon set, only the feeble light of the stars coming in the front of the wagon. Yvonne moved slowly and carefully, pulling away from Tangeree. The girl stirred and murmured in her sleep, and Yvonne waited a moment and moved again. She tucked the covers around the girl as she pulled away from her, and she quietly climbed out of the wagon.

The orderlies and wounded soldiers were still asleep. A lantern at one side of the others was burning brightly, the globe cleaned and the wick trimmed. Dawson was sitting by it with his overcoat pulled around his shoulders, smoking a cigar. A wide smile spread across his face and he shrugged off his coat and stood as he saw Yvonne approaching out of the darkness. Then his smile faded as she walked into the light of the lantern and he saw her expression. Yvonne looked up at him, then looked away.

"Charles, I'm not sure of where in California we're

going, so do you know where you'll be going after
the War? Or is there some way I'd be able to get in
touch with you?"

"Yvonne, I've been thinking about this, and I've
thought of several ways that I can see that you and
Tangeree will be—"

"No, Charles, I've made up my mind. I want to get
myself and Tangi away from this war, and there are
other things involved."

He puffed on the cigar, looking down at her. "It's
Tangeree, isn't it?"

Yvonne sighed, nodding. "Partly, but there are other
things as well. There are many things involved,
Charles."

"Yvonne, there's nothing that I couldn't put right to
keep from being separated from you. Let me go talk
to her, and I'll explain how—"

"No!" she snapped, then she smiled apologetically to
soften the sharp reply. "No, Charles. Perhaps a time
will come when things will work out for us, but not
now. I've made up my mind, and it's a waste of time
talking about it."

He looked away, his features taut with bitter disappointment, and he tossed the cigar over the rail.
The burning tip glowed redly as it arced through the
air and disappeared into the darkness. He heaved a
deep sigh and rubbed his chin, thinking, then looked
back at her. "I have a friend in Virginia City, Nevada.
That's a mining town just across the mountains from
California, and the main route into California passes
near it. The man's a doctor and his name is Sam
Leggett, and he would be able to advise you and perhaps help you get settled down. I'll see if I can contact him and stay in touch with him."

Yvonne silently nodded. They looked at each other for a moment, then he took her into his arms, the clinging force of his embrace expressing the intensity of his unwillingness to be separated from her. Yvonne kissed him, then pulled away from him and walked back toward the wagons. Her eyes burned, but her tears had been exhausted. She felt drained and lifeless.

Tangeree was still asleep. Yvonne quietly undressed and lay down again, slipping under the cover. The girl stopped snoring and muttered, turning toward Yvonne. She nestled against Yvonne and began snoring again, and Yvonne held her and looked into the darkness.

The darkness became thicker, then the faint, first gleam of dawn came to the front of the wagon. The boat changed direction, and the drumming vibration of the wheel turning slowed. The voices of men moving about carried across the deck. The boat changed direction again, then once again, and the wheel slowed more. Then the wheel spun in a burst of speed and slowed until it was barely turning as the boat drifted backwards. The boat brushed something solidly, and the wheel stopped turning.

Tangeree stopped snoring and lifted her head. She listened, then lay her head back down and moved closer to Yvonne. Men called out, and footsteps moved back and forth across the deck as the orderlies and crew carried the wounded soldiers off the boat. Minutes dragged by. Tangeree lifted her head again and looked at Yvonne, her face a vague blur in the dim light. Yvonne kissed her and patted her. Tangeree put her arms around Yvonne and squeezed her affectionately, then pushed the cover aside.

There was a tense silence between them as they dressed, the sounds of activity continuing and the minutes passing. Tangeree finished dressing and sat down on her pallet, and she broke the silence. "Well, I guess you'd like to go say goodbye to him."

"Yes, I would."

"Well, I don't care."

Yvonne stepped to the front of the wagon and climbed down to the deck. A few stars still shone in the west in the stark, gray half-light of dawn. Mist hung over the river, a filmy, fleecy layer of fog that covered the water to the height of the rail. No one was stirring around the other wagons, and the orderlies and crew were carrying off the last of the wounded soldiers. Yvonne crossed the deck and stood by the oxen pen.

The town was no town at all, just a few shacks at the top of the bank and a muddy, rutted road between them that came down the bank to a sagging, spindly wharf. The stretchers were in rows in the weeds by the road, and Dawson walked among them, looking down at the soldiers. The crewmen came back along the wharf. Two of the orderlies cast off the ropes, and crewmen gathered them in as rumbling vibrations came from the interior of the boat and the wheel moved. Dawson turned and looked at the boat. He waved. Yvonne waved.

The utter contrast stirred the memory of another departure, bringing it back in sharp, clear detail. In the happy, carefree days of youth, she had gone with her husband on a trip to Baton Rouge to buy horses, and they had gone downriver from Vicksburg on *The Pride of Natchez*. The captain of the massive riverboat had accepted a challenge to break the record on the run, fortunes had been wagered, and excitement had built up for days. On the day of the departure,

business had come to a standstill in Vicksburg.
Throngs had jammed the waterfront, people had filled
small boats among the docks, and crowds had lined
the levee. A cannon in the fort had fired, signaling
the stroke of noon and the start of the run.

And then *The Pride of Natchez* had surged away
from the wharf with a thousand bales of cotton in
her holds and her tier of decks filled with passengers,
banners streaming, flags snapping in the wind, and her
wheel churning the water to foam. In her splendor,
she had seemed imbued with life rather than a structure of wood and metal, the thunder of her cannons
and sonorous blare of her horns smothering the frenzied jangle of the banjo band on the main deck and
the swelling, hysterical roar from the crowds.

And now tendrils of fog crept up the muddy bank
where the wounded soldiers lay on their stretchers.
The growing light silhouetted the shacks at the top of
the bank. The bow of the old stern-wheeler swung
away from the bank. The horn tooted, and the wheel
thrashed, clanked, and turned jerkily. Dawson waved.
Yvonne waved.

Her tears blinded her, and she continued waving
as details of the bank blended together and it became a dark blur from the bright light of the rising
sun behind it. The boat moved on out into the river,
angling upstream, and the point on the bank where
the town was located became lost in the distance and
the glare of the sun. Yvonne continued waving. The
boat rounded a bend, and she dropped her arm. She
wiped her eyes, turning away from the rail.

Tangeree was standing behind her, waiting. A
bruise on her cheek from the slaps the night before
stood out in sharp contrast with her fair skin. She

smiled radiantly, holding out her hand for Yvonne's. Yvonne put out her hand, trying to smile. Tangeree took it, and she laced her fingers tightly through Yvonne's as they walked toward the wagon.

9

TANGEREE'S FEATURES TWISTED with pain, her eyes closing tightly and her lips becoming thin and taut across her teeth. She stood behind the sagging, bony cow with a stained canvas parturition apron wrapped around her to protect her dress and her right sleeve rolled up to her shoulder, her right hand and most of her arm in the cow's vagina. The cow's back arched slightly, and Tangeree rose on her toes and hissed between her teeth as the contraction of the uterus squeezed her arm between the calf and the cow's pelvis, a forceful, relentless pressure that ground muscles against bone and cut off the circulation, numbing the wrist and fingers. The cow looked into the distance with a mild, bored expression as the contraction intensified; then it passed. Tangeree relaxed, panting softly and leaning against the cow's flank as she groped inside the cow.

"I have one of the rear feet back, Ma."

"Tangi, I had one of them back three times," Yvonne sighed, rubbing her right arm and flexing her fingers. "I'm beginning to think that it doesn't have but one rear leg."

Tangeree giggled, then her smile faded as she con-

137

centrated, moving her hand and feeling the calf inside the cow. The water bag had broken well over an hour before Yvonne and Tangeree had been called to assist the cow, and the calf had been knotted into a tightly-packed ball of flesh in the dry birth canal, solidly blocked against the narrow point near the end of the passage. For the past thirty minutes, they had been trying to ease the calf back along the canal without injuring it, and sort out the tangle of limbs so they could arrange it into a position in which it could pass into and through the narrow point.

Brush and deep weeds rustled as Spencer stepped along the side of the two wagons parked on the trail and looked at Yvonne. "Ain't you got it out yet?"

"Are we catching up with the other wagons?" Yvonne replied acidly. "Or do you think I'm waiting here to pass the time of day?"

"I didn't ask for the sharp edge of your tongue," Spencer grunted. "I just wanted to know if you'd got it out yet."

"You'll know when we get it out. If you'd kept an eye on this cow and called me when the water bag broke, it would have taken ten minutes. As it is, it might take another hour."

Spencer looked at her stolidly, trying to stare her down. Yvonne glared back at him. He was a tall, saturnine man, from a large city in Ohio, something of an anomaly and misfit in the largely rural group, and he was totally self-centered. When they had pulled out of the wagon train and stopped, Yvonne had immediately unyoked and hobbled her oxen so they could graze, but his were still yoked to his wagon. He treated his animals and his family with callous disregard, and Yvonne felt an intense antipathy toward him. They had exchanged heated words several times during the trek, and he had tried to stare her down before. He stared, and she stared. His eyes fell, and he stamped back along the wagons, muttering under his breath.

Yvonne looked back at Tangeree and the cow. Some cows were indifferent to manipulation of a calf when they were experiencing difficulty in delivering it, but this cow was one of those that reacted with uterine contractions that kept forcing the calf back into the breached position when it was moved. But Tangeree's small hand and slender arm didn't appear to bother the cow as much, and she seemed to be able to anticipate and avoid a degree of movement of the calf that would trigger a contraction.

"Do you want me to take another turn, Tangi? Your arm must be feeling like it's been in a clothes press."

Tangeree shook her head, frowning in concentration as she leaned against the cow's rump and gingerly moved her arm, pushing and feeling. "I have the other hind leg, Ma. Now if I can just get it back without hurting the calf." Her voice faded as she bit her lip and frowned in concentration, moving her hand inside the cow.

Yvonne nodded, looking away, and shivered as the breeze stirred the tall evergreens that towered upward on both sides of the trail, casting it into deep shadow. It was cool at the high altitude, even though summer had arrived weeks before, while they had been traveling along the Platte River. Full summer on the plains had brought fierce, blinding dust storms that had ripped tents and shredded wagon cover, and it had brought violent thunderstorms with crackling displays of lightning, shattering claps of thunder, and pelting hail followed by drenching rains.

Full summer on the plains had also brought the

threat of the raging fury of tornadoes on muggy afternoons when the sky had been filled with black clouds
and the air had been breathlessly still, with a feel of
tension and of forces precariously balanced on the
point of being unleashed. And it had brought heat—
suffocating, blistering heat from a glaring, torrid sun
that had beamed down from a brassy sky as the
wagons crept along the trail, a row of tiny motes in
the proportion of the enormous spaces of the vast, rolling plains stretching off to distant horizons on each
side.

The heat and monotony of the prairies had been left
behind at the Black Hills, a low, broken chain of
mountains that took their name from the dense, dark
growth of cedars and pines that covered them, and
the top of Laramie Peak had risen six thousand feet
in the center of them and served as a landmark for a
distance of a hundred miles. Then the trail had
climbed steadily upward toward South Pass, the gate-
way across the Rocky Mountains. It had wound along
the narrow banks of rivers foaming and roaring
through granite gorges, crossed high, barren plains
and fertile valleys covered with deep grass and thickets of trees, and gone up precipitous slopes where the
heavier wagons had been painfully hoisted to the top
with ropes and crude windlasses.

High mountain storms had lashed the wagons, there
had been broken wheels, accidents, and other damage
to repair, and the patient oxen had toiled on as massive, snow-capped mountains in the distance had
gradually moved closer. Then the mountains had
loomed up all around and the aspect of the wilderness
had become more remote and forbidding as the trail
became more difficult, winding around bluffs where
the wagon wheels cast stones from the trail into the

bottom of deep canyons hundreds of feet below, crossing and recrossing raging rivers, and passing over high saddles and rocky ridges covered with gnarled, wind-blasted trees clinging precariously to the thin soil.

The days were cool and the nights cold, the breeze carrying with it a frigid chill of the snowy slopes high above. The summer sun shone down brightly on fleecy puffs of clouds in the sky above the ceiling of foliage over the trail, but the air was almost as cool as the coldest day of winter in Mississippi. And there were other differences. West of St. Joseph, the War had suddenly become distant. On the last day on the riverboat, the War had still been an ominous threat in Yvonne's mind and a constant topic of conversation around her. It had been an almost palpable and omnipresent danger that could still strike in the form of renegades, the clash of armies, or martial law authorities who could rule that a widow and her daughter were vagrants. On the next day it had been gone, people's minds occupied primarily with other concerns.

Across the Missouri from St. Joseph, they had met a large extended family named Seeton, a family with origins among those who had been in the van of the people on the edge of the frontier as it moved west. Jacob Seeton, a man of fifty and the leader of the group, had been a fur trader, surveyor, and guide in the West since his boyhood. He, his sons, and various other male relatives in the clan, had gathered their families to take them west, and they had been preparing to set out when Yvonne and the Dowds had arrived. Others had arrived, a few escaping the War but most of them men who had come from the West for their families, and a train of over twenty wagons had been formed. And from the time Yvonne had met the Seetons and the others, most of the talk around her had centered on wagons, animals, and prospects in the West. There had been conversation about the War, but most of it had been references to the few people on the Overland Trail as a result of the War.

Along the Nemeha, Blue, Sandy, and Platte rivers east of Fort Kearney, scattered settlers were edging onto the plains, most of them immigrants drawn from Europe by broadsides about the Homestead Act. Those who spoke English had talked about the War, because incoming immigrants were being screened for able-bodied men to conscript into the Army, one or two husky boys being taken from each large family. But they had talked more about their sod houses, the wells they were digging and the windmills they were building to drive their pumps, and the crops they were planting. In the small settlements along the way, there had been factions that favored the North and South, but it had been bloodless arguments more than feuds. The raids and other ripples of conflict that had passed had long since faded, and a tornado or hailstorm that had ruined crops the previous year had been of more concern.

The wagon train had camped overnight at some of the Overland Mail stations, and had been at them a few times when stages had arrived. The drivers and passengers had mentioned the War, but they had talked more about famous gunfighters, marshals, gamblers, saloons, and gold bonanzas. At Fort Kearney, conversation had focused mainly on a threatened uprising of the Pawnees and Sioux, and at Fort Laramie it had been about the new ferry being built across the Laramie River. At Fort Bridger, all anyone had talked about was the trip Jim Bridger was making

with General G.M. Dodge to survey a route for a
railroad that would come west from Council Bluffs.

It had been almost like passing into a different
world, and even the herbs were different, familiar
leaves changing or disappearing. That had been a
cause for concern for a time, even though Yvonne had
an ample supply of seeds and dried roots to transplant,
because the properties of herbs could change when
they were grown in other than their native soil. Then
Yvonne had met an herbalist at Ford Bridger who had
sources of supply for herbs in the East, and who would
send them on to California by stage. And while the
climate, foliage, and other things had changed, more
fundamental things remained unchanged. An aged
relative among the Seetons had died and been buried
on the Platte, and two days later one of the Seeton
women had given birth to a baby who had been
named after the deceased. Three days before, a cow
belonging to another family among the wagons had
eaten poison sumac and died, and Tangeree was
toiling to bring a new calf into the world.

The cow had another contraction, Tangeree wincing
and raising on her toes from the powerful constriction
around her arm. The contraction passed, and Tangeree
slumped again, groping inside the cow. Then a
weary, triumphant smile spread across her face. "I've
got both of them, Ma! I have both hind feet back!"

"Are you sure both of them are hind feet, Tangi?"
Yvonne replied as she rose. "I've been fooled several
times."

"No, I can feel the hocks—they're both hind feet."

"All right, just ease back on them a little and keep
them straight," Yvonne said, walking to the cow and
looking. The vulva was swollen and distended far
more than usual, suggesting the dreaded possibility

of a prolapsed uterus as the calf was born, and Yvonne shook her head worriedly. "Tangi, I sure hope we don't have a cast calf bed here."

Tangeree sighed and nodded, pushing at her hair with her free hand. "As hard a time as she's had, I wouldn't be surprised, and it feels pretty dry and loose in there. If she does cast it, we'll have our hands full keeping the blowflies off it and getting it back in her out here."

"Well, we'll have to wait and see," Yvonne said, stepping to the cow's head, and she patted the cow's neck and scratched her ears. "Now just give us a good push or two, old bossy, and we'll get this over with."

The cow seemed to sense that relief was near, and she spread her feet wider, arched her back, and uttered a soft, high-pitched moo when the next contraction began. Tangeree leaned back, exerting a gentle pressure, and her arm slid out of the cow's vulva, smeared with blood and sticky, drying fluid from the water bag. Thick drops of the fluid dribbled out as Tangeree's hand emerged, two tiny hoofs clutched between her fingers. The toes of the hoofs were pointed downward, and Yvonne nodded as she looked at them.

"I hope that the legs aren't twisted and that the belly's down. If it is, things should be easy now."

"I believe it is, but if you want to hold the feet for a minute, I can go back in."

"No, trying to turn it now might make the difference between having to get her calf bed back in her and not having to do it. If it's on its back, you can hold the hind legs and I'll get the front out. Or do you want me to spell you now? You must be getting tired, Tangi."

"No, I can finish it, Ma."

Yvonne stepped back to the cow's head and patted her, talking to her soothingly. The cow gathered herself for the supreme effort, knotting her muscles and lowing shrilly as the next contraction began, and Tangeree leaned back against the hoofs. The calf came in a rush, slithering out as Tangeree pulled and the cow strained. Tangeree's weary right arm became weak, and she almost dropped the calf as she gathered it to her and lowered it to the ground. Yvonne stepped back along the cow, looking at her. The uterus had reamined in place, and the vulva was closing rapidly as blood and fluid ran from it and drained down the cow's legs.

Tangeree fumbled with the calf hastily, trying to lift it, and Yvonne grasped it by the rear legs and picked it up, letting the head dangle. She shook the calf vigorously to drain the fluid from its lungs, then lowered it to the ground and knelt by it, shaking its head. The small, blank eyes had a preoccupied light, gazing into the distance. Then they brightened, the tiny nostrils twitched, and the small chest stirred as the calf began breathing. Yvonne looked at the calf and felt its limbs and neck, and nodded in satisfaction. The calf didn't appear to have suffered from the difficult birth. And it was a heifer, the source of continued life. Yvonne stepped to the corner of the wagon and called out to the woman at the wagon in front.

"Mary, we need a couple of buckets of water and some old rags!"

"Ain't you got no water?" Spencer replied from in front of the wagon.

"I have a barrel of water!" Yvonne shouted angrily. "And if you can tell me why I should use my water to wash your calf, then I will!"

Spencer muttered and grumbled in front of the

wagon. A small girl came around the wagon with a
wad of rags under her arm, and a woman and a boy
followed her around it with wooden buckets. They
filled the buckets from the barrel on the side of the
wagon, and carried them toward the rear of Yvonne's
wagon. The woman was in her thirties and looked
twenty years older, with a habitual worried, harried
expression on her drawn, pale, deeply lined face. All
three of them were thin and ragged, and they looked
furtive, cowed by Spencer. Yvonne felt sympathetic
toward the woman, but she also felt an irritated impatience toward her for her lack of spirit.

"You have a nice little heifer, Mary."

"Well, we appreciate what you've done. Mr. Spencer
doesn't always get around to saying everything he
should, but we appreciate your help."

Yvonne nodded, taking the bucket from the woman
and the rags from the girl. "I was glad to do it for the
cow's sake."

The children looked at the cow and calf curiously
and the woman took the bucket from the boy and
sent them back to the wagon in front, believing in
the folk superstition common among urban people
that knowledge of birth processes would jeopardize
the girl's innocence and would prematurely arouse
the boy's sexual desires. The cow expelled the afterbirth as Yvonne washed and dried the calf, and Tangeree washed the blood and fluids off the cow's legs
so the cow wouldn't be bothered by flies. They washed
their hands and arms, and examined the cow and afterbirth as the woman took the buckets back to the
other wagon. The afterbirth was complete, and the
cow looked sufficiently recovered to travel, nuzzling
and licking at the calf as it lay on the ground with its
legs folded under it. The woman returned for the

calf and took it to the other wagon, and the cow followed her, her ears cocked forward as she sniffed at the calf in concern.

Yvonne and Tangeree put away the canvas parturition aprons, buried the afterbirth under a sapling by the trail, and yoked the oxen to the wagon. The Spencer wagon was disappearing from sight around a curve in the trail as Tangeree climbed into the wagon, the cow following and lowing anxiously as she lifted her head to sniff at the calf in the rear of the wagon. Yvonne put on her shoulder holster and linen dust coat, and gathered up the halter ropes. She tugged on them, and the oxen leaned into the yoke.

The trail was a wide, shallow ravine, winding up a gradual grade that was thickly forested with the lofty evergreens. It had been gouged into the earth by the iron rims on the wheels of countless wagons that had passed along it, and it was scored and pocked with gulleys and holes from the runoff of rain. Several of the Seeton men had been along the trail two and three times, and they had talked about their experiences on other trips while sitting around the campfires at night. One had told of pulling off the trail between Fort Kearney and the Platte River Ford to replace a wheel rim, then of waiting four hours for a break in the solid line of passing wagons before he could get back on the trail. The story was easy to believe, because the trail had become a feature of the terrain along most of the way, a deep, indelible mark carved into the land by a nation spreading westward.

The trail was strewn with debris left by tens of thousands and with the signs of misfortune suffered by many, parts of broken wagons, weathered yokes, and the whitened bones of oxen. Valleys below steep grades were littered with belongings that had been abandoned to lighten the loads, boxes of fine china, linens, farming implements, furniture, and other things representing the labor of lifetimes. The shredded and rotting remains of lace petticoats, wedding dresses, and intricately sewn quilts had been tangled among broken crockery and glass, and collections of daguerreotypes, heirloom clocks, furniture with the stamp of age and Old World manufacture, and other treasures of past generations had been left behind so a generation could go forward. Weeds had grown up and the sun, snow, and rain of the passing seasons had come and gone, and the belongings had settled into a rubble of mute remnants of dreams and memories, of evidence of poignant moments of sorrow suffered by those who had left the things behind.

There were also grave markers, evidence of times of heartbreak. Some had been weathered until they were only symbols that a human being had been buried there, and others had been legible, identifying children, men and women, and entire families. The Seeton men had talked about the dread cholera and other epidemics that had swept through parties and decimated them, and of strong, healthy men and women who had fallen ill in the forenoon and been buried the following morning. When the trail had been filled with long lines of wagons, the water holes had been fouled, the graze had been used up, and the game had been frightened away by those who had risked a lingering winter and set out early. And disease and hunger had been rampant.

Even those who had left early hadn't escaped illness, and Yvonne had found herself enthusiastically welcomed by the Seetons, to the extent that Jacob hadn't charged her a fee for joining the wagon train, and he had made an allowance in what he charged the

Dowds because Yvonne and Tangeree ate with them. The water holes had been clean and the graze had been good during the trek, because there had been only one large train of twenty wagons several days ahead of them on the trail. They had passed the wagon train near Fort Laramie, where it had stopped because of widespread illness among the people, and the commanding officer of the fort had ordered the wagon train to camp at least two miles away so the illness wouldn't spread to the fort. When Yvonne and Tangeree had stopped, a few in their wagon train had wanted to leave them behind, but Jacob Seeton had said that the wagon train would wait for a day farther along the trail.

The ill among the people in the wagon train had been infected with a type of grippe Yvonne had never before seen, and a tea of yellow root and balsam had seemed to give them more relief than the other things she had tried. She and Tangeree had worked through a day and a night, assisted by the few among the wagon train who weren't ill. The people had been grateful, and the leader of the party, a lean, leathery man named Elder, had been almost in tears because of the improvement in his wife's condition. Yvonne had refused payment, because the people had been very poor and she wasn't sure she had helped them significantly. In the early hours of the morning, she and Tangeree had made a supply of the tea to leave with the people, then had set out to catch up with their wagon train.

There had been no trouble with Indians during the trip, and Yvonne and Tangeree had been separated by a short distance from the main body of the wagon train in numerous other instances. They had frequently stopped with other wagons to see to an ailing animal or person and had stopped to gather herbs, and Yvonne enjoyed the relative calm and quiet away from the clamor of the other wagons and people. The disturbance in the forest caused by the passage of the wagon train had long since settled, and the activity of the forest had resumed, bird calls ringing through the trees, squirrels chattering, and a porcupine rustling in the underbrush.

A raging forest fire had swept across the top of the slope years before, and the trail was more bumpy, with patches of bedrock laid bare where wagon wheels had scoured away the thinner soil. The late afternoon sunshine beamed down on the goldenrod and evergreen saplings that had grown up among the burned and rotting logs and stumps, and wild phlox, valerian, and other flowers were muted splashes of color in the shade of the saplings. The Spencer wagon came into sight again, going around a curve below the top of the slope; then it disappeared behind trees. Tangeree gathered in the rope on the brake lever as the trail began slanting downward. The yoke chains slackened and dragged against the ground as the wagon started easing forward toward the oxen, and Tangeree leaned back against the rope. The rawhide pads on the brake blocks squealed against the iron rims on the wheels, and the yoke chains became taut again.

The wagon train had stopped for the night in a glade at the bottom of the slope, gathering around an abandoned station of the defunct Pony Express Company. There was daylight left, but Jacob Seeton led the wagon train at a casual and unhurried pace that reflected his approach to life, an attitude that had allowed him to reach a substantial age in good health. Seeton had several men helping him repair the corral at one side of the decaying log buildings, the Dowds had parked their wagons by the charred remains of a bunkhouse, and Hester and the other women were building a fire in the stone fireplace. Yvonne led the oxen off the trail and parked the wagon by the ruins of the bunkhouse, and Tangeree climbed down to help unyoke the oxen and lead them to the corral.

The skin diseases and rapid inflammation of wounds that Yvonne had been accustomed to in the hot, humid Mississippi lowlands had been left behind, and other things had taken their place. The dust along the Platte had made many among the group suffer respiratory system irritations, and the dry heat had given many of the children earaches because of hardening of their earwax. Chest congestions had become more frequent in the cold, thin air of the mountains, the cold had aggravated the aches and pains of the older people, and toothaches and other common complaints continued.

Accidents and mishaps also continued. A young boy among the Seetons had been bitten by a rattlesnake four days before, a girl had fractured a forearm a week before, and an ox that belonged to a man named Biggs had developed an infection in an injured dewclaw. Yvonne walked through the wagons and examined the people she had been treating, then went to the corral. Tangeree had put the oxen in the corral and was cautiously looking at the ox with the infected dewclaw, stepping out of the way as the ox kicked at her. The infection was clearing up, and they went to look at Spencer's cow and calf. The vaginal discharge from the cow had diminished to a normal watery ooze, and the cow had become possessive over the calf, muttering in her throat and shaking her horns threateningly at Yvonne and Tangeree as they

looked at the calf. The calf had dried off completely
and it was beautiful, a pale red with white spots. Its
long, frail legs were still shaky, but it was rapidly
gaining strength and was slobbering greedily at the
cow's teats.

Abigail Dowd was waiting for them when they returned to their wagon, holding her baby and one of
the small earthenware bowls. "Ma Dowd says supper's
about ready, and I wonder if I could get some more
of that salve you gave me for little Bobby Bownay.
I've used up every drop of it."

"Yes, of course, Abby," Yvonne said, and she
reached for the baby as Tangeree took the bowl and
walked toward the rear of the wagon to mix the salve.
"How is the rash now?"

"There's not a sign of it now, but I wanted to use
that salve a while longer to make sure it stays gone.
He fretted a lot for a while there."

Yvonne held the baby, looking down at him. He had
a sunny disposition, and he gurgled and smiled widely
as Yvonne touched his cheek and bounced him in her
arms. She looked back at Abigail. "How are your
nipples?"

"Oh, they've healed right up. And it's a wonder, the
way little Bobby Bownay goes at them, but that stuff
you gave me was really good. But the way he's going,
he'll be eating right along with everybody else before
you know it. This noon he ate most of a baked potato
and drank a whole cup of water."

"Yes, he's getting to be a big boy," Yvonne said,
handing the baby back. "You're making sure he gets
only boiled water, aren't you?"

"Yes, I boil up a fresh bottle every night. Pretty
soon I'm going to have to find another bottle, though,

because he's got to where he drinks might near a whole bottle during the day. . . ."

Abigail continued in the inexhaustible discourse of a young mother when talking about her offspring. Then Tangeree returned with the bowl filled with salve and they walked toward the stone fireplace. The sun was setting, and woodsmoke eddied across the clearing as it bustled with noise and activity. Children chased each other in and out of the abandoned buildings, women called to the children and rattled pans and dishes by the fires, and the men finished chores and gathered around the fires.

Darkness fell as Yvonne and Tangeree sat with the Dowds in front of the stone fireplace and ate dinner. The wagon train was within days of leaving the Rocky Mountains, bringing the end of the trek close enough to become a topic of conversation, and the Dowds had begun discussing what they were going to do when they reached California. Dowd and Whittacker were planning on establishing farms, but Jason and some of the other Dowd sons were more interested in prospecting for gold. They talked about it again and the discussion bordered on becoming an argument, as it always did.

They became silent as Jacob Seeton stepped into the light of the fire, carrying an empty whiskey bottle. He was a tall, heavy-set man with long, white hair, beard, and mustache, and he wore a wide trapper's hat, a fringed buckskin jacket, and dark drill trousers tucked into heavy boots. A bowie knife and a tomahawk were thrust into the front of his wide belt, and a long, heavy Colt Patterson five-shot revolver hung in a holster on the right side of his belt. He nodded to the men and women as they spoke, then looked at Yvonne and lifted the bottle.

"Mrs. Beaunais, could I bother you for some more of this medicine you gave Martha for her lumbago? She drank the last of it awhile ago."

"Yes, of course, Mr. Seeton. How is she feeling tonight?"

"She's feeling good enough, and she'll be all right as soon as we get out of these mountains." He smiled widely at Tangeree and handed her the bottle as she rose to take it, and his eyes twinkled under his grizzled eyebrows as he looked back at Yvonne. "Are you sure I couldn't trade you a couple of my loutish boys for this girl of yours, Mrs. Beaunais? I might even throw in a good yoke of oxen to boot."

"No, I couldn't do without Tangi," Yvonne laughed as Tangeree flushed and smiled, picking up the kettle by the fire and turning toward the wagon. "Little Silas looks like he's getting over that snakebite."

"Yes, he ate supper with everybody else tonight," Seeton replied. "I'd say he's on the mend."

"Here, sit down here, Mr. Seeton," Dowd said, moving over. "Would you like some coffee?"

Seeton shook his head as he sat down between Dowd and Whittacker. "No, I'm obliged, but I've had my fill. I see you got the tongue on that one wagon replaced."

"Yes, we found a tongue that somebody had left along the way. It's hickory and just as solid as iron, so we put it on. We were sitting here and talking about what we're going to do when we get to California, Mr. Seeton. Jase here and a couple of the other boys have gold on their mind, but to my way of thinking a farm offers a man a lot more he can depend on. What do you think?"

"Well, I lean toward your way of thinking," Seeton replied. "I have in mind a valley up by Mineral Summit where I'm going to do some farming as well as some hunting and trapping, and that suits me fine. I had my chance at plenty of gold and let it pass by to go trapping instead, and I've never regretted it."

"Were you in California when gold was discovered at Sutter's Mill, Mr. Seeton?" Jason asked.

Seeton smiled, looking into the fire and stroking his beard, and he shook his head. "No, I wasn't, but I knew there was gold in California a long time before then. In 1825, Jedidiah Smith was leading a trapping brigade for the American Fur Company, and my older brother John was among them. Smith took his brigade along the Humboldt and across the Sierras, then down to southern California and back up along the eastern side of the Sierras. They trapped a little here and there, and one of the places they trapped was on Mono Lake. And Smith picked up a pocketful of gold nuggets there as well."

There was a startled murmur among the people around the fire as they looked at each other in surprise. Dowd looked back at Seeton. "This was in 1825? Didn't this man Smith do any more about it?"

"Yes, when he got back he told the owners of the company. And right away they outfitted him to make a prospecting trip, but he run into a war party and got killed, along with most of his brigade. So it was dropped then and there, and that's how things stood until Marshal found gold in the race at Sutter's Mill."

"Did you hear about it from your brother?" Dowd asked.

"Yes, he got sick and didn't go on the second trip. When he got well, he came up to Three Forks where I was staying with my brother Lewis, helping him with his trading and trapping. I was about fifteen at the time, and I remember that John and Lewis talked some about the gold. But talk was all it amounted to, and we joined a trapping brigade instead of going after it. And like I said, I've never regretted it."

"Then the gold rush could have taken place a lot sooner, if things had turned out a little different," Dowd said.

"If Smith hadn't run into that war party, it could have," Seeton agreed, nodding. "The people who were running the company were just interested in money, but they didn't know exactly where the gold was. And the few who knew where it was were all like my brother John, more interested in trapping and hunting than in prospecting. And I'm the same. Money's never meant that much to me, and it don't now. I'm just going to settle in that valley I have in mind, and spend what days I have left there."

"You don't think you'll be traveling the Overland Trail again, then?" Dowd asked.

"No, and before long I don't think anybody will be traveling it," Seeton replied. "Jim Bridger is helping General Dodge lay out a route for a railroad, and if Jim is involved in it, I opine it won't be very long until you'll see a railroad. I've known Jim a good while, and he's not a man to waste time and effort. . . ."

Yvonne listened and looked at Seeton as he continued talking quietly, looking into the fire and stroking his beard. In St. Joseph, people had been almost reverentially respectful toward him, and stage drivers and others along the trail had shown a similar attitude, going out of their way to exchange a few words with him. When the wagon train had arrived at Fort Bridger, the older boys among the substantial brood of children borne by James Bridger's three Indian

wives had swarmed out of the fort and greeted Seeton boisterously, knowing him well.

The old man was a living legend, one of those who
had opened the West in the way Daniel Boone and
others had opened the Kentucky Wilderness. And
when he talked he spoke reminiscently of other legen-
dary names; William Ashley, the Sublette brothers,
Broken Hand Fitzpatrick, John Fremont, Kit Carson,
James Pattie, and others. His life had been woven into
the fabric of the history of the West, and he spoke
familiarly of events ranging from the early explora-
tions to the disaster met by the ill-fated Donner
Party and other later events.

The fire crackled in the fireplace, the light of the
flames shining on the faces of the people sitting on
logs, makeshift benches, and upended buckets around
the ruined hearth. Children slumped sleepily, and
the adults listened raptly to the old man. He looked
like a living legend, with his flowing white beard and
hair, his greasy buckskin jacket, and the familiar ease
with which he carried his weapons. He was a huge
man, the patriarch of his large clan of family, relatives, and followers, and an old man, but he moved
with the light, lithe step of a child and with the silence of a shadow. Friendly but capable of towering
rages, experienced and wise but with a childlike sim-
plicity, and following a drumbeat that only he could
detect, he seemed the personification of the mountain
men who had forged their way into the wilderness
and made trails for others to follow.

Tangeree returned with the bottle filled with infusion. Seeton took it and left, and Yvonne and Tangeree returned to their wagon and built a small fire
by it. They had gathered jimsonweed, larkspur, and

burdock during the past few days and had hung them
in linen bags in the wagon to dry, and they took out
those that had dried completely and sat by the fire
to put them in jars, carefully breaking the flower pods
from the jimsonweed stems and selecting the choice
leaves of the larkspur and burdock. The penetrating
chill of evening was settling, and Yvonne looked at
Tangeree as she moved closer to the fire and shivered.

"Do you need your coat, Tangi? I don't want you
catching a croup."

Tangeree tossed a handful of stalks from the herbs
into the fire and nodded as she stood. "I guess I'd
better get it. From what they're saying, though, it
won't be long until we'll wish we had some of this
cool air."

"That's what they say, but we're not there yet. It
wouldn't hurt to have a mint toddy to ward off the
chill, would it?"

Tangeree smiled and nodded her head as she
walked toward the rear of the wagon. Yvonne put
more wood on the fire, and moved the kettle closer
to the flames for the water in it to heat. Tangeree
climbed back out of the wagon with their pipes and
tobacco, and a jar of molasses, a large earthenware
jug of corn whiskey, a glass jar of mint leaves, and
their cups. She crushed mint and dropped it into the
cups, poured an inch of whiskey into each one, and
stirred a spoonful of molasses into the whiskey. They
filled their pipes and lit them, and Tangeree poured
water into the cups and stirred them when it began
boiling. She took a sip of hers and nodded as she
puffed on her pipe.

"That tastes like toddy to me, Ma."

Yvonne took a sip of hers and winced as she reached
for the kettle to pour more water into it. "It has

enough whiskey in it to ward off the chill, no doubt about that. . . . Everybody else has been talking about what they're going to do when they get to California, but we haven't done much talking about it, have we?"

"Well, we'll do what we've always done, won't we, Ma?"

Yvonne stirred her cup and took a sip from it, looking across the fire at the clearing. The activity had settled, and most of the other people had gone to bed. The fires had died to smoldering embers, and the pale moonlight shone down on the wagons and decaying buildings. All along the trek, the surroundings had been a constant reminder that they were far from the East and the medical colleges there. Yvonne sighed, puffing on her pipe. "Yes, it looks that way, Tangi."

10

THE FOLIAGE CHANGED again as the trail led down out of the mountains, the tall, dense evergreens gradually thinning out to be replaced by stands of oak, beech, and smaller pines and cedars covering the rolling slopes, with cottonwoods and willows along the creeklines. The more direct route taken by the Pony Express Company had varied from the Overland Trail in many places, cutting across loops and bends, where the wagon trail followed the line of least resistance in the terrain and kept to the valleys and the more gentle grades. The two routes joined through the western foothills of the Rocky Mountains, the abandoned relay stations at regular intervals of ten miles along the trail serving as silent reminders of a brief, closed chapter of history that had been brought to an end by the line of poles supporting the telegraph wires that linked the West with the East.

The Overland Mail Company stations were at irregular intervals along the trail, some at former Pony Express stations. Most had bunkhouses and a dining room for stage passengers, and all had barns filled with fodder, blacksmith shops for shoeing horses and making minor repairs to stages, and large corrals filled with horses to exchange for the lathered teams that pulled in. A few Indians lived around many of them, drawn by the activity, availability of whiskey, and possibilities for trading with stage passengers. Old trappers and hunters had also settled at some of them. The company advertized an enroute time of twenty-five days between St. Joseph and San Francisco, and the company had equipment and drivers to fulfill the promise. The small, solidly built coaches were light enough for the three teams of horses to pull at a dead run on level ground and up moderate grades, and the drivers vied with each other for reputations for speed, skill, and daring. The stages careened past the wagon train in one direction or the other every three or four days, the drivers shouting and whipping the panting, laboring horses. Three or four suffering inside passengers would look numbly out through the small window in the door as the coach shot past, and two or three outside passengers would be standing on a ledge at the rear of the coach and clinging grimly to the baggage rail through rain, mud, dust, frigid cold, and stifling heat.

The daytime temperatures increased as the wagon train moved along the winding trail through the foothills and down into the parched, sandy terrain north of Great Salt Lake, where patches of desert sedge, mesquite, and wiry brush covered the broken, rocky hills. The stagecoach stations were located at the more reliable sources of water in the arid, hostile region. They resembled tiny settlements, with trading posts at most of them, numerous Indians and white people living in huts and shacks around them, and wandering prospectors using them as bases of operation. The wagon train stopped at the station at Cooper Springs to prepare for the first trek across a long stretch without water, and they remained at the station for an extra day, letting the animals graze, drink their fill of water, and rest. They left at first light the following morning, maintained a hard, steady pace as the long, hot day passed and darkness fell, and arrived at Willow Flats well after dark.

A stagecoach approached the station at Willow Flats as the wagons were leaving the next morning. It bounced and swayed on the road as it neared the station, dust boiling up from it and the driver whipping the horses to a faster pace to make a dramatic arrival, and two men moved about in the corral, picking out horses to repleace the teams pulling the stage. A handful of Indians and loiterers gathered under the sagging, ramshackle porch in front of the adobe station building to watch the stage arrive as the first wagons slowly lumbered away from the station and onto the trail. Yvonne held the halter ropes and watched the approaching stage as she waited for the other wagons to sort themselves out into their usual traveling order and leave.

The pounding hoofbeats of the horses became a drumming tattoo, and the steady cracking of the whip and rumble of the stage jolting along the road became louder as it neared the station. Then it veered off the trail and onto the wide, dusty expanse in front of the station, two wheels lifting and slamming back down as the long double line of horses swung sharply. The Indians on the porch watched silently and woodenly, and the loiterers on the porch cheered, whooped, and whistled shrilly as they leaped up and down and waved.

The sweaty, gasping horses stretched out in a hard run toward the porch, foam streaming from their mouths. The driver stood in the box with the brim of

his hat turned back against the crown and his thick
mustaches flying in the wind as he gripped the
traces in his left hand and wielded the whip with his
right. The dusty coach lurched and bounced wildly,
with the two outside passengers clung to the rear of
it. The driver swung the horses parallel to the porch
as they approached it, then leaned back on the traces
and stamped on the brake lever by the box. The two
front wheels on the coach stopped turning, and it
skidded sidewards in a cloud of dust as the three
teams of horses dissolved into a plunging, rearing
mass, fighting the abrupt pressure on the bits.

As the dust swirling around the stage began dissipating, the two men in the corral ran out to take the traces
and unhitch the horses. The driver leaped down. The
doors on the stage opened and the inside passengers
stumbled out, and the outside passengers climbed
down and limped toward the porch, beating the dust
from their clothes with their hats. The driver ran
around the stage and toward the wagons moving out
onto the trail, shouting interrogatively, and people in
the wagons pointed at Yvonne. The man turned and
trotted toward her.

"Are you the woman who does the doctoring?"

The swelling at the side of the man's mouth became
visible under his dusty, bushy mustache as he approached. Yvonne nodded. "Yes, that's right."

"Can you knock out a tooth for me?"

"Yes, go fetch a chair or a stool from the station,
and I'll park my wagon by the corral."

The man walked toward the station, and Yvonne led
the oxen to the corner of the corral and tied them.
The bustle of noise around the stagecoach station began fading as the last of the wagons fell into line on
the trail and rumbled away, and the two men un-

hitched the teams from the stage and led them into the corral. Tangeree stepped back through the wagon to put the case of dental instruments on the tailgate as Yvonne lowered it, and the driver came out of the station with a heavy wooden chair. He was a tall, thin man in his forties, dust caked on his clothes and drifting from him as he walked, and dust covering his lower face, mustache, and the long hair hanging from under his wide hat.

"I saw Shorty Givens up at Apache Pass, and he said I ought to stop and see you about this tooth," he said as he approached. "He said that stuff you gave him for his colic has him in the finest fettle he's been in since he was a colt."

"I'm glad he's feeling better. If you're chewing tobacco, spit it out."

"I wish I was," he chuckled ruefully. "I ain't had a chaw for two days because of the misery this tooth's been giving me."

"Let me have the chair, and I'll see what we can do for you."

Yvonne took the chair and placed it so the morning sunlight would be on him and he would be turned away from the instruments Tangeree was putting out, and he sat down and took off his hat. Dust puffed up from the hat as he dropped it by the chair, but his forehead was bright, clean, and pale from the hat being pulled down to his eyebrows. Yvonne tilted his head back and looked in his mouth. His teeth were stained from chewing tobacco but were in moderately good condition. The one causing the trouble was the first upper molar on the left side. Yvonne selected a probe and began checking it.

The tooth couldn't be saved. Tangeree mixed the olive oil and morphine paste in an earthenware bowl,

and Yvonne numbed the tooth. The two men replac-
ing the teams finished harnessing the fresh horses to
the stage, and they walked over to watch. Three of
the passengers came out of the station with their tin
plates and cups of coffee, and they ate and drank as
they watched. The driver was in extreme pain from
the tooth and appeared unafraid, but Yvonne kept his
head tilted well back and the instruments out of his
line of vision. The tooth unseated smoothly from the
socket when Tangeree struck the dowel with the mallet, and Yvonne twisted it out with the pliers and
pulled the hardwood block from his front teeth as she
stepped back.

It surprised him completely, and he blinked in shock
as he closed his mouth. He probed with his tongue,
then a wide smile spread across his face as he stood
up. "Well, I'll be horsewhipped! That's the slickest
tooth knocking I ever had! What do you think,
fellows?"

The others chuckled and nodded, and the driver
put on his hat, spat out a mouthful of blood and
saliva, and took out his purse. "Yes, I can see why
folks talk about you the way they do, m'am. Shorty
said he met a train of pilgrims up by Steamboat
Springs who couldn't say enough about you."

"That must be the Elder party," Yvonne replied.
"How are they?"

"Shorty said they was all alive, and that they was
giving you credit for that. How much do I owe you?"

"Whatever you can afford—ten cents or so will do.
I'm pleased to hear that the Elder party is doing well,
because I wasn't able to stay with them as long as I
would have liked."

"Well, they said you and your girl worked straight
through a day and a night helping them, and every-

body else shunned them like the plague. And I can believe it now that I've met you. I believe a tooth-knocking as good as that one calls for a half a dollar at least. And you fellows got to watch while it was my toenails pushing through the soles of my boots, so you can ante in a nickle or a dime apiece. Just step over here and put a nickle or a dime by this fifty cents. And I'm much obliged to you, ma'm."

"Thank you for being so generous."

The driver shrugged and nodded, and spat out another mouthful of blood and saliva as he picked up the chair. The other men smiled and chuckled good-naturedly as they took out their purses and put coins by the fifty-cent piece on the tailgate, then walked back toward the station with the driver as Yvonne and Tangeree began cleaning the instruments and putting them away.

The men came back out of the station as Yvonne and Tangeree were leaving, the driver gobbling food from a tin plate and gulping coffee from a cup as one of the men who had changed the teams walked by him and talked to him. Yvonne untied the halter ropes and led the oxen toward the trail. The passengers boarded the stage, the inside passengers climbing in and slamming the door and the outside passengers clambering onto the ledge at the rear of the stage and taking a firm grip on the baggage rail.

The driver handed the cup and plate to the other man, took a plug of tobacco from his pocket and bit off a large chew, leaped onto a front wheel and scrambled into the box, unwrapping the traces from the brake lever and snatching up his whip. He uttered a shrill whoop, and the whip uncoiled and cracked explosively over the horses' heads. The horses lunged into a headlong run, jerking the coach into motion.

The long double line of horses wheeled into a turn toward the trail, dust boiling from their pounding hoofs. The coach snapped into the turn behind them, two wheels lifting and slamming back down. The driver lifted his hat with his whip hand and waved it at Yvonne, grinning widely. The inside passengers waved through the window, and the outside passengers waved and quickly gripped the baggage rail again as the coach jolted through a rut and bounced off the ground. Yvonne smiled and waved. The driver clamped his hat back down on his head and cracked the whip rapidly, wheeling the line of horses onto the trail.

The stage and horses made a large cloud of dust on the trail ahead of Yvonne, rapidly drawing ahead and drifting off to the side of the trail in the gentle breeze. The stage became smaller as the driver let the horses settle to a canter; then it disappeared over the top of a long, gradual incline ahead of Yvonne. Yvonne walked along the trail with the halter ropes slack, letting the oxen set their own pace. When she reached the top of the incline, the dust was a light spot in the far distance across the rolling, rocky terrain, where the trail came into sight at the top of another long rise. A larger, thinner cloud of dust rose from behind a closer hill, that from the wagon train as it moved along the trail.

It was a short day of travel, with the wagon train scheduled to arrive at Wolf Creek and spend the night before a longer trek to the next source of water on the following day. The temperature rose as the sun climbed higher in the clear, brassy sky, beaming down on the parched, sandy hills. Yvonne walked slowly along the trail, with the oxen trudging along behind her. The cloud of dust from the wagon train remained

at about the same distance ahead of her, and the
wagons occasionally came into sight where the trail
went around the brow of a hill, the canvas tops a line
of small white dots that danced in the distance in the
heat waves rising from the arid ground. When the
fiery heat of the afternoon settled, the dry, hot air became breathlessly still and the smell of dust hung over
the trail from the wagon train far ahead. During midafternoon, Yvonne reached the top of a low rise between two hills, and the line of bright green foliage
of Wolf Creek came into sight in a valley ahead.

The wagons were in a wide, level clearing in the
trees by the creek, a haze of woodsmoke rising from
fires around them, and the lowing of a cow became
audible at a distance from the wagons. There were
several cows with the wagon train, two belonging to
the Dowds, several belonging to the Seetons, and
others, all of which had been allowed to run dry and
hadn't been bred so they could make the trek more
easily. The only one that had calved during the trip
was the one that belonged to Spencer, and the lowing
had the distressed sound of a cow in pain or one
calling her calf.

The Spencer wagon was near the edge of the trail,
the cow tied to the tailgate and lowing almost constantly, and her calf wasn't with her. Yvonne looked
at the cow as she led the oxen off the trail, and she
stopped the oxen, handed the halter ropes to Tangeree, and walked toward the wagon. The Spencers
were by it, the man chopping wood and the woman
building a fire, and they looked up as Yvonne approached.

"Where's your calf?"

"I knocked it on the head, if it's any of your business," the man replied curtly. "And I'm fixing to do the same for that cow if she don't shut up."

"You killed a heifer calf?" Yvonne said in astonished disbelief, looking at him, then fiery anger swelled in her. "You're the one who should be knocked on the head!"

"It's none of your goddamned business what I do with what's mine!" he snarled. "If I figured that calf was more use to me as grub, then it was mine to eat!"

"Yes, it was yours, all right!" Yvonne replied angrily. "And I delivered it for you, so I want to be paid! That'll be five dollars!"

"Five dollars?" he sneered. "I ain't about to give you five dollars! We didn't make any bargain, and you don't charge anyone else!"

"What I do or don't charge anyone else is none of your business! You sent for me to deliver that calf, I delivered it, and now I want to be paid! That'll be five dollars!"

"You need a husband to take you in hand and teach you how to talk to a man is what you need!" Spencer bellowed. "It's none of your goddamned business what I—"

"And you need to learn how to talk to a lady!" Jacob Seeton barked in his deep, rumbling voice as he approached. "And I'm more than ready to do that right now, Spencer!"

Silence fell, and Spencer's dark frown became wary ss he looked at Seeton. Seeton walked toward the wagon with slow, deliberate steps, the fringes on his buckskin jacket swinging and his eyes narrow and cold. Others looked and moved toward the wagon, and Seeton stopped, glancing between Yvonne and Spencer. "Now what's this all about?"

"I knocked my calf on the head, and she's talking like it was hers," Spencer muttered, jerking his head toward Yvonne. "And now she's saying that I owe her five dollars. I ain't about to pay her five dollars."

"Yes, somebody told me you'd knocked that calf on the head," Seeton said in a soft, scornful tone, glaring at Spencer. "I've heard of people who'd eat their seed corn, but you're the first one I've met."

"That calf was mine," Spencer grumbled defensively. "I don't see what everybody else has got to do with it. And I'm fixing to knock that cow on the head if she doesn't stop carrying on like that. She ain't worth anything to me, because she doesn't give enough milk worth having."

"That's because of the way you've been treating her!" Yvonne snapped. "You can't mistreat an animal and then expect anything from it!"

"The way I've been treating her?" Spencer replied sarcastically. "I've never had to grin at a bucket to get a drink of water out of it, and I'm not going to start now!"

"A cow isn't a bucket! And what are those marks on her side? Have you been kicking that cow?"

"I said I'm going to knock her on the head if she keeps carrying on!" Spencer shouted. "Why are you so worried about that cow? Do you want to buy her? I'll sell her to you!"

"How much do you want?" Yvonne barked back at him angrily.

Spencer hesitated, blinking, then nodded. "By God, I will sell her to you. I paid twenty-five dollars for her in St. Joe, and I figure bringing her this far is worth something. I'll take thirty-five dollars, and then you can talk and worry about her as much as you like, because she'll be yours."

"Now just a minute," Seeton said. "Twenty-five dollars is top dollar for a cow, and that's a long way from being a top cow. And to my way of thinking, she done more to get herself here than you did. Along with that, you still owe for having the calf delivered." He looked at Yvonne. "How much do you think the cow's worth?"

Yvonne looked at Seeton, at Spencer, then at the cow. Things had happened rapidly. She didn't want the cow, and she couldn't afford it. Charges for ferries at the river crossings during the trek had taken far more than the few dollars she had received for treating people, and she had less than forty dollars left. The cow began lowing again, a soft, mournful hooting sound. The cow was bony and bedraggled, with scuff marks on her sagging, dusty belly where Spencer had kicked her, dung on the back of her rear legs from watery bowels, and she shook her head frequently to snap her ears, apparently having some kind of ear infection. Yvonne sighed, thinking, then looked back at Spencer.

"I'll give you twenty dollars."

"That sounds like a pretty good deal to me," Seeton said quietly as Spencer started to argue and bargain. "I'd advise you to take it."

Spencer looked at Seeton, his lips tight with anger, then looked back at Yvonne and nodded. "Give me the money."

Yvonne took out her purse and counted out the money. Then she untied the cow's halter rope and led her toward the wagon. Seeton motioned Spencer to one side and talked to him warningly in a quiet, angry rumble, and the other people moved back toward their wagons. Tangeree stood holding the oxen's halter

ropes and looked at the cow and Yvonne with a quiz-
zical smile as she approached.

"What did you want that cow for, Ma?"

Yvonne sighed and shrugged. "Tangi, honey, I really
don't want to talk about it."

"Well, I like the idea of having a cow, but that
doesn't look like much of a cow, Ma. She doesn't have
enough milk to founder a cat."

"I don't want to talk about that either, honey,"
Yvonne replied. Pointing to the Dowd wagons, she
said, "Come on, and let's get the wagon over here and
get the oxen out of the yoke."

The cow continued lowing as they parked the
wagon, unyoked the oxen and put them to pasture
with the others, and built a fire. Yvonne had never
administered a tranquilizer to a large animal and
wasn't sure of the dosage, and she made a half gallon
of lady's slipper and ginseng infusion, funneled it into
a drenching bottle, and poured it down the cow's
throat in pint doses at five-minute intervals until the
cow stopped lowing. The cow became calm and relaxed and tried to chew on Yvonne's skirt, an indication of extreme salt starvation. Tangeree poured
salt in a pan, and the cow greedily licked it up and
began placidly cropping the grass around the wagon
as Yvonne and Tangeree examined her.

The cow was a young brindle, no more than three or
four years old, but she had been badly neglected and
mistreated. Her hoofs were cracked and worn down,
her udder was a limp, flaccid sack with only a small
amount of milk in it and scratches and bruises on it,
and it was dangerous to stand around her head as she
snapped her ears and waved her sharp horns about.
There were bruises on her belly where Spencer had
kicked her, but her stomach muscles hadn't been

ruptured. She wouldn't give down her milk when Yvonne tried to milk her, because of obstinance and the pain in her scratched, bruised udder, and the milk was thin and watery when Yvonne worked patiently and filled a small bowl. Yvonne and Tangeree oiled and trimmed the cow's hoofs, mixed powdered speckled alder with olive oil to pour in the cow's ears, and led her along the creek to a patch of thick, deep grass.

Yvonne always took the last place in the wagon train, putting herself in a position to stop if someone pulled out of the train because of illness of a person or animal, and following at a sufficient distance to escape the dust from the others. The other wagons gradually pulled away from her the following day as she walked slowly along with the cow tethered to the tailgate of the wagon. She stopped at intervals to let the cow rest, eat a bundle of grass, and drink from a bucket. It was late afternoon when Yvonne caught up with the other wagons, parked in a pasture by another Overland Mail Company station. After the wagon was parked and the oxen were pastured, Yvonne went to see the manager of the station to buy corn to grind and make bran for the cow.

The infection in the cow's ears cleared up, the cow's ribs began disappearing after a few days of care and abundant food, and Tangeree became possessive toward the cow. She washed it each night, combed out the tuft of hair on its tail and polished its horns, and found bits of ribbon to tie on the tips of its horns. The cow responded to the care and affection, her udder began filling with milk that was rich and creamy. Yvonne milked the cow each morning, and put the milk in the wagon in a wooden churn she borrowed from Hester Dowd. By evening, the heat and jolting of the wagon turned the milk into buttermilk, with large clots of butter floating around in it, and the cow's udder was heavy and sagging with milk again. The cow's hoofs were slower to heal, but the rough trail turned into a road when they reached Nevada Territory, giving the new hoof a chance to gradually grow out and replace the cracked, ragged hoof.

The road became smooth and well-traveled when they reached Lassen's Meadows, a supply point for itinerant prospectors and temporary mining settlements in the area. The town had grown up around trading posts established to supply food and other essentials to incoming wagon trains in past years and was a community of substantial size, with two dusty streets of stores and saloons and a permanent population of several hundred people. The wagon train was something of a curiosity to the people in the town because few had arrived during the summer, and townspeople straggled out to the creek at the edge of town as the wagons pulled off the road.

Some of the townspeople brought baskets of vegetables to sell, some of the men in the wagon train wanted iron to make new shoes for oxen before starting across the Sierra Nevada, and people milled back and forth between the wagons and town. The activity diminished as sunset approached and cooking fires blazed up around the wagons, townspeople going home for dinner and the men from the wagon train returning to the wagons. Yvonne and Tangeree ate with the Dowds and went back to their wagon. There was a festive atmosphere among the people in the wagon train because of the approaching end of the journey. Some of the men from the wagon train went to the saloons in town after dinner, and a few people from the town returned to the wagons.

A mounted man rode in among the wagons, dismounted, and talked to the people at a fire. Then he led his horse toward Yvonne's wagon, its hoofs clopping softly in the dust. He stopped and touched the brim of his hat as he stepped into the light of the fire. "Mrs. Beaunais? My name's Sam Leggett, and I'm a doctor from Virginia City."

He was the man Charles Dawson had mentioned, and was a small, spare man in his late forties. His short, neat beard and mustache were streaked with gray, and he wore a brown tweed suit, a string tie, a wide hat, and a long, heavy revolver on his right side. Yvonne nodded, standing.

"I'm very pleased to meet you, Doctor Leggett. This is my daughter, Tangeree."

They greeted each other, Leggett's brown, leathery face wrinkling in a smile, and he looked back at Yvonne. "It seems that you have all the stage drivers talking about you and singing your praises, Mrs. Beaunais. I happened to be out this way, so I thought I'd stop by and say howdy."

"I'm very pleased that you did, Doctor Leggett. Would you like to sit down?"

"Yes, I believe I will," he said, stepping to the end of the wagon and tethering his horse to a wheel. "I've put a lot of trail behind me today, and me and my horse both could stand a rest. How has your trip been?"

"It's passed tolerably well thus far. We had one death, but that was mostly a result of age, and we've had no serious injuries or illness."

"Well, that's good to hear. It's a lot different when the trail is crowded, as I'm sure you noticed."

"Yes, we saw many graves along the way. Would you care for a mint toddy, Doctor Leggett?"

Leggett nodded as he folded his legs and sat down by the fire, sighing heavily. "Yes, I don't mind if I do. I could use something to slake the dust in my throat."

Yvonne put the kettle on the fire and glanced at Tangeree. She rose and went to the rear of the wagon, and Yvonne looked back at Leggett. "Did you hear from Charles, then?" she asked quietly.

Leggett glanced at the rear of the wagon and leaned toward Yvonne, nodding. "Yes, I got a letter from him a little over a month ago, and he said you'd be coming through. I heard the wagon train was coming in and I had some business up this way, so I came on up and waited for you to get here."

"I'm much obliged for your trouble. Where is Charles, and how is he?"

"He was fine when he wrote the letter, and he said he was being sent to Vicksburg. I guess you've heard of what's happening there."

The siege of Vicksburg by Union forces and other developments in the War had been mentioned by people on stages and others along the way, and Yvonne nodded. "And it was over a month ago that you received the letter?"

"Yes, and close to three since he wrote it. I answered it, but it's hard to get letters through now. He asked me to help you out if I could, which I'll be glad to do, of course." The corners of his eyes wrinkled in a smile. "And he told me not to mention him around the girl."

"Yes, things have been difficult for Tangeree, and it hasn't been that long since her father was killed."

"You don't have to explain it to me," Leggett chuckled. "My pa died when I was about her age, and when my ma got married again I kicked up a rumpus like a bull buffalo in a brush fire." He looked beyond Yvonne to Tangeree as she came back around the corner of the wagon, and sat up straight and began talking in a normal tone again. "I heard from a stage driver that a wagon train back along the trail had stopped because everybody had got sick, and that you got them back on their way again."

"Yes, that was the Elder party. We weren't able to stay with them as long as I would have liked, and I was glad to hear that everyone recovered."

"From what I heard, the time you did stay with them was well-spent. Well, have you decided on where you're going to settle and what you're going to do?"

"I've been giving it some thought. We've traveled with the Dowds all the way from Mississippi, and it appears that the most logical thing to do is to settle where they do in California. They're going to buy a farm, but I'm sure they'll be close enough to a town or to other people for me to have plenty to do."

Leggett lifted his eyebrows and nodded doubtfully. "Yes, that makes sense, all right. But just how well it will work out for you depends on exactly where they're going to settle. They have ordinances on who can practice medicine in a lot of places over there."

It was an unexpected problem, and Yvonne frowned as she looked into the fire, thinking about it. With few exceptions, the title of doctor was a title of courtesy, because extremely few physicians had a doctorate degree in medicine. Many had attended a series of lectures at a medical school and served a period of preceptorship under the supervision of a practicing physician, and others had done one or the other. And some had simply bought a few books, instruments, and a supply of medicines, and begun practicing medicine. There was no general standard of qualification for physicians, but there were places where widespread abuses by unqualified medical practitioners had resulted in enactment of ordinances establishing minimum qualifications. In those places, the minimum qualifications were always attendance at a medical school and a period of preceptorship, qualifications she didn't have.

Yvonne looked back at Leggett. "The Dowds have been talking about a place called Sonoma. Do you know if they have an ordinance there?"

"No, I don't. But they've also been talking over there about a state law on medical licenses, and that's something you might care to think about."

"In other words, regardless of where I go in California, I could eventually end up not being able to do anything except deliver babies."

Leggett shrugged and nodded morosely. "That's about what it amounts to. I hate to be the one to tell you, but that's the way it is."

Tangeree glanced up at Yvonne worriedly and looked back down at the cups as she mixed the drinks. She poured water into one, handed it to Yvonne, and poured water in the other two. Yvonne handed Leggett the cup, and took hers. Leggett lifted the cup in a silent toast, and took a deep drink. His eyes widened, and he gulped, coughed, and cleared his throat.

"Here, let me put more water in it for you, Doctor Leggett," Yvonne said, reaching for the kettle. "Tangi mixes a strong toddy."

"No, no, it's good," Leggett chuckled. "I just jumped at it when I should have sidled up to it. This is mighty tasty, and I like a drink with body."

"I think I can do with a little less body," Yvonne said, smiling at Tangeree and pouring more water into her cup. Her smile faded as she put the kettle back and stirred the cup. "I didn't expect that about those ordinances, and now I'm not sure what to do."

"Well, you could always settle in Virginia City," Leggett replied, shrugging. "Personally, I like it better than California."

Yvonne took a sip from her cup and shook her head doubtfully. "I don't like the idea of settling in a mining town. They come and go, and I want to settle somewhere permanently. And a mining town wouldn't be a place for a young girl like Tangi."

"Virginia City ain't just a mining town," Leggett laughed, shaking his head. "There's a lot of families there, and a lot of other girls just like yours. And churches, meeting halls, theaters, and places like that. Of course there's also saloons and a bunch of other places that can get pretty wild, but you don't have to worry about being permanent. Virginia City is going to be there for a long time to come."

"Would there be work for me there?"

"I don't see why not. They keep me so busy that I have trouble getting away as much as I like. There's one other doctor there, an old boy named Cummings. He saws on some bones now and then, but he spends most of his time fooling with mining stocks."

"Are there houses available?"

"Plenty," Leggett replied, nodding. "And I know of a house that might suit you. It's out on the edge of town and it's good and big, and it has a little barn and so forth. The price on it is two thousand, and the mortgage on that would pay out at about twenty-five dollars a month."

"Twenty-five dollars a month?" Yvonne replied, wincing. "And two thousand dollars?"

"That ain't much," Leggett chuckled. "It's no trouble to find houses there going for thirty thousand, because there's millionaires in Virginia City. I took a look at that one myself when it came empty, but I decided it was a little too far out for me. But if you're interested in Virginia City, I'll mosey on down that way with you and help you get settled. I ain't in no hurry to get back to work."

Yvonne looked at Tangeree. "What do you think, Tangi?"

Tangeree shrugged and shook her head. "I don't know anything about it, Ma. It's up to you."

"Well, I don't know any more about it than you do," Yvonne sighed, looking into the fire. "But it appears we don't have a lot of choice." She pursed her lips, musing, then shrugged as she looked at Leggett and lifted her cup. "Here's to Virginia City, I suppose."

Leggett laughed and nodded, lifting his cup. "Here's to Virginia City. The best in the West."

PART THREE

VIRGINIA CITY

11

VIRGINIA CITY sprawled across the barren slopes and ravines of Mount Davidson in a mingled patchwork of contrasts between makeshift and permanent, functional and decorative, humble and luxurious. Blocky, dusty, warehouse-like hulks of superstructures squatted over mineshafts, housing the ventilation equipment, pumps, and elevators extending deep into the earth, and mountains of tailings trailed away from them. Large restaurants with fanciful facades and brick hotels with uniformed doormen occupied corners, and narrow side streets led past clapboard boarding houses and open-fronted cafés filled with trestle tables and benches. General stores, grocers, butchers, and furniture stores stretched along arcaded boardwalks with assay offices, banks, and law offices. Noisy saloons, gambling parlors, theaters, lodge halls, and restaurants crowded together on other streets. There were large mansions with spool-railed balconies, steamboat gingerbread trim, and cranberry porch lamps; streets of staid, modest houses on the edges of the town; warrens of tenements near the mines; and clusters of shacks in the sagebrush fields around the town.

Churches maintained croquet lawns and sponsored

picnics, sports events, and evening conversational gatherings for the devout and moral. And the nights were alive with the activities of the unfaithful and immoral. Glassware clattered and music blared in saloons, dice rattled and cards slapped in the gambling parlors, shrieks of feminine laughter came from behind thick, red drapes on the windows of large houses on side streets, hoofbeats drummed along the streets in impromptu races between saloons and other places of entertainment, and there were occasional staccato roars of gunfire.

Some participated in both, went to the theaters to see the Chapman Family and Adah Isaacs Menken, and to the horse races at the track at Lousetown, at the foot of Mount Davidson. And there were other activities in the town, but the pulsing, throbbing heartbeat of the town was the steady, crunching roar of the mill stamps crushing the ore so the gold and silver could be extracted.

The sound faded to a distant, rumbling mutter under the noise of the activity of the day and evening, and it rose to a drumming thunder in the quietness of late night. It permeated the town, becoming a background to every activity. And it was comforting and reassuring, an audible contact with the river of wealth that flowed from the mine shafts and broke into a multitude of streams in every direction, providing trickles to porters, tradesmen, laborers, barkeeps, ministers, and all the others who contributed and supported. It was the central sound of the town, the sound of the purpose of the town.

The sound set the town apart from those places where the mill stamps no longer pounded, where veins of ore had dwindled and disappeared into worthless rock, where vacant windows stared down at weeds

growing in empty streets. And when it stopped for a
boiler to be cleaned or for repairs to be made, the
silence was uneasy. People were distracted, listening
for the sound to resume. Then when smoke belched
from the tall stacks and the gears began turning
again, and when ore tumbled down chutes and the
massive steel shoes began lifting and dropping on the
steel faceplates again, the atmosphere relaxed. People
smiled more easily and worked more industriously, because the heartbeat of the town had been restored.

Gamblers, pedlars, and loiterers came and went between Virginia City, Gold Hill, Bodie, Austin, Aurora,
Pioche, and other mining towns, and world-famous
lecturers, musicians, magicians, theatrical groups, and
revivalists entertained in the theaters and opera
houses. Speculators traded rumors about mines that
had struck bonanza outcroppings and others that were
struggling to keep from being flooded by an underground reservoir, and they cultivated acquaintances
and recruited informants among the miners roaming
between saloons and gambling houses. Maids, porters,
clerks, and day laborers speculated in dollar shares
with their wages, and gathered outside the offices of
broker to guardedly discuss their choices and read
the quotations telegraphed from the exchange in San
Francisco. The streets were crowded with drays,
wagons, carriages, riders, and pedestrians, and the
bustling activity had a sharp, frantic edge from the
scent of wealth in the air.

The road across the Sierra Nevada and through the
bleak, arid Washoe Mountains around Mount Davidson was heavily traveled, a flood of commodities coming in, and Wells Fargo stages carrying bullion out.
Drovers herded cattle and swine along the road, and
huge drays loaded with timbers for the mines lum-

bered along it. Wagons brought costly furnishings
that had arrived at the docks in San Francisco, and
foodstuffs from farms in the Sacramento Valley. The
hopeful rode in wagons and stages, and the wealthy
in large, luxurious carriages. Fast carriages brought
seafood delicacies from San Francisco and snow from
the high peaks of the Sierra Nevada to cool cham-
pagne, and express riders fetched starched shirts and
linens from laundries in Sacramento that were favored
by mine owners and their wives.

The house Charles Dawson had recommended was
a hundred yards up the hill from where the road
passed through the western outskirts of the town. The
street had a few other houses on large lots along it,
and a livery stable and a blacksmith shop occupied
the corners of the intersection of the street with the
road. On days when the breeze was from the north, it
brought with it the dust from the road and the odor
of the livery stable and blacksmith shop, but the street
was quiet and the house was comfortable, well-built,
and abundantly large. There was a front room for a
waiting room, a large porch to take the overflow from
it, a parlor for an examination and treatment room,
three spare bedrooms for patients, and an enormous
kitchen, and the former occupants had left a few sticks
of furniture and a large stove in the kitchen.

The wealth in Virginia City attracted charlatans of
every description, including faith healers, mesmerist
healers, and pedlars of nostrums and cure-all potions,
and neither the waiting room nor the porch were
needed at first. Yvonne sold the oxen and wagon to
the livery stable owner and talked to him, but he was
noncommittal about consulting her on treatments for
his animals. Neighborhood women came to visit and
become acquainted, and their reaction was similar to

that of the owner of the livery stable. Someone had dug up part of the stony ground behind the house at one time or another to try to make a garden, and Yvonne and Tangeree carried manure from the cow's stall in the barn and mulched a patch to try to grow herbs in the spring, made curtains for the windows in the house, and found other things to do to occupy their time.

An old man awakened Yvonne and Tangeree late one night, pounding on the door and half-crazed with pain from an abscessed tooth. The man returned the next afternoon after having slept for a full twelve hours and for the first time in days, beaming with gratitude and driving a mule pulling a cart loaded with furniture. He was a furniture-maker, and he brought a large settle for the waiting room, benches for the porch, and a table and chairs for the kitchen. The old man also told the blacksmith at the end of the street about it, the blacksmith sent a man who had fallen against the forge in the shop and severely burned himself, and sent travelers along the road who complained of illness. The owner of the livery stable came for Yvonne late one night after he and his helpers had tried most of the day to deliver a foal, and Yvonne and Tangeree delivered the foal alive and in good condition without injuring the mare.

Word gradually spread and others came, bringing their illnesses along with gossip about the town and its leading citziens. The pan-and-shovel prospectors who had discovered the Comstock Lode had long since faded into obscurity, their places taken by those who were more resourceful, ambitious, and wealthy. William Sharon was the leading figure among banking and financial interests, and William Stewart and John Mackay were prominent among politicians and mine

owners. George Hearst had accumulated the founda-
tions of a vast fortune in Nevada mines, with shares
in the Comstock, the Toiyabe Range, and in the El-
dorado, Cortez, and Sheba mines, and mine stocks
rocketed and plummeted in response to rumors about
his intentions.

Matthew Lassiter was a wealthy man from Boston
with a mysterious past. He was reputed to have been
a Union Army commissary and to have accumulated
a fortune by shipping stolen supplies through the
blockade to the South; it was said he had escaped ar-
rest through influence with the federal government.
He was rumored to hold interests in the Virginia Consolidated and Ophir mines, two of the richest-produc-
ing mines on the Comstock Lode, and he was known
to have influence throughout Virginia City and Nevada and to be the owner of a saloon and brothel in
the town. Samuel Clemens, a reporter for the local
newspaper, the *Territorial Enterprise,* wrote entertaining commentary on daily events under the name
of Mark Twain. Six Fingers Skelly was a notable
resident gambler at the Aces High gambling parlor,
and Tombstone Jack Ferris was a local gunfighter who
was reputed to have been hired numerous times to
make out-of-court settlements on disputes over mining
claims.

There were other stories and gossip, but little
money. The people in the town were relatively young
and the weeding-out process of the arduous journey
on the Overland Trail or by sea had eliminated many
of the weak and old, and illnesses among them were
less common than usual. The wealthy consulted doctors in Sacramento or San Francisco, and others consulted Leggett and Cummings. For the most part,
Yvonne's patients were the few old people in the town,

and the poor. They brought food, pieces of furniture, and gratitude, but little money.

For the first time, Yvonne was forced to regard healing as a means of earning a livelihood. In the rural South, virtually everyone lived in extended family groups that supported each other and shared fortune and misfortune. It hadn't been unusual for up to six or eight women and two or three men to accompany a single ill child, and a porch and yard full of people had usually meant a half a dozen to ten sick people. Attending one member of the family had placed an obligation on an entire extended family, and while she had received little cash money, she had received all the necessities of life in abundant surplus.

There were no extended families in Virginia City, and the people reflected it. The old were without the invigorating influence of the young around them, the young were without the wisdom and moderating influence of the old around them, and the children lacked the love, affection, and guidance of a wide range of relatives. Even those obviously from rural areas had urbanized rapidly. They lacked the support of others to give them a grasp of their own worth, and the rootlessness and being surrounded by strangers inclined them to be hostile, defensive, and suspicious. Virginia City was different from the rural South, and the necessities of life included a twenty-five dollar mortgage payment each month and other expenses that had to be paid in cash.

The first month's mortgage payment came out of the money she had received for the oxen and wagon. Some patients were coming and she was receiving foodstuffs and some money by the time the second month's payment was due, but she still had to take eight dollars out of the money from the oxen and wagon. During the third month she received more than enough money to pay the mortgage payment, but she had to order a supply of several herbs from the woman at Fort Bridger and had to buy supplies of several staple foodstuffs, and she took another sixteen dollars out of the money from the oxen and the wagon.

The weather turned cold during the fourth month, and the price of all foodstuffs went up because of the difficulty in transporting them across the Sierra Nevada. More of the patients gave what money they could rather than food, and it appeared that she was going to receive more money than she spent during the month. But then she had to buy firewood and lamp oil, which meant taking another four dollars from her diminishing funds. Leggett visited occasionally, and Yvonne told him she was doing well. From all appearances she was, because she had a growing number of patients. Leggett perceived more than she told him, however, and he casually mentioned that a mortgage payment could be deferred by paying a month's interest and a small additional charge. And Vicksburg had fallen to the Union forces, but Leggett hadn't heard from Charles Dawson.

The first snow of the season came, the first snow Yvonne and Tangeree had ever seen. It brought the most severe cold Yvonne and Tangeree had ever experienced, and it also brought an influx of patients with grippe and other respiratory system complaints. A woman who worked as a maid in a hotel in town brought a child, and she brought two luxuriously warm and heavy coats for Yvonne and Tangeree in payment. Yvonne was suspicious about how the woman had come into possession of the expensive coats, and she questioned her about them. They were coats

that had been left at the hotel, the woman assured
Yvonne, over two years before, and no attempt had
been made to claim them. The woman offered to
have a seamstress she knew alter and dye them, and
dire need and worry about money made Yvonne
hesitate in what she knew was a clear moral choice.
And she felt ashamed of herself because of her hesitation. Finally she sent the coats back, bought material
in town for a coat for herself and Tangeree, and gave
it to the woman to have her friend sew the coats.

Even after buying the material for the coats and
another supply of firewood, the large number of people who came in brought in enough money to pay the
month's expenses. But there was little over and for a
time it appeared that Christmas was going to be
bleak. Then a teamster from the Sacramento Valley
arrived late on a Sunday afternoon with his son, who
had broken his arm during the trip. The man was
obviously prosperous, both he and his son wearing
expensive fur coats and boots. The large, snowcaked
dray was filled with foodstuffs for delivery to Virginia
City, a costly cargo in the winter season, and the three
yoke of oxen pulling the dray were young, powerful,
and expensive animals.

The boy was a tall, strong, and healthy youth of
fifteen named Timmy, and he was in very little pain
from the simple fracture of his left forearm, barely
wincing as Yvonne set it in splints and wrapped it
firmly. At the same time, the arduous trip across the
Sierra Nevada in winter was dangerous even for the
most capable, and the man intended to start back
immediately after he unloaded. The boy looked fa-
tigued from the trip over. Yvonne gave the boy a
drink of lady's slipper and ginseng infusion to relax
him, left him on the table in the examination room,

and went back into the waiting room to talk to his father.

"If you think he should stay with you, then he'll stay," the man agreed quickly. "The man down at the blacksmith shop said that everybody says you know what you're talking about, so he'll stay. I'll be back over on Wednesday to bring turkeys and geese for Christmas, and I can pick him up then."

"Yes, that'll be about right, Mr. Cargill. He won't be able to use his arm, but at least moving about won't put him in danger of having his arm grow back crooked. I'm afraid I'm in a position that I'll have to ask for money in advance, though."

The tall, burly, bearded man frowned, moving his chew of tobacco in his mouth. "Well, I'm leaving my boy for pledge," he said curtly. "Ain't that enough good faith that I'll pay?"

"I didn't make myself clear, Mr. Cargill. His keep between now and Wednesday might have to come out of my savings, and I daresay Timmy is a hearty eater."

"Oh, is that what you're talking about?" Cargill laughed as he turned to the door. "You've guessed that boy right, because he knows how to hide some vittles, but I can do better than pay in advance. You just stand in your trace chains a minute."

Yvonne stepped to the door as he went out, and watched him. He climbed onto the dray, tossed down a hundred pound bag of potatoes, a large bag of onions, a bag of carrots, a ham wrapped in burlap, and other packages. Then he began carrying them in. There were bags of rice, beans, dried apples, and dried peas. Yvonne's conscience twinged.

"Mr. Cargill, all this is worth far more than you should pay for having Timmy's arm set and for his keep for a few days. Now I really can't accept all this—"

"Oh, it ain't that much," Cargill chuckled, puffing from carrying the heavy bags. "I got storerooms full of all this, and I ain't out that much. And I don't mind saying that I was worrying some about that boy's arm, because I wasn't likely to find no sawbones sober and at home tonight. Beyond that, it's near Christmas, ain't it? I don't pay no attention to it myself, but I know a woman sets store by it and likes to have extra vittles in the house."

"Yes, that's true, Mr. Cargill. This is still far too much, but I'm very grateful for it and I assure you that Timmy will have the best of care."

"I'm sure he will, ma'm," Cargill replied, turning back to the door. "And you're more than welcome for the vittles."

Yvonne smiled and nodded as she followed him out onto the porch. She folded her arms and shivered from the cold as Cargill went to the top of the steps and spat a stream of tobacco juice.

"Well, I guess I ought to have a word with your man," he said as he turned back around, wiping his mouth with the back of his hand. "I guess he's a miner, ain't he? I wouldn't expect nobody else to be working on a Sunday night. Which mine does he work at?"

"No, my husband is dead, Mr. Cargill. He was killed at Fredericksburg."

Cargill frowned, chewing his tobacco and looking away. "Well, now I ain't so sure that leaving that boy with you is such a good idea. He can be a handful."

"Mr. Cargill, you can't be serious," Yvonne laughed. "I'm an adult woman, and I assure you I can deal with a fifteen-year-old boy."

"You don't know that boy," Cargill said, shaking his head doubtfully. "Him and his three brothers kick clean out of the chains sometimes, and they're a handful for me. I ain't got no doubt that you can handle your girl, but I ain't so sure about that boy. He's a feisty one."

Yvonne smiled and shook her head. "Mr. Cargill, be assured that I can deal with Timmy. And you can also be assured that I won't be cruel if I have to discipline him."

Cargill grunted, shrugged, and sighed as he started down the steps. "I'm more worried about you than I am that boy, because you ain't big enough to hurt him. If I can't you sure as hell can't, and I've tried. And I don't think you know what kind of yoke you're putting your shoulder to, but I'll leave him if you say so."

"Please don't worry about it, Mr. Cargill. Instead, you should worry about your trip. And you should really rest before you start back, because that's a dangerous trip."

He looked back at her with a nettled expression. "Well, I don't need nobody to tell me what to do, ma'm. I aim to hit deep snow at daybreak and be out of it by nightfall tomorrow. I know what I'm doing."

Yvonne smiled, placidly and nodded. "I didn't mean to imply that you don't, Mr. Cargill, I was only expressing concern for you. I live in Virginia City, and I'm well aware of the situation we would be in if it weren't for you brave men who bring us the things we need."

Cargill looked at her blankly, his lips parted. Then his mouth snapped closed and he flushed furiously in embarrassment. He turned and stamped down the steps, then spat tobacco juice, cleared his throat, and looked back at her. "Thankee, ma'm," he said awkwardly. "I guess you ain't got no brother or somebody nearby you could call if that boy kinks his back, have you?"

"Mr. Cargill, please put your mind at rest on that score. I wouldn't want to think you were worrying about that when you should have your attention on what you're doing on your journey."

"Oh, I'll be all right," he chuckled, and motioned toward the oxen. "I've got on old Ned and old Buck on my lead yoke, and they don't start pulling good until the snow's a foot above their horns."

"Those are certainly some of the most beautiful oxen I've ever seen. You take good care of your animals."

Cargill nodded, his smile fading as he reluctantly moved toward the dray. "Well, I'll see you again come Wednesday."

"Very well. Goodbye, and Godspeed, Mr. Cargill."

Cargill stopped and looked back at her, scratching his beard. He started to say something else, then he changed his mind and nodded again as he spat and stepped to the lead oxen, taking their halter ropes. The massive oxen leaned into their yokes, effortlessly pulling the huge dray, and it turned ponderously in the road, its large, wide wheels grinding through the thin, dirty snow and pulverizing small rocks.

The animals were well-broken. Cargill tucked the halter ropes over the head of one of the lead oxen and walked back to the side of the dray to pull down on the brake lever rope and keep the dray from building up speed on the downward slope in the street. Yvonne stood on the corner of the porch with her arms folded, shivering in the cold. Cargill was a large, gruff man, but she knew that he would look back when he reached the road. He looked back and waved. Yvonne waved, and went into the house.

She built a large fire in the fireplace in one of the spare bedrooms to take the chill off the room, then went back to the examination room. Timmy had dozed off on the table from the effects of the tranquilizer and his fatigue, and he was disgruntled when Yvonne told him his father had left him. Helping him into the bedroom was awkward, because he was two or three inches taller and forty or fifty pounds heavier than her, and he didn't want to be helped. He tried to lie down on the cover with his boots on, and he was surly when Yvonne started to help him take them off, pulling away from her impatiently. Then he grumbled in his throat and frowned darkly when she spread the comforter over him and tucked it around him.

Yvonne had been planning on having corn gruel enriched with pork fat for dinner, which wouldn't have satisfied the boy, and it was impossible to resist a degree of extravagance with the unexpected windfall of food filling the food safe, the cupboards, and one corner of the kitchen. Yvonne cut thick slices from the smoked ham, and they put on rice seasoned with bits of the ham and made mashed potatoes and biscuits. Darkness fell outside, spots of light danced on the ceiling and floor as the roaring flames in the stove licked around cracks in the firebox, and the lamp on the table cast a soft glow over the center of the kitchen. The room was comfortably warm and filled with the delicious smell of the ham frying. Yvonne felt more cheerful than she had in weeks, her worries forgotten for the moment and Tangeree ebulliently happy as she looked forward to the meal. Then Yvonne went to get the boy.

"I don't want no supper," he muttered in a sullen, sleepy voice as he jerked away from Yvonne's hand on his shoulder. "Leave me alone."

"No, you must have dinner, Timmy. You can sleep after you've eaten."

"I don't want no goddamned supper!" he shouted. "I've been up since before daybreak, crossing them goddamned mountains! I'm tired and I don't want no goddamned supper, so leave me alone!"

Yvonne turned and walked out of the room, stiff with rage. Tangeree sat at the table and looked straight ahead, carefully avoiding any expression that Yvonne might find aggravating. Yvonne looked in the firewood, picked out a billet, and carried it to the chopping block outside the back door, leaving the door open so the light would fall across the block. She split a flat piece four inches wide and a little over a foot long from the billet, trimmed down one end of it with the axe so it would fit her hand, then went back inside.

The boy had dozed off again, and he woke with a start and snort of surprise. He tried to fight her off, but Yvonne gripped his right wrist, used his momentum to flip him onto his stomach on the bed, and twisted his right arm up behind his back. His weight was on his broken arm, and he gasped with pain as he tried to get it from under him. Yvonne held his right wrist tightly and began beating him on the buttocks with the piece of wood.

Dust rose from his trousers, and he squealed with pain as he struggled harder, bouncing on the bed. Yvonne pressed his weight down on his broken arm, and pounded harder. He churned his legs and twisted from side to side, pinned firmly on his broken arm and unable to lift himself with it because of the pain in it, his right arm locked tightly behind his back.

Then the boy stopped struggling and tried to endure the pain. But it wasn't only pain he was enduring, as he had when he had been thrashed by his father, a man. It was too much for him. He began weeping, but the tears were only those of anger, and Yvonne continued whipping him. Then the weeping turned into hurt and humiliation, and she stopped. She dropped the piece of wood, pulled him up to a sitting position on the bed, and sat down by him, pulling him to her and patting him.

"Leave me alone," he sobbed, jerking away from her. "After what you done to me!"

"I did that because you had it coming, Timmy, as you well know," she said, pulling at him. "Now we can forget it. Come here."

"I ain't forgetting a goddamned thing! I ain't about to—"

"You stop that, Timmy!" Yvonne hissed, slapping him sharply across his face. "You stop that cursing!"

"See, you're still hitting me," he whimpered, shaking with sobs and flinching from her upraised hand. "Now how am I supposed to forget about anything. . . ." His voice faded into a wail as he began weeping brokenly.

"If you'll stop cursing so I can stop hitting you, then we can both forget it," Yvonne said firmly, pulling him to her again. "Now just rest your head on my shoulder, and you'll feel better in a minute."

"I ain't no baby," he muttered tearfully, halfheartedly pulling away. "I don't need no woman to baby me."

"Yes, everyone has a little bit of a baby in them, Timmy," Yvonne murmured, pulling him closer and patting his face. "I do, you do, and the biggest man in the world does. But it takes a really big man to recognize it and admit it. Everyone hurts and wants to be comforted now and then."

"Well, you're the one who done it to me."

"And you know full well why I did it, Timmy, so there's no reason to even discuss it. But I certainly didn't want to do it."

"You sure went at it like you wanted to."

"I did it because it had to be done, and I wanted to get it over with. Now it's over and done with, and I want to forget it. I want you to like me, and I want to like you. And I won't have any trouble liking a big, handsome lad like you as long as you'll behave."

Yvonne pulled his head down to her shoulder, holding him to her. The light from the fireplace shone on his face as he looked up at her from the corners of his eyes, tears trickling down his cheeks, and his lips parted as he continued sobbing softly. Yvonne smiled down at him, pushing his hair away from his forehead, and leaned down and kissed him. He dropped his eyes, an expression of offended dignity on his face, but it wasn't convincing. Yvonne kissed him again, pulled his head firmly against her shoulder and wrapped her arms around him, and began rocking back and forth with him, humming softly. He slowly relaxed against her, his shoulders occasionally moving convulsively in the shuddering aftermath of his tears.

Tangeree didn't look up when they walked in. Her eyes were on the dishes on the table, her lips pursed in regret as she looked at the cold rice, globby potatoes, and the scum that had formed on the gravy. Timmy's expression reflected awareness that Tangeree had heard his thrashing, and he avoided her with his eyes as he sat down. Yvonne and Tangeree passed dishes back and forth, and Yvonne filled Timmy's plate and put it in front of him.

The boy's fierce, proud independence and resentment of control was as strong and healthy as his father's. At the same time, he had a yearning need for attention, affection, and love. Yvonne had made a contact with him, and he wanted to please her. The atmosphere relaxed as they ate and Yvonne chatted with the boy, and he talked about the trip across the mountains, how he had broken his arm, and about his family. He was the next to youngest of four sons, their mother had died years before, and their father had remarried three or four years before.

And the woman had left. It appeared likely to Yvonne that the woman had left to get away from the four rowdy boys, and what Timmy said confirmed it. She had been a large woman of Russian extraction from Fort Ross, suggesting that size had been a criterion in Cargill's choice, and Timmy talked about the things the four boys had done and the severe thrashings the woman had given them. Then one of them had put a snake in the flour bin.

"Cletis just had in mind to fun her a little," Timmy said musingly, chewing. "To show her he didn't hold no grudge because she flailed him with that fence rail, I expect. But she took it wrong and broke clean out of the pen, and we ain't seen hide nor hair of her since. And Clete told us we'd get it from him if we let on to Pa about what happened, because he was afraid Pa would kill him for running her off."

Yvonne smiled wryly and shrugged as she pushed her plate away and picked up her coffee cup. "It probably scared the life out of her. I know I wouldn't want to put my hand in a flour bin and get a handful of snake."

"Well, we figured it would make her hop around some," Timmy chuckled. "But we didn't look for her to break out of the pen. What would you have done? I guess you would have whaled the lights out of all of us, wouldn't you?"

Yvonne shook her head, taking a drink of coffee. "No, that wouldn't have done any good. I never have made any snake biscuits and I don't know how they would taste, but that's what you boys would have had. And you wouldn't have had a bite of anything else to eat until you ate them."

Timmy looked surprised, then he sat back and slapped the table with his palm as he roared with laughter. "Snake biscuits! By gonny, a body has to be careful about what they put in your flour bin, don't they? But it would have been worth eating my share just to see Clete eat his'n. Something like that would set plumb sideways in his craw. I wonder why she didn't think of that?"

"The woman was probably at wit's end. If you're through eating, you can help Tangeree with the dishes, Timmy."

He started to offer an objection, then he nodded and smiled amiably as he pushed back his chair and rose. "Well, I'm through. That was good grub and I wished I had somewhere to put more of it, but I'm out of room."

The boy had devoured almost everything on the table that Yvonne and Tangeree had left, and he had recovered his composure enough to notice that Tangeree was a girl. They carried the dishes to the sink as Yvonne sat at the table and sipped another cup of coffee, and the boy grinned and moved closer to Tangeree as they began washing the dishes. Tangeree's hostility toward males remained and had caused some friction with youths among the Seetons during the trip. When the circumstances were such that she could forget that a youth or man was male, as when they were ill, she regarded them as she did women. But sex was clearly in evidence as Timmy brashly moved closer to her. She moved away several times, then she picked up the large wooden mixing spoon and rapped his left arm with it, a firm, solid blow. The boy staggered and almost fell, the color draining from his face.

"Don't hurt his arm, Tangi," Yvonne said mildly. "If you do, we'll have something to settle between us."

"Well, you get over here and let him rub up against you!" Tangeree barked in exasperation. "I'm not going to just stand here while he slobbers around me!"

"You don't have to, but you didn't have to hit him that hard, honey," Yvonne replied, and looked at the boy. He was leaning against the sink, his knees sagging. "If it had been most, we'd be picking him up off the floor and carrying him to bed. Most people with a broken arm carry on like a guinea hen with a snake after its eggs, but he didn't make a sound while I was setting his arm."

Tangee looked at Yvonne disdainfully, then sighed and nodded in resignation as Yvonne frowned. "Yes, he can take pain better than most people. . . ."

It was halfhearted, but it was enough to stimulate the boy's vanity and he straightened up with an effort and began helping with the dishes again. And he gave Tangeree more than enough room in front of the sink.

He apparently considered a quick rinse enough effort to expend on a dirty dish, and he was bemused by the thorough scrubbing in hot, soapy water that Tangeree gave them. Cleanliness in general didn't appear to cause him any significant amount of concern, because his clothes were wrinkled and grubby and his hair was dirty. Yvonne took her cup to the sink and handed it to Tangeree, and pulled Timmy's head down and looked at his hair.

"You've got a little shaggy, Timmy, so I'll trim you up and wash your hair first thing in the morning."

"During the winter?" he replied in alarm. "I'll catch my death, and it ain't been that long since I washed my hair."

"You can sit by the stove and dry it, and you might have fallen in a creek or something this past summer, but I think it's been a while since there's been any soap on that head."

"Well, if it has to be washed, I can wash it. I don't need nobody to wash my hair for me. . . ."

"No, that job needs two hands, and I want to look you over good while I'm at it to make sure you don't have any nitties hiding in that mop."

The boy muttered and continued objecting, but a pleased smile tugged at the corners of his mouth even as he protested, and he reminded her about it the next morning when he thought she had forgotten it. Yvonne washed his hair in the sink, then boiled his clothes and dried them on a rack behind the stove as he sat at the table with a blanket pinned around his neck and devoured a large stack of johnnycakes soaked in molasses. And he buttoned his shirt with the buttons in the wrong holes when he dressed, and went to lengths to make Yvonne notice it so she would unfasten it and button it for him.

He made peace with Tangeree during the day through talking to her about his broken arm. Tangeree took out an anatomy book, showed him the bone that was broken, and explained the process it would go through in mending itself. The situation had a high potential to make Tangeree jealous over the attention Yvonne devoted to the boy, and Yvonne compensated for it by being more attentive to Tangeree than usual. Jealousy didn't become a problem, and somehow the fact of the difference in sex between Tangeree and the boy became sufficiently obscured that she became more tolerant toward him.

The boy was strong and energetic, and he did a number of useful chores around the house in spite of his broken arm. He swept out the snow and dirt tracked in by people coming to see Yvonne, chopped up all the firewood behind the house, cleaned out the cow's stall in the barn, and repaired loose boards there that were letting cold drafts blow through it. Drafts were also coming in through cracks around several of the windows in the house, and he painstakingly cut thin slivers of wood from billets of firewood to chink the cracks. Then he cleaned out the ashbox in the kitchen stove and tightened the loose plates in the stove.

A woman whose husband was a dealer in sundries brought in her child and offered to pay in cash, but Yvonne asked for knitting wool instead. When Tangeree and Timmy were asleep, Yvonne worked rapidly to knit a pair of mittens for Timmy and a thick muffler for his father, and she finished them on Tuesday night. The boy's mood was subdued the next day, and even his appetite had deserted him. He was so downcast that Tangeree made an effort to assist Yvonne in cheering him up, initiating conversation and chatting with him. The boy smiled wanly as Yvonne and Tangeree talked to him, and he gloomily roamed around the house, looking for things to repair that he had missed before.

The last of the ill people for the day left during late afternoon, and the three yoke of powerful oxen and the snow-covered dray turned onto the street a few minutes after. Timmy was sweeping the snow and dirt off the porch, and he came back in, put the broom away, and went for his coat and cap. Yvonne checked the wrappings on the splints on the boy's arm and adjusted the sling around his neck, and she talked about the opportunities he would have to return for a visit as she helped him on with his coat. He nodded and grunted morosely, glancing toward the door as the jangle of chains and rumble of heavy wheels on the road became audible. As Yvonne straightened Timmy's coat on his shoulders and buttoned it, Cargill's heavy footsteps came up the steps and across the porch. Yvonne went to the door and opened it.

Cargill's eyes were cautious and worried as they moved quickly around the room, darting to Tangeree, the boy, and back to Yvonne, studying the expressions. Then he smiled tentatively as he stepped inside. "Well, then, how's the boy doing?"

"He's coming along very well, Mr. Cargill," Yvonne replied. "And he's been a great help to me while he's been here, haven't you, Timmy? He's done all sorts of repairs and other work about the place, even with one hand." Tangeree had the mittens, and Yvonne turned and took them from her. "And here's a little Christmas present for you, Timmy. You won't be able to wear but one right now, but you do as I told you and you'll be using both hands before you know it."

Timmy took the mittens and looked at them, swallowing, then put them in his coat pocket. "I don't want to get them dirty."

"Very well, Timmy," Yvonne chuckled, and she straightened his cap, pulled him down, and stood on tiptoe to kiss him and pat his face. "But do put one on if your hand gets cold. And come back and see us when your arm heals."

The boy nodded, swallowing again and almost in tears, and turned toward the door. Then he turned back, put his right arm around Yvonne and squeezed her tightly, and stepped to Tangeree and silently extended his hand. Tangeree shook hands with him, and he wheeled around and brushed past his father, ducking his head and hurrying out.

Cargill looked on with a dumbfounded expression, turning and watching the boy as he crossed the porch and went down the steps. He shook his head as he pushed the door closed. "Well, I seen it, and I don't believe it," he muttered in wonder. "I'm ready to jerk my eyeballs out of my head and call them liars to their face."

"Timmy wasn't an unruly boy, Mr. Cargill," Yvonne said. "He isn't hard to deal with."

"Well, you ain't see what I've seen," Cargill replied. "I had a woman who'd make four of you, and she couldn't do nothing with him or his brothers. They run her clean off."

"That was your fault as much as hers, Mr. Cargill," Yvonne said firmly. "A lot of oxen will back off the yoke in a left turn, right turn, or some other particular situation, and it's up to the yoke partner to pull harder. Yoke partners should make up for each other's weaknesses, whether they be oxen or people.'

Cargill looked down at her, his beard moving as he chewed his tobacco, and he nodded as he took out his purse. "I can't argue with that, ma'm. And I'm seeing a steadiness in you that I didn't notice before, so I got an idea of what that boy run up against if he commenced some of his capering with you. Well, I'll settle my tally."

"No, Mr. Cargill, you don't owe me anything. After all the food you left the last time, I owe you."

"I wasn't out nothing on that, and I'll leave five dollars," Cargill replied, taking five silver dollars from his purse and putting them on the table by the door. "It's worth more than that to see what you done with that boy. And if some of it rubs off on his brothers, it'll be worth more yet."

"I'm very grateful, Mr. Cargill, even though I don't feel I've earned it. And I have a small Christmas present for you." She turned and took the muffler from Tangeree, and smiled up at him as she handed it to him. "Merry Christmas, Mr. Cargill."

"Well, now, ain't this nice," Cargill said as he chuckled heartily, taking the muffler. "This is something that I can use, because I've got this open spot right here at the front of my collar where the wind gets me just like a knife. I'm much obliged, ma'm. I got a little present out on the dray for you and the girl here."

"Mr. Cargill, you've given us far too much already," Yvonne protested. "Honestly, I couldn't take anything more than—"

"No, I put it on the dray especially for you and the girl," Cargill said, turning to the door. "Just step on out, and I'll put it on the porch for you."

Yvonne smiled and nodded in resignation as she and Tangeree followed him out. Timmy was sitting forlornly on the snow-covered bags at the front of the dray, his legs hanging over the edge. He stood as Cargill walked to the dray and climbed on the wheel, and he helped his father lift down a lumpy burlap bag. Cargill put the bag on his shoulder and carried it to the porch, and put it on the edge of the porch.

"Well, Merry Christmas, ma'm."

"Thank you, Mr. Cargill, and the same to you. Merry Christmas, Timmy!"

Timmy forced a smile and silently nodded. Yvonne and Tangeree stepped to the corner of the porch as Cargill returned to the dray, wrapping the muffler around his neck and tucking the ends into his coat. Then he took the halter ropes on the lead oxen. The oxen turned, and the dray swung around in the street. Timmy waved all the way along the street as Cargill walked by the wagon and pulled on the brake lever rope. Yvonne and Tangeree shivered in the chill, waving. At the bottom of the street, Cargill looked back and waved.

The dray turned onto the road and disappeared behind the blacksmith shop, and Yvonne and Tangeree carried the bag inside. A large frozen turkey was in the top of the bag, neatly plucked and wrapped in grease paper. A smaller bag under the turkey contained two dozen large, juicy oranges, a rare and costly delicacy in Virginia City during winter.

The spicy scent of the oranges filled the house as Christmas approached, an odor that was poignantly reminiscent to Yvonne of childhood Christmases. The five dollars paid for a new dress for a present for Tangeree, the turkey and abundance of other food promised a memorable Christmas dinner, and what had been the threat of a drab, dismal holiday season turned into joyful anticipation.

Then a woman came for Yvonne and Tangeree as they were decorating a tiny evergreen in the kitchen on Christmas Eve. They gathered up the herb chest and their other things, and left with the woman. Christmas wreaths were silhouetted by the cheerful glow of warm fires and yellow lamplight in the windows of houses, the ringing sound of merry voices hung in the night air as caroling groups went from house to house, and the lantern the woman carried made a puddle of dim light on the dirty snow as Yvonne and Tangeree followed her through the streets.

The woman led them to a squalid, hulking tene-
ment building near the mill. The dark, narrow alley
past the doorways smelled strongly of urine and feces,
and the pounding of the mill stamps almost drowned
the sounds of revelry in the flats and in nearby streets.
The woman was a neighbor, and she disappeared as
Yvonne and Tangeree went inside. Three ragged, hun-
gry-looking children were huddled in a corner of the
tiny, grimy front room. The man was almost drunk,
and the woman had been drinking. The woman lit
another lamp, and led Yvonne and Tangeree into a
bedroom.

The boy on the bed was seven or eight, frail, thin,
and dirty. His temple was bruised from a fall or a
cuff, there was a large sore in the corner of his mouth,
and he had the furtive, hangdog look of an abused,
neglected child, a child who was a by-product of
copulation rather than an object of affection and love.
His mother said that he had been bothered periodical-
ly with bowel congestion during the past two or three
years. When he had complained the previous day, she
had obtained a strong laxative tonic from a neighborhood midwife and given it to him. He was burning
with fever, in agony with pain in his obdomen, and his
lower abdomen was discolored and swollen. And
through some mercilessly cruel anomaly, he remained
fully conscious and completely aware of his surroundings.

They returned to the front room, and Yvonne told
the woman. She uttered a wailing cry and collapsed
against the man, sobbing. The man's lips trembled, and
his eyes filled with tears as he held the woman.
Yvonne and Tangeree returned to the bedroom. Tangeree took the lamp and went to the kitchen to look

for water and a clean cup to dilute the tincture of opium. Yvonne sat with the boy in the darkness, holding his hand and trying to sooth him.

Tangeree returned with the lamp and the cup, and Yvonne began giving the boy sips of the liquid. The man left, and returned with a minister. The minister had been drinking heavily, and he prayed loudly in a rambling, senseless torrent of words. The man and woman stood at the foot of the bed and wept in alcoholic, maudlin self-pity. The boy was terrified for a time, then the opium began overcoming that and the pain.

Then peace descended. The minister left. The woman sat in a chair on the other side of the bed and dozed off. The man went to sleep in the front room. The boy's pain and fright disappeared. Death's hand rested on him, turning his face ashen and making dark circles under his eyes. And still he remained conscious and aware of his surroundings, his frail body battling valiantly for survival. Yvonne put mint on his tongue to take away the taste of the opium. He smiled, his small, thin face radiant with relief from the pain and with pleasure from the attention and affection. Yvonne held the small, cold hand, Tangeree touched his arm, and they talked with him. And they waited with him. The mill stamps pounded nearby, a rhythmic, drumming roar, and the minutes and the hours of the death watch passed.

The end came as daylight was creeping through the dirty pane and picking out the peeling paint on the wall and the ragged edges on the coverlet. Yvonne used the small mirror from the herb chest to make sure there was no breath, then closed the boy's eyes and pulled the coverlet over his face. Tangeree gathered up the things, and Yvonne woke the woman and told her. Then Yvonne and Tangeree walked home in the cold, gray Christmas morning.

The house was cold and the small tree in the kitchen looked shabby, part of the decorations on it and some of its needles already beginning to fall. It was uncomfortably suggestive of the small boy, a young life prematurely ended. Yvonne put the tree outside, and they built up the fire in the stove and put the turkey in the oven to bake. Then they went to bed.

Tangeree snored softly in her room. Yvonne lay and looked up at the ceiling. The daylight behind the curtain over the window kept her awake. And the slight, nagging pain stabbed in her lower abdomen again. She wondered if the events of the night had brought it on or made her more conscious of it.

12

A MURMUR of feminine voices raised in a heated exchange came through the door to the waiting room, and Yvonne looked up from the small girl on the table and exchanged a glance with Tangeree. She looked back down at the girl and smiled at her as she patted her shoulder. Then she turned away from the table and went to the door.

Four women, three children, and a man were in the waiting room. One of the women had arrived since Yvonne had last looked into the room, and she was sitting away from the others on a chair in a corner. Her face was powdered and rouged heavily, she had on a bright red silk dress, an expensive fur coat, and a wide hat decorated with a large pink plume. A strong scent of lavender cologne wafted across the room from her.

A buxom, aggressive-looking woman on the settle looked at Yvonne for support, then back at the woman in the corner. 'This is a place for decent people, not for your kind! Get on back to where you belong!"

"Piss on you, you fat old bitch!" the woman barked back. "If I listened to every goddamned fat old bitch like you, I'd never—"

"Just a moment," Yvonne interrupted in a quiet,

firm tone, looking at the woman in the corner. "What is your name, please?"

The room became quiet. The woman sat back in her chair and cleared her throat, a wary, defensive expression on her face. "I'm Crystal Brixton. Are you Mrs. Beaunais?"

"Yes, that's right, and I'm pleased to meet you, Miss Brixton. I'll ask you not to use that sort of language here, because this is my home and there are children here." She turned her head and looked at the woman on the settle. "I am the one who will decide who comes here and who doesn't. And anyone who is ill and wishes to see me is welcome here."

The woman's face flushed as she stiffened, glaring at Yvonne. She started to reply, then she bit back the words and looked away, fuming with anger. The other two women frowned darkly in disapproval, the children looked frightened and curious, and the man darted surreptitious glances at Crystal from the corners of his eyes. Crystal was about thirty, with a voluptuous attractiveness that was marred by her brassy, predatory bearing. She looked uncomfortable and unsure of herself in her surroundings, but she smiled gratefully and nodded as Yvonne went back through the door.

Yvonne listened for another outburst of arguing, but there was only a steely silence in the waiting room instead of the usual hum of conversation and whining and crying of children.

The buxom woman on the settle was next. She was sullen and brusque as Yvonne examined her child and asked questions, and she put only five cents on the table when she left. The man wanted a tooth extracted, and while Yvonne was waiting for Tangeree to prepare the olive oil and morphine paste mixture, she heard a woman and child come up the steps and across the porch, and enter. Then the sound of an indignant snort came faintly through the door, the front door slammed, and the woman stamped back across the porch and down the steps.

The other two women still looked disapproving when they brought in their children, but they were courteous. One left fifteen cents, and the other left twenty-five cents. Then it was Crystal's turn, and Yvonne called her in. The scent of the lavender cologne filled the room as she undressed and Yvonne examined her, and Tangeree went to mix the guaiac and lobelia infusion and the bichloride of mercury salve as Crystal put her clothes back on.

"I don't think there is a medicine that will cure it completely," Yvonne said. "Lues is a very difficult disease to treat."

"But the sore will go away, won't it?"

"Yes, keep the salve on it and drink a sip of the infusion after every meal. You should see a change in about two or three days, then the medicine will work more quickly and the ulcer should be gone within a week. But it'll probably come back."

"I'll worry about that when it happens," Crystal chuckled, moving her shoulders and tugging on the waist of her dress to adjust the bodice. "And I'm much obliged to you for not acting as though you think you're so much better than I am, like those old bitches out there."

"I don't believe it's up to me to judge you. At the same time, that doesn't mean that I approve of what you do, so make no mistake about that."

Crystal smiled nonchalantly and shrugged, picking

up her reticule and opening it. "You still don't treat me like I'm dirt under your feet, and I like you for that. How much do I owe you?"

"Whatever you can afford. Twenty-five cents or so will do."

"Twenty-five cents?" Crystal exclaimed in astonishment, then laughed and shook her head. "No, you should charge more than that, Mrs. Beaunais. Doc Cummings charges two or three dollars just to talk to someone, and then he charges for medicine on top of that. And that's when you can find him. Mr. Lassiter gave me ten dollars to come here with, and you might as well take it all."

"No, twenty-five cents will be enough."

"Well, I'm going to put a dollar here, and I'm not going to take it back even if you throw it at me," Crystal said, placing a silver dollar on the table. "Mr. Lassiter has several men that run around and do things for him, and it's usually one of them who tells us what to do. But he talked to me himself about coming here, because he wants to know about you."

"Why would he want to know about me?"

"He's heard of you, and I think he's getting tired of trying to deal with Doc Cummings. And I won't have anything but good to tell him about you, you can depend on that. If he wants me or the other girls to come here, would you rather we came at night? That would probably be better than being here at the same time as a lot of other people, like I was."

"There usually aren't more than one or two people here and a lot of times there aren't any, but that doesn't make any difference to me. When someone is ill, they can come here at any time."

"You're sure different than Doc Cummings, because

he just wants us to come at night. And then we have to use the back door. Mr. Lassiter also told me to ask you about arrangements for restoring regularity. As you can imagine, we get caught every now and then."

"I won't perform an abortion," Yvonne said, shaking her head firmly.

"Are you sure? Doc Cummings charges a double eagle for it, and that's good money."

"No. I won't perform an abortion for any amount of money."

Crystal sighed and shook her head as she picked up her coat and put it on. "Well, Mr. Lassiter isn't going to like that."

Yvonne chuckled dryly and shrugged. "I don't care whether he does or not, Miss Brixton."

"Don't ever let him hear that you said anything like that, Mrs. Beaunais," Crystal said, frowning warningly. "When he wants something in this town, he gets it. I know you're in a lot different position toward him than me, but you still shouldn't let him hear that you said anything like that. There's no point in hunting for trouble, is there? And I'll just tell him you said you don't know how to restore regularity, all right?"

"You will not!" Yvonne laughed, stepping to Crystal and helping her adjust her hat. "If he asks you, you tell him exactly what I said. I don't want any misunderstanding on that, Miss Brixton. I won't perform an abortion under any circumstances."

Crystal looked at Yvonne worriedly and started to say something, then Tangeree came in with the bottle of infusion and small bowl of salve. The woman took them and looked back at Yvonne, shrugging in resignation. "All right, I'll tell him, Mrs. Beaunais. I'm much obliged to you for being so nice to me."

"You're more than welcome, Miss Brixton. If you don't see a change in the ulcer within three days, come back and see me."

Crystal smiled and nodded, and nodded to Tangeree as she went out. Yvonne glanced in the waiting room to see if anyone else had come in, then began helping Tangeree put things away.

The dollar was still on the table, and Yvonne picked it up and tossed it in her hand as she looked at it. During the three weeks since Christmas, more of the patients had been from families of tradesmen and others in town who were relatively prosperous. Two had been miners who had been injured in accidents, and Leggett had begun telling his patients to come to her when he was out of town, which was often. A number of them had left a dollar or more, and one of the miners, a critically ill child, and a woman who had had a difficult childbirth had spent a few days in the extra bedrooms, which had brought in more money. The total she had received was already far more than the month's expenses.

It appeared that a corner of sorts had been turned and that worries about money would become a thing of the past. But even if the trend continued, it would still be impossible to save enough within any reasonable length of time for Tangeree to go to medical college. And there were subjects she should be studying in preparation for medical college, but there were no academies in Virginia City. Yvonne sighed as she put the dollar in her pocket and continued helping Tangeree put things away. The strong scent of lavender cologne still hung in the air, and Yvonne smiled to herself as she thought of the women's umbrage over Crystal Brixton's presence in the waiting room.

* * *

Crystal Brixton's visit continued to have repercussions. A woman who brought in a child the following day was the one Yvonne had heard arrive and leave abruptly while Crystal had been in the waiting room. The woman told Yvonne about it indignantly, and said that Cummings allowed the bordello women in his office only at night.

"I'm not ashamed of anything I do, Mrs. Appleby," Yvonne replied. "Anyone who is ill is welcome here, and I wouldn't have anyone here under cover of darkness that I wouldn't have during the day. And it appears that Doctor Cummings is wasting his time trying to conceal what he does if everyone knows about it."

"Well, I don't think it's right for good people to have to be around the likes of her," the woman said irately. "And I sure don't want my little Martha around something like her and asking questions about her. It spoils children's minds to know about things like that."

Yvonne smiled down at the small girl on the examination table and shook her head. "I disagree. Ignorance can harm a child, but not knowledge that is presented properly."

"I ain't going to argue with you about it. But if I ever see something like her out there in that front room again, then I ain't coming back here no more."

"That is up to you, Mrs. Appleby."

The woman subsided into angry silence, waiting for Tangeree to return with the eucalyptus salve and infusion for the child's chest congestion, and she put five cents on the table and left without speaking, her back stiff and her features drawn in a dark scowl. Others who came in during the day referred to the incident more indirectly, having heard of it from someone else.

Some indicated disapproval, and others indicated indifference. It was mentioned and hinted at on the
following day, and Yvonne overheard two women
whispering about it as she walked through the waiting
room to the kitchen. Then it was gradually forgotten
as other subjects of newer interest arose to gossip
about.

The salve and infusion Yvonne had given Crystal
Brixton were a combination of treatments she had
learned from her mother and Charles Dawson and they
were efficacious most of the time, but not always.
Sunday came, the third day since Crystal Brixton's
visit, a rare day for anyone to come unless they or a
child were seriously ill. On Monday, a woman returned
who had been there at the same time as Crystal, reminding Yvonne of the woman. She didn't come in
during the day, and Yvonne concluded that the salve
and infusion must have been effective.

On Tuesday night, Yvonne and Tangeree were
washing the dishes after dinner when they heard a
carriage approaching rapidly along the street. It turned
off the street and pulled up by the house, the wheels
bouncing over ruts and the horses stamping and pawing as they stopped, then footsteps raced across the
porch and there was a loud knock at the door.

"Mrs. Beaunais! Mrs. Beaunais!"

It was Crystal Brixton. Yvonne wiped her hands and
picked up the lamp from the kitchen table, and
Tangeree followed her through the house to the front
door. Crystal called out again in an imperative, frightened voice, and her hand was lifted to knock again as
Yvonne opened the door. Her hair was down around
her shoulders and her makeup was thicker than before,
and she had her coat pulled around her shoulders
over a long nightgown that was cut low in front and

revealed most of her breasts. She was holding a lantern, and she lifted it and pointed over her shoulder.

"We have Rosie Gibbs here, Mrs. Beaunais, and she's real bad off. Could you see if you can do something for her?"

A large, tall man was standing behind her, holding a long, shapeless bundle. Yvonne stepped back from the door and opened it wider. "Yes, of course. What's wrong with her?"

"She went to get her regularity restored, and it took her real bad," Crystal said, stepping inside. "Bring her on in, Mort."

"I hope you know what you're doing," the man grunted in a deep, gruff voice, moving toward the door.

"Well, goddamn it, we had to do something!" Crystal snapped. "If Mr. Lassiter gets mad and wants to take it out on somebody, he can take it out on me!"

"You watch how you talk to me!" the man barked angrily. "You'll get my fist along the side of your head!"

"Just get her on in here, and I won't have to talk," Crystal said in a placating tone. "Come on, Mort, she's real bad off."

The man was ugly, with grossly heavy features that were battered and scarred, and his eyes were small and cruel, glaring at Crystal as he walked in. He was large and hulking, carrying the woman effortlessly in a bundle of silk sheets and a purple velvet coverlet that hung down and trailed along the floor. Tangeree ran toward the kitchen, and Yvonne opened the door to the examination room and put the lamp on a table at the side of the room, motioning toward the examination table. The man put the woman on the table and walked back out, dusting and tugging at his sleeves, and Yvonne moved the lamp closer and looked at the woman's face. She was young, no more than twenty, her face was blanched under her thick, smeared make-up, and she looked barely conscious.

"Mr. Lassiter wasn't there," Crystal said worriedly. "I told Mort that we had to do something before we lost another one. He really didn't want to without talking to Mr. Lassiter, but I—"

"Another one?"

"Well, you know how it is about restoring regularity. Sometimes it takes a body real bad, and I've seen it happen to a few. And in that place I was at in San Francisco before I came here, it seemed like we were losing one a month for the longest—"

"What was done, when was it done, and who did it?"

"She went to Doc Cummings early tonight, about dark, I expect. And I don't know what he did, but I went to her room a while ago and she looked like it had took her real bad . . . ."

Yvonne started to open the bedclothes, and saw blood long before she saw the woman. The abortion had been done mechanically, because there was too much blood too soon for it to have been a drug or herb to induce miscarriage. She pulled the bedclothes back together and leaned over the woman's face. The woman looked like she was probably spiritless and had a cringing personality, lacking the all-important courage and will to fight for her life. Yvonne slid a hand under the woman's head and lifted it, smiling at her.

"You're going to be all right, Rosie!" she said loudly. "We're going to help you, and you're going to be all right! Do you hear me?"

The woman's eyes focused, and she blinked. Her lips twitched in a suggestion of a smile of acknowledgment. Crystal stepped out of the way as Tangeree rushed in with a pan of hot water. She put it on the table by the wall, looking at Yvonne.

"I built up the fire and put on more water to heat, Ma."

"All right, Tangi. This woman has had an abortion through someone pushing a rod, a stick, or something like that up her vagina. I'd say either the womb, vagina, or both have been cut or torn, depending on what was used. If she's still bleeding, and she probably is, we'll rinse her out with baneberry and put in a linen tube soaked in baneberry to make it clot."

Tangeree winced, rolling up her sleeves. "You're going to start with baneberry?"

"We don't have any time to lose if she's still bleeding, because she's lost a lot of blood. And I don't want to move her around too much, so let's work fast. You wash her so I can see if there's fresh blood."

Tangeree nodded, turning to the table by the wall and tearing a rag into pieces. Yvonne began pulling the bedclothes open. Crystal chuckled, looking from Tangeree to Yvonne.

"That little Tangeree is more like a doctor than Doc Cummings. She always knows just what she's doing, and she's so—"

She broke off as Yvonne reached the blood-stained sheets and began unwinding them. Gouts of blood had streamed from the woman while she had been moved about, and the silk sheets were sodden and heavy with it. The woman had on a thin silk nightgown, and it was soaked with blood in front and sticking to her thighs and stomach. Yvonne gripped it tightly and tore it open, then ripped it open from the woman's stomach to her knees. Her pubic hair, upper thighs, and a pad that had been tied over her vulva were a gummy,

matted mass of blood. Crystal made a retching sound
in her throat and clapped her hand over her mouth as
she wheeled and ran to the door.

Yvonne ripped the pad off and tossed it into the
refuse container on the floor by the table, then cautiously lifted the woman's knees and parted them,
nodding to Tangeree. The front door slammed, and
the sound Crystal made in vomiting over the edge of
the porch was faintly audible. Tangeree lifted a rag
from the basin of water and daubed it on the woman's
vulva. She tossed it into the refuse container, bloody
water dripping from it, and took another rag from the
basin. Her features were neutral and her lips pursed
in concentration as she bent low over the woman,
gently sponging the blood away. She moved back, and
Yvonne gingerly spread the woman's vulva open with
her thumb and forefinger. Fresh blood was trickling
from the woman's vagina. Tangeree threw the rag into
the refuse container and quickly washed her hands in
the basin as Yvonne pulled the bedclothes back together over the woman.

The man was slouched on the settee, the lantern on
the floor at his feet. His eyelids drooped sleepily, and
he glanced at Yvonne and Tangeree and looked away
disinterestedly as they came out of the examination
room and walked toward the kitchen. They mixed an
infusion of baneberry in a bowl, let it steep and
strained it into another bowl, and carried it back
through the house. Crystal had come back in and was
sitting in a chair in the waiting room, her face drawn
and haggard under her make-up in the dim light of the
lantern.

Tangeree took the large india rubber bulb from a
shelf and filled it with infusion as Yvonne looked at
the woman. She was still hovering on the edge of un-

consciousness, her pulse weak and her breathing shallow. Tangeree put the large nozzle on the bulb, handed it to Yvonne, and helped Yvonne lift the woman's knees and part them. There was a danger of dislodging blood clots that might have begun forming if there was too much pressure, and a danger of not reaching all areas of the wound with the styptic liquid if too little pressure was used. Yvonne inserted the end of the nozzle and squeezed the bulb gently, and a mixture of the infusion and blood began pouring back out of the woman's vagina and onto the blood-soaked nightgown and bedding. There was a light tap on the door, and Crystal called out.

"Mrs. Beaunais?"

"Yes?"

"We have to go now. Is Rosie . . . is she going to be all right?"

"I don't know."

There was a murmured exchange between Crystal and the man, then she called out again. "Mort says that somebody will be here tomorrow to see how she is."

"Yes, all right."

"Good night, Mrs. Beaunais. And we're much obliged."

"Good night, Miss Brixton."

Their footsteps went out, the front door closed, and they crossed the porch and went down the steps. A moment later, the carriage moved away from the house. Tangeree finished rolling a tube of linen and held it in front of Yvonne's eyes as she bent over the woman, and Yvonne shook her head. "That's a little too wide and not hardly long enough, Tangi. I don't want to force it, and I'd like to get it all the way up to her womb, if I can."

Tangeree turned away from the table and rolled another tube of linen, and showed it to Yvonne. Yvonne nodded, pressing the bulb flat and squeezing the last of the infusion from it. Tangeree soaked the linen in the bowl of infusion, handed it to Yvonne and took the bulb. Yvonne began cautiously inserting the linen. There was a tight resistance.

"Tangi, see if she can hear you and if you can get her to relax a little."

Tangeree leaned over the woman's face, smiling down at her and talking in a loud, cheerful tone. "You're going to be all right, Rosie! We're taking care of you, and you're going to be all right! Just relax, Rosie, and we'll—" Her voice faded, and she thumbed back one of the woman's eyelids. "She's fainted, Ma."

"That's all right, it's going a little easier now. Fill the bulb again and put the thin tube on it."

Tangeree stepped back to the table, took the nozzle off the bulb, and began filling it again. Yvonne pushed on the tube of linen with a careful pressure until all but the end was inserted. Then she plucked at the end, spreading the roll and flaring it. Tangeree handed her the bulb again, and she pushed the long, thin nozzle up through the center of the roll. Yvonne squeezed the bulb, saturating the tube of linen, and the mixture of infusion and blood began showing at the end of the tube when the bulb was half empty. She stopped squeezing and pulled the nozzle back out, and Tangeree picked up the lamp and held it between the woman's knees. They watched the end of the linen for a moment, and the faint color of blood on it didn't become darker. Yvonne sighed and shrugged.

"Well, maybe we got it, Tangi."

"Do you think the vagina could be torn all the way

through somewhere and she's bleeding inside rather than outside?"

"If it is, we have a death watch tonight. And we'd better not try to move her yet, so go get a childbirth pallet and some blankets while I get her cleaned up."

Tangeree put the lamp back on the table and went out, and Yvonne took a rag and sponged most of the blood off the woman's stomach and legs. She tore the nightgown all the way up the front and carefully pulled the woman's arms out of it. When Tangeree returned with a pallet and roll of blankets, they gently lifted the woman to push the nightgown and bed-clothes off the table, pulled the pallet under her, and covered her with the blankets. Tangeree went for clean water to wash the india rubber bulb and nozzles, and Yvonne built up the fire in the fireplace in the examination room and brought in two chairs from the kitchen.

When the woman stirred or sighed, one of them rose to look at her. She remained unconscious, but her pulse felt stronger and her breathing was deeper. At about midnight, they lifted the blankets and looked at the end of the linen tube. It showed somewhat more blood than before, but the bleeding had been arrested and there was no indication of stomach swelling, the deadly signal of internal bleeding.

Hours later, a sound woke Yvonne from a light doze. The lamp was guttering and the fire had burned down, and Yvonne turned her head to look at the woman in the dim light. The sound hadn't come from the woman; a horse was approaching the house at a slow walk. Tangeree snapped awake, blinking her eyes and listening. The horse stopped by the porch, slow, heavy footsteps came up the steps and across the porch, and there was a light knock at the door. Tangeree yawned and tossed a piece of wood on the fire, and Yvonne rose, picked up the lamp, and turned up the wick as she walked toward the door.

The man was tall and well-built, wearing a black swallowtail coat, tight black riding breeches, shiny knee boots, and a black hat with a wide brim and flat crown. His features were darkly tanned, and thick black sideburns extended down the sides of his face. And he was so handsome he was almost pretty. But it was a cruel, deadly masculine beauty, the glossy sheen and perfect symmetry of a diamondback. He took the thin cheroot from his mouth and took off his hat as he bowed. "I'm Matt Lassiter, Mrs. Beaunais. I apologize for coming at this late hour, and I wouldn't have knocked but for the fact that I saw a lamp burning. May I see Rosie?"

Yvonne nodded coldly, stepping back and opening the door wider. A heavy gold chain bobbed on his vest and a diamond stickpin in his necktie glinted in the light of the lamp as he stepped inside. Yvonne closed the door and led him into the examination room, his heavy boots thumping against the floor behind her. He stopped and bowed to Tangeree. Tangeree stood by the fireplace with her back stiff and her chin lifted as she looked at him from the corners of her eyes with a hostile, suspicious glare, the way she looked at most men. Her only acknowledgement of his bow was a narrowing of her eyes and a more belligerent thrust of her chin as she lifted it higher.

Lassiter puffed on his cheroot, looking at the pile of blood-stained bedclothes in the corner, then at the woman on the table. "How is she?"

"We've stopped the bleeding for now. If we can

keep it stopped and keep infection from developing, she'll live."

"I take it that you believe this shouldn't have happened."

"You take it correctly. The young woman isn't married, so she shouldn't have become pregnant. Having become pregnant, she should have borne the baby naturally."

Lassiter smiled faintly and started to reply, then glanced at Tangeree. "Perhaps it would be better if we discussed this elsewhere."

"I see no reason to. It would surprise me to no end if you knew a fraction as much about childbirth or the human body as my daughter. Or about life or death, for that matter."

Lassiter nodded, still smiling faintly. "Very well, Mrs. Beaunais. I don't operate a lying-in house, as I believe you know. In the future, I'll have you consulted in cases like this."

"I will not perform an abortion, Mr. Lassiter."

"I can promise you upwards of twenty dollars a week in steady income, Mrs. Beaunais. You will be consulted in all illnesses and all cases like this. Cummings has done this to me once too many times."

"Doctor Cummings didn't do this to you, Mr. Lassiter, he did it to the young woman on the table. And I will not perform an abortion under any circumstances."

"Then let's say upwards of fifty dollars a week, Mrs. Beaunais. I believe that should be enough to—"

"You aren't listening to me, Mr. Lassiter. I will not perform an abortion under any circumstances."

He puffed on his cheroot again, looking down at her, then exhaled. "I believe you'll change your mind, Mrs. Beaunais."

Yvonne had been prepared for bluster and threats, but there was no suggestion of physical threat, the slight smile was still on his face, and his voice was quiet, a steely quiet like the taut, hushed stillness before the onslaught of a tornado. Yvonne shook her head. "No, you'll change your mind, Mr. Lassiter. You see, you've had to do with whores until you've forgotten what it is to deal with a woman who's on an equal footing with men. And I am."

His lips twitched as his smile widened, and he bowed to Tangeree again and turned toward the door. "Many men find it convenient to do as I wish, Mrs. Beaunais. We shall see who changes their mind."

Yvonne followed him to the front door and held it as he went out. He stopped outside the door and bowed, still smiling. Yvonne nodded coldly. He put on his hat and crossed the porch, and Yvonne closed the door and walked back toward the examination room as the horse's slow footsteps moved away from the house.

Tangeree was still standing by the fireplace, and she was frowning anxiously. "I wonder exactly what he meant, Ma."

Yvonne was thinking about the same thing. She pushed it out of her mind and shrugged as she put the lamp on the table. "We have this woman to worry about right now, Tangi."

13

At DAYLIGHT the woman's pulse and breathing were stronger. Tangeree and Yvonne made a fire in the fireplace in one of the extra bedrooms, moved the woman to it, and cleaned up the examination room. After the cow was milked and breakfast was finished, Tangeree napped, lying on the bed by the woman and holding the woman's hand, her mind attuned to the woman so she would be awakened by any sound or movement she made. It was a slow, peaceful winter morning. Only the owner of the livery stable came, bringing a horse that had a wheezing rattle in its lungs; then no one else as the hours dragged by.

The woman stirred during late morning, pain arousing her to a dazed semi-consciousness. Her features twisted as she sighed and murmured softly. Yvonne sent Tangeree to the butcher in town for liver to make rich broth for the woman, and she spooned sips of diluted tincture of opium into her mouth. Tangeree returned with the liver and boiled part of it down into a thick broth, and they held the woman up and spooned it into her mouth.

During the afternoon, Yvonne napped on the bed with the woman. Many of those who came regularly trusted Tangeree's judgment in most situations, a lot of them perceiving her as a repository of information and as someone apart from the rules that normally governed what people were at various ages. There was only one patient and a woman who wanted more of an infusion for a child during the afternoon, and Tangeree took care of both of them.

Yvonne and Tangeree divided the vigil of the night, giving the woman more broth and tincture of opium, and watching over her. Tangeree woke Yvonne during the early hours of the morning, when the woman became feverish. It was the ominous signal that infection had set in, and Yvonne tried febrifuge infusions at first in an attempt to hold down the woman's temperature while her body fought the infection. She began with milder herbs and changed to the more potent herbs and stronger infusions, but the woman's temperature continued rising, and her automatic swallowing reflex ceased as she became more feverish and weaker. The infection was too powerful for her body to fight without assistance, and it presented one of the frequent dilemmas in treating the ill: any attempt to treat the infection directly would cause some bleeding, and it might trigger a fatal hemorrhage.

Yvonne delayed, hoping that the combination of the febrifuge infusions would begin to act, and that the woman's body would rally and fight the infection. But much of the problem lay in the woman's lack of a driving, deeply seated will to cling to life. She was ebbing away, passively relinquishing life. Shortly before daybreak, they carried the woman into the examination room and prepared a strong infusion of sanicle, and Yvonne rinsed the woman's vagina with it. The bleeding began again as soon as they removed the roll of linen. Yvonne fought against the panic rising within her as the infusion poured back out of the woman, richly colored with blood and carrying bits of precious clots that had been dislodged by the washing action of the infusion. Tangeree handed Yvonne a fresh roll of linen and she put it in place, and they carried the woman back into the bedroom.

Daylight came, and the day was long and busy, with whining, whimpering children and impatient, argumentive adults. The people came at intervals that were just long enough to prevent Yvonne from resting, and there was just enough activity for her to need Tangeree all the time. And there seemed to be more of the frustrating situations than usual, at a time when Yvonne didn't feel like dealing with them. A woman and her mother-in-law came with a thin, sickly baby that vomited most of its milk, and Yvonne perceived the problem in listening to the woman and her mother-in-law rather than in examining the baby and the woman's breasts. There was nothing wrong with the baby or woman, but the mother-in-law was critical, domineering, and ill-tempered, and the baby's condition was a physical result of its mother's resentment. The solution to the problem lay in either poisoning the mother-in-law or tranquilizing the baby's mother, and Yvonne had Tangeree prepare lady's slipper and ginseng infusion for the woman to take in small doses through the day and in large doses before feeding the baby.

A woman who had been taking burdock and peppermint infusion for her stomach returned to complain because a lifetime of overeating and cultivating a sour disposition couldn't be overcome within a week, and there were others. Yvonne found herself starting to doze when she stood still and her concentration wandered. The cow had to be milked, the meals had to be prepared, and other household chores had to be done. As the day dragged to a close, Yvonne bruised her foot while chopping wood for the fires during the night, and Tangeree burned her hand while making a pot of strong coffee for the night's vigil with the woman.

The rinse with the sanicle infusion hadn't brought any change, other than starting a slow, steady loss of blood, and the woman still burned with fever. Yvonne sat by the bed and struggled to think clearly as the night wore on, and she talked with Tangeree about the woman. It frequently took the sanicle infusion hours to act when infection was well-established. It was sometimes necessary to apply it repeatedly, and there was a possibility that she had been too cautious and fearful of starting a hemorrhage, and hadn't reached all the infected area with the infusion.

The woman seemed to be sinking and something had to be done. Yvonne decided to use the sanicle and baneberry infusions again. They carried the woman into the examination room and prepared the infusions, and Yvonne inserted a fresh roll of linen and pushed the thin nozzle on the india rubber bulb up through the center of it to saturate it with the baneberry infusion. Then they built up the fire in the fireplace in the examination room and waited.

After an hour, the bleeding appeared to have stopped, but the woman's temperature was still rising, her skin hot to the touch. They went outside and scraped up sooty, late-winter snow that had drifted into thin smears around protected corners of the house and barn, wrapped it in rags, and packed it around the woman on the table. Yvonne sat in her chair by the fireplace as they waited again, listening to the faint, labored rasp of the woman's breathing and looking at Tangeree's young face, drawn, lined, and haggard with fatigue. She dozed off, and was awakened by Tangeree's soft, gasping sobs. Her tears were those of relief, not of despair and defeat. The woman's fever had broken, her pulse was stronger, and her breathing was deeper.

The next day was another slow day, only one young woman coming during the morning to get warts removed from her hands. Crystal Brixton came in a carriage shortly before noon. She was a bright glow of color on the cold, gray day, wearing a striped lemon and pink silk dress, a bundle of bobbing plumes on her large hat, a beauty patch on her cheek, and jangling bangles and rattling beads. She exuded a strong odor of lavender cologne as she expressed exuberant happiness over Rosie Gibbs's likelihood of recovery, and concern over the possibility of trouble between Yvonne and Lassiter.

"He don't look like what he is, Mrs. Beaunais," she said worriedly. "The man who owned that place in San Francisco was as ugly as a bullfrog, but he was an angel compared to Mr. Lassiter. He can get really mean."

"What he wants is something I won't do, Miss Brixton, and there's nothing he can do to bother me or mine."

"How do you know? He owns a lot of this town and holds a mortgage on a lot more, and you'd be surprised how many people he can call on when he's a mind to. Judges, and people like that. And don't tell anybody I told you, but have you heard of that constitutional convention thing? Well, he's right in the middle of it, and a lot of the delegates are friends of his. He's mixed up in a lot of things like that."

There had been talk among patients and articles in

the newspaper on the convention, a preliminary to establishing statehood in Nevada, as well as news about Union Army victories in the South and other things. Yvonne nodded and shrugged. "I can see much in common between his kind, politicians, and the like. Regardless of who he knows or anything else about him, what he wants is something I won't do."

"Well, now, you must have done things before that you didn't want to do, Mrs. Beaunais. Everybody has, haven't they? And it seems to me that you—"

"People can find themselves in situations and circumstances outside their control, Miss Brixton. I didn't necessarily want to come here, for example. But within their situation and circumstances, people have the choice to make of themselves what they will. I've done things that I didn't want to do, but I've never done what I don't do."

"Well, I'm not really sure of what you mean, but I know I've got my back up about things sometimes and I would've been a lot better off if I'd just thought twice before I spoke. Things can strike a body wrong at first look, and they'll seem different if a body just backs up and takes a second look."

The conversation continued for a time, and Yvonne recognized that it was pointless, senseless discussion. It involved a matter of principle and of morality, which was foreign to Crystal Brixton and which she couldn't understand. Before she left, she offered to pay Yvonne for what she had done for Rosie Gibbs, and Yvonne remembered that Lassiter had given Crystal money to come and see her before. And she wondered if the woman's visit was a ploy of Lassiter's in an attempt to change her mind about performing abortions.

Rosie Gibbs regained consciousness that night,

awakening Tangeree as she lay on the bed by her and held her hand, and Tangeree came to Yvonne's room and woke her. The woman's pulse was firm and most of her fever was gone, but she was wracked with pains in her stomach. Yvonne administered diluted tincture of opium while Tangeree made a bowl of broth, and the woman slipped into a deep sleep after eating.

The woman improved slowly, the massive loss of blood making her feeble and continuing pains in her stomach keeping her bedridden for another three days, then Yvonne and Tangeree began taking her out of bed and helping her on short walks through the house. Rosie then began improving more rapidly, walking about the house without assistance and eating at the table. And Yvonne tried to persuade her not to return to Lassiter.

"You can stay right here in the house, Rosie, and no one will bother you. I won't let them."

"Oh, I guess I'd better go back, Mrs. Beaunais."

"But you've seen how much that man thinks of you, Rosie. You've seen what that kind of life leads to. And I know you don't like it. You're a young, pretty girl, and you have much of your life ahead of you. I hate to see you throw your life away, Rosie."

"Oh, I guess I'd better go back."

"I want you to understand that you don't have to, Rosie. If you don't want to go back, there's nothing that Lassiter or his men can do. All you have to do is stand behind me, and no one will bother you. I'll protect you from everyone. Or do you think that I might not be able to?"

"Oh, no, it ain't that, Mrs. Beaunais."

"If it is, I have friends in California, and you can go there and stay with them. I dislike asking people to do things for me, but I'll do it for you, Rosie. And then Lassiter won't know where you are, because I certainly won't tell him."

"Oh, I guess I'd better not, Mrs. Beaunais."

Yvonne persisted in trying to persuade her, feeling the close involvement that she always felt toward a patient, and frustrated by her inability to make the woman see that what she was doing was unnecessary and irrational. The conversation was repeated numerous times, with several variations as Yvonne thought of other things to say to her, but always with the same result.

The woman had a pitiable desire to be liked and avoided doing or saying anything that might make someone angry at her, and the lack of will that had been a factor in treating her was a pronounced characteristic in her personality. She was completely passive, perferring to always take the path of least resistance and accept what life offered her rather than assume the responsibility of making a decision for herself. The woman seemed to be intimidated when Yvonne talked to her, shrinking from her, and she was also awed by Tangeree, a servile smile on her face whenever she talked to the girl. She was much more at ease with Crystal when she visited, laughing and chatting with her freely.

It was apparent that Yvonne's intentions toward Rosie were transmitted through Crystal to Lassiter, because Crystal and a man came to take Rosie away ten days after she had arrived, a few days sooner than Yvonne thought wise. Crystal brought clothes and helped Rosie dress in her room, and walked out with her. Yvonne made a last effort and tried to get near Rosie to touch her hand, to offer herself as protection, to invite Rosie to step behind her and be protected. But Rosie avoided Yvonne, hastily saying goodbye and rushing out with the man, and Crystal opened her reticule and fingered coins in it.

"Well, I know money can't pay you for what you've done, Mrs. Beaunais, but we have to make some kind of reckoning. How much do you think would be enough?"

"Seven dollars."

"Seven? But Mr. Lassiter gave me fifty dollars here."

"No, it'll be seven dollars."

"Well, if you say it's seven dollars, that's what it is, then. Here you are, and we're much obliged, Mrs. Beaunais."

"You're welcome."

"Goodbye then, Mrs. Beaunais."

"Goodbye."

Crystal left, and Yvonne went to the front window in the waiting room and watched the carriage move away from the house and along the street toward the road into town. She thought about the bitter, exhausting struggle to drag the woman back from the brink of death, and she felt a sense of crushing defeat and disappointment. The carriage passed out of sight behind the blacksmith shop, and she turned away from the window. Tangeree was standing in the doorway on the other side of the room, a morose musing expression on her young, wise face. She sighed and shrugged as she turned to go into the kitchen to begin preparing dinner, and Yvonne followed her.

Yvonne heard a horse approaching the house shortly after dinner, then heavy footsteps came up the steps and crossed the porch. It sounded like Lassiter, and it was. His smooth, tanned face shone faintly in the dim light of the lamp, and the large diamond on his stickpin glinted as he stepped inside, taking off his hat. He took the cheroot from his mouth and bowed to Yvonne, then to Tangeree.

"Mrs. Beaunais, I came to thank you for what you did for Rosie."

"That wasn't necessary, Mr. Lassiter. I did it for Miss Gibbs, not for you."

The corners of his lips lifted in the faint smile that seemed characteristic of him. "I also came to see if you would reconsider your charge for what you did. In my opinion, it was far too little."

"I charged what I considered fair. That's all I want, Mr. Lassiter."

"And I came to ask you if you've reconsidered your answer to the proposition I discussed with you before."

"I haven't, and I won't."

His smile widened, and he nodded as he puffed on his cheroot. "The next time we discuss this, Mrs. Beaunais, you'll have to come to me. And I believe you will."

"Never, Mr. Lassiter."

He looked at Yvonne in silence for a moment, smiling and puffing on his cheroot, then he bowed to her and to Tangeree and walked out, putting on his hat. Yvonne closed the door and returned to the kitchen, frowning in perplexity as she puzzled over what he had said and over the absolute assurance in his attitude when he had said it. Again, there had been a total lack of any hint of physical threat in his manner, and Yvonne couldn't think of any way he could bring pressure on her in an attempt to make her change her mind.

And at first she didn't recognize it for what it was when it happened. The number of people coming to see her and the calls to other houses was erratic. Some days were long and filled with frantic activity and others slow and peaceful, and it took her a few days to observe that the overall number had diminished. And it took another day or two for her to notice that those who had stopped coming were from the families of tradesmen, clerks, laborers, and others who had been the source of most of the money she had been receiving. Then she realized what had happened. Lassiter had friends, business associates, people owed him money, and others who would do as he wished. All those had people who worked for them, owed them money, did business with them, and would do as they wished. Word had gone out through that network of influence, and it apparently included most of Virginia City.

It was confirmed on an afternoon two weeks after Lassiter had come to see her. Several days had passed since the owner of the livery stable had called on her to see to any of his animals, and she had observed a horse in the corral with an abscess on a foreleg. She and Tangeree were returning from a call at a house along the road into town, and the owner of the stable was at the corral fence adjacent to the edge of the road. He didn't observe her and Tangeree until they were passing; then he nodded, touched the brim of his hat, and started to hurry away. Yvonne stopped him.

"Mr. Grayson, that mare in the holding pen over there will go lame if something isn't done about that abscess."

Grayson flushed and cleared his throat, looking at the mare, at Yvonne, then away. "Oh, I've had a look at her and doctored her up a little, and I think she'll be all right."

"That's your mare, Mr. Grayson, but she's in pain and she isn't going to be all right."

His face flushed and he frowned angrily. "Mrs. Beaunais, I owe Mr. Lassiter money and I depend on him for a lot of business, and I ain't going to get crossways of trouble you might have with him," he blurted, then he looked away and cleared his throat again. "And I got my family to think about."

Yvonne realized she had humiliated the man, and she smiled apologetically. "Of course you do, Mr. Grayson. And I sincerely beg your pardon for mentioning the matter."

His face turned crimson, and he was more embarrassed than before. He nodded and shrugged awkwardly. "I hope eveything turns out all right for you, Mrs. Beaunais."

"I'm sure it will. Good day, Mr. Grayson."

"Good day, ma'm."

As Yvonne walked on along the road, it occurred to her that it had been several days since the owner of the blacksmith shop had sent anyone to see her, and previously there had been at least two or three a week, travelers along the road who had become ill or whose animals were ill. He did all of Grayson's farrier work, and it was possible that he was also indebted to Lassiter or had some other relationship with him. A small cluster of people had gathered on the porch during her absence, and they moved about and looked along the street expectantly as she approached. They were ragged, thin, and feeble, the old and the poor, most of them with only their gratitude to offer in return for relief from their pains and illnesses.

When Leggett heard about what had happened through his patients, he came to see Yvonne and angrily denounced Lassiter and offered to see him. Yvonne pointed out that Lassiter had done nothing more than let it be known that he preferred people not to do business with her, which wasn't an unusual practice among businessmen when friction developed. Leggett offered to loan her money if she needed it, and she quickly refused and thanked him for his offer.

Cargill also heard about it and wanted to confront Lassiter, and Yvonne declined to let him become involved. But he wouldn't accept a refusal of food he brought, and he stolidly carried it into the house over her protests. When the snow started melting out of the passes through the Sierra Nevada, he began his spring and summer schedule of one trip a month with three large drays and all of his sons, and he always brought bags and baskets of fruit and vegetables, slabs of bacon, and other things to the house. Yvonne prepared dinner for him and his sons in a token effort of repayment. He and his four large sons seemed to fill the house with tons of exuberantly virile manhood, which appalled Tangeree, but they were friendly and well-behaved, and there was always abundant food in the house when the flow of money coming in diminished to a trickle.

There was another offer of help that came unexpectedly. A tall, weather-beaten man wearing a fringed buckskin coat and knee-length moccasins was waiting at the house when Yvonne and Tangeree returned from making a call one early spring afternoon. His horse was tethered by the porch, weary from traveling and loaded with heavy saddlebags and a pack behind the saddle. The man remotely reminded Yvonne of Jacob Seeton. He was about Seeton's age, and his bearing was reminiscent of Seeton, a reserved expression but a cordial, kindly light in his frosty blue eyes. He was heavily armed, with pistol and bowie knife on his belt and a shotgun and buffalo rifle on his saddle.

He rose from the steps and touched the brim of his battered hat as Yvonne and Tangeree approached. "You'll be Mrs. Beaunais, I expect. My name's Carson, and I have a tooth that's pestering me, if I could bother you to look at it."

"I'll be glad to, Mr. Carson. If you like, you could unsaddle your horse while I'm getting things ready. He looks as though he's been a mile or two, and he could probably use the rest."

"He could, and I'll do that, ma'm."

Yvonne and Tangeree went inside as the man unsaddled the horse and put the saddle on the edge of the porch. Tangeree went into the kitchen for a chair, and Yvonne put the herb chest they had taken with them on a shelf and took down the chest of dental instruments. The man walked into the waiting room, moving silently in his moccasins, and followed Tangeree into the examination room. Yvonne took the chair and placed it by the table.

"Have a seat, Mr. Carson, and I'll see what we can do. From the appearance of your horse, you've just come across the mountains."

Carson nodded as he sat down. "I've just come from seeing some friends of yours, as a matter of fact—the Seetons. They told me to come by and see how you was doing, and this tooth must have figured out that I was on my way here. They said to say that they was thinking about you."

"I'm pleased they are, and I think about them often. How are they?"

"Oh, they're all fit as fiddles. Jacob looks feistier than I've seen him in years."

"I'm glad to hear that. You've known Mr. Seeton a good while, then?"

"More years than I like to think about."

Yvonne smiled, selecting a pick from the instruments, and the man opened his mouth and pointed to the second lower premolar on the right side. The man's teeth were in exceptionally good condition for his age. He still had most of them and they were stained with tobacco juice, but they were firm and solid in the gums, with few spots of decay. The tooth that was aching looked as though part of the crown had been chipped off, and decay had eaten down into it. Yvonne probed at the tooth with the pick and examined the gum around it, and stepped back.

"How much has that tooth been hurting, Mr. Carson?"

"I've had worser ones. It was the cold air up on the mountain that got it started, I believe. And cold water on it will make my eyeballs crack together across my nose."

"I might be able to save it. It would cause some pain to scrape it out and I'd have to charge you for the gold to fill it, but I can try, if you like."

"I'd like to keep her, if I can."

"I'll see what I can do, then. If it gets too painful or if the decay is too deep, I'll go ahead and remove it. Would you get some water and a basin, Tangi?"

Tangeree put the bowl of olive oil and morphine paste on the table and went out. Yvonne opened and closed drawers in the chest of instruments, selected heavy scrapers, gouges, and reamers and placing them in a row. Carson shifted to a more comfortable position on the chair, folding his arms and looking up at Yvonne.

"It took me some looking around and asking to find your house, ma'm. And while I was asking, I got the understanding that you've been having some trouble with a man here in town."

"Matthew Lassiter and I have had a disagreement, but it's no great cause for concern, Mr. Carson."

"That may be, but I'd feel that I hadn't done what I should if I didn't do something about it. So if'n it's all the same to you, I'll go by and see this man Lassiter before I leave. If you'll just tell me what it is you want him to do or to quit doing, I think I can oblige you."

The man suddenly looked even more like Seeton, a slight smile on his seamed, brown face but a potential for savagery in his icy blue eyes. Yvonne smiled and shook her head. "Thank you, but that won't be necessary, Mr. Carson."

"Well, I ain't one to run somebody else's trapline, but I wanted to make myself available."

"I didn't interpret your offer as interference, and I'm very grateful for the thought, Mr. Carson. But it isn't a matter for concern." She started to open another drawer in the chest, then hesitated and looked down at him again. "You say you've known Mr. Seeton a long time. You wouldn't happen to be Mr. Christopher Carson, would you?"

"Yes, ma'm. Most folks call me Kit."

"Well, this is a surprise, Mr. Carson. I didn't occur to me who you were until I thought about your knowing Mr. Seeton for a long time. I've heard so much about you and the things you've done, as has everyone else."

Carson chuckled and shrugged. "Well, I've heard a lot about you, too, ma'm."

Yvonne laughed and turned back to the table. Tangeree returned with a pitcher of water, a cup, and a basin, and Yvonne took the pick and bent over Carson, using the pick to flow drops of the numbing mixture into the cavity in the tooth and under the gum around the base of the tooth. She waited for a moment for the tooth to become numb, then she selected a pointed gouge and dug down into one side of the decayed area with a twisting, driving pressure. The brown, decayed fabric of the tooth shredded under the tip of the gouge with a grinding, splintering noise, vibrations traveling through Carson's lower jawbone as Yvonne gripped it tightly with her left hand.

White, undecayed tooth began showing through the decay crumbling under the tip of the gouge, and Yvonne stepped back. Tangeree poured water into the cup, held it for Carson to take a mouthful and rinse his mouth, and held the basin for him to spit into. Yvonne leaned over Carson again, and dug the gouge into the other side of the cavity. The decay on that side extended up under the intact crown of the tooth, and Yvonne put the gouge back on the table and picked up a larger one with a hooked tip. The enamel on the tooth was extremely hard, and the tip slid off the side of the decayed area as Yvonne tried to chip the crown away to get down into the decay. Tangeree leaned close, watching.

"Chisel?"

Yvonne nodded, put the gouge back on the table, and used the pick to flow more of the numbing mixture into the cavity as Tangeree moved around her to the instrument chest. Tangeree stepped back, holding three tiny chisels and a small hammer. Yvonne selected a chisel, placed the tip of it a fraction of an inch from the edge of the cavity, and tapped it sharply with the hammer. The portion of the crown that had been undercut by the decay collapsed, and Tangeree reached for the cup and basin as Yvonne stepped back, looking down at Carson.

"Is the pain very bad, Mr. Carson?"

He took a mouthful of water from the cup and rinsed his mouth, and shrugged as he spat the water and piece of tooth into the basin. "Things have happened to me that felt better, but I've had worser as well."

Yvonne smiled and nodded, and reached for the gouge again. She drove it down into the side of the cavity that had been concealed under the crown, and stepped back when white, undecayed tooth began to show. Tangeree gave Carson another mouthful of water and held the basin for him to spit, and Yvonne selected a small reamer. Irregularities in the sides of the cavity crumbled as the reamer ground straight down into it, forming it into a cup-like depression in the tooth. Yvonne took a larger reamer and widened the cavity, and the sides became smooth and even, with only a few streaks of decay remaining. She took a scraper and dug them out, and stepped back again. Tangeree gave Carson a mouthful of water and held the basin for him, and Yvonne examined the cavity carefully. There were a few brown spots and loose fragments of tooth in the bottom of the cavity, and she dug them out with the pick and filled the cavity with the numbing mixture as Tangeree opened the box of gold wire and laid out the punches.

Tangeree fed lengths of the thin gold wire into the cavity, and Yvonne compacted it into place, using a punch with a tiny tip at the bottom of the cavity and changing to punches with wider tips as the cavity filled up. Tangeree changed to wire of a thicker gauge, and Yvonne began tapping the punch harder with the small hammer, forming the gold into a solid mass with no air pockets that would cause pain. When the cavity was filled, Yvonne smoothed off the surface with a tiny file and had Carson close his mouth as he held his lips apart and looked to see how the surface of the gold filling matched the tooth above it. The teeth met smoothly, and Yvonne nodded as she stepped back.

"That should do, Mr. Carson. It'll hurt for a day or two, then the pain will go away and it won't bother you anymore."

Carson smiled wryly and nodded as he stood, feeling the side of his jaw. "It knows something has had ahold of it, but I'm more than glad for the chance to keep it instead of having it knocked out. How much do I owe you, ma'm?"

"The gold is two dollars, and twenty-five cents or so will do for filling the tooth."

"Oh, no, it ought to add up to a five dollar job at least," Carson said, taking out his purse. He opened it and put a five dollar gold piece on the table. "And I'm much obliged along with it, Mrs. Beaunais."

"Thank you for being so generous, Mr. Carson. We'll be having dinner before long, if you'd like to stay and eat. And we have extra rooms, if you'd like to spend the night."

"I'm much obliged for the offer, ma'am, but I've got more trail than I have time. I might come back through here during the summer, and I'll try to stop in if I do."

"You'll be welcome any time," Yvonne said, walking toward the door with him. "Did you happen to see any of the Dowds while you were in California? They've settled near Sonoma, I believe."

"I didn't, but Jacob mentioned them. He said the older ones in the party had settled on farms, and that a couple of the younger ones had caught gold fever. A one-legged boy and his brother, he said."

Carson continued as they walked outside and he saddled his horse, talking about the various people

that had been in the wagon train, what they were doing, and what had happened to them. Then he
mounted his horse and settled himself in the saddle.

"Are you sure you've thought enough about that
other we talked about, ma'm? It wouldn't be no
trouble at all for me to put that right, and I'd be
more than glad to do it."

Yvonne hesitated. People in the West revered their
legends, and Kit Carson was a towering figure among
them. South of Virginia City was the Carson River,
named by the explorer Fremont for his guide, Kit
Carson. The place most people favored as the capital
when Nevada achieved statehood was Carson City.
And there was the Carson Valley, Lake Carson, and
other places. He was a giant among the legends, and
the situation would disappear after a few words from
him. But it was her battle, and the victory would belong to another. There had been battles when there
hadn't been a Kit Carson to win them for her, and
there would be others. She smiled and shook her head.

"I'm very grateful for your offer, Mr. Carson, but
there's no reason for concern."

He nodded, gathering his reins and turning his horse
as he touched the brim of his hat. "All right, ma'm.
Goodbye."

"Goodbye, Mr. Carson, and Godspeed."

The horse turned onto the street and cantered slowly along it, the weapons and heavy pack behind the
saddle swaying, and Yvonne stepped to the corner of
the porch. Carson reined up at the end of the street
and waved. As Yvonne lifted her arm, she was acutely
aware that she could beckon him to return, and he
would ride back to the house. She hesitated, then
waved in farewell. Carson waved again, and turned
his horse to the left on the road, away from town.

14

THE FIVE DOLLARS from Carson went for material to make two dresses for Tangeree, because she had begun growing again during the winter. She had been taller than Yvonne for a year or more, and suddenly the tall, thin girl was no longer thin and her bustline was much larger that Yvonne's. She was less particular about clothes than many girls of her age, with a total lack of concern about a band of different color by a seam that was glaring evidence the seam had been let out, but she was self-conscious about her abrupt blossoming and wouldn't wear a dress with a tight bodice.

Yvonne helped Tangeree let out the seams in some of her dresses, but many were old and their seams had been let before. There was enough material in some to make separate bodices and skirts, but her hips were also wider and pulled the hems on some of the skirts above the tops of her shoes, making them too short to wear out of the house. A few weeks before, when money hadn't been a worry, Yvonne had bought new shoes for her. But they seemed to be wearing out very rapidly, and Yvonne found herself scolding Tangeree with unnecessary severity for dragging her feet when she walked.

Just when it appeared that the need for large amounts of firewood was ending for the year, it turned cold again and Yvonne had to buy more. There were other expenses, and Yvonne castigated herself for not having been more frugal when money had been coming in. In the false sense of security that the steady income of money had given her, she had ordered larger quantities of herbs from the woman at Fort Bridger than were absolutely necessary, and she had bought other things that weren't completely indispensible, spending that seemed foolish in retrospect. And there was no margin of savings, because the money from the sale of the oxen and wagon hadn't been replaced.

The realization that she wasn't going to have enough money for the mortgage payment filled her with panic. Several days before the payment was due, she still needed a little over eight dollars. The days dragged remorselessly by, time closing in far too rapidly for the thin trickle of money to fill in the difference. The amount she needed diminished to over seven dollars, then to over six as she sat at night and counted and recounted the money, stacking the coins in front of the lamp on the kitchen table. And it became evident that the due date was going to arrive and the amount in the cash box was still going to be well short of twenty-five dollars.

The day before the payment was due, Yvonne went to the bank. The teller walked around the high partition across the center of the room and held a swinging gate open for her, and showed her into the manager's office. The manager was a portly, well-dressed man named Abercrombie. He had an effusively unctuous manner and a hearty, beaming smile that didn't reach his calculating, watchful eyes. He seated Yvonne in a straight chair in front of his desk and sat behind it, nodding and puffing on his cigar as he listened. Then he sighed gustily and shook his head regretfully.

"It is true, Mrs. Beaunais, that we occasionally accommodate a client in temporary financial straits by taking only the interest and a small additional fee in lieu of a full mortgage payment. However, as much as I would like to, I'm unable to do that in this instance. You see, the bank doesn't hold your mortgage."

"The bank doesn't hold my mortgage? But I arranged for the mortgage here, and I come here to pay the monthly reckoning."

"Yes, we service your mortgage, but we don't own it. You see, there are people who invest monies in mortgages, and that gives us the opportunity to recover the funds we have expended on mortgages and use them elsewhere."

A nagging suspicion formed in Yvonne's mind as she thought about what he had said, looking at him as he sat back in his chair and puffed on his cigar. "Who bought the mortgage, Mr. Abercrombie?"

Abercrombie pursed his lips and looked away in a display of hesitation, then looked back at Yvonne. "Well, we don't normally discuss our clients' affairs, but I'm sure he wouldn't mind if I told you. It was Mr. Matthew Lassiter."

"And does Mr. Lassiter buy mortgages from you frequently, Mr. Abercrombie?"

"We have numerous dealings with Mr. Lassiter, but I really can't discuss them in detail. But it's been my experience that he is a very reasonable and congenial man. If you were to see him and discuss this with him,

I'm certain some satisfactory arrangement could be made."

His smile was wide, and his eyes were cold. And the message from Lassiter was clear. Yvonne nodded, rising. "Thank you, Mr. Abercrombie."

"You're more than welcome, Mrs. Beaunais. And if there is any other way I can be of assistance, please don't hesitate to contact me."

Yvonne walked back through the streets to the house, thinking of the cow, the one valuable asset that she could sell. It had become Tangeree's pet. The girl washed and brushed it, polished its horns and hung ribbons on them, and fed it treats. And she had few things to lighten her life of grim, onerous dedication to healing. Yvonne's mind shrank from the thought of selling it, but she steeled herself against her own sorrowful reluctance and the pain it would cause Tangeree.

Tangeree was in the kitchen preparing lunch, and she trotted through the house as Yvonne climbed the steps and crossed the porch. The girl's hopeful smile faded as Yvonne entered the waiting room. "They wouldn't do it?"

"No, they wouldn't, Tangi." She started to broach the subject and get it over with, but a vacillating weakness made her delay for a moment. "Has anyone been in?"

"Only that Mrs. Bissel, and she wanted some more slippery elm infusion for her husband. She didn't have any money, but she brought a nice crocheted antimacassar."

"That would be handy if we had a cushion chair to put it on."

Tangeree chuckled and nodded, and turned to go back into the kitchen. Yvonne followed her. It was easier to say with the girl's back turned. Yvonne drew in deep breath.

"We're going to have to sell the cow, Tangi."

Tangeree stiffened and stopped, not turning. Then she nodded and began walking again, and Yvonne followed her into the kitchen. The girl suddenly sobbed, and she clutched her hands to her face, weeping. Yvonne stepped to her and put her arms around her.

"I'm sorry, Tangi. I'm really sorry."

"There's no reason for you to be sorry, Ma," Tangeree said, pulling away and wiping her eyes. "It isn't your fault. There's nothing you can do, and you won't take her to the stock market, will you?"

"No, not if I can keep from it. I'll take her to that dairy place down the road and see if they'll buy her there."

"Do I have time to feed her?"

"I don't want her acting like she's off her feed, Tangi. And I want to be done with it."

"Well, lunch is about ready, Ma."

"I don't feel like eating, honey."

Tangeree nodded, wiping her eyes as she stepped to the stove and moved a bubbling pot to one side. Yvonne looked at her, trying to think of something to say, then sighed heavily and walked toward the back door.

The dairy was a quarter of a mile along the road away from town. Barns, stock pens, sheds, and chicken coops were scattered around a wide hollow off the road, and an open-fronted shed by the road was filled with neat, clean dairy wagons that trundled into town early each morning to deliver milk, butter, and eggs to restaurants, cafés, hotels, and the homes of the wealthy. The owner, a stocky, brusquely businesslike man named Johnson, started to shake his head as

Yvonne talked to him. Then he looked at the cow again, lifted her head to glance in her mouth, and walked around her.

"I'm not in the market for cows, but this cow looks as good or better than any I have. How much do you want?"

"Twenty-five dollars."

"No, I can't pay that much, but you might be able to get it at the market."

"I don't want to take her there. How much will you pay?"

"I'll give you twenty dollars. That's my top dollar, and it's about as much as I pay for any cow. They're cheap in California, and I buy them there and drive them across the mountains."

"You'll be good to her, won't you?"

"Well, I ain't going to take her to the house for supper, but she'll be looked after and took care of as long as she gives milk."

"All right, I'll take it."

Johnson counted out the money, and the cow pulled at her halter rope and tried to follow Yvonne as she walked away. Yvonne went into town to make the payment on the mortgage, then returned home. Lunch was cold, and neither she nor Tangeree had an appetite. The crock of butter milk on a stand in the corner of the kitchen was almost full, but neither of them could drink it and they poured it out.

There was almost fourteen dollars left after making the payment on the mortgage, and it was relatively easy to accumulate the rest to make the next payment. Then another month began with three dollars and a few pennies in the cash box. The rate at which the amount grew was tediously slow, while the days fled rapidly.

Yvonne began to realize that Lassiter's influence was far from as absolute as she had first thought. When she pondered the situation at length, she recognized the fact that he could retaliate against one, two, or even half a dozen who went against his wishes, but he would ostracize himself through any attempt at widespread retaliation. His influence existed because he was believed to have influence. When that belief disappeared among people at large, his influence would disappear with it. And he had come perilously close to the mistake that had to be avoided by a leader who valued his position. He had broadcast an order that people might not follow.

A woman whose child was ill had priorities in which her husband's business concerns were of a secondary nature. Yvonne's reputation was well-established, Leggett was frequently gone, and Cummings wasn't widely trusted. Slowly, people began returning; a hotel clerk suffering with an abscessed tooth, a baker's wife in desperation over a child burning with fever. The processes of nature were far removed from any influence that Lassiter could exert, the skill with which Yvonne and Tangeree delivered babies was a topic of conversation when women met to talk, and frantic husbands came for them at night.

One person took courage from another in the waiting room, and there were indications that word was quietly spreading. The cracks in the dam multiplied, promising collapse and a flood, but it happened too slowly. The weather had turned warm and belated spring had arrived, chronic complaints had subsided, and there were fewer illnesses. The coins added up to another dollar and then another, but it appeared that the amount was still going to be short of twenty-five dollars on the day the mortgage was due. Leggett and the Cargills came again, and it was more tempting than ever to ask for a loan in the knowledge that it was only a matter of time before Lassiter would have to concede. But the temptation wasn't enough to overcome pride. And another concern overcame Yvonne's worries about money during Leggett's visit, because he brought news that Charles Dawson had been wounded at Vicksburg.

"At Vicksburg?" she exclaimed in consternation. "But that was months ago! Why did it take so long to hear about it? And is he all right?"

Leggett had called her outside on the pretense of looking at his horse to get her away from Tangeree. He patted his horse, glanced at the front door, and looked back at Yvonne. "It took him a while to get to where he could do anything, Yvonne, and he won't be over it completely for some time to come. Somebody else wrote the letter for him, because he's lost his right arm."

Yvonne gasped in anguish, tears filling her eyes. She turned away, drawing in a deep breath and controlling herself. "What did he say about me, Sam?"

"He got my last letter, and he said that he was glad that you and the girl was settled good."

"And that's all?"

"He's lost his right arm, Yvonne."

"Sam, Charles Dawson is an intelligent, educated man. He isn't like some drover or some workman who—"

"He's a human being, Yvonne. You know as well as I do how something like that can take some people, and I've seen some drovers who take it better than some lawyers. You might as well make up your mind to give him the time to get over it, because he's going to take the time whether you give it to him or not. It might take him years, and he might never get over it. Now you know all that just as well as I do."

Yvonned swallowed, fighting back the sob that tried to rise in her throat. "And he didn't say he wanted me to write?"

"Yvonne honey, I told you what he said," Leggett sighed. "And that's all he said. I wish there was something else I could tell you, because I sure as hell hate to be the one to tell you this."

"Yes, I know, Sam. Well, thank you."

"When I write to him, I'll tell him you're thinking about him."

"No, tell him I send my love, Sam."

Leggett looked at her in gruff, discomfited sympathy, and he nodded as he tossed his horse's reins over its neck and stepped into the saddle. "All right, Yvonne. Are you sure you don't need no money?"

"I'm getting plenty of calls, Sam."

"Yes, and you're getting all the people I run from, because I have to eat and feed my horse. I'll carry a few, but I've got to live. And you'd be wise to look at it the same way."

"I'll manage. Let me know when you hear from Charles again."

Leggett looked down at her and sighed, starting to say something. Then he silently nodded and touched the brim of his hat as he turned his horse toward the road. Yvonne walked back up the steps to the porch, drying her eyes before she went back in to Tangeree.

The crushing news about Charles Dawson cast a gloomy cloud of depression over Yvonne, making her situation seem even more hopeless as the last week before the payment was due arrived. She still needed several dollars to make the payment, and the amount in the cash box grew in tiny increments as the days passed, rapidly. Then there was a remotely familiar face in the waiting room late one morning, when Yvonne and Tangeree were struggling with a spoiled, fractious boy of ten in the waiting room.

The boy had an abscessed milk tooth that had begun loosening, and he was in pain from the abscess. But he was also in panic-stricken terror because of stories about chisels, augers, and other instruments of torture he had been told by other boys, and Tangeree had been bitten and Yvonne had been kicked twice while the boy's mother stood at one side and wrung her hands helplessly. Yvonne heard a man's heavy footsteps in the waiting room as she moved away from the boy and his mother began trying to calm him again, and she stepped to the door and opened it.

The man's tall, lean face was tantalizingly familiar, and she struggled to place it as a wide, beaming smile spread across his features and he extended his hand. "Howdy, Mrs. Beaunais. I'm George Elder, if'n you don't remember me."

The man had been the leader of the wagon train stopped by sickness near Fort Laramie, and Yvonne had seen their faces through a daze of fatigue. The name brought back a sharp, clear memory of the long, weary day and night and the frustrated sense of helplessness in trying to diagnose the illness. Yvonne smiled, shaking hands with him. "Of course I remember, Mr. Elder, and it's very good to see you again. How are you?"

"Well, I'm fine now that I've found you," he laughed. "We been asking high and low about you, you know. A lot of people know about you, but some said maybe you was here and some said maybe you was there. And we didn't know for a fact where you was until me and my Mary met a Horace and Hester Dowd down in Sacramento about two weeks ago."

"Are they living in Sacramento now? They had a farm near Sonoma the last I heard of them."

"No, they're still there. They had come to get some things they needed, the same as me and my wife. They're fit enough, and they said they think about you a lot."

"I think about them often, because they were good friends to me and my daughter. How is your wife?"

"Well, that's one of the things I come to talk to you about, when you get time." He glanced past her and into the examination room, and chuckled as he looked back at her. "It sounds like you've got your hands full right now."

"I have," Yvonne laughed wryly. "It shouldn't take too long, so just have a seat."

"Take your time, take your time," Elder replied, turning to the settle. "Now that I've finally found you, I can sure wait a minute to talk to you."

Yvonne smiled and nodded, but her smile faded as she turned back into the room and closed the door. The woman was sitting on the chair and holding the boy on her lap, crooning and cooing as she stroked his head, and the boy glared up at Tangeree with his lower lip pushed out in a pouting, sullen frown. Tangeree looked down at him from the corners of her eyes, her features neutral and her fingers stroking the handle of a mallet among the dental instruments on the table. Yvonne sighed silently as she walked toward the chair. Any child was easy to like, but the boy was less easy than most.

"Mrs. Richland, I could give you some medicine that

will relieve most of the pain. A permanent tooth is coming in under the one that's hurting, and it won't be long until—"

"No, no, that won't do, Mrs. Beaunais," the woman interrupted emphatically. "I come here for him to get rid of all the pain, and getting rid of just some of it won't do at all. I can't stand another night of listening to this poor little thing crying when he's trying to go to sleep."

The boy approached being as large as his mother, sprawled on her lap as she patted him and murmured comfortingly, and he glowered at Yvonne petulantly. Yvonne cleared her throat and looked away, nodding. "Very well, but I think it would be better if you went into the front room."

"Now I told you I couldn't do that, Mrs. Beaunais!" the woman replied impatiently. "That trashy bunch we've got living on that street now has scared the life out of him with the things they've told him, and I've got to stay in here with him. He's liable to get so scared that he'll have a spasm."

Yvonne nodded again, stepping forward. "Then put him on the chair and stand by the wall there, Mrs. Richland. And stay there."

"All right, but you be as easy on him as you can," the woman said, rising and putting the boy on the chair. "Now you set there and be good for Mrs. Beaunais, Billy, and she'll fix that nasty old tooth for you."

The boy bounced up from the chair and started to follow his mother as she moved toward the wall. Yvonne took his shoulder, pulling him back to the chair. He snarled as he wheeled and kicked at Yvonne's leg, and the toe of his boot whipped her skirt as she sidestepped the kick. Yvonne gripped his shoulders, pushed him off balance as he was recovering from the kick, and slammed him down into the chair, nodding to Tangeree. Tangeree gripped the boy's wrists, pulled his arms around the back of the chair, and put her knee against the back of the chair, holding the boy firmly. The boy shrieked deafeningly, and the chair bounced up and down as he kicked furiously. The woman moved forward, wringing her hands in anguish, talking to the boy soothingly, and telling Tangeree to be more gentle.

Picking up a hardwood block and the hooked pliers from the table, Yvonne turned to the chair. Tangeree gripped the boy's wrists with one hand, seized his hair with the other, and pulled his head against the back of the chair. Yvonne put her knee firmly on the boy's thighs, and pinned them to the seat of the chair. The boy screamed in terror and outrage, his feet a blur of motion as he kicked them rapidly. The woman moved closer, almost in tears, and the toe of one of the boy's boots connected solidly with one of her knees. She howled in pain, almost falling as her knee buckled.

The boy snapped viciously at Yvonne's fingers as she held the hardwood block against her left palm with one finger and extended the other fingers toward his mouth. Yvonne popped the narrow side of the block between his teeth and twisted it deftly, propping his mouth open, and put her hand against his forehead to pin his head against the back of the chair. The boy struggled frantically, his gagging scream becoming shrill and piercing, and Yvonne gripped the tooth with the pliers. She twisted it out, and plucked the hardwood block from between the boy's teeth as she took her knee off his thighs and stepped back. Tangeree released his hair and wrists at the same time, and the boy lunged out of the chair and threw himself at the woman, sobbing wildly. He threw his arms around her and buried his face against her, almost knocking her off her feet as she rubbed her knee. The woman recovered her balance and held the boy, patting him and stroking him.

"Now don't take on, honey, because it's all over with now. It's all over with, and that nasty old tooth ain't never going to bother you no more." She lifted her head, looking at Yvonne. "I must say that it seems to me like you went at it sort of rough, Mrs. Beaunais. Everybody says how good you are, but it looked kinda rough to me."

"I'd be more than glad to listen to advice on an easier way of doing it, Mrs. Richland. He can spit in the bucket there."

"Yes, well, here, honey, spit in the bucket. Honey, you're getting blood all over Mama's dress, and . . . well, it don't make no difference. This is an old dress, and I need to get you right home in case your little arms is sore or something, don't I? That girl of yours has got a good size on her, Mrs. Beaunais, and I'll bet she could break somebody's arm if she put her mind to it. Well, how much do I owe you?"

"Whatever you can afford. Twenty-five cents or so will do."

"I think I've got about ten cents here, so could I give you that and bring some more again? It's a few days before my man gives me my money."

"Yes."

"All right, let Mama get the money out, Billy," the woman said, patting the boy and fumbling with her reticule. She opened her purse inside the reticule and put ten cents on the table, then limped toward the door with her arm around the boy. "I'm much obliged to you for taking care of his tooth, Mrs. Beaunais."

"Thank you for coming in, Mrs. Richland."

They left, the woman holding the boy and murmuring to him as he whimpered pettishly. Elder stepped into the examination room doorway, grinning widely.

"It sounded like you had a hard time throwing that one."

"Yes, I did," Yvonne laughed. "He can kick like a mule, but his ears aren't as long as a mule's and it's hard to ear him down. Come on in, Mr. Elder. You said you wanted to talk to me about your wife?"

A beaming smile spread across his face as he stepped into the room. "Well, I got a couple of things I wanted to talk to you about, and that's one of them." His smile faded as he folded his arms and stroked his chin musingly. "The reason I wanted to talk to you about Mary is that she's going to have a baby directly. And you might remember that I told you she's had three before, and all three of them was borned dead."

Yvonne didn't remember, but she did recall that the Elders didn't have children. "Did she carry them the full nine months?"

"Yes, everything was fine each time right up to the end, but they was borned dead every time. Now I'll tell you straight out that I think a lot more of Mary's peace of mind than I do about children, but I think they're wrapped up together. And that's one reason I've been so lathered up about finding you. Horace and Hester Dowd allowed that if anybody could deliver a live baby for Mary, it would be you. That's what me and Mary think as well, and that's what everybody who knows you says."

"I'll be more than glad to do what I can. How far along is she?"

"She reckons it's due in about a month or so."

"Has it been moving?"

"Yes, but they did every time."

Yvonne nodded absently, thinking. There were instances when everything seemed normal, but the baby would be dead for no apparent reason. And three previous stillbirths was ominous. It suggested an inherited weakness that was passed along to the baby, a deficiency in some vital organ.

"Now I was mighty glad when I seen how you was fixed up here," Elder continued. "Because what I had in mind was just bringing Mary over here to let her spend the last weeks with you. And I'd like to bring her sister, too, if it won't put you out too much. I'll see you right on everything, but I was just thinking that you might find things to do ahead of time that nobody would know about."

The man continued talking his quiet, earnest tone reflecting his concern for his wife, and the burdensome worry of the financial situation returned as the central thought in Yvonne's mind, a crushing, depressing weight. And it was more frustrating than ever. She needed a little over nine dollars to have enough to make the mortgage payment. Another one or two payments, and the month or two that would provide, might be enough to erode Lassiter's influence to the extent that it would make no difference.

What Elder wanted to do offered hope for the next mortgage payment. There would be no cash outlay in providing for the two women, because there was ample food in the house from what Cargill had been leaving. Ten dollars didn't seem an unreasonable amount to ask, and Elder could afford it, because his appearance was far different from his ragged state of before. All the people in his wagon train had appeared penniless, and he had apparently prospered in California. His clothes were of good quality and almost new, his boots were new, and his tweed coat was an expensive one. But asking for the money in advance might take him aback, and he might not have it with him. And she had to have the money within the next three days.

Elder had stopped talking, and he was looking at her unsurely. "Of course, if you'd rather not take them in."

"No, no, I'll be more than glad to," Yvonne replied quickly, smiling. "I was only thinking about . . . how best to accommodate them. Well, it's almost time for lunch, and we can discuss it over lunch, can't we?"

"I'd like to stay for dinner, but I'd better head on back. You see, me and Mary was worried that you might have moved on to somewheres else, and I'd like to let her know that I found you for sure and that everything's settled."

Yvonne looked away, biting her lip. "Well, I did hope that you could stay for lunch, because I wanted to discuss, well, I'd like to find out about the other people who were in your wagon train."

His wide smile of before returned, and he nodded. "I was fixing to tell you about them, and that brings me to the other thing I come to talk to you about. Now a lot of us settled around Hangtown, including me and Mary, the Gooches, the Howards, the Robinsons. . . ." He continued naming off the families that had been in the twenty wagons, those that had settled in Hangtown, the ones who had settled near Nevada City, and the few who had gone on to the Sacramento Valley. Then he got to his point.

". . . and I guess it wasn't no secret that we didn't have much when we come here, but since we've settled we've all done right good. And a lot of us get together now and then, and one of the things we've talked about is doing something for you to show you what we think of what you done for us. And we took up a collection after I found out where you was." He took a canvas bag from his coat pocket and put it on the table. "And there it is. I had in mind about twenty-five dollars a wagon, but I didn't hardly make that. What we got together was four hundred and sixty-two dollars, and that's our way of saying we're much obliged, Mrs. Beaunais."

A dental instrument rattled on the table as Tangeree dropped it and looked at the bag with a stunned expression, her cheeks pale. Yvonne's mouth felt dry as she looked at the bag. She opened her mouth to speak, then cleared her throat and tried again. "Mr. Elder, that is far, far too much money. Perhaps a few dollars, but not—"

"Mrs. Beaunais, that money ain't nothing to what you and your girl done for us. We was there with our friends and kinfolk fixing to die all around us. My Mary couldn't lift her hand, and I didn't know nothing to do for her. The Army told us they'd show us the wrong end of their cannon if we come within three miles of their fort. We seen stages pass, and we seen riders pass. And nobody would even stop to see whether we was dead or alive. Then the wagon train you was in commenced passing, and we allowed it was more of the same."

He drew in a deep breath, his smile gone and tears standing in his eyes. His lips and chin trembled, and his voice quavered as he continued. "And then we seen your wagon pull off and stop. And we seen you and your girl build your fire and commence cooking your medicines. And we seen you and your girl going amongst the sick, not stopping through the day and not stopping through the night . . . ."

His voice broke as his tears overflowed, and he turned and stepped quickly to the door. He stood in the doorway and leaned against the jamb with his back to the room, wiping his eyes and controlling himself. Tangeree looked at the bag, her lips a tight, thin line and tears trickling down her cheeks. Yvonne's eyes burned with tears, and she fought back a sob that tried to rise in her throat. Elder sighed heavily as he turned.

"That money ain't nothing, Mrs. Beaunais. It ain't a pissle to what I'd give you if I had it, and if there's another two like you and your girl, I don't know where on God's green earth I'd go to look for them. But that's what we got together for you, and we want you to have it."

Yvonne swallowed and nodded, wiping her eyes. "I'm very grateful, Mr. Elder. I'm so very, very grateful."

"And you're more than welcome. Well, then, when would you like me to bring Mary and her sister over?"

"As soon as you can."

"I'll make it a week from Wednesday, then. Should I have her lay down on something during the ride over?"

"No, have her sit, but on deep padding or in a well-sprung carriage."

"All right, I'll do that, and I'll see you again come a week from Wednesday. Goodbye, Mrs. Beaunais."

"Goodbye, Mr. Elder, and Godspeed."

He went out and closed the front door quietly, and his footsteps crossed the porch. The clopping of his horse's hoofs moved away from the house, and Yvonne and Tangeree stood looking at the bag. Tangeree wiped her cheeks as she stepped to it and touched it, and she looked at Yvonne.

"Ma, will you buy my cow back?"

"If he'll sell her, Tangi. Go put out my green dress for mè."

Tangeree went out, and Yvonne crossed the room to the bag. She untied the rawhide thong and opened the top, looking in it. Most of the coins were silver dollars, but there was a sprinkling of other coins among them. She saw a double eagle and took it out, and raked her fingers through the coins, looking for another one. There was another near the bottom, and she took it out and looked at the two coins. If the people at the bank believed the fat, heavy bag contained double eagles, it would appear that she had over four thousand dollars instead of over four hundred. She put the double eagles on the table by the bag, tied the top of the bag, and went to her room to get ready.

She put on her best dress and her coat, and walked through the streets to the bank with the heavy bag under her coat and the two double eagles clenched tightly in her right hand. The bank was crowded, with a line in front of the teller's window. Yvonne stood in the line and moved forward as people moved away. Through the heavy steel bars across the teller's window, she could see Abercrombie talking to a man at a table against the wall. The last man in front of Yvonne moved away, and she stepped to the window and rested the bag on the ledge in front of the bars. The teller looked at the bag then at her, and smiled and nodded.

"Good day, Mrs. Beaunais."

"Good day. I'd like to pay the month's reckoning on my mortgage, please."

The teller reached on a shelf below his stool for a ledger. Yvonne looked at Abercrombie from the corners of her eyes. He glanced around as he talked to the man, then looked back at her. The man said something to him, and he nodded absently, moving away from the man and puffing on his cigar as he looked at Yvonne and the bag. The teller thumbed through the ledger and opened it, then picked up a pen and dipped the tip in an inkpot.

Abercrombie stepped closer as the pen scratched. The teller put the ledger aside, and looked at Yvonne expectantly. She plucked at the knot in the rawhide thong and untied it, put her right hand in the bag, then took it back out and put the two double eagles on the ledge, pushing them under the bars. Abercrombie craned his neck and looked at the double eagles, and he took another step closer as Yvonne retied the rawhide thong on the bag. The teller opened his cash drawer, put the double eagles in it and pushed a five-dollar and ten-dollar gold piece under the bars, and began filling out a receipt. Abercrombie moved closer, his lips stretched in a wide smile and his eyes penetrating and curious.

"Good day, Mrs. Beaunais. It appears that the business affairs of physicians are doing very well."

"Good day, Mr. Abercrombie. No, business is actually quite poor just now, but I made an investment some time ago that has paid off handsomely."

"Yes, I can see," Abercrombie chuckled heartily. "Handsomely indeed, I would say. But it isn't wise to carry funds of that amount about, you know. You could leave it on deposit with us, if you wish."

"Thank you, but I had in mind leaving it on deposit at Washoe Bank."

"Washoe Bank?" Abercrombie laughed. "My dear, Washoe pays only six percentum interest on funds left on deposit, and we pay eight."

Yvonne smiled placidly and nodded. "Yes, but Washoe Bank didn't sell the mortgage on my house to a whoremaster, Mr. Abercrombie."

The teller jerked convulsively, and his pen left a large blot of ink on the receipt. There had been a murmur of conversation in the line behind Yvonne, and there was sudden silence. Yvonne smiled blandly at Abercrombie. His smile became sickly as color spread up his face from his neck, and he made a sound in his throat as he turned and walked back to the man at the table. The conversation in the line began again, becoming louder than before, and people's feet scuffled as they moved around each other to look at Yvonne. The teller blotted the receipt and completed it, his face crimson as he contained his laughter, and he pushed the receipt under the bars, smiling widely at Yvonne.

Yvonne left the bank and walked on along the street to Washoe Bank. She kept seventy-five dollars and deposited the rest of the money, then walked along the streets and the road out of town to the dairy. Johnson was talking to two men sorting through baskets of eggs on a table in front of one of the sheds. Yvonne walked toward him. He turned and looked as one of the men spoke to him and nodded toward her, then he walked toward her.

"Good day, Mrs. Beaunais. You don't have any more cows to sell, do you?"

"Good day, Mr. Johnson. Has she been a good cow for you, then?"

"I've had a lot that are easier to handle, because she's used to getting her own way, but I've never had a better milker. I wouldn't sell her for what I paid for her."

"How much would you sell her for?"

His eyebrows drew together in a puzzled frown. "What do you mean?"

"The reason I sold the cow was because I had to, Mr. Johnson, and she was my daughter's pet. My financial problem has been eased considerably, and I'd like to buy her back if I could."

Johnson's frown became thunderous as he looked away, scratching the stubble on his chin. He sighed heavily, then pointed to one of the barns and began walking rapidly toward it. Yvonne followed him, lifting her skirt and walking around piles of cow manure. Johnson went into the barn and led the cow out, and the cow lowed softly and rushed toward Yvonne as she recognized her. Yvonne patted the cow, looking at Johnson as he tied the halter rope to a fence rail.

"How much do you want for her, Mr. Johnson?"

"Give me twenty dollars."

"No, it's only right that you should have some—"

"Give me twenty dollars," he interrupted impatiently, then he smiled thinly and shrugged. "I heard about your money problem and about what caused it. And I ain't glad to sell the cow, but I'm glad you've got the money to pay for her."

"Thank you, Mr. Johnson, and I'm grateful to you for selling her back to me."

"Well, just give me the money before I change my mind."

Yvonne opened her reticule and counted out the money, and thanked him again as she gave it to him. He grunted and nodded brusquely as he put the money in his pocket and walked back toward the two men, and Yvonne untied the cow's halter rope and led her toward the road.

The cow hadn't been milked since early morning and her udder was heavy and sagging with milk.

Yvonne led her slowly along the road and turned up the street to the house. Tangeree was standing on the porch and watching the street, and she ran down the steps and along the street. The cow cocked her ears and flared her nostrils, looking at Tangeree, and began lowing loudly and running, dragging Yvonne along by the halter rope. Tangeree slid to a stop by the cow, throwing her arms around the cow's neck as the cow nuzzled and pushed against her, almost knocking her off her feet. She took the rope and led the cow on along the street, beaming with happiness as she scratched the cow's ears and talked to her.

There was milk to go with dinner for the first time in weeks, and a happier atmosphere at dinner than there had been for months as Yvonne and Tangeree talked about the money. As they were cleaning off the table, a horse turned off the street and stopped in front of the house and there was a knock at the door. It was Lassiter. Suppressed anger smoldered in his eyes as he and Yvonne looked at each other silently in the light of the lamp she held. She moved back, opening the door wider, and he stepped inside and bowed as he took off his hat. Tangeree walked in from the kitchen, wiping her hands on her apron. He bowed to her, then looked back at Yvonne.

"There's a girl down at my place who's been plagued by the vapors lately," he said quietly. "And another one has bellyaches all the time. Do you want to see what you can do for them?"

"Of course I will. There's no need to ask."

"I wanted to make sure."

"Anyone who is ill is welcome here."

Lassiter nodded musingly, looking at Yvonne, then he put his cheroot in his mouth and puffed on it as he reached into his coat and took out a folded sheet of paper. It was the mortgage she had signed. He put it on the table by the door, and took his cheroot back out of his mouth, exhaling. "I don't like to lose, and I don't very often. But when I do, I pay off."

"I don't want that, Mr. Lassiter," Yvonne said, shaking her head. "I want only what I have earned."

Lassiter made a sound of amusement in his throat as he turned back to the door and put on his hat. "You earned it. Good night, Mrs. Beaunais."

15

ON THE DAY Mary Elder and her sister Elvira arrived, what residents of Virginia City called a Washoe zephyr was blowing, a near-tornado-force wind that ripped loose boards from houses and barns and filled the air with flying shingles, clumps of sagebrush, and choking clouds of sand and dust. Elvira was a widow of about fifty, a heavy-set woman with a placid, imperturbable good nature and a twinkling smile. Mary was about fifteen years younger, a strong, healthy woman with a disposition much like that of her sister.

The unborn baby was positioned properly. It didn't move and flex its limbs as energetically as most, but the degree and force of movements among unborn babies varied. Mary had torn on each of the three previous deliveries, and there was scar tissue that would make the stitching more difficult, which was common. Yvonne and Tangeree differed by a few days in their estimate of when the baby would be born when they measured the expansion of the uterus by finger-widths up the front of Mary's stomach, but their margins of error overlapped. In all respects, Mary appeared to be in the final stages of a normal pregnancy, but it worried Yvonne that the woman had experienced three previous stillbirths. And the woman had a fatalistic conviction that she was going to have another.

The two women moved their belongings into one of the spare bedrooms and took over all of the housework and cooking. They blended into the household routine as they dug up and mulched more of the garden area behind the house that Yvonne and Tangeree had worked on in spare moments, transplanted saplings and placed them around the house and barn, and took walks into town and along the road.

Sundays were normally quiet and peaceful, but the second Sunday after the two women arrived was one of unbroken activity. On Saturday evening, a pregnant woman in a family from one of the settlements between the Washoe Mountains and the Sierra Nevada began premature labor while the family was enroute to Virginia City, and the blacksmith sent them to the house. The labor was routine and relatively easy, and the baby was born early Sunday morning. It was a few days short of full term and small, but it was active and healthy and the people loaded the woman and baby into their wagon and left.

Two women with ill children and a man who wanted a tooth extracted came to the house, and there was a call to a house where a young boy had been injured. Carpenters had been working on the house and the boy had been prowling about on the scaffolding. He had fallen, lacerating and breaking a leg. Yvonne and Tangeree set and bandaged the leg and gave the mother instructions for checking the wound for infection. A large, expensive carriage was waiting at the house when they returned. Leggett was out of town and one of his patients, a daughter of a superintendent and part owner in one of the mines, had gone into labor.

The carriage took them to one of the mansions on the street overlooking the center of the town. The woman's mother, sister, and other female relatives and friends were in the elegant, luxuriously-furnished parlor, and the husband, father, and other male relatives and friends were in the library. Servants moved about silently, and the housekeeper led Yvonne and Tangeree up a wide, sweeping staircase to the bedrooms. The woman having the baby was young and it was her first, but she was less worried than anyone else, a cheerful gamine of twenty with a comical sense of humor.

The servants brought linen, basins, and boiling water, and put a silver coffee service and trays of delicacies in an alcove at one side of the bedroom. The woman was totally fascinated with Tangeree and her experiences, and they chatted between contractions. Tangeree wanted to smoke to help her stay awake as the night wore on, and an impassive, expressionless maid brought her a choice of a cigar and box of cigarettes on a tray. The baby was born at four, a large, healthy boy. Everyone was still awake, and they filed into the bedroom after the maids had cleaned it. Yvonne and Tangeree gathered up their things, the people thanked them and the father gave Yvonne an envelope containing a five-dollar bill. Dawn was starting to break in the east as the carriage took them home.

Voices and activity in the house woke Yvonne three hours later. Hurried footsteps moved about, a door opened and closed, a deep, resonant man's voice rumbled in a concerned tone, and Mary and Elvira replied. Elvira went to Tangeree's room and called her, and she replied sleepily as she scrambled out of bed. She coughed and sniffled as she dressed hurriedly, and walked rapidly out of her room and toward the front of the house. Yvonne sighed wearily as she pushed the covers down and climbed out of bed.

The man was standing in the waiting room and looking worriedly at the closed door of the examination room, a tall, beefy man nearing sixty, with a ruddy complexion, muttonchop whiskers, and a full mustache. His hair was tousled, his clothes were disheveled from being hurriedly pulled on, and the curly gray hair on his chest showed at the open collar of his shirt. He turned and looked at Yvonne. "Mrs. Beaunais? I'm Christopher Woodruff, and Doctor Leggett told me to consult you whenever he's away. My daughter Christina was feeling a bit out of sorts yesterday, and this morning she was very ill when the maid started to dress her."

His name was very familiar, that of the owner of the Yellowjacket Mine, and Yvonne recalled a recent newspaper article that said the shaft in the Yellowjacket had gone directly from one bonanza into another that assayed at thousands of dollars per ton of ore. "I'm pleased to meet you, Mr. Woodruff," she said, opening the door to the examination room. "I'll talk with you in just a moment."

He frowned anxiously and nodded, and Yvonne went into the room and quietly closed the door behind her. The girl on the table was flushed and looked groggy with fever as Tangeree bent over her, listening to her chest and talking to her. She was surprisingly young for a man of Woodruff's age to be her father, about twelve or thirteen. Tangeree's eyes were puffy and red from lack of sleep, but her smile and voice were cheerful and warm as she talked to the girl.

"And it hurts when you breathe, Christina?"

"Yes."

"It hurts mostly on this side, doesn't it?"

"Yes."

"And you feel a little sick at your stomach?"

"Yes."

The girl was pretty and had a slight lisp when she talked. Her brown hair was a mass of long curls that came almost to her waist. She was wearing a bright, silky dress with an intricate lace bodice, the frills of her snowy pantaloons showed below the hem of her dress, and her shoes were small and dainty. It was impossible to keep from comparing the girl's clothes with Tangeree's. She had on a faded bodice and skirt that had been made from her old dresses, she had buttoned the bodice in the wrong holes in her hurry and her petticoat showed below it as she bent over the girl, and the hem of her dress was above the tops of her scuffed, blocky shoes. The girl on the table looked like she was accustomed to having maids dress her and to the other things that went with a life of leisure and plenty—the afternoon parties with others of her age, the selected comedies at the theater, and the croquet matches. Tangeree looked like she lived for the sole purpose of serving the needs of the ill.

Tangeree stepped out of the girl's line of vision and mouthed the word as Yvonne approached the table. It was pneumonia. Yvonne smiled down at the girl and patted her arm, then leaned over and put her ear to the girl's chest. The wheezing, gargling rattle was clearly audible in the girl's lungs as she breathed shallowly, and the girl was burning with fever. Yvonne smiled down at the girl again as she straightened up, and she walked back toward the door.

Yvonne pulled the door closed and looked up at

Woodruff as he leaned toward her, breathlessly intent. "It's pneumonia, Mr. Woodruff."

For an instant, Yvonne thought the man was going to burst into tears. His features twisted, and he turned and sat down heavily on the settle, resting his elbows on his knees and burying his face in his hands as he shook his head. "And it's my fault," he groaned in a muffled voice. "We were in the mountains on Saturday, and we played in the snow. I knew it might make her ill, but she wanted to . . . ."

The large, heavy-set man had strong, authoritative features and a commanding presence about him, a charisma that set him apart from others. He looked like a man of prestige and influence, a man capable of dealing with his wealth and with the lives and fortunes of others. And the thought of his playing in the snow with the girl would have been amusing, if it hadn't been for the girl's illness. But the situation was clear. The girl was very pretty and charming, the child of his autumn years, and an object of adoration. Yvonne sat down on the chair by the settle. "And did she possibly become overheated and take off her coat?"

"Yes," he sighed nodding. "That's precisely what happened. I made her put it back on, but she had it off for several minutes." He drew in a deep breath and released it in a gusty sigh, sitting up. "How serious is it, Mrs. Beaunais?"

"Pneumonia is always serious, but she's a strong, healthy girl, Mr. Woodruff. I see no reason for despair."

He nodded and pursed his lips musingly, looking away, then looked back at her. "Mrs. Beaunais, I intend no slight to you when I say this, but I want the best possible medical care for my daughter. Doctor

Leggett speaks very highly of you and I've heard others speak well of you, but my daughter means the world to me. Are you absolutely certain that my daughter will recover under your care, or should I take her to a physician in Sacramento or San Francisco?"

"I'm a parent, so I don't consider a parent's questions a slight, Mr. Woodruff. I recommend strongly that you don't take her across the mountains, because she's too ill for such a trip. And no one can give you absolute assurance of being able to cure your daughter, but I've cured many people of pneumonia. If you want me to treat her and you also want to bring a doctor here, I've no objection. But you should bear in mind that there might be disagreement with my treatment simply for the sake of disagreement. If the doctor happened to be someone like Doctor Leggett, though, there shouldn't be any problem."

His eyes were those of the keen, analytical businessman rather than the father for a moment as he looked at her in silence, evaluating both her and what she had said, then he slowly nodded. "Thank you for being frank with me, Mrs. Beaunais. I'd like you to see to my daughter. If Doctor Leggett returns while she's under your care, I might ask him to look at her. Otherwise, I'll leave it up to you. You think she should stay here rather than return home, then?"

"Yes, I do. In its normal course, the illness will get worse for a day or two and then reach a crisis, and she should have more or less constant care until she passes the crisis."

"I see. Would you have any objection if I remained here for a while?"

Yvonne shook her head as she rose and walked toward the examination room. "No, of course not. Mary and Elvira are preparing breakfast, and you're more than welcome to go in and have breakfast or some coffee."

Woodruff forced a thin smile of thanks as he rose and walked toward the kitchen, his shoulders slumped despondently and his footsteps slow and·dragging, and Yvonne went back into the examination room.

Christina had a higher temperature than most did in the early stages of pneumonia and it was a cause for concern, because it was sapping the strength her body would need when the illness reached the crisis stage. Yvonne sent Tangeree to prepare an infusion of cinchona bark for the fever and an infusion of butterfly weed, pennyroyal, and ginseng to combat the illness. She took the girl to an empty bedroom and put her to bed, wrapping her warmly in blankets. Tangeree brought in the infusions, and they began administering them to the girl. The powerful febrifuge acted almost at once, her temperature began falling, and she began breathing more easily.

Yvonne left Tangeree with the girl, and went to the kitchen for breakfast. Woodruff was sitting morosely at the table over a cup of coffee, and Mary and Elvira had eaten and were moving around in the kitchen. Yvonne told Woodruff that the girl's temperature was falling, which made him momentarily less gloomy, and he talked for a few minutes, asking her about the normal progress of the illness, and the procedures and medicines she used in treating it. Elvira took Tangeree's breakfast to the bedroom, with a bowl of hominy grits flavored with cinnamon and brown sugar for Christina, then she went outside and began doing the washing as Mary washed the dishes.

Woodruff became silent again, his chin propped on his hand as he looked down at his cup and moved it around on the table. The fresh, cool air of the early spring morning came through the back door, and the birds chattered cheerfully outside. Elvira sang tunelessly and splashed clothes in the tub and boiling washpot outside the back door, and Mary hummed as she moved back and forth in the kitchen and rattled dishes in the sink. Woodruff looked up, then straightened as Tangeree came in with the dishes from the bedroom.

"Did Christina eat anything, Miss Beaunais?"

Tangeree nodded as she put the dishes on the sink. "Yes, sir. She ate most of it, then went to sleep."

"She must be feeling a lot better, then."

"Yes, sir, she feels better now that her fever's down. It'll go back up slowly, then it'll break completely and she'll start recovering. It should break late tomorrow or tomorrow night, shouldn't it, Ma?"

"Yes, I'd say it'll be about then, Tangi."

Woodruff nodded, looking back down at his cup. Tangeree took her coffee cup to the stove and refilled it, and looked in the wood box for a long splinter. She still had the box of cigarettes from the night before, and she put one in her mouth and pulled a splinter from a stick of wood. Mary stood at the sink and wiped a dish, trying to conceal her mixed fascination and disapproval as she watched Tangeree light the cigarette. Tangeree tossed the splinter into the stove, picked up her coffee cup, and puffed on the cigarette as she walked back out of the kitchen. Woodruff glanced at her, then blinked in surprise and looked. His eyes reflected amusement as he watched her leave the room.

"Your daughter is a very remarkable young woman, Mrs. Beaunais. When I was talking to her this morning, it was difficult for me to keep in mind that she's scarcely more than a girl. It was more like talking to Doctor Leggett."

"Yes, Tangi's been working with sick people since she was ten," Yvonne replied. "She has a lot of experience and she's good at it, but that's all she has, instead of the things other girls her age have. That's why I let her smoke and do just about anything else she wants."

"It's very admirable for a person to devote themselves to some valuable service to others," Woodruff said. "And she appears to get satisfaction from it."

"Yes, she likes it, but it's really all she's ever known. As her mother, I regret the things she's missed and will miss. But a lot of people are alive and well through what she's done."

"I wouldn't mind letting her deliver this baby I'm fixing to have," Mary said, stacking the dishes on the sink. "There ain't many doctors that girl couldn't learn a lot, I'll tell you, and none her mother couldn't. Half of the people on our wagon train owe their lives to them two."

Woodruff nodded, looking at Mary, and looked back at Yvonne. "Did you come on the same wagon train?"

"No, we came with the Seeton party, and Mary's husband was leading another wagon train. They had sickness among them when we caught up with them at Fort Laramie, and we stayed with them for a day and treated them."

"There's a lot more to it than that," Mary said emphatically, shaking her head. "A whole lot more. I was so sick I don't even hardly remember it, but half of our people was dying. The Army wouldn't let us come close to their fort, and nobody wouldn't stop nor come close to us. Then our prayers was answered when Mrs. Beaunais and her girl got there. The first thing I remember good is that girl Tangeree looking down at me with that sweet little smile of her'n, and saying that I was going to be all right. And you know, I'll be durned if I didn't start perking up. . . ."

There was a knock at the front door, and Yvonne rose and walked through the house to the door as Mary continued relating the story. An old man and old woman named Jessup were at the door, a frail, penniless couple whose only ailment was the ruin wrought by years. They came every week for their medicine, a pint of infusion of burdock and ginseng mixed with a pint of whiskey. The old woman held the bottle and the old man's arm as he leaned heavily on his cane, and they smiled up at Yvonne. A young woman was walking up the street toward the house, carrying a child. Yvonne shrugged off her fatigue and lack of sleep and smiled at the old couple. She reached for the bottle as they stepped feebly over the threshold.

Others came and Yvonne needed Tangeree's help, but Woodruff needed reassurance that his daughter was receiving attention, and Tangeree needed the rest she could get by dozing in the chair by the bed. It took Yvonne longer to see to the people by herself, and she became more sleepy and sluggish as the hours of the morning dragged by. Woodruff's carriage had remained at the house and he went home for a few minutes and returned wearing his tie and hat, and Mary and Elvira set a place for him at the table for lunch. Elvira took lunch in to Tangeree and Christina, and Yvonne went in with her. The girl's temperature was almost normal and she was resting comfortably, and Tangaree was well rested and alert.

After lunch, Yvonne sat with Christina and rested. A woman brought in a boy with infected sores on his mouth during late afternoon, and Tangeree came for

Yvonne and sat with Christina again while Yvonne attended to the boy. Three men had come to see Woodruff and were sitting on the porch with him, talking to him and showing him papers as he smoked a cigar and listened absently. The three men left at sunset, and Woodruff came back in the house and sat in the kitchen. He picked at his food during dinner, and sat at the table and conversed listlessly with Yvonne as Mary and Elvira washed the dishes and cleaned up the kitchen. After Mary and Elvira went to bed, Woodruff stood for a moment in the doorway of Christina's room and looked at her in the dim light of the shaded lamp on the table by the bed, then he left.

Yvonne and Tangeree divided the night, taking turns dozing on the bed by Christina and waking her to give her drinks of the infusions. Woodruff returned early the next morning, his eyes red and bleary from lack of sleep. Christina's temperature was higher in spite of the febrifuge infusion and she had no appetite for breakfast, the first indications of the approaching crisis in the illness. Yvonne left Tangeree with Christina and attended to the people who came in. It was a slow, peaceful morning with only two patients— a young woman who wanted a sty removed from her eye and a couple with a boy who had a hoarse, rasping cough.

Christina didn't want the broth Elvira made for her lunch, and her temperature had risen more. By nightfall Christina's temperature had stabilized at a safe level, but she was semiconscious and beginning to have extreme difficulty breathing.

Mary and Elvira went to bed and the house became quiet. Yvonne and Tangeree sat by Christina's bed and bathed her face with cool water as her breathing became more irregular and labored. Woodruff sat at the table in the kitchen, his face pale and drawn. He looked up at Yvonne when she came in for fresh water, and looked away when she shook her head. Then the abrupt turning point of the crisis came during a period of thirty minutes just after midnight. Christina's breathing rapidly became stronger and more regular, her temperature began dropping, and she passed from semiconsciousness into a deep sleep. Yvonne went to the kitchen and told Woodruff. He came and stood in the doorway for a moment and looked at Christina, tears of relief standing in his eyes and his features trembling; then he averted his face and walked rapidly out of the house.

Christina's healthy constitution asserted itself, and she began recovering rapidly, eating ravenously and regaining her strength. Woodruff brought handkerchiefs for Mary and Elvira, scarves and perfumed soap for Yvonne, boxes of cigarettes for Tangeree, and bonbons, toys, and games for his daughter. Most of the toys and games were favorite ones from their house, and for a time Yvonne was puzzled by the fact that some of them weren't of a kind that would normally interest a thirteen-year-old girl. And that perplexity was a key to a more complete understanding of Christina and a deeper insight into the relationship between the girl and her father as Yvonne watched them while they were together.

Woodruff's wife had died several years before, and his only other child was a son who was at a university in the East, a man for all practical purposes. He and his daughter had no other close relatives living in the West, and they loved each other deeply. There was every reason why the girl should be spoiled, but instead she had a charming disposition. And when

Yvonne understood Christina better, she realized the girl had more than a share of the precocious maturity acquired by some children living in constant contact with adults.

The bonbons brought outbursts of excited squeals and furious rattles of paper as the girl ripped them open, Woodruff watching and beaming in delight. Then after all the excitement, noise, and gasps of anticipation to express gratitude, the girl never ate more than one. When Christina and her father played with the games and toys, she hesitated until her father chose one. Then they played noisily, Christina giggling and shrieking and her father roaring with laughter. And Yvonne saw what the girl was doing. In her love and a deep wisdom far beyond her years, Christina entertained her father by making him believe he was entertaining her. The man hadn't played in the snow with his daughter. It had been the other way around.

After the fourth day, Christina was moving around the house in a silky dressing gown and slippers, and both the girl and her father importuned Yvonne to allow her to return home. Tangeree thought she still heard a suggestion of rattle in Christina's right lung, and Yvonne wasn't completely satisfied with the color of the whites in the girl's eyes and her general appearance. Yvonne firmly refused, warning Woodruff of the deadly danger of a recurrence of pneumonia, when the body was still weak. Christina continued improving, full color returning to her cheeks and her eyes clearing. She began sitting on the porch with her father during the warmth of the afternoons, and Yvonne agreed to allow her to return home on the seventh day.

Then shortly after lunch on the sixth day, Mary dropped the dishcloth with a gasp of pain as she was

standing at the sink and wiping the dishes. She
clutched her swollen belly and leaned against the
sink. Yvonne called Tangeree from the front of the
house and Elvira from outside, and they took Mary
to the bedroom. Woodruff and Christina were on the
front porch, and Yvonne went to the front door and
called him inside. She told him that Mary had begun
her labor, and he frowned with concern.

"But it isn't time for it yet, is it?" he asked. "Is everything all right?"

"Yes, it's close enough to her time, and no one ever
knows exactly when it's going to happen," Yvonne replied. "The baby's the one who decides that. But it
probably wouldn't be best for Christina to be here
while Mary is in labor."

"Yes, that's right," he agreed, turning back to the
door. "I'll bring her in and collect her things, and I'll
get my driver to help carry them out."

Yvonne nodded, and walked through the house to
the bedrooms as he went back out on the porch, calling
Christina. Tangeree and Elvira were stripping the bed
and putting a childbirth pallet on it as Mary sat on a
chair in the corner of the room and held her stomach,
and Yvonne took out a loose shift and began helping
Mary undress. Christina chattered happily in the next
room, her father chuckled and replied in his deep
voice, and the driver's boots thumped against the floor
as he walked back and forth and carried things out.

Tangeree and Elvira finished preparing the bed, and
rearranged the chairs and other furniture in the room.
Yvonne dressed Mary in the shift and helped her onto
the bed, and went back out as Christina and her father
were leaving. Christina embraced Yvonne and kissed
her, and Yvonne walked through the house to the
front door with them. The girl darted out the door

and ran across the porch and down the steps toward the carriage, shouting and beckoning her father. He laughed and nodded, but his smile faded as he turned and looked down at Yvonne.

"There's no way I can express my thanks, Mrs. Beaunais. Anything I could say wouldn't be enough."

Yvonne nodded toward Christina as the girl hopped onto the step of the carriage and swung on the open door, looking up at the driver and laughing and talking with him. "There's my thanks. She's a strong, healthy girl."

Woodruff looked at the girl, then looked back down at Yvonne. "You mean that quite literally, don't you? I've never met anyone as dedicated as you and your daughter, Mrs. Beaunais. And during these past days, I've come to regard you and your daughter as friends."

"It pleases me very much that you feel that way, Mr. Woodruff. I'd like to regard you as a friend."

Woodruff smiled warmly and nodded, then looked at the carriage and chuckled as Christina shouted and beckoned. "I'd better get Christina home, I suppose," he said, walking toward the steps. "She has a lot of things to catch up on." His voice faded, and he turned back around at the top of the steps. "I forgot to pay you."

"I'm sure you have it," Yvonne laughed. "It can wait until later."

Woodruff laughed, and started to turn toward the steps again. Then he stopped and looked into the distance, his lips pursed and his brows drawn in contemplation. Christina shouted at him again, and he looked at her and nodded absently, still musing. Then he looked at Yvonne again. "I'd also like to know how Mary and her baby are, so I'll be back later."

"Very well, Mr. Woodruff."

Woodruff walked down the steps and toward the carriage, and Yvonne stepped out on the porch, wondering why he had hesitated and what he had been thinking about. He still seemed preoccupied as he walked toward the carriage. Christina shouted at him impatiently, and he smiled at her and walked more rapidly.

He got in the carriage, and Christina leaned out the window and waved as the carriage moved away from the house. Yvonne waved, and started to go back in the house. As the carriage turned onto the street, she saw Woodruff through the window. He was sitting back in the seat and looking down as he stroked his chin, deep in thought.

16

THE HOUSE was quiet after the days of Christina's chatter and laughter during her convalescence, and Mary's labor settled into the routine of childbirth after the initial flurry of preparations, her contractions gradually becoming more intense and at closer intervals. Yvonne and Tangeree sat in chairs on opposite sides of the bed, talking to Mary and encouraging her, and Elvira was in and out of the bedroom, finishing the dishes in the sink, hanging out the washing, putting a roast and potatoes in the oven to bake for dinner, and returning to the bedroom.

The warmth of midafternoon settled, with a sultry touch of heat that warned of the torrid, dusty summer in the parched Washoe Mountains. During the time Mary had been at the house, she had kept the pessimistic conviction that the baby was going to be born dead, despite her invariably cheerful outlook on life in general and Yvonne's efforts to change her attitude. She murmured about it weakly between contractions, telling Yvonne and Tangeree that it wouldn't be their fault and talking about how disappointed her husband would be. Yvonne scolded her gently and talked about other things, trying to get her mind off it.

Then when final labor came, it didn't have the characteristic feel or the smooth, steady rhythm of the average, uncomplicated childbirth. It advanced at a faltering pace, with the energy and pain of some of the contractions being wasted instead of exchanged for progress. In many respects it seemed like the delivery of a first rather than a fourth baby. Elvira sat at the head of the bed and wiped Mary's face with damp cloths, and Yvonne and Tangeree used massage, bent over Mary and encouraged her, and urged her on to greater efforts during the contractions. And still the labor didn't gather momentum and develop the surging pulse of the forces of nature pushing new life into the world.

The first sign of trouble came when the bag of waters finally broke. Tangeree was at the window too long, sniffing and examining the fluid on her fingers. Her eyes were apprehensive as she walked back from the window, and she nodded toward the fluid soaking into the pallet and to the window as she washed her hands in a basin on the table. Yvonne dabbled her fingers in the fluid, and went to the window. There was just a hint of the pungent odor of fecal material and a few tiny, brownish-green flecks, indicating partial umbilical strangulation or some other abnormal condition.

Elvira murmured comfortingly to Mary, and Mary sighed something plaintively in reply. Yvonne washed and dried her hands, and sat back down. Tangeree sat on the other side of the bed and looked at Yvonne, waiting for instructions, and Yvonne pondered worriedly. Something was wrong, but there was no indication of disaster. Some babies suffered partial umbilical strangulation during birth, there were accidents and other circumstances that caused the presence of traces of fecal material in the fluid, and the babies suffered no apparent lasting ill effects. Mary was in no danger, and using the paddles was always dangerous for the baby as well as increasing the risk of vaginal infection.

There were many things that dictated against using the paddles. Balanced against that was the fact that the baby was in some degree of distress, and an intuitive feeling that she should get the birth over with as rapidly as possible. And Tangeree felt the same way. The wise, ageless blue eyes in the young face across the bed were troubled. Yvonne nodded, and Tangeree rose.

A vaginal rinse with sanicle infusion had to be used to fight infection after using the paddles. Tangeree handed Yvonne the bowl of eucalyptus oil and morphine paste she had mixed and went to the examination room to get the india rubber bulb and nozzles. Yvonne daubed the mixture on the soft area below the woman's vulva to numb it before cutting it, and Tangeree returned and moved back and forth around the table, rolling the knife in a fold of linen and oiling the smooth, hardwood paddles. Mary stirred, turning her head to look around uplifted knees at Yvonne.

"That feels really funny," she whimpered weakly. "What are you doing? Have you already figured out that it's dead or something?"

"Mary, if you don't stop saying that, I'm going to take advantage of the fact that I have your ass right here handy, and I'm going to use the sole of my shoe on it."

"What are you doing, then?"

"You're getting as slow as molasses on a winter morning, and we're just going to help you along a little. Now just relax, Mary."

Elvira wiped Mary's face with a cloth, murmuring to her and hushing her. Tangeree prepared the needles and thread, and the strings to tie off the umbilical cord. Then she sat down, taking the bowl from Yvonne and handing her the knife and paddles in cloths. Yvonne put them on the edge of the bed and waited a moment for the morphine to penetrate, then took the knife out of the cloth and touched the area with the sharp point. Mary didn't move. The crown of the baby's head was showing, and Yvonne put two fingers into the vaginal opening, pulled it away from the baby's head, and sliced down through the flesh. The keen blade hesitated as it passed through thick scar tissue from times when the flesh had torn, and Mary flinched and whimpered in pain as blood began coursing down from the cut. Yvonne put the knife aside and reached for the paddles.

Mary screamed in fright and pain as Yvonne inserted the first paddle, and Tangeree leaned forward, ready to hold Mary's thighs apart if they started to close. Yvonne groped gingerly with the paddle, feeling for the side of the baby's neck with the curved tip, then picked up the other paddle. A contraction began as she positioned the paddles, and she pressed the handles together and pulled. Mary uttered a shrill scream as she tensed, pushing, and the baby's head slid smoothly out, momentarily interrupting the flood of blood from the cut as the face pressed down against it. Tangeree caught the head in her hands to support it, and Yvonne put the paddles aside and leaned forward.

The paddles had left marks on the sides of the baby's head that would fade in a few days, and there had been no damage, but the baby was the wrong color. Instead of the normal bluish color, it was pallid, sickly gray—the color of a baby in dire distress. Yvonne's fingers touched Tangeree's as they both groped around the baby's slippery neck, feeling for the umbilical cord to pull slack into it. It wasn't there. And the baby didn't feel right. All newborn babies were limp as they emerged into the world, but they had a feel of tension, of living flesh. The baby felt like a wet rag, loose and flaccid.

Yvonne and Tangeree looked at each other, their faces inches apart as they leaned over the woman. Something had to be done, and quickly. Yvonne pushed her fingers in past the baby's neck and pressed its shoulder, turning it into position to come past the narrow exit of the birth canal. Mary screamed again, her hips lifting off the pallet. The baby's head slowly rolled in Tangeree's hands. Yvonne slid the tip of a finger under the baby's tiny arm and tugged with a steady, gentle pressure. The baby slithered out.

Tangeree knotted the lengths of string around the umbilical cord, her deft fingers moving swiftly. Yvonne cut the cord. Tangeree picked up the baby, sucked the mucus from its mouth and nose and spat it into a basin, then bounced it in her hands. Then she bounced it higher. Then she took the extreme measure to make it draw in breath, holding its feet between the fingers of her left hand and letting it dangle as she smacked its buttocks sharply with her right hand. The baby swung lifelessly back and forth from the blow, its arms flapping limply.

It was a beautiful baby. A female, large and sturdy. It appeared perfect in all respects, except for its color. And except for the fact that it was dead.

"It's dead, ain't it?" Mary whimpered, lifting her head. "It's another dead one, ain't it?"

"Yes, it is, honey," Elvira sighed sadly, pushing

Mary's head back down. "Now just lay your head down and be quiet."

"Oh, God Almighty, why did you do it?" Mary wailed, bursting into tears. "After all this, and it's just another dead one. Why did God do this to me, Elly?"

"Hush, hush, honey," Elvira said, wiping Mary's face with a cloth. "Now just be quiet and don't take on about it. . . ."

They continued, Mary moaning and weeping, and Elvira trying to calm her. Tangeree looked at the baby and at Yvonne in consternation, and she cradled the baby in her left arm and bent over it, blowing gently in its mouth. The baby's head fell limply to one side. Tangeree cupped the baby's face with her right hand, squeezing its mouth open with her fingers, and held it tightly against her, pressing its stomach in just above the umbilical cord with the tips of her left fingers. Then she began taking quick, shallow breaths and blowing into the baby's mouth.

Yvonne sighed, looking away. She had heard talk about attempts to breathe life into others, and she had seen it tried on drowned people. And it didn't work. And it wouldn't work. The baby was dead. A crushing sense of defeat swelled within her. Attempting to shrug it off, she sat up in her chair. Tangeree's cheeks were flushed and she was becoming breathless from taking in the rapid puffs of air and blowing into the baby's mouth. Yvonne felt sympathetic, understanding and sharing the girl's frantic, frustrated urge to do something, anything.

But the immediate necessity in a stillbirth was to end it, to get the dead baby out of sight, and to get the mother's mind onto something else. And Mary was becoming hysterical, weeping and wailing as Elvira tried to comfort her. Yvonne leaned over and touched Tangeree's arm. Tangeree pulled away, not lifting her head from the baby's face. Yvonne leaned farther over and caught Tangeree's sleeve, jerking on it. Tangeree twisted in her chair, pulling the sleeve out of Yvonne's fingers.

"Tangeree!" Yvonne barked impatiently.

Tangeree rose, swaying on her feet, and her chair fell over with a clatter as she bumped against the back of it. She weaved from side to side as she walked blindly to the door, and she ran into the doorjamb with a heavy thud, then went through the door and disappeared. Yvonne stood, calling out to her irately, and started to go after her. Then she looked at Mary, and stepped closer to her and leaned over her.

"Mary, now you stop that and be quiet! Do you hear me, Mary?"

"I ain't blaming you, Mrs. Beaunais," Mary moaned, sobbing. "I know it ain't your fault."

"And it isn't yours either! Now you stop taking on that way, or you'll make yourself sick!"

"But I just don't know how I'm going to face George and tell him that I've had another—"

"George is more worried about you than he is about any baby, Mary. That's what he told me himself, standing right in there. So if you're thinking about George, then you should be thinking about yourself. Now you stop this before you make yourself sick. Hand me the rag there, Elly."

Elvira handed Yvonne a cloth from the basin, and Yvonne wiped Mary's face and eyes, talking to her in a more gentle tone and calming her. As the hysterical frenzy faded from the woman's sobs and she began weeping quietly, Elvira took the cloth and talked to Mary in a soothing tone, daubing at her eyes. The afterbirth was being expelled, and it was complete

when it emerged. Yvonne filled the india rubber bulb
with sanicle infusion and rinsed the woman's vagina
with it, then carried the basin containing the threaded
needles to the bed and sat down.

The scar tissue resisted the needles and the stitching
caused the woman some pain, but it also seemed to
take her mind off the baby. Tangeree usually pulled
the knots into place and she could do it more skillfully
with her long, slender fingers, and Yvonne felt intense-
ly aggravated with the girl as she fumbled with the
knots. She got them tied and the bleeding diminished
to a negligible amount, then Yvonne went back to the
table and prepared the pad soaked in sanicle infusion.

"Help me lift her, Elly."

Elvira smiled at Mary and patted her shoulder as
she rose. She stepped along the bed and helped Yvonne
lift the woman's hips put the pad in place and tie it.
She leaned close to Yvonne and whispered softly.

"What did Tangeree do with the baby?"

"She took it in there."

Elvira nodded knowingly. Yvonne finished tying
the pad in place, then gently straightened Mary's legs
and tugged the shift down. Elvira moved back to the
chair at the head of the bed and sat down again, smiling at Mary. Yvonne gathered up the knife, paddles,
and cloths from the bed, put them on the table, and
returned to the bed for the basin that had contained
the threaded needles.

A baby cried in the kitchen. It was a thin, weak
whisper of sound, a feeble wail. There was a pause,
an instant of silence, then the cry exploded into a
lusty, ringing shriek. Yvonne's hands went weak as she
looked at the doorway, stupified. The basin fell from
her hands and clanged to the floor, water splashing
from it, and it rolled toward the door.

"That's my baby!" Mary screamed at the top of her voice, sitting up and starting to get off the bed. "My baby's alive! I hear my baby! My baby's alive!"

Yvonne wheeled and leaped to the bed, and she gripped Mary's shoulders and pushed her back down. "Mary, you lie down there! You're going to hurt yourself! Elly! Elly, help me hold her!"

Elvira was looking toward the doorway with a stunned, wild-eyed expression. She slowly turned her head and looked at Yvonne as she shouted again. Then she moved quickly, seizing Mary and pinning her to the bed.

"I hear my baby!" Mary shrieked, struggling frantically to get free. "I want my baby! My baby's alive, and I want—"

Her voice broke off as Yvonne slapped her sharply across the face. "You stop that!" Yvonne barked, slapping her again. "Stop it! Stop it!" The woman's eyes focused, and she flinched as Yvonne poised her head threateningly. "Now you stop that! Do you hear me?"

"I hear my baby," Mary moaned, relaxing. "I hear my baby, and I want it!"

"Then you stop that, and I'll go get it," Yvonne said, stepping back from the bed. "If you pull those stitches out, you'll really hurt yourself. Now you lie there, and I'll go get it. And you keep her there, Elly."

Elvira nodded numbly, holding Mary's shoulders and looking between Yvonne and the doorway in dazed disbelief. Mary motioned Yvonne toward the doorway, sobbing. Yvonne crossed the room and walked through the door, then she ran.

Tangeree was lying on the floor in the back door, propped on an elbow. Her face was blanched and drawn, and deep, rasping sounds came from her throat as she tried to breathe, and retched and choked at the same time. She was holding the baby to her with one arm, and its small limbs were flailing as it howled, its tiny face twisted and its mouth wide open. Yvonne crossed the kitchen and knelt by Tangeree, taking the baby. It was a rich, healthy red color, and it almost wriggled out of her hands as she took it. She held it with one arm, putting her hand on Tangeree's shoulder.

"Tangi, are you all right?"

Tangeree nodded, retching again, and waved Yvonne away. Yvonne climbed to her feet and took a step away, then hesitated, looking at Tangeree. Tangeree glanced at her, gasping hoarsely and waving her away again, and pointed to the baby as she tried to say something. Yvonne cradled the baby in her arms and walked back toward the bedroom.

Elvira struggled to keep Mary from sitting up as Mary moaned wordlessly and eagerly reached for the baby, tears of ecstatic joy in her eyes. Yvonne put the baby in her arm, and Mary cuddled it and talked to it in a crooning, sobbing voice as it howled angrily. Elvira leaned over and looked at it with a beaming smile. And Yvonne looked at the baby in wonder, reaching down to touch its limbs and trying to comprehend what had happened. It had seemed totally lifeless, but it was unquestionably alive.

Yvonne took the baby back, washed it, and wrapped it in clean linen as Elvira moved Mary off the soaked pallet, and rolled it up, and put a clean shift on her. Mary dozed off peacefully when Yvonne put the baby in her arms again, and Yvonne and Elvira cleaned up the room and carried the things into the kitchen. The threshold of the back door and the back step were soaked with water where Tangeree had washed away the vomit, and she was sitting on the chopping block behind the house and smoking a cigarette, her elbows propped on her knees and her shoulders slumped wearily. As Elvira went back into the bedroom, Yvonne walked outside.

"Tangi, how did you know what to do?"

Tangeree looked up, then looked away and puffed on the cigarette. She exhaled, shaking her head and shrugging. "I don't know, Ma. I just thought that maybe it didn't know how to breathe and I should show it, or maybe . . . I don't know, Ma. Maybe I just had to do something, and that's what I did."

"I noticed you were pushing your fingers into its stomach. Why did you do that?"

"So the breath would all go into its lungs instead of its stomach."

Yvonne put her hand on Tangeree's shoulder and looked away. The answers hadn't satisfied her, hadn't told her what she wanted to know. But her questions hadn't pinpointed what she wanted to know, because she didn't know what to ask. A baby had been dead and now that baby was alive, and it appeared that the vital secret in that fact was the mystery of life itself. Tangeree had responded intuitively, knowing what to do through that deep rapport she had with others. The baby had needed breath, and she had given it.

The sun was deep in the west, casting a ruddy glow of sunset over the rocky, sandy peaks around the town, and a haze of smoke hung over the town from evening fires. Yvonne patted Tangeree's shoulder and looked down at her. "I've seen people try to do that before, and it didn't do any good. But they were grown people, so maybe someone can give enough breath for a baby and not for a grown person."

"It could be, Ma. And maybe I was working harder than I had to or something, but I feel like I've loaded ten hay wagons."

Yvonne smiled, patting Tangeree's shoulder again, and her smile faded as she thought of other stillbirths. "The thing that sticks in my mind is that I can think of other babies that might be alive today if I'd thought to do that."

"They might, or they might not be, Ma," Tangeree sighed, puffing on her cigarette. "I'm sure there are all kinds of things that can be wrong with a baby, and that's just one. And you've said yourself that we learn all the time. We do the best we can, and we learn."

"Yes, I suppose so, Tangi. Dinner's in the oven, so come on in and have a bite and then you can lie down."

Tangeree dropped her cigarette and stepped on it as she rose, and she grimaced as she rubbed her stomach. "I don't want anything to eat, Ma."

"All right, come on in and lie down, then."

Tangeree nodded tiredly as they walked toward the door. Elvira was moving around in the kitchen, taking dinner from the over and preparing a plate for Mary. Yvonne gathered up the soiled childbirth pallet and put it in the washing pot outside the back door, carried water to cover it so it would soak overnight, and took the afterbirth and buried it under one of the small trees by the barn. Darkness was falling as she returned to the house. The lamp was burning on the kitchen table, and the wailing of the baby carried through the house and out the back door. Elvira was stacking dishes in the sink, and she glanced over her shoulder at Yvonne as she came in.

"I put your supper on a plate in the oven, Mrs. Beaunais. Mary's in too much of a tizzy to eat, and so am I, for that matter. But you ought to see that little one going after its dinner."

"Yes, it turned into a lively one once it got started, didn't it?"

Elvira laughed and nodded. "Yes, and its crying will lift the shingles off the roof." She turned away from the sink, wiping her hands on a dishcloth. "You know, Mary's been talking about asking you if she could name it after you."

"Tangi was the one who saved that baby, Elly."

"I know, but we sort of think of you all as going together. And it ain't just for that. We're a long way from forgetting what you all done for us at Fort Laramie, you know."

"Well, it would please me if that's what she wants to do, Elly."

Elvira smiled and nodded as she put the dishcloth on the sink and walked toward the doorway. Her footsteps went back through the house to the bedroom, the baby continued crying for a moment, then the house was silent. Yvonne washed and dried the basins and instruments, took them to the examination room and put them away, and returned to the kitchen. She took her dinner out of the oven and ate, then filled her pipe and sat back down at the table, puffing on her pipe and musing about the baby and what Tangeree had done.

A carriage rumbled rapidly along the street and turned off in front of the house. Yvonne carried the lamp through the house to the front door as Woodruff's characteristic footsteps came up the steps and across the porch. He looked more like a mine owner than he had in his often untidy state of dress during his daughter's illness. His muttonchop whiskers and full mustache were trimmed and combed, and his tweed hammerclaw coat was perfectly tailored to his wide, heavy shoulders. The sedate color of his coat was offset by his bright tie, flowered vest, and buff trousers, and he wore a short stovepipe hat and carried a mahogany cane with a large golf knob. He smiled widely and bowed, glancing around as he took off his hat and stepped inside.

"Everything seems quiet, so I take it that Mary's baby has arrived?"

"Yes, it's a girl, and they're both fine," Yvonne replied, closing the door. "But that's a delivery I'll remember for a long time."

"Indeed? What happened?"

Yvonne told him about what Tangeree had done as they walked through the house to the kitchen. "And I still don't understand it or how she knew to do it," she said as she put the lamp on the table and sat down. "But I do know that Tangi has a feel for a lot of things that I don't."

Woodruff put his hat and cane on the table and sat down, frowning musingly and nodding. "She's a very remarkable young woman in many ways, isn't she?"

"Yes, she is. Is Christina in bed?"

Woodruff chuckled and nodded. "We went to a restaurant for dinner, and she had to go shopping and first one thing and another. She could scarcely keep her head up when we got home, and she went to bed early. That gave me an opportunity to come here and see how Mary and her baby were. And to settle with you for treating Christina, of course."

Yvonne nodded and shrugged. "Five dollars or so will do. But you've brought presents here that are worth more than that."

"It was worth more than the presents for me to see Tangeree smoking her cigarettes," he replied, smiling. "And don't you usually tell people that the charge is what they can afford?"

"I'm sure you can afford five dollars," Yvonne laughed.

Woodruff laughed and nodded. "Yes, I can afford five dollars. But I've been thinking about somewhat more than that." He looked away in silence for a moment, his smile fading, then looked back at her. "Have you ever considered sending Tangeree to a medical college?"

"Considered? I've dreamed about it for years, but . . ." Her voice faded, and she looked at him in shock as the full meaning of his question dawned on her. Then she remembered his hesitation on the porch when he had left the house during the afternoon, and she realized he had been considering the matter at length.

"I believe it's something she deserves,". Woodruff said. "As I said before, it's admirable for a person to devote themselves to a valuable service to others, and she at least deserves an opportunity to develop herself to her full ability. And the circumstances are very favorable. There are a number of medical colleges in Philadelphia, and I happen to have some very good friends there by the name of Randolph. I'm sure they'd be happy to accomodate Tangeree, and you could be assured that she would be in proper surroundings."

Yvonne looked at him numbly, shaking her head. "But it would cost thousands."

"Yes, several thousand when all of her expenses are considered. But I have more than my son and daughter will ever use, I'm accumulating still more, and I occasionally make an investment in some worthwhile purpose that promises benefit to people at large. As this does. But it would cost you something more valuable to you than the money is to me."

"I don't understand."

"It would cost you your daughter for a period of several years. She should have an arts degree to get the full benefit of medical college, and that will take time. It would probably be best for her to go to San Francisco for that, and I have several friends there who could accomodate her. But that will take years, and medical college will take years. Would you be willing to do that?"

"Yes, I'd be more than willing, but. . . ." Tears suddenly flooded her eyes, and a tight constriction formed in the back of her throat. She looked away, wiping her eyes. "I'm sorry, Mr. Woodruff, but this is something I've dreamed of so long, and I never really thought . . . ."

"It's also come as a surprise, it's very late, and you've had a very busy day," he said, standing, and he shook his head and gathered up his hat and cane as she started to rise. "No, I'll see myself out, Mrs. Beaunais. Let's both give this some thought, and then we can discuss at length the arrangements we wish to make."

"Very well, Mr. Woodruff. And I'm so very grateful!"

"You deserve it no less than Tangeree. Good night, Mrs. Beaunais."

"Good night, Mr. Woodruff."

Yvonne stopped trying to restrain her tears and sat with her face in her hands and sobbed as he walked quietly through the house. The front door opened and closed. The carriage moved away from the house, and there was silence except for the distant pounding of the mill stamps. Yvonne sat up, wiping her eyes. The night breeze coming through the back door made the flame in the lamp gutter and flicker. She went to the door and closed it, then walked toward the bedrooms.

The sound of Tangeree's soft snores came through the door of her bedroom. Yvonne opened the door. "Tangi?"

Tangeree stopped snoring with a snort. There was momentary silence, then a flurry of movement as she began scrambling out of bed and reaching for her clothes in the darkness. "What is it, Ma? Is it Mary or the baby?"

"No, they're all right. Come into the kitchen, Tangi. I have something to tell you."

PART FOUR

THE DOCTOR

17

RANDOLPH FOLDED a letter and pushed it back into the envelope, then put it on the silver tray at one side of his plate and glanced at the other morning mail. Then he took off his spectacles and put them on the tray as he took a sip of coffee and looked down the long, gleaming table at Tangeree. "Well, Miss Beaunais, do your studies continue to progress satisfactorily?"

"Yes, thank you, sir."

"Very good, very good," he said heartily, pulling his napkin from its silver ring. He picked up his knife and fork and began slicing the scrapple on his plate. "And what will you be studying today?"

"Pathology this morning, and *materia medica* this afternoon, sir."

"Path . . . ah, yes, I see. A lecture hall is a dull place on a spring day like today, what? I can remember the job I had making myself go when I was at Harvard, and I'm happy that's long since done with. Do you have any trouble staying awake?"

"I don't believe I will this morning, sir. I'll be in the laboratory."

"Laboratory? Yes, yes, I see. Well, I never had any

of that myself. Mixing things in beakers and all that, what?"

"No, sir, not in pathology. We'll be dissecting."

Randolph blinked, his fork poised halfway between his plate and his mouth as he analyzed the implications of the word. The maid standing by the sideboard looked up at the ceiling, her cheeks flushing faintly as she pressed her lips together and kept her features in neutral, expressionless lines. Claire, Randolph's daughter of nineteen, looked at Tangeree from the other side of the table and ducked her head over her plate as she smiled. Phoebe Randolph, a bosomy, formidable matron of forty-five with intimidating features, multiple chins, and a high pompadour hairstyle, sat at the opposite end of the table from Randolph. She put down her fork and swelled visibly as she picked up the pince-nez hanging on a gold chain across the front of her dress and looked through them at Randolph, her chins quivering. Randolph cleared his throat uncomfortably, and put the bite of scrapple in his mouth and chewed rapidly.

"Yes, well . . . yes, I see. Well, Phoebe, with the weather turning off the way it has, we have the promise of a good display for the flower festival, what?"

The woman nodded as she dropped her pince-nez and picked up her fork again. "Let's hope it's better than the dreadful showing we had last year. I can't remember when we had a worse one, it was hardly worth the effort, was it? And now that the weather's turning warm, you'll want to be looking for another hunter for Pejoe when he comes home, won't you?"

"Oh, I think the black he has in the stable will do, won't it? Its leg has come right along, and beyond that, Pejoe's the one who did it, wasn't he?"

"I don't think Pejoe's at fault in any way because his horse stumbled, Julian, and it wouldn't do for him to have a lame, would it? And once the season begins, there won't be any good hunters here and it'll be too late to send to Kentucky. . . ."

They continued talking about a horse for their son Percival Joseph, who would be coming home on summer vacation from Harvard within a few weeks. Tangeree had met him the previous summer, and he seemed much like his father, with a bumbling, vapid amiability, a hearty enjoyment of good food, wine, and companionship, and an intellect that was distinctly less than keen. And he seemed destined for a career much like his father's.

Julian Randolph had graduated from Harvard with a law degree years before, but apparently had never practiced law. His family owned a large interest in a shipping firm in Philadelphia, and had other investments, all of which were managed by employees. Through family connections, he was on the board of governors of an insurance firm and a bank in Philadelphia, both of which were operated by hired managers and administrative staffs. He was on the board of trustees of the museum and opera company, a member of an exclusive men's club, a committeeman for the summer regatta, flower festival, and other civic activities, and a key member of a foxhunting club. But Tangaree hadn't found anything that he actually did.

The discussion about the horse continued, the woman seeking her son's best advantage without regard to cost, and the man taking a more detached viewpoint, as usual. Then the woman ended it.

"Very well, Julian. If you think the black will do,

then we'll keep it. But I daresay that Papa will want to get him another one even if you don't."

Randolph stopped chewing and looked at her. "Papa? I see no reason why Papa should have to be bothered with this, Phoebe."

"Neither do I, Julian, but I'm sure he wouldn't want his grandson and namesake on a horse that might go lame. And suppose it happened during the June courses? It would ruin the entire season for him, wouldn't it?"

"Well, if you think that might happen, Phoebe, perhaps I'd better talk to one of the grooms about going to Kentucky. . . ."

A threat to consult her father was a weapon that Phoebe occasionally used to settle disagreements with her husband. And it always worked. In contrast to Randolph, Phoebe Randolph's father, Percival Joseph Wyndham, was both highly intelligent and tirelessly industrious. He was a doughty, acerbic widower of seventy or so who was immensely wealthy and who was a figure of authority in his clan and in Philadelphia at large.

Since Randolph had imperturbable good nature, being bested in a disagreement with his wife didn't ruffle him, and he chatted with her about the coming flower festival as he ate with gusto. Scrapple was a breakfast food unique to Philadelphia, made from the liquid of boiled pig's head mixed with cornmeal and highly seasoned, and recooked until it thickened sufficiently to be sliced when it cooled. It was rich and filling, along with the fried eggs, fried potatoes, crisp rolls and whipped butter, and coffee with thick, heavy cream, but Randolph always ate several helpings. The maid carried the trays from the sideboard for him to refill his plate, started to move quietly back to the sideboard, and hesitated and glanced at Tangeree's plate. Tangeree shook her head at the maid, touching her lips with her napkin, and Randolph looked at her.

"You haven't had enough have you, my dear? My word, you hardly eat enough to keep a bird alive."

"Yes, it was delicious and I've had so much I'm quite breathless, sir. And I shall have to hurry or I'll miss my train." She looked at Phoebe. "May I be excused, please?"

"Certainly, Miss Beaunais. And do be careful on the streets in the city, my dear."

"Yes, I shall. Good morning."

Randolph half-rose from his chair as Tangeree stood and pushed her chair back to the table. She bobbed in a token curtsy to him and his wife, and exchanged a nod and smile with Claire as she turned away from the table.

The house was a massive two-storey brick structure in Georgian style. The lower floor was on two levels, the rooms at the front raised above the kitchen, scullery, and servant quarters, and other rooms at the rear. It was elegantly furnished and decorated, with matching fawn furniture and drapes in the receiving rooms, blue and white damask sofas and chairs in the parlor, mahogany in the dining room, and crystal chandeliers, ornamented mantels, and ormolu mirrors in all of them. The central hall was a wide expanse of gleaming parquet floor, with two huge chandeliers hanging from the vaulted ceiling above, long mirrors and ormolu sconces on the walls, and staircases on each side leading up to a mezzanine that overlooked the hall. It was an old house, but it had been modernized, with gas lighting fixtures, coal-burning fireplaces and stoves, and hot water from a central reservoir.

Tangeree lived in guest rooms at the end of one of the short hallways at the rear of the staircases, not upstairs with the family and not in the rear with the servants. The bedroom was neat and comfortable, and the bathroom had a marble washstand, an iron bathtub on claw feet, and a porcelain water closet of European design. The sitting room was furnished with chairs, bookshelves, and occasional tables, with a fireplace in a corner and a desk under a window that overlooked a flower garden at the side of the house.

She went into the bedroom and picked out a wide picture hat trimmed with ribbons and net that matched her dress, stood in front of the mirror on the chiffonier to pin it on, and tucked wisps of hair up under the hat as she walked back into the sitting room. Her satchel was on the floor by the desk, and she opened it on the desk and put notepads, pencils, and textbooks into it. A letter from her mother had arrived the day before, and she picked it up and glanced over it again.

The letters had come weekly, from the first days of the agony of loneliness and acid bath of customs, courtesies, and etiquette in San Francisco, and during the past period of almost two years in Philadelphia. They were always long, several pages filled with her mother's tiny, frugal handwriting and phonetic spelling, and occasionally there would be a pocket made on the reverse of a center page with a scrap of paper and flour paste, containing a five or a ten dollar piece. Until a year before, they had always been somewhat disorganized, written over a period of a week as she made spare moments. Then Jason Dowd had been embroiled in a fight in Auburn and had been killed, and

Abigail Dowd had brought Bobby Bownay to Virginia City and taken over the housekeeping, cooking, and other chores. The letters had become more coherent, the narration of the week's events less fragmentary and easier to understand, but there had been no substantial change in tone. They had always been warmly affectionate and encouraging, reaching out to maintain contact. But at times it seemed that the barren Washoe Mountains of Nevada were a very long distance away.

There was a light knock on the door as Tangeree was putting the letter back in the envelope. She turned to the door, saying "Come."

It was the housekeeper, a tall, thin middle-aged woman with lined, stony features, a strong Irish accent, and a thick bunch of keys at the waist of her severely plain black dress. She was tireless and ruthlessly efficient, and she was treated with respect by the Randolphs and with fear by the household staff. "Henry has the cab at the side door, Miss. And my sister asked me to thank you for the medicine. She says it's ever so much better than Doctor Shipley's Rheumaticon Elixir."

"I'm pleased it helped her, but do stress to her that she's to take it only after eating. It may cause upset on an empty stomach."

"Aye, well, she had to find that out for herself, and not ten minutes after I'd told her it and all. But she knows it now, no fear, because I've never heard such groaning in my life. Will you be here for lunch, Miss?"

"No, I'll have a full day today, Mrs. Delaney."

"I'll have someone bring you a tray when you return, then. But I won't make it so plentiful that it'll take away your appetite for dinner. The family will be having beef Wellington for dinner, and you'll enjoy that, I'm sure."

"Yes, I'm sure I will. Thank you very much, Mrs. Delaney."

The woman smiled thinly and nodded, closing the door, and Tangeree fastened the top on her satchel and prepared to leave. The phrasing the woman had used in the comment about dinner had been the signal that the Randolphs weren't having guests and she would be expected to join them. The system of communication wasn't totally unlike the system Woodruff used for her financial transactions. An assistant manager at a bank in the city gave her pocket money each month and wrote checks against an account in the bank to pay for her books, clothes, and other needs, serving as a neutral third party so all contacts between her and Woodruff could be kept on a personal level. Similarly, the housekeeper was a neutral third party for communications between her and the Randolphs to avoid embarrassment and awkwardness. There were occasions when Claire Randolph didn't dine with guests, and there were more times when Tangaree's presence at dinner would have placed the Randolphs in an impossible situation.

The Randolphs' social circle was a closed group associated with each other in a complex tangle of relationships by blood, marriage, and financial interests. Few outsiders were admitted, and that circle was closed to a young woman with the temerity to enter a male profession in which most of what she learned was improper for a young woman to even know. In addition to that insurmountable barrier, her antecedents were unacceptable, she had a thick Mississippi accent that had been the despair of elocution tutors in San Francisco, and she was from the distant reaches of the wild and unsettled West.

At the same time, the Randolphs had exerted themselves to make her welcome in the household. She had been invited to parties and other gatherings organized for Claire and Pejoe Randolph, Phoebe Randolph had taken a limited motherly interest in her, and Randolph had a paternal attitude toward her. They were hospitable people by nature; they understood her position, and it was clear they didn't want to alienate Woodruff. Their connection with him went back to the time of the opening of the Erie Canal, when Woodruff had lived in the East years before. As a result of the opening of the canal, the exchange of produce and manufactured goods between the East and West had begun going to New York, by river down to New Orleans, or over the newly constructed and macadamized National Road through the mountains to Baltimore.

As a further result, Philadelphia had been eclipsed and its existence as a major port had been threatened. Woodruff had been a key figure in the financing and development of the Pennsylvania Railroad, which had resolved the situation and assured the financial wellbeing of a number of prominent Philadelphia families involved in shipping and commerce. The Randolphs were pleased with the situation, because by doing something Woodruff wanted, they were discharging a group obligation and obligating the Wyndhams, Wrexlers, Bordens, and several other prominent families to them.

The only real snobbery Tangeree had detected had been from some of the household staff, who were paradoxically far more severe than the Randolphs in their judgment of people and their antecedents. But the housekeeper had vented her fury whenever she perceived any deviation from the standards of service and courtesy she set for house guests, and the driver of the small, two-wheeled cabriolet waiting at the side entrance of the house was neatly attired in his driver's coat and tall hat, and his boots gleamed. He opened the half-door on the side of the cabriolet and handed Tangeree in, then stepped onto the driver's stand behind the hoodlike top of the vehicle and clucked to the horse, turning it around toward the drive at the front of the house.

The grounds in front of the house were carefully tended, with expanses of trimmed grass between groves of trees in the light green foliage of spring, box hedges surrounding statuary, and a walk leading to a detached gazebo on a high point off to one side of the house. The drive led through the grounds, and to the densely-wooded road to the village and the train station. Other drives turned off to each side of the road at long, irregular intervals, and there were glimpses of other large, imposing houses through the trees. Drays were parked on the drive to a house owned by a family that followed the old custom of living in a townhouse in the city during winter and moving to the cooler, more pleasant, and more salubrious surroundings of Germantown for summer. But like the Randolphs, most families along the road had moved permanently to their summer homes since the railroad into the city had been completed a few years before.

The trees along the road thinned out, pastures and crop fields bordered the road, and farmhouses and other buildings were in groves at the end of narrow roads on each side. The road widened and became paved with cobblestone as it entered the seventeenth-century village, and the aura of the centuries was heavy, many of the solid, settled beam and plaster buildings marked with bullet holes from the American

Revolution and from skirmishes in the War of 1812. The meeting hall for the foxhunting club was a large, new building with paddocks at the rear, the racquet club occupied a building in front of its lawns and nets that reflected its more modest circumstances, and there were a few houses, shops, and an old church. The train station at the end of the village was the focus of most of the activity, with carriages, cutters, cabriolets, and wagons moving about and people walking through the gate in the fence by the road. The driver snapped the traces and urged the horse into a trot to make a smart arrival, then wheeled the cabriolet around near the gate and stepped down to open the door and hand Tangeree out.

A cluster of men stood inside the gate, chatting and smoking cigars. Several of them tipped their hats and bowed, and Tangeree averted her gaze and nodded in the accepted form as she walked past them to climb the step to the platform between the long, low train station and the tracks. The engine was a gleam of brass and red paint. Steam hissed from it softly and smoke trickled from its funnel-shaped stack, and its row of half a dozen small, boxy cars stretched along the platform. People stood on the platform and chatted. Those near the engine were mostly couples, the women in large plumed hats and bright flowing dresses decorated with gathers and pleats, with sun veils or parasols to protect them, the men in tall hats, starched, snowy stocks, and Prince Albert coats with flowers in the left lapels. The people at the other end of the platform were noisier, more unrestrained in their conversation and laughter, workmen in rough boots, caps, and baggy coats, and servants in mob caps, bonnets, and dull, shapeless dresses.

Some stopped just short of observing Tangeree and acknowledging her presence, their eyes approaching no closer than a few degrees to one side of her, but most women nodded and most men bowed and touched their hats. Her position in the household of the Randolphs conferred a degree of acceptability, and most were confident enough of their own position to be egalitarian to some extent. Others seemed to regard her as so exotic that she was completely outside the normal standards, and Tangeree had heard gossip about a few who appeared inclined to be more friendly. The Harrisons had a son who had married an Irish housemaid shortly after his return from Harvard, and he had taken some kind of job and was busily producing a swarm of red-headed children. But he had demonstrated enough tact and regard for his family to bury himself in Boston. A daughter of the Loudens had married a mechanic and tinkerer from Baltimore and had settled in a poor district of Philadelphia to flaunt the disgrace she had inflicted upon her family.

Word had also spread that Tangeree was a source of advice and assistance on dandruff, halitosis, menstrual pains, and other matters on which doctors were ignorant and regarded as frivolous, and some made an effort to cultivate her acquaintance. The Colburns stopped Tangeree as she moved along the platform with her heavy satchel, and she stood and talked with them. San Francisco had prepared her to deal with and understand the Randolphs and the situation in Philadelphia in the same way that her arts degree had prepared her for medical college, but there were still many things about people she failed to understand. The people stood on the platform and the empty train waited on the tracks by it, but anyone who boarded the train before time would be the object of cool glances because of their unseemly haste.

Tangeree and the Colburns were joined by the Bealors, staunch prohibitionists with a robust glow from their morning tonic of Hostetter's Stomach Bitters, which was almost fifty percent alcohol by volume. Most of the conversation was about the flower festival, and Tangeree nodded, smiled, and made appropriate comments. Then the station master came out of the station, looked at his watch, and signaled the driver in the engine. The whistle on the engine squeaked politely. Colburn took Tangeree's satchel to carry it onto the train as people moved toward the doors at the ends of the cars.

The car swayed from side to side and vibrated heavily as the wheels bumped and thudded on the tracks, the engine snorted, and the whistle shrieked. The distance into the city was just over five miles, and the tracks went through a long belt of trees and grassy meadows by the Schuylkill River where there had once been country estates that the Randolphs had talked about. Navigation on the river had been obstructed by the Falls of the Schuylkill until a dam and lock had been built in the long curve between Philadelphia and its western outskirts, and the backed-up water had bred mosquitoes and made the area damp and unhealthy. Crumbled walls and shells of some of the large houses still remained, curiosities for families on Sunday outings from the city to explore, and long, squat barges loaded with hundreds of tons of coal moved slowly down the river toward the port.

The train went around a curve and the city came into sight. Other cities sprawled in unplanned, haphazard growth, but Philadelphia had been laid out in squares across the narrow waist of the band of land between the Delaware and Schuylkill rivers. Masses of trees buried some streets that hadn't been completely filled and there was some fragmenting into winding roads around the edges, but the center was in even, orderly lines, pointed spires of churches and square, blocky tops of larger buildings jutting up above others and the greenery. The tracks passed a large colliery with its black mounds and blackened drays, and scattered buildings flicked past.

There was a large mill where Quaker flour was processed and bagged, a name familiar to Tangeree since childhood, and other manufacturers were located along the river. One was a factory built by a carriage maker who had started building miniature carriages for the children of the wealthy as a novelty years before, and had discovered a lucrative market among people at large who preferred to push children in miniature carriages rather than carry them. There was a plant where ice cream was made, and a factory where belts, pulleys, and tires for carriages were made from india rubber, owned by a man named Charles Goodyear.

The buildings closed together and rushed past on both sides, other tracks appeared by the train as the car rocked violently and the whistle shrilled, then the train slowed and pulled into the dim, dingy spaciousness of the station. It squealed to a stop, and the people getting off the train with Tangeree melted into a crowd of strangers as they blended with others in the smoky, noisy bustle of the station. Carriages for hire were lined up on the street outside the main station, and the crowd that came out of the station around

Tangeree began thinning out and breaking up, some walking away and some climbing into the carriages at the front of the line.

Others streamed along the sidewalk toward the side street by the station, and Tangeree walked around the corner with them. There was a line of horse cars at the curb, long, open-sided vehicles with rolled-up curtains for inclement weather and seats for twenty-six people. Tangeree walked along the line, looking at the numbers on the front of the cars, and joined the line, climbing the steps into one of them. The man ahead of her in the line tipped his hat and took her satchel as she lifted the hem of her skirt and climbed the steps, then tipped his hat again as he put the satchel down by her seat and walked along the aisle between the seats to the rear. The driver moved along the aisle and collected the fares, then stepped across the bench in front and sat down on it, gathering up the reins and clucking to the team.

Vendors were beginning their daily rounds, and merchants' errand boys were putting out awnings and sweeping the sidewalks along the wide streets of shops. Drays loaded with lumber, brick, stone, and other building materials moved along the streets; construction was in progress in many locations. The city was growing rapidly, and it had become a major supplier of coal, locomotive engines, ships, and other things. Numerous colleges had also been established in the city, and it had become a center of medical education for the country. There was a women's medical college in the city, and Tangeree and everyone else involved had anticipated that she would attend it. The entire curriculum consisted of lectures, as it did in most medical colleges, and graduates were expected to serve a period of preceptorship under the supervision of a qualified physician for practical experience. Tangeree's practical experience exceeded that of many physicians, and her arts degree combined with medical college qualified her for the award of a doctorate in medicine rather than a certificate of completion and a title of courtesy. But during the recent past, there had been many developments in equipment, techniques, and medicines that couldn't be learned in lectures.

After her arrival in Philadelphia, she had found out about Arundel Medical College and the fact that it was organized on the European model, with an associated infirmary. The college had a teaching staff, and the infirmary had a medical staff who served as consultants for local physicians, carried on private practices, and provided advanced training for students in the college. There had been times when she had wistfully wished that Woodruff could have made arrangements for her to live with a family that was less socially prominent and wealthy, but it had been of distinct advantage when her request for enrollment at Arundel had been summarily rejected because she was a woman. Randolph had referred the matter to Percival Joseph Wyndham. Arundel's license to teach and operate an infirmary in the city had been called into question, and she had been promptly enrolled.

Her concept of colleges, which had been formed in San Francisco, changed when she saw Arundel. The college was off Lombard Street, in an older section of the city near the river, and it occupied three buildings on a corner of a street of small, grimy shops, warehouses, and other old structures. One was a decrepit hotel that had been converted into offices on the lower floor and laboratories and lecture halls on the upper floors. Another was a clapboard building that had been

erected adjacent to the hotel building to house the
infirmary, and the third was a dingy greystone building that had been converted to accommodate lecture
halls and a surgical amphitheater.

The three buildings roughly represented the three
years of instruction, the greystone building with its
amphitheater and lecture halls for the lectures and
demonstrations of the first year, the former hotel building with its laboratories and lecture halls for the inter-
mediate students, and the infirmary for the advanced
instruction in diagnosis and treatment of patients under the supervision of a physician. Unlike many medical colleges, graded examinations were administered,
and there was a heavy attrition of students between
the first and second years. Some students left to apply
themselves to learning to read and write before again
attempting medicine, others left to go to colleges less
determined to keep them from pursuing a career in
medicine, and others remained in the first year of
instruction to try again.

A group of about twenty men was standing in front
of the greystone building. They were all first-year
students and less accustomed to seeing her, and several of them whistled and catcalled as she crossed the
street and went up the steps of the old hotel building.
A half-dozen men were standing and talking on the
steps, all second-year students who were accustomed
to her presence. A couple tipped their hats and spoke;
the remainder ignored her.

There was a quiet murmur of activity in the rooms
off the dim, expansive lobby, and two of the instructors
were arguing in a room along a corridor off the rear of
the lobby. Carpeting that had been on the wide,
sweeping staircase had been removed, and her heels
clicked against the bare wood of the steps as she

climbed the stairs. There was still a suggestion of the feel of a hotel about the place, the scent of people and clothes and an atmosphere of transience, and it was blended with the sharp odor of chemicals and the sweet, clinging stench of death. Tangeree turned into the wide corridor on the right at the top of the stairs, and walked along it. It was dim, the only light coming through a dirty window at the end. Most of the tall, heavy doors on each side were blocked, because the partitions between the rooms had been torn out to make them into larger rooms for laboratories and lecture halls. She stopped at the last door on the right, opened the door and went in.

The room was warm and bright from the sunlight streaming in the bare windows; the walls were lined with sinks, workbenches, and cabinets. A group of men varying in age from twenty to thirty stood by the windows. One of them took off his hat and bowed mockingly to Tangeree, looking at her with a sarcastic smile.

"Good morning, Miss Beaunais. I'm so pleased that you arrived before the unveiling."

"Why don't you shut up, Stokes?" one of the other men barked at him, then he looked at Tangeree and nodded. "Good morning, Miss Beaunais."

"Good morning, Mr. Carroll."

Stokes grunted and chuckled sourly, a couple of the other men smiled and spoke to Tangeree, and others nodded. Tangeree walked to a bench, put her satchel on it, opened it and took out her textbook. Of the ten men, one was hostile, three were friendly, and the remainder were either something in-between or indifferent. It was about the average for all the students.

During the first year, there had been some who had regarded her presence at the college as a joke.

That attitude had disappeared when the results of the examinations at the end of the first year had been posted in the lobby, and her name had been at the top of the list. Tangeree had succeeded in gaining the respect, and even admiration, of her fellow students and doctors alike.

18

THE DOOR OPENED quietly, and Doctor Frazier walked in with a bundle of notes and papers under his arm. He was a small, thin man who wore his black, thinning hair combed back tightly. The skin on his smoothly-shaven face was shiny and taut across the sharp bones of his face, and his small eyes were dark and piercing. Tangeree had heard a rumor that he had given up medical practice because he had made an error in diagnosis that had resulted in the death of a family member, and he was a bitter man. His habitual expression was a mocking half-smile, he was given to caustic, sarcastic comments, and he was an exacting instructor.

The men were suddenly silent. Frazier walked to a bench in a corner, put the papers on it, and thumbed through them. "Jones."

Jones jerked convulsively, then walked rapidly toward Frazier with an apprehensive expression. "Yes, Doctor Frazier?"

"Either you did a report on a kidney section while looking at a lung section, or you need to learn to write," Frazier said in a quiet, acid tone, cramming a sheaf of papers into Jones's hands. "Do it over. Plummer."

Plummer marched toward him, his face flushed. "Yes, Doctor Frazier?"

"You have written at length on how a heart functions," Frazier said, pushing a sheaf of papers at him. "What I wished to know is what you found that might indicate why it stopped functioning. Do it over."

The two men walked back toward the others, glumly looking through the papers while Frazier indulged in the casual cruelty of standing with his back to the room as he continued thumbing through the papers. Everyone waited tensely. Tangeree knew her report had been concise, accurate, and well-substantiated, but her heart pounded as the seconds dragged by and a minute passed. Then Frazier put the rest of the papers into a cabinet over the bench and closed it, and the collective soft sigh of relief was faintly audible. Frazier folded his hands behind his back as he walked away from the bench, and looked at Tangeree.

"Beaunais, the analysis of the urea content in the blood to determine kidney dysfunction was very astute. But kindly satisfy my curiosity and tell me why I find you continually fascinated with urea."

"I intend doing my thesis on urea analysis, Doctor Frazier."

There was a muffled sound of amusement from one of the men as Frazier nodded, and Frazier's eyes darted toward the man. "Please share your cause for mirth with us, Beck."

Beck was a tall, freckle-faced man with an irreverent sense of humor and a reputation as a comic. He grinned and shook his head. "I was just clearing my throat, Doctor Frazier."

"Indeed? In the unlikely event you matriculate, what do you intend writing your thesis on, Beck?"

Beck glanced around, scratching his head and grinning, and shrugged. "I hadn't thought about it much, Doctor Frazier. Hypogastria, I guess."

It was a term used by quacks who peddled elixirs and powders that purported to cure premature ejaculation, nocturnal emission, and other sexual dysfunctions in men. There was a stir of amusement, then silence. Then the silence stretched out. Frazier stared at Beck with his small, penetrating eyes, his lips twisted in his mocking half-smile. Beck's grin became strained, then it became sickly and faded. He looked away, then glanced back at Frazier. Frazier continued staring at him. Beck flushed hotly, and beads of sweat became visible on his face. The silence continued as Frazier stood motionless, his hands folded behind his back and his eyes riveted to Beck's face. Then Frazier turned and walked toward the tank, and Beck relaxed, wiping his face with his hand.

Frazier gathered up the canvas on top of the tank and tossed it onto a bench. "Let's take a look at our patient and see what we can determine by visual examination. What do you think brought him to his present state, Graham?"

The men trooped over to the tank and Tangeree walked toward it, and Graham looked in it, pondering. "It could have been a heart seizure, Doctor Frazier. The way the face is twisted indicates great pain."

"Most things that bring on a terminal condition also bring pain, Graham. Birth and death are painful undertakings. As is life. Mead?"

"Perhaps he strangled on something, Doctor Frazier. It looks like he was trying to breathe . . . ."

They continued, and Tangeree stood at one end of the tank and looked at the cadaver. The man had been about fifty, a little below average height, and about a hundred and forty pounds. There had been great pain, because it was still reflected on the features even though the man had been dead far longer than necessary for the muscles to relax and sag. The skin was a faint brownish-purple and the entire body was swollen, indicating advanced decay. But the lower stomach was more swollen than the rest of the body, and it was slightly darker in color.

Frazier looked at Tangeree. "Beaunais?"

"Perityphlitic abscess, Doctor Frazier."

Frazier looked at her unblinkingly for several seconds with his sneering smile, then slowly nodded. "On what do you base your diagnosis, Beaunais?"

"The discoloration and swelling in the iliac region, Doctor Frazier."

Frazier continued staring at her for a moment, then looked away. "I believe you're right, Beaunais, so we shall see. And you may be our surgeon for the day as a reward for agreeing with my diagnosis, so kindly prepare yourself. Plummer, see if your intelligence and mechanical ability are equal to the task of hooking up a water hose for the tank. Beck, you will enjoy the humor involved in searching for instruments and specimen trays. The rest of you see if your carousing of last night left you with sufficient strength to turn the tank so our surgeon may perform."

The men moved around, and Tangeree went to a row of rubber aprons hanging on wall hooks in a corner of the room. She took one down, took off her hat and hung it on the hook, then put on the apron and tied it. Her hair began coming down, and she pinned it back up and opened a cabinet by the wall hooks to get a pair of gloves. A wisp of hair came loose and hung over her face, and she pushed it back, looking through the gloves for a small pair.

"Beaunais, when you are quite finished with your toilette, your audience and your patient are waiting."

Tangeree pushed the door of the cabinet closed and walked back across the room, pulling on the long, heavy gloves. The tank was parallel to a bench and two feet from it, and the steel specimen trays and instruments were on the bench. She stepped around the tank and stood between it and the bench. Frazier stood on the other side of the tank, and the men gathered around him.

"Beaunais, bear in mind that the students enjoying the stimulation of their first year of lectures and demonstrations take our leavings, so we must arrange for some portion to remain intact. Now, where do you wish to begin carving on the goose?"

"In the abdominal region, Doctor Frazier."

"Very well. If you have espied something you wish to gaze at and meditate upon, we will wait. Otherwise, please proceed."

Tangeree picked up a scalpel with a straight, one-inch blade, turned back to the tank, and leaned over it. She placed the tip of the blade by the point of a pelvic bone and pressed down on it, drawing it across the body. The wall of the abdomen spread apart behind the blade from the pressure of the swelling, and a putrid stench of decay rose from the tank. There was a scuffle of feet as some of the men stepped back, choking and coughing, and others took out handkerchiefs and held them over their noses and mouths.

Her years of daily exposure to the excreta and odors of the ill had built up a defense against discomfort and disgust, and her only limitation was that she had to

be able to breathe. The foul, thick odor was just short
of being so powerful that it could overcome her. She
continued leaning over the tank, lifting the flap of
flesh on one side of the incision and cutting through
the skin, muscles, and peritoneum as she guided the
blade of the scalpel up toward the ribs. She turned
back the flaps, then cut in the other direction to the
edge of the pubic hair and laid back the flaps.

Frazier leaned over the other side of the tank and
looked at her with his mocking smile, impervious to
the odor. "I enjoy watching an enthusiastic surgeon at
work, Beaunais. Indeed, when you come to amputate
a leg, I believe you will amputate the patient and
leave the leg in place. But I fear you have dispersed
your audience, so perhaps you should use some water
to see if you can dispel some of the odor and draw
them back."

The water hose connected to the tap in the sink was
draped across the workbench between the tank and
the sink, and coiled in the bottom of the tank. Carroll
stepped to the sink and turned on the tap, and Tangeree picked up the end of the hose. It jerked and
spluttered, then water began gushing from it and
Tangeree put the end in the abdominal cavity. Water
filled the cavity and moved the intestines gently as it
began pouring out the sides of the cavity, thick with
the slimy fluids of decay. Some of the men opened windows, and fresh air swept into the room, dissipating
the odor.

"If we have removed the odor sufficiently to keep
from offending you, perhaps we can proceed," Frazier
said, glancing around at the men. "Each of you take
a specimen tray, and our surgeon will dole you out a
select portion of our goose for you to examine and
report upon. Plummer, let me prevail upon you not to

dwell upon the function of your portion. This is not anatomy, Plummer. What I wish to know is your findings on the changed state of the portion as compared to a perfect specimen. And don't use the word 'rotten,' Plummer. That is a most unscientific term . . . ."

He continued in his acid, biting voice, and the drain gurgled as the water flowed out of the cadaver and across the bottom of the tank. The internal organs bobbed, shreds of the peritoneum and other tissues floated on the surface of the water, and ropy strings of semi-solid fluids of decay swirled out of the stomach cavity and floated in the water toward the drain. A spot of lighter color surfaced near the large intestine and disappeared again. Tangeree looked, and leaned closer. The tiny organ normally attached to the lower curve of the bowel appeared to be missing. She became aware that Frazier was talking to her, and she looked up.

"I beg your pardon, Doctor Frazier. The veriform appendix is gone."

"That is an inaccurate observation," he replied caustically. "If you will examine closely, you will find some portion of it remaining. It isn't uncommon for the more delicate tissues to deteriorate very rapidly when perityphlitic abscess occurs, Beaunais, as you should know. And further deterioration is occurring even as we ponder the matter. Meanwhile, we have Beck standing here with his specimen tray and eager for his portion so he can see if he can find something amusing about it. As our surgeon, what portion do you suggest we give him?"

"Perhaps the spleen, Doctor Frazier?"

Frazier blinked, his twisted smile almost changing to one of amusement, then it changed back to a sneer as he nodded. "Beaunais, I perceive that Beck isn't the

only one among us with a view toward the lighter side
of life, and I agree that he could well do with more
spleen. By all means, serve him an additional portion."

Beck moved closer, holding a specimen tray and
grinning widely. Tangeree plugged the end of the
hose into the drain as she picked up the scalpel. She
fished in the water in the body cavity for the organ,
cut off a small slice of it, and put it in the tray. The
others were in a line behind him with trays, and they
moved forward and passed the tank as Frazier kept
up a running commentary in his mocking, caustic voice
and Tangeree cut slices from the internal organs and
dropped them into the trays. There was a small, tumor-
like growth on one side of the stomach, and she cut it
and a slice of the stomach off and put it in Carroll's
tray.

"Excellent, excellent," Frazier said. "Your youth and
manly beauty have rewarded you with an opportunity
to do a comparative report, Carroll. But I fear we have
more guests than we have portions presently available,
Beaunais, so perhaps you should bare more of the
goose."

Tangeree sliced open the skin up the center of the
chest with the scalpel, then took the bone saw off the
bench, sawed up through the sternum to the top of
the rib cage, and opened the chest cavity. The rest
of the men filed past as she cut slices from the chest
organs and put them in the trays, and the men scattered around the room and stood at the benches, examining the specimens and separating fragments to put
on glass slides for microscopic examination. Frazier
walked around the room, looking and commenting,
and Tangeree leaned over the tank and examined the
large intestine.

Part of the wormlike veriform appendix remained

on the deep curve of the intestine, but it was hollow and open on the end. The water was settling in the stomach cavity, becoming dark, thick, and putrid, and she put the hose back in it. The spot of lighter color swam to the surface of the water near the large intestine again, and she dipped her hand under it as it started to sink. The water drained off the palm of the rubber glove, leaving a small, spongy ball of matter half the size of a marble. She took a specimen tray off the bench, dropped the specimen into it, and looked at it closely.

"Didn't you have breakfast this morning, Beaunais? Or are you simply attempting to make your eyes serve as a microscope?"

Tangeree looked at Frazier as he stood on the other side of the tank with his hands folded behind him, bobbing up and down on his toes. She held out the tray, and he shrugged.

"It appears that you have managed to discover a bit of putrescence in a decaying body, Beaunais. Do you find that remarkable?"

"I found it right here, Doctor Frazier. And the end of the veriform appendix is open. Do you think this might have come from it?"

"I think we have here a classic instance of peri-typhlitic abscess, and I think I prefer to leave speculation to others, Beaunais. And, unlike many of my colleagues, I readily admit that there are many things that we don't know."

"Have you ever seen anything like this before, Doctor Frazier? And have you seen the veriform appendix in this condition in other cadavers?"

"I have, yes. And if you remember our dissection of a month or so ago, the entire caecum was open. If you will recall my comment of a few minutes ago, the more

delicate tissues deteriorate very rapidly when perityphlitic abscess has been the cause of death. As to
whether or not I've seen anything like that before, I
don't recall having done so. But if it interests you, by
all means do a report on it." He turned and walked
away from the tank, glancing around. "I require two
assistants with strong backs and weak minds to remove
the tank so the students in the next building may revel
in the mysteries of anatomy, and I see I am spoiled
for choice here. Beck, perhaps you will find the
undertaking amusing. Jones, judging from your girth,
you could well do with some exercise . . . ."

Tangeree lifted the large intestine to cut off the
veriform appendix. The intestine was iridescent and
swollen with decay. But, strangely, it was empty, col-
lapsing in her hand. She cut off the veriform appendix
and the portion of the intestine immediately around
it, put it in the specimen tray, and turned off the water
in the sink. Beck and Jones walked over to take the
tank away, and she put the plug in the drain and dis-
connected the drain hose. They put the canvas cover
on it and wheeled it away, and Tangeree washed off
the gloves and apron, took them off and hung them
on the edge of the sink to dry, and carried the specimen tray over to the bench where she had left her
satchel.

The veriform appendix appeared to have ruptured,
rather than deteriorated through decay. Tangeree
looked at the tiny shred of tissue through the microscope, turning the knobs on the side of the base to
move the slide back and forth a fraction of an inch,
then took out the slide and cut another tiny piece from
the fragmented edge of the organ. She put it on a
slide and placed it in the base of the microscope, then
focused the lens again. Fibers had frayed from the

edge as a result of the action of the water, appearing like thick ropes through the microscope, but the edge was as thick as any other part of the wall of the organ. If it had deteriorated through decay, the edge would be thin and a mass of fibers. She took a notepad and pencil from her satchel, and began sketching the microscopic view of the section of organ.

The duration of many of the laboratory classes was a matter of choice, and some of the men began leaving. Tangeree probed at the spongy ball of matter in the specimen tray with a scalpel, separating it. It appeared to be coagulated pus, not unlike the core of a boil or some other infection. Then the tip of the scalpel ground through something more solid and a different material. She carefully scraped the matter away from it. It was a tiny brown ball embedded in the matter and it was decayed, crumbling as the blade of the scalpel touched it. She leaned closer, looking. It was strangely like a seed or something similar, about the size of a small cherry pit. She took slides out of the box and laid them in a row, put daubs of the brown material and the yellow matter on them, then went to a cabinet for the materials to stain the slides.

There was the scuffle of a shoe on the floor by her as she bent over the slides on the bench, staining them in sets of different colors, and she looked up. It was Carroll. He leaned against the bench, smiling down at her.

"Thank you for the tumor."

His tone was humorous, inviting a joking rejoinder. And he was handsome and pleasant, with strong, smoothly shaven features and a twinkling, amiable smile. But his approach was a preliminary to coaxing her to go to lunch with him or for a walk in one of the parks after the day's instruction was over. He was a vibrantly masculine man, and one part of her mind glowed with satisfaction from his attention. But that same quality stirred memories of cruel faces smiling down at her, fists striking her, pain and degradation, distant memories in which details had melted into a penetrating terror that made her mouth dry and her heart race.

"You're welcome."

It was a gauche, cloddish reply, and she felt her cheeks flush as she looked back down at the slides. He leaned closer to look at the slides, his tall, muscular body looming over her and almost touching her. One part of her mind interpreted it as an immediate, dire threat, and another knew that he wasn't going to attack her. Her hand trembled as she steeled herself and kept herself from leaping away from him, and a drop of stain fell from the dropper and splashed on the bench. He didn't appear to notice, and he moved back, looking at the sketches on the bench by the microscope.

"I wish I could draw like you do. That's almost like looking at a tintype. Did they teach drawing at the college in San Francisco?"

"Yes."

He made a sound in his throat, nodding. Then there was silence. Another talent she had developed in San Francisco was conversational ability, and she could maintain a flow of polite chatter to keep silence from developing. But only with women and couples. She licked her lips and steadied her hand as she dipped the dropper and stained another slide. Carroll looked at the door, then back down at her.

"There goes Beck, and I could use some cheering up after pathology. But it would cheer me up even more if you'd have lunch with me. There's a very good restaurant not far away."

"Thank you for the invitation, but this will keep me for some time, and I'd like to prepare for the class on *materia medica* this afternoon."

His lips tightened slightly and his eyes momentarily reflected disappointment, then he smiled and silently nodded as he walked away from the bench. Tangeree looked back down at the slides. The first ones she had prepared were dry, and she picked up one and put it in the microscope.

The yellow matter was coagulated pus, a mass of fatty tissue serum, dead blood corpuscles, and debris from fragmented corpuscles. And the brown material was some kind of vegetable fiber. She frowned in perplexity as she looked at all the slides, then she went to the instrument cabinet for tweezers and carefully pulled the material in the specimen tray apart. The brown ball embedded in the pus looked more and more like an ordinary cherry pit, and there even seemed to be an outer hull that was tougher than the interior. She pulled off fragments of it and prepared more slides, staining them different colors to select the best contrast. Frazier left, the other men finished and left, and the room was quiet around her. She picked out the best of the slides, then began painstakingly sketching. The distant sounds in the building faded away, and the only noises were those coming through the windows from the street.

After an hour, footsteps began moving along the halls again, and there were faint sounds of laughter and voices. Tangeree finished, dumped the remainder of the specimen into a waste can, and washed the tray, slides, and instruments. She put on her hat and gathered up her things, and walked back along the corridor to the stairs. Students were walking along the hall, a few spoke, several nodded, and a couple looked at her with sneers. She went up another flight of stairs, along the corridor, and into a lecture hall. A dozen men were seated in the rear of the room, three spoke and smiled, several nodded, and one stared at her insolently. She could feel his eyes on her as she sat in the front row, sorting through her pencils and taking out a notepad. Then the instructor came in and walked to the lecture podium, and there was a shuffle in the rear of the room as the students sat up, taking out pencils and notepads.

The lecture was on general anesthetics, one of a series on anesthesia. Both nitrous oxide and sulphuric ether had been used for years as recreational intoxicants, and they had gradually found their way into use in medical practice as general anesthetics. Ether had become preferred, because it was liquid and easier to handle and use, but it had several serious shortcomings. It frequently produced headaches and nausea in a patient, and it was highly explosive. Chloroform had been developed, and had largely replaced ether. But the use of anesthetics at all was sometimes debated in general practice. Some patients refused to be anesthetized, and some doctors refused to administer anesthetics to women in childbirth because of the Biblical reference to pain during childbirth.

The instructor commented on the controversy, and looked at Tangeree and smiled. "We're uniquely fortunate in this class, because we can have a different viewpoint on the matter. What do you think, Beaunais?"

"I wouldn't hesitate to administer anesthetic to a woman during childbirth, Doctor Rochester."

"But you are familiar with the verse in *Genesis?*"

"Yes, but I don't interpret that as divine prohibition to administering anesthetic to a woman during childbirth, Doctor Rochester. In the same book in the Bible it relates how God made Adam sleep to remove his rib, and I don't think anyone would want to suggest that a woman is more capable of bearing pain than a man."

Laughter broke out in the rear of the room, and Rochester laughed heartily. He was one of the senior staff members in the college, and he had at first been extremely disgruntled over her enrollment. Then he had found her presence much easier to tolerate when her tuition had been paid promptly in advance every three months, in contrast to the irregular, piecemeal, and frequently late payments from many other students.

Rochester had both a Snow and a Clover inhaler, devices designed to cover a patient's mouth and nose and produce a chloroform vapor, and he had a bottle of chloroform. Two of the students volunteered to be anesthetized, and they moved chairs around and arranged them so they could lie down. Rochester demonstrated the use of the inhalers and how to gradually awaken a patient with cold compresses on the head, then the class broke up and the students straggled out, the two who had been anesthetized still unsteady on their feet and chuckling wryly as the others laughed at them.

It was midafternoon, the streets and sidewalks were busy, and the horse cars were crowded, people standing in the aisles and on the steps. A man gave Tangeree his seat, lifting his hat and pushing back into the people standing in the aisle to make room for her to sit down. She thought about the classes and puzzled over the fact of finding what appeared to be a cherry pit in a cadaver as she rode the car back to the train station. When she was on the train, she took out her sketches and notes and leafed through them and studied them as the train rocked and rumbled along the tracks to Germantown.

The groom was waiting at the station with the cabriolet, and Tangeree began looking through her stacks of medical journals for references to perityphlitic abscess as soon as she got to her rooms. At the same time that she had bought her books, she had bought a complete set of the *Columbia Journal of Medicine*, which she hadn't completed reading, and there were articles in other journals that she couldn't remember in detail and that might contribute to her understanding. A maid brought in a tray, and Tangeree munched the sandwiches and sipped the milk as she leafed through the journals, folded them open at articles on the subject and put them in a stack, and looked at others. The maid came and took the tray away. It seemed only minutes later that it was becoming too dim in the room to read, and she lit the gaslight on the wall and the lamp on her desk.

The housekeeper knocked on the door and called her to dinner. After dinner, the Randolphs usually sat in the parlor to have their coffee, and it was accepted practice for Tangeree to excuse herself when she had to study. She returned to her room, and continued looking through the journals. The stack of journals folded open at articles grew and the pile of journals she tossed aside turned into a mound, and the stack remaining to be looked through diminished. Then she finished, lit a cigarette, and began reading.

As in many things, there were divergent schools of thought. The condition had been known to the ancients as colic or iliac passion, identified by the symptoms of low-grade fever, nausea, constipation, and varying degrees of pain in the lower torso. Numerous anatomic, pathologic, and physiologic studies had established that the disease was an inflammation, but the origin of the inflammation hadn't been definitely established. It was generally thought that the point of origin was the caecum and general region of the head of the colon, which was the genesis of the name perityphlitis, meaning inflammation of the peri-caecal tissues.

A minority of opinion that wasn't supported by the resounding, well-known names of medical authority suggested that the inflammation might originate in the veriform appendix. An article in one of the journals related the experience of a physician who had introduced a needle into the iliac region of patients on three different occasions and drawn off pus, temporarily relieving the condition. The physician had aimed the needle toward the veriform appendix. Another article described a pathological examination of a patient who had died from perityphlitis. The death was attributed to inflammation of the veriform appendix that had been caused by a foreign body. The physician had found a watermelon seed that had become lodged in the veriform appendix.

And there was personal experience. Fever, nausea, constipation, and pain in the lower torso described bowel congestion, which was treated by a purge. But she could remember intuitive warnings against a purge in some instances. The fever had seemed a little too high, the pain a little too severe. She could remember a pattern she had found among instances of chronic stomach pains over a period of time and severe illness and death following a purge, and she could remember a Christmas Eve long before when she had sat through the night and looked at a pale, wan face as the mill stamps pounded and death drew near.

The week was divided into three full days and two half days of instruction, with two classes each week in physiology, pathology, chemistry and *materia medica*. The report on the specimen didn't have to be turned in until Thursday of the following week, and she had a long report in chemistry that was due on Monday. But the subject was intriguing, giving her a feel of leaving the well-worn paths and venturing into relatively new territory, and she worked feverishly through the weekend to finish the chemistry report and have the pathology report ready on Monday.

The report was enormously long and thick, with the sketches of the microscopic views and all the applicable references from the journals written out in full. On Sunday afternoon, she had the chemistry report finished and she was hesitating over the conclusions in the pathology report, unsure of whether or not to include a comment on the possibility that the inflammation had been brought to an acute stage by a purge. The conclusion was based primarily on experience, but the caecum in the cadaver had felt empty and it could be attributed to an observation. She continued working on the report, and had it finished late that night.

Frazier looked at the report when she gave it to him the next morning, thumbing the edges of the pages and weighing it in his hand. "You produced this book as a result of that bit of putrescence you found, Beaunais? I'll have to watch that you don't come into possession of a gallstone, or you might have me reading until winter."

"The analysis led to some general observations and

conclusions on the nature of perityphlitic abscess,
Doctor Frazier."

Frazier grunted sourly and looked at her with his
habitual sneering half-smile as he tucked the report
under his arm and moved away, but Tangeree had
become accustomed to some of the nuances in his
mannerisms and she could see that he was pleased by
the thick report. Of all the staff, he had been the one
most unconcerned over the presence of a woman
among the students. She had received her share of the
gratuitous scathing remarks he made to everyone, but
in a number of ways he had tacitly acknowledged the
fact that she was far more advanced than most of the
students. And she had received more than her share
of attention from him, because he devoted more effort
to students he considered more promising.

He was impatient with customary courtesies and
rarely observed them with anyone, staff or students,
but he usually spoke to Tangeree when they met outside the laboratory. However, she passed him as she
came into the building the following day and spoke
to him, and he didn't reply. He looked at her with his
mocking smile, then silently nodded and brushed past
her. Tangeree thought about it uneasily, wondering
if he were in a particularly bad mood, or if it might
have something to do with the report.

On Thursday, he had the report among the papers
under his arm when he came into the room. The reports were due from the others, and they gathered
around him to submit them. Then he handed back a
couple of reports that had been rewritten and still
didn't satisfy him. Tangeree waited nervously as he
castigated the others and pushed the reports at them.
Then he put the stack of papers in a cabinet without
calling her name.

He had borrowed a library of dried tissue slides from a medical college in Boston, and Tangeree found them fascinating, but she had difficulty concentrating on them and the sketches she made as she wondered why he had brought the report to class with him. The less diligent of the students finished looking at the slides and making an effort to sketch a few, and they left. Others began leaving as the hours dragged by, and Tangeree became involved in sketching a series of slides of malignant tumor tissues. Then she finished, and the room seemed quiet. She glanced around as she began collecting up her notepads and putting the slides back in the wooden box. Frazier, standing in front of a window with his back to her, was the only other person in the room.

Frazier took the report out of the cabinet as she put the box of slides with the others, and he leafed through it as he walked toward her. "You prepared a very interesting report here, Beaunais. And it is long, but certainly it isn't too long for its span. Somehow you leap from the morsel of pus you found to the conclusion that the demise of our cadaver was occasioned by his taking a cathartic."

His tone lacked the biting, scathing intensity that warned of a tirade, but it was still heavy with sarcasm. Tangeree cleared her throat nervously. "The caecum was empty, Doctor Frazier."

"Did Doctor Beckman omit mentioning the function of the sphincter muscle in your anatomy lectures, or were you asleep when he mentioned it?"

"There is ordinarily some fecal material remaining in the caecum after the sphincter muscle relaxes, Doctor Frazier."

"That is an unwarranted generalization, Beaunais. If someone died of starvation, for example, one would hardly expect to find a glutted caecum, would one? It is true that there is usually a certain amount of fecal material in the caecum in most cadavers, and its absence might be noteworthy for one reason or another. However, a pathologic finding of involvement of a cathartic in a death would depend upon a chemical analysis of the contents of the intestines and determination of the presence of a cathartic. It is not sufficient to squeeze the caecum and remark that it seems empty, Beaunais."

Tangeree hesitated, then nodded. "Yes. While writing the report, I allowed my conclusions to be influenced by my experiences while working with my mother."

"Ah, yes, your mother the herbalist," he chuckled dryly. "Did she purge so many to death that it influences you that deeply?"

"My mother has never purged anyone to death, Doctor Frazier," Tangeree replied firmly, her temper stirring. "My mother is a physician of great talent and ability. And she deals with illness far more effectively than many doctors."

Frazier suddenly laughed, shaking his head. "Beaunais, hod carriers would deal with illness more effectively than many doctors. At least they would leave the afflicted alone so they might recover, instead of bleeding, purging, and puking them to death."

It was the first time Tangeree had seen him laugh. She smiled, and looked at the report. "Shall I rewrite the report, Doctor Frazier?"

He shook his head, looking down at it and leafing through the pages. "No, I see no reason to, Beaunais. I don't agree with your conclusion that the veriform appendix is the site of inflammation in perityphlitis. And this fellow who found the watermelon seed might

have found a cantaloup seed instead if he had been
eating one of those before he did the post mortem,
because it very likely got in there on his cuff or lapel.
But your conclusion is supported by the views of
others, and this sketch here is undeniably vegetable
matter of one kind or another. The report is thought-
provoking, and it's more than satisfactory."

"When I saw you had it with you, I thought it was
because you were going to return it, Doctor Frazier."

"No, I was going to suggest that I show it to one of
the infirmary staff and talk to him about beginning
your training there a few months early. It won't be
long until I'll be hard pressed to keep you busy for
more than one class a week, because you actually approach being as well-informed as you consider yourself. Doctor Rochester feels the same. You now have
two free afternoons, and that would give you four
afternoons each week for training in the infirmary.
Shall I talk to someone there?"

Tangeree's smile had been growing as he talked,
and she nodded. "Yes, please, Doctor Frazier."

"I happen to be on fairly good terms with Doctor
Palmer. Shall I talk to him?"

Palmer, the most well-known doctor on the staff,
had trained in Edinburgh and Vienna. He was also extremely selective in choosing students to work under
his supervision. The other doctors had six to eight
students to supervise, but Palmer always had visiting
doctors working with him and supervised only two
students. Tangeree's smile became brilliant, and she
nodded eagerly. "Yes, please, Doctor Frazier!"

19

TANGEREE'S HEELS clumped against the rough wooden stairs as she climbed them, holding up the front of her skirt with one hand and carrying her satchel in the other. There were no risers between the steps, the walls were of the same rough, unpainted wood as the stairs, and long, dim rooms opened off both sides of each landing. They were like caverns, with tightly spaced rows of crude wooden bunks on each side of the center aisle from which movements were vaguely visible, hands lifted and pleading for help. A loud, rising and falling chorus of moans and groans came from the rooms, which emanated a powerful stench of urine, feces, unwashed bodies, and suppuration—the sounds and odors of a hospital.

She reached the top of the stairs. A small laboratory across the landing had a desk in a corner, several chairs around the walls, and medical journals and other reading material scattered around, but no one was in it. Other rooms opened off a short corridor to the left, and a long room for patients was at the end of the corridor. Here the bunks were spaced farther apart, it was light from sunshine beaming in the windows, and it smelled strongly of carbolic acid. Several men

were standing at the end of one of the bunks near the
door, discussing the patient. Tangeree walked along
the corridor toward the room.

A patient jerked a light, dingy blanket over himself
as she stepped into the doorway, and other lifted their
heads and looked at her. The conversation between
the men at the end of the bunk began dying away as
they turned and looked. Tangeree looked at the large
red-headed man in the center of the group as he
turned.

"Doctor Palmer, sir? I'm Beaunais."

Other patients stirred as they heard a feminine
voice, lifting themselves to an elbow and looking at
her curiously. Palmer looked at her, holding a sheaf
of papers and stroking his beard, then nodded. "Well,
come on in, Beaunais. This is Phelps, that's Murphy,
there's Doctor Henderson, Doctor Griffin. . . ."

There were seven of them. Two were a little older
than her and students, and the other five were doctors
who varied in age from thirty to fifty. They all nodded
as Palmer introduced them, their attitudes ranging
from friendly to neutral. The only disapproval was on
the oldest doctor's face, and it had distinctly fatherly
overtones.

Palmer was about forty-five, a large healthy looking
man whose head was a blur of tones of red with his
ruddy complexion and red hair, beard, and mustache.
He looked amiable enough, but he also appeared to be
unsure of what to do with her. The patients craned
their necks and the silence stretched out as Palmer
finished introducing the others and looked at her
again, stroking his beard. Then he looked at one of the
men.

"Show her around, Murphy."

"Yes, sir. Show her everything?"

"Whatever you need to know, she needs to know," Palmer replied impatiently, turning away and looking at the patient and papers in his hand. "All right, we used ten percent carbolic in linseed oil on this one as well, but this time we have some suppuration. . . ."

His voice faded to a rumbling murmur behind Tangeree as she stepped back into the corridor and walked along it with Murphy. He motioned toward the laboratory. "You can leave your satchel in there, and we'll start downstairs."

Tangeree put the satchel in a corner in the room, and they walked down the stairs to the first floor where they began going through the infirmary, Murphy pointing and explaining. Most of the patients were charity cases, for whom the city paid the college a small amount for care and treatment. They had various diseases and injuries and were crowded together into the long, noisy, odorous rooms, with one or two orderlies to clean each room and attend to the patients. The orderlies were informally trained through experience, most of them older men who risked contracting contagious disease because they were unable to get work elsewhere, most of them moving stolidly about at their own pace, hardened and indifferent to the wails of the feverish, pain-racked forms on the bunks around them.

Conditions here were better than at most hospitals. In some, the incidence of blood poisoning and hospital gangrene was always high, and stumps of amputated limbs that became honeycombed with pockets of pus were almost normal. Many hospitals were abandoned and burned down because they became pestilential with erysipelas and pyemia, the mortality rate for patients with open wounds reaching sometimes as high as one hundred percent. Those conditions had been avoided in the infirmary by periodic scrubbing of the floors and walls with carbolic acid, boiling bedclothes in carbolic acid, and using other procedures developed by Lister. There was still some inflammation of wounds and cross-contagion between patients because of the crowded conditions and the method of the indifferent orderlies, and as a result of the fact that not all doctors who worked in the infirmary were supporters of Lister's techniques, but it wasn't epidemic.

Palmer was a staunch supporter of Lister's techniques, and Murphy pointed out Palmer's patients as they worked their way back up the stairs to the upper floors. Most of the patients on the upper floors were laborers and others who were either in critical condition or couldn't be cared for at home for one reason or another, and they were paying for their treatment and care. The rooms had better ventilation and more lighting, they were less crowded, and the orderlies there were more industrious. The patients gaped in shock and snatched at bedclothes as Tangeree entered the rooms and walked through them with Murphy. Murphy talked about the patients, and he also tried to talk to Tangeree about herself. She evaded his questions and turned the discussion back to the patients, but he was persistent and rapidly became more friendly toward her—more friendly than she liked. Then his questions about her stopped when he asked where she lived.

"With friends," she replied. "The Randolphs, in Germantown."

They were walking up the stairs to the top floor, and he stopped and looked at her in surprise. "You live with some of the Randolphs? In Germantown?"

"Yes."

"*The* Randolphs?"

"Julian and Phoebe Randolph."

His eyes moved down her, then back up to her face. "Why are you attending medical college?"

"To learn how to help people who are ill and injured."

He scratched his chin musingly, looking away, then nodded and began walking on up the steps. "Come on, and I'll show you the surgical room that Doctor Palmer uses."

The surgical room was equipped for Lister's techniques, and it reeked of carbolic acid. There was a large atomizer machine for spraying carbolic acid into the air while surgery was in progress, there were pans for washing instruments in carbolic acid solution, and trays where instruments were kept under cloths saturated with carbolic acid solution. Cabinets held rows of instruments, chloroform inhalers and other equipment was on shelves, and the surgical table was an adjustable type, with which the patient could be raised to a sitting position or lowered to a lying position. Murphy went for the key to the medicine room. When he unlocked it, Tangeree saw that it was lined with shelves filled with surgical dressings and boxes and bottles of medicines. The laboratory, which was fully equipped, also served as a sitting room, with chairs, reading material, ashtrays, and a pan for making coffee over a burner.

Tangeree and Murphy returned to the room where Palmer and the others were examining and discussing the patients. Tangeree stood on the edge of the group and tried to ignore the curious stares of the patients. As she listened to the aside comments from the group, she found out that one of the doctors was from Philadelphia, and the other four had come from various

cities in the East to work with and learn from Palmer.
In listening to their discussion, she found out that
using Lister's techniques was anything but an established and standardized routine.

The objective in the techniques was to kill the bacteria that caused suppuration in open wounds, but
circumstances sometimes made it difficult. A putty
made of whitening and a solution of carbolic acid in
linseed oil was the preferred dressing for a wound, but
there were some types of wounds for which it was
necessary to use cloth dressings. And while most of
the surgical patients in the room were there for amputations and limb or torso injuries, there was one
who had a head injury and carbolic acid couldn't be
used because of the danger to his eyes. Unknown fac-
tors were also present, because a given dilution of
carbolic acid would prevent inflammation in some instances and not in other similar instances. And there
was the human factor. Palmer examined a long, deep
wound on the thigh of the patient in the bunk by the
door, then began upbraiding him for scratching it.

"But that itching drives me plumb crazy sometimes,
Doctor!"

"You'll wish you had it there to itch if you keep on
scratching it!" Palmer barked irately. "If you get inflammation started in that leg, it's going to have to
come off there!"

"Well, I'll do my best, Doctor."

"You'll do better than you've been doing, or I'll fix
you so you will," Palmer said warningly as he moved
away from the bunk and toward the door, pointing
his finger at the man. "If I find one more scratch
mark on there, your hands are going to be tied to the
head of that bunk!"

The man looked away and nodded, his face red

with chagrin, and the doctors chuckled and talked with Palmer as they followed him out and along the corridor. Tangeree followed the others, stopping with them at the end of the corridor. The doctors made parting comments and left, their shoes thumping heavily down the stairs, and Palmer nodded to Murphy and Phelps and they left. He looked at Tangeree and motioned toward the laboratory, and she followed him into it.

"I liked your paper on perityphlitis," he said as he walked to the desk and sat down. "I don't like to have more than two students at one time, and I've never before taken a student who wasn't in the third year. And needless to say, I've never had a student who was a woman. But Doctor Frazier recommended you highly, and I liked the cast of mind that your paper indicated. And I liked the viewpoint, because I'm leaning toward the veriform appendix as the origin of inflammation in perityphlitis."

"I'm flattered that you liked the paper, Doctor Palmer, and I enjoyed doing it. Nothing I read holds out any promise of cure, however."

"No, there's no cure. I've incised and put in a trocar to try to drain off the inflammation, but I've had very poor success."

"You've incised the abdomen?"

He nodded and shrugged. "When a patient is going to die, I do whatever I can. I've incised for that and ovarian tumor, but it's a last resort, of course. Even with Lister's techniques, inflammation is almost inevitable when the abdomen is incised, and it's always fatal." He sat back in his chair, stroking his beard. "When you're in surgery you'll get soaked in carbolic, so we'll have to think of some way to keep you from leaving here smelling like a carbolic factory."

"I can do the same thing that Phelps and Murphy do, Doctor Palmer."

"No, the smell of carbolic might very well be an improvement over how they would otherwise smell, but it wouldn't be for you," he chuckled, and nodded toward a closet at the side of the room. "That's full of clutter, and you can clean it out and use it for changing. Bring an old dress and whatever you wear under it, and you'd also be wise to bring a rubber swimming cap or something to cover your hair. You can leave them there and keep them locked in the closet."

"Very well, Doctor Palmer. I appreciate your consideration."

Palmer nodded in dismissal, gathering up papers from his desk and looking at them. Tangeree went to the corner for her satchel and started to leave, but Palmer's voice stopped her.

"Incidentally, Beaunais, what's your mother's name?"

"Yvonne," she replied, turning back.

"Yes, that's right," he chuckled, nodding. "When I first heard your name, I thought it was very familiar. Then when Doctor Frazier mentioned that your mother was an herbalist, it began coming back to me. I used to have a friend who spoke very highly of your mother."

"Was it someone my mother treated?"

"No, he was a doctor who worked with her, Doctor Charles Dawson. Is the name familiar to you?"

Tangeree blinked, taken aback. Then she nodded. "Yes, sir. My mother spoke of him often, and I met him once. That was years ago, during the War."

"During the War? Was that before he was wounded?"

"He was wounded?"

"Yes, he lost his right arm. And it took all the life out of him, I understand. It does that to many, and I understand how it would be particularly bad for a doctor, because a doctor needs his hands. He was in some little town in Mississippi the last I heard of him, teaching or something. . . ."

His voice faded and he looked away, pursing his lips and frowning sadly as he mused. Then he shrugged and sighed heavily as he shuffled the papers and looked at them again, and Tangeree turned and walked toward the stairs.

The mention of Charles Dawson had cast a pall over the pleasure and excitement of working in the infirmary under Palmer's supervision. The memory of much of the trip on the riverboat was blurred by time, but the memory of the night Charles Dawson had been on the boat was still sharp and clear, etched in her mind. Adulthood had brought an understanding of her mother's viewpoint, and understanding had brought tormenting guilt over what she had done to her mother. In the twisted, tortured complex of reactions to the rape by the renegades and the terror of fleeing for safety from the War, she had violently rejected the thought of sharing any aspect of her mother's life with another. She had demanded everything from her mother. And her mother had given her everything.

During the brief time she had spent in Virginia City after college in San Francisco, she had tried to broach the subject with her mother so she could apologize or at least say something in acknowledgement of the sacrifice her mother had made. Her mother had veered away from the subject of Charles Dawson, apparently still finding her own memories of that night on the riverboat too painful to discuss. And Tangeree's guilt had become excruciating, an agony of remorse every time she thought about the subject.

Hearing about Dawson placed her in a quandary of indecision. If she couldn't broach the subject in person, with the advantage of being able to detect and convey nuances of communication, it seemed unwise to attempt to address it in the blunt, crude contact of a letter. At the same time, it seemed reasonable that her mother might want to know about Dawson. But it was also possible that whatever relief or pleasure her mother would gain from hearing about him would be more than offset by the sorrow of knowing that he had been wounded, that he had lost an arm, and that the loss had affected him emotionally, as it did so many.

A possible solution was to contact Dawson herself. They had met and discussed medicine and what she wanted to do, and it shouldn't seem strange to him to receive a chatty letter from her telling him about college. It was logical to assume that he didn't know where her mother was, particularly in view of the change of destination from California to Virginia City, and he might be eager to write to her if he could find out. But she had to find out where Dawson was before she could write him.

Her attempts to find Dawson's whereabouts were made more difficult by her changed schedule. Frazier and Rochester had expressed confidence that she could manage pathology and *medica materia* with only one class each week, but it was difficult. The schedule of five full days each week was grueling. She had to work until late each night and through each weekend to keep abreast of the necessary studying, reading, and reports, and the four afternoons each week with Palmer were filled with things that were new to her. Dawson wasn't listed in the register of doctors in the college library and Palmer didn't encourage idle conversation, but during a relaxed moment in the laboratory she found out that Dawson had been in Livermore.

Livermore was near Natchez, and another doctor on the staff was from Natchez. From him, Tangeree got the name and address of a Doctor Elmo Johnson in Natchez, and she wrote to him and inquired about Dawson, referring to him as a family friend. Johnson replied, informing her that Dawson had moved from Livermore some years before and gone to Meridian, and he included the name and address of a Doctor Clarence Ryan in Meridian in his letter. Then her search came to a dead end. Tangeree wrote Ryan, and he wrote back that Dawson had left Meridian two or three years before and he didn't know his whereabouts.

It was tempting to mention Dawson in a letter to her mother, to try to relieve her guilt to at least some degree by telling her mother the little she had found out about him, but she resisted the temptation. Her mother's letters continued arriving at their unvarying weekly intervals, and the one she wrote after learning about Tangeree's change in schedule and assignment to the infirmary was ecstatic. She mentioned the many things she had read about Palmer and his accomplishments, and she asked for details on Tangeree's training in the infirmary. There was little to relate at first, because Tangeree spent hours rolling bandages and coating silk and linen thread with beeswax and shoemaker's wax, and twisting it into two- and four-ply strengths for ligatures and sutures. She learned how to dilute carbolic acid with linseed oil and mix putty for dressings, and how to sterilize the instruments in carbolic acid and put them in a rigidly designated order on the trays in the surgical room. And she learned how to sharpen scalpels, honing the edges on whetstone, then leather, and then oiled silk to bring them to keen perfection.

The patients and orderlies became accustomed to seeing her. Palmer occasionally let her change a dressing, and he nodded in satisfaction at the strong, neat wrappings. Some of the patients had to undergo surgery several times for repairs to mangled limbs and to have stumps of amputated limbs cleansed of infection caused by bacteria that had found a gap in the antiseptic procedures, and Palmer began allowing her in the surgical room. She learned anesthetic procedures, assisted in passing instruments, and pumped the handle on the carbolic acid atomizer machine as it hissed and filled the surgical room with a reeking mist that burned the eyes and stung the nose and throat.

She also learned diagnostic procedures, the careful analysis of the symptoms and the combinations of symptoms, and the use of the clinical thermometer, the improved stethoscope, the laryngoscope, the ophthalmoscope, and the other diagnostic instruments. The diseases and conditions were familiar from childhood, but the names used to identify them were different in most instances and the method of arriving at conclusions was different. Instead of evaluating all the symptoms together to identify the disease or condition, the symptoms and evidence from the diagnostic instruments were used as paths to wend through the various possibilities of diseases and conditions. And instead of heating water to make an infusion of some fragrant herb, the pharmacopeia standard for the disease or condition was taken from the shelf in the medicine room.

There was a constant flow of patients through the

infirmary, the destitute staggering in, being brought in by the police, or being brought in by equally destitute relatives, and others arriving in wagons and carriages. The infirmary was close enough to a foundry, several mills, and other manufacturing concerns along the river to receive many accident victims, and a large proportion of the patients were injured rather than ill. The infirmary almoner divided the patients among the doctors, and Palmer's reputation brought him a larger share of those who were able to pay. Palmer attended to patients in his private practice during the mornings and spent the afternoons at the infirmary, and there were indications that he had a highly remunerative practice. The doctors who came to work with him and to learn from him were there for varying periods, some for two or three weeks and others for a month or more, and there were four to six of them all the time.

The doctors usually observed in surgery, with Phelps and Murphy assisting Palmer. Palmer gradually allowed Tangeree to do more and to occasionally assist him. He grunted and nodded in satisfaction at the tiny, neat ligatures she tied and at her straight, even rows of sutures. When she administered anesthetic or pumped the atomizer machine and watched, she winced inwardly at the huge, clumsy knots that Phelps tied in ligatures with his thick, spatulate fingers, and both Murphy and Phelps pulled sutures tighter than necessary, which made the lines of flesh crooked and uneven as they healed.

What bothered her most was the general lack of consideration for the patients. The reputation of hospitals at large made most people regard them as the portals of death. And there was an even more widespread fear of general anesthesia because of the unbalanced view prompted by newspapers through publicizing the few errors and ignoring the many successes. Patients in agony from injuries were also stiff with terror when they were brought in. A chloroform inhaler was clamped on their face as they struggled weakly, and they passed into insensibility, every factor in the situation encouraging them to flee into death and draining them of the vital will they needed to fuel their body in its fight against the injuries and the assault with scalpels and saws. The method of treatment went against everything she had learned from her mother about the care of patients, and against what she had seen proven successful.

It also went against instinctive, imperative impulses that had been instilled in her from early childhood. These impulses asserted themselves on an afternoon during her second month of training in the infirmary. The almoner rushed up the stairs, with two workmen in grimy, sweat-stained clothes following him and carrying a third on a door, an accident victim with a crushed leg. Tangeree and Phelps were preparing dressings in the laboratory; Palmer and the others were with the patients. Tangeree snatched her rubber swimming cap out of the closet and led the men toward the surgical room as Phelps went for Palmer.

Tangeree pulled a sheet off a shelf as she walked into the surgical room, whipped it onto the table, and pulled on the cap and pushed her hair under it as the men lifted the injured man onto the table. Then the sight of his pale, pain-racked face struck a responsive chord within her as their eyes met, his glazed with terror. He wasn't a young man, and he didn't look like a strong-willed man. His left leg was crushed, a seemingly boneless, bloody appendage up to the knee, he had bled heavily, and he was panic-stricken. And he was in mortal danger of giving up. The other two men were following the almoner and carrying out the door they had used for a stretcher, and Tangeree called to them.

"What's his name?"

The men had looked at her curiously, as usual. The question puzzled them. They glanced at each other and looked back at her. "It's Shorty Cullen," one of them replied.

Tangeree nodded, stepping toward the table as the men went out and the heavy, hurried footsteps of Palmer and the others came along the corridor. She looked down at the man, smiling. "You're going to be all right, Mr. Cullen."

His eyes focused on her face, and he licked his lips dryly, his breath coming in shallow pants. "The wagon hit me . . . run right over me. . . ."

"Yes, I know, Mr. Cullen, but you're going to be all right now."

Palmer and the others rushed into the room in a heavy thudding of footsteps on the wooden floor, Palmer glancing at the man and barking orders. The man's lips moved, and Tangeree leaned lower and put her ear close to his lips, straining to hear what he said. It was a faint whisper of sound, in an interrogative tone. And it was something about dying.

She slipped effortlessly back into the pattern developed years before, smiling warmly and cheerfully, touching his face lightly and communicating concern, talking loudly, and encouraging him to summon his will. "No, you're going to be all right, Mr. Cullen. Your friends brought you here in plenty of time, and you're going to be all right. Doctor Palmer is going to take care of you, and he's done this many, many times. You're perfectly safe, and you don't have anything at all to worry about."

Fear still lurked in his eyes as she talked to him, but the terror disappeared. His lips twitched in a wan smile. Then Tangeree became aware of the silence in the room, and she glanced around. Two of the doctors were looking at her in amusement, one in perplexity, and one in understanding. Phelps and Murphy looked puzzled, glancing between her and Palmer. Palmer looked at her thoughtfully, rinsing his hands in a basin of carbolic acid solution. He glanced at Phelps, then looked back at Tangeree.

"Give her the inhaler, Phelps."

Tangeree took the inhaler from Phelps and twisted the valve on the chloroform chamber to start it trickling into the felt in the front of the inhaler. She looked back down at the man on the table. "Now just breathe deeply, Mr. Cullen. This won't hurt you, because we use it all the time and it's perfectly safe. I'll put this over your mouth and nose, and you'll get sleepy. Just go ahead and go to sleep, because it's perfectly safe."

The apprehension started to intensify in his eyes as he looked at the inhaler, but it faded as she continued talking to him. She put the inhaler over his mouth and nose, smiling and talking encouragingly. He looked into her eyes, breathing deeply, and his eyelids began drooping.

The others moved around the room, preparing, and the atomizer began hissing and filling the room with its spray. The man's eyelids closed, and Tangeree put the strap on the inhaler around the man's head and placed her finger on the pulse at the side of his throat. His pulse was steady and strong. She thumbed back one of his eyelids and looked, then nodded to Palmer.

The ragged, bloody trousers leg flopped into the can under the surgical table. The bone saw grated and whined minutes later, Palmer grunted with effort, and the leg thumped into the can, the shoe sticking up above the top. Palmer stepped away from the table and washed and dried his hands, watching Phelps suture and put on the dressing. Phelps finished, Palmer nodded to Murphy at the atomizer, and the machine stopped hissing.

"That's a good stump, Doctor Palmer," one of the doctors said, then laughed. "But I thought Beaunais was going to talk his leg off before you got to it."

Palmer smiled and shook his head, stepping to the table and feeling Cullen's pulse. "In Edinburgh, I knew a man named Soames who used to do that all the time. Any patient of his who died had to get away from him, because he talked them into living. And feel his pulse—it should be going fifty to the dozen, but it's as steady as mine."

One of the doctors snorted skeptically. "I'll depend on a sharp knife and a fast saw myself."

Palmer nodded and shrugged. "I will, too, because I have trouble talking the iceman out of a quarter's worth of ice for twenty-five cents. Murphy, go get some orderlies and get him into a bunk. Beaunais, you and Phelps clean up in here. Gentlemen, we can return to what we were doing and finish it up, if you like."

They left, talking about the surgery, and two orderlies came in to take Cullen out as Tangeree and Phelps were sterilizing the instruments and cleaning out the surgical room. It was late afternoon, and the doctors were leaving when Tangeree finished. She went into the closet in the laboratory, changed into the clothes she had worn to the infirmary, combed out her hair and pinned it up again. Everyone except Palmer had left when she came out of the closet. He was at the desk, reading a medical journal.

"How much do you know about vaginal rectocele, Beaunais?"

Tangeree pushed her hat into place and pinned it, and shook her head. "I've read about it, but that's been some time ago, Doctor Palmer."

"Here's an article that'll tell you all about it. I have a patient who has one, but her modesty is more of a problem than the rectocele. She doesn't mind me so much, but she won't have two or three men around her when she's exposed. And I have to have an assistant to do any surgery. Perhaps she won't mind your being there, and perhaps you can talk to her as effectively as you did that amputation. She's a little worried about surgery."

"I'll certainly try, Doctor Palmer."

"Very well, here's all the information I have on her. Study that and the article in the journal, and I'll make an appointment for us to talk to her tomorrow. Be here at noon, and I'll have my carriage here."

Tangeree nodded, taking the handwritten sheets of paper and folding them into the journal. Being asked by Palmer to assist with a private patient was completely outside the scope of training in the infirmary and a distinct compliment, and she glowed with satisfaction as she walked toward the door.

When she was on the train, she read the papers and the article. The woman was fifty-two, and for the past fifteen years she had suffered with headache, backache, and nausea, and she had been bedridden for periods of time. Her condition had been diagnosed as a displaced uterus, for which the accepted treat-

ment was to push the organ back into place and keep
it in position by packing the vaginal cavity with gauze.
An alternative and more controversial treatment was
the insertion of a mechanical metal support called a
pessary.

Both treatments had been tried. The only result had
been increased discomfort and irritation of the vagina,
and the woman had called on Palmer. He had diagnosed the condition as a rectocele, a hernial projection
of a part of the vagina through a laceration in the retaining perineum that had occurred during childbirth.
The article in the journal described the usual surgical
procedure, returning the protruding tissue to its place
and repairing the perineum. It required a long period
of complete inactivity while the perineum healed and
became strong enough to retain the swollen tissue,
and Palmer had scratched through lines, made notes in
the margins, and drawn a small sketch of his procedure, a radical removal of the rectocele.

Tangeree read the article and the papers several
times, and studied Palmer's procedure, learning it
thoroughly. His carriage was on the street in front of
the infirmary when she left her chemistry class the
next day, and they went to a large mansion in a fash-
ionable district on Brandywine Street. The house and
the luxurious parlor the housekeeper conducted them
to suggested that the woman might be haughty and un-
approachable, but she was amiable, gracious, and
motherly. Palmer introduced Tangeree as his surgical
assistant. The woman was modest, but she wasn't
squeamish and she was interested in her condition, and
Palmer hadn't fully explained it to her. She was also
intrigued by Tangeree's experiences and the fact she
was in training to be a doctor. Tangeree explained the

condition in detail and chatted with her, a cordial rapport quicly developing between her and the woman.

Tangeree and Palmer returned to the house at noon the next day, with a case of surgical instruments, equipment, and dressings, and a portable carbolic acid atomizer. They set up a temporary surgical room in an alcove off the woman's bedroom and sterilized the instruments, then Tangeree anesthetized the woman and pumped the atomizer as Palmer performed the surgery and sutured the wound. The woman awakened from the chloroform a few minutes after they put her in bed, cheerful, relaxed, and in very little pain. Tangeree and Palmer gathered up the things and returned to the infirmary.

Palmer regarded the surgery as routine, but the woman was at the forefront of Tangeree's thoughts that evening and the following morning. When her morning lecture was finished, she hurried to the infirmary and up the stairs. Palmer was at his desk in the laboratory, and he nodded as Tangeree came in, asking about the woman.

"She's doing very well, and she'll be up and about within a day or two. And most importantly, she doesn't have a temperature."

"Then she's out of danger from inflammation."

Palmer nodded, standing and digging in his pocet. "If there's no temperature rise within twelve hours, the patient is safe. Here, this is yours."

Tangeree held out her hand as he extended his, then looked at the double eagle in her palm. "Twenty dollars? What for, Doctor Palmer?"

"It's your assistant's fee." He lifted his hand and chuckled dryly as she started to shake her head and demur. "Considering what I'm being paid for that surgery, you more than deserve an assistant's fee, Beaunais. What are you going to do this summer?"

"Do?" she replied blankly, then shrugged and shook her head. "Well, I studied last summer and caught up on all of my reading."

Palmer pursed his lips and looked up at the ceiling in elaborate nonchalance. "Phelps and Murphy will be graduating and leaving, and you may work here with me this summer, if you wish." He laughed as her eyes widened, and he nodded toward the closet. "Go change your clothes, Beaunais, and get that silly-looking cap ready to put on."

Tangeree nodded and smiled ecstatically, digging in her reticule for the key to the closet as she walked toward it.

20

As SUMMER APPROACHED, the Randolphs talked more frequently over breakfast about Pejoe's return home for the summer vacation. Tangeree felt guilty over her attitude about it, because it was presumptuous and reflected less than full appreciation for the Randolph's hospitality, but Pejoe's return wasn't an event she looked forward to with anticipation. The tranquillity of the household had been upset from time to time the previous summer by garden parties and other social gatherings organized for Pejoe and Claire, and she preferred the quiet and solitude of the winter season.

She had been invited to the gatherings, and had gone to some. But hours of idle talk and posturing bored her, she had been the object of unwanted attentions by too many young men, and she had found many of the attitudes of the young, idle, and wealthy to be irritating. After the first parties, she had used the excuse of having to study, and she had spent her time reading and studying in her room, and in a private nook she had found in the rear of the formal gardens behind the house.

The outlook for the summer became even more discouraging at breakfast one morning when the Randolphs discussed a letter from Pejoe. He had recently befriended Dennis Selfridge, of a socially prominent and wealthy Boston family. Selfridge's parents were spending the summer in Europe, and Pejoe was bringing Selfridge home with him for the summer.

The skill in dissimulation that Tangeree had developed during the years of working with the ill was taxed heavily as she listened to the Randolphs with a bland, polite smile and shrank inwardly. During the social gatherings the previous summer, many of the young men had approached her with the apparent attitude that she had been in some sort of stasis all of her life awaiting their arrival, which had infuriated her. But at least they hadn't been staying in the house, and it had been possible to avoid them.

The Randolphs' viewpoint toward the visit became more ambivalent when another letter from Pejoe arrived. Selfridge had a sedentary nature, he wasn't a foxhunter, he didn't like sailing because he was prone to seasickness, he didn't play racquets, and there were other things he didn't do. They talked about it over breakfast, and Randolph shook his head musingly.

"One would wonder what he does with his time, wouldn't one? Did you say his family makes sausages or something like that?"

"They have to do with meat packing or something of the sort," Phoebe replied. "But that shouldn't have anything to do with it, should it? It could be that he collects things or something, like your cousin Cecil. And perhaps he might enjoy the flower festival . . . ."

They continued discussing it and the subject came up again when other letters arrived from Pejoe, Randolph becoming vaguely doubtful that Selfridge would enjoy his visit, and Phoebe suggesting things that hopefully Selfridge might enjoy. Tangeree listened to the conversations, reflecting that Selfridge sounded less threatening than before, and feeling less concerned about the matter than she had before Palmer had asked her to work with him during the summer.

The time approached for graduation at the college, and Phelps and Murphy were gone occasionally, seeing to their affairs and making preparations to leave. A number of second-year students who would be remaining in Philadelphia during the summer made requests to the various doctors on the infirmary staff to work under their supervision during the summer, which was a means of gaining a foothold for training with preferred doctors the following term, and Palmer received several. He accepted one from a man named Williamson, and he made arrangements to have Tangeree hired as an infirmary staff member for the summer. The wages were a token amount, but it became a matter of record that she was a staff member of the infirmary and surgical assistant to Palmer, and there was a promise of a substantial amount in assistant's fees.

Graduation day came and passed, and the incidence of suppuration in amputations and wounds became more common as the weather turned warmer. Palmer began giving Tangeree more latitude and more responsibility, allowing her to examine patients and change dressings when he was attending to his private practice during the mornings, and watching over her as she cleansed shallow pockets of infection that developed in the wounds. She began working on the deeper infections in the surgical room, carving into the wounds and cleansing them as Williamson pumped the handle on the atomizer. Palmer watched over her shoulder, and the visiting doctors stood on the other side of the table, watching and commenting. Then she did her first amputations, a man from the foundry whose arm had been crushed in a machine and a railroad worker whose leg had been caught as he was coupling cars.

The Randolphs' preparations for the arrival of their son and his guest reached a peak and seemed to hang there for a period of days, then it melted into the background of other household activities. One evening there was a carriage loaded with luggage in front of the house when Tangeree returned home, and grooms and gardeners were carrying the suitcases in. Pejoe's booming voice and loud laughter came from somewhere in the house as she went to her rooms, and there was a bustle as the grooms and gardeners rushed in and out. All of Tangeree's forebodings returned as she changed her dress, put up her hair, and prepared to go to dinner.

The family was in the parlor. Tangeree grimly steeled herself as she crossed the entry hall toward it. Randolph and Pejoe were laughing and talking, almost drowning the sound of Phoebe's and Claire's voices, and there was a quiet, subdued sound of another man's voice. Tangeree stepped into the doorway, and Randolph looked at her and smiled widely, standing.

"Come in, my dear, come in. You remember Pejoe, of course."

"Yes, of course," Tangeree replied as she smiled and walked into the room. "It's so good to see you again, Mr. Randolph."

"And it's a pleasure to see you again, Miss Beaunais," he replied, standing and bowing, and he pointed to the man on the corner of a sofa. "This is my friend Dennis Selfridge. Dennis, this is Miss Beaunais."

The man was totally unlike what she had expected. He looked younger than Pejoe, and almost boyish.

And somehow he looked small, even though he wasn't particularly small. There was the most vague resemblance to someone Tangeree had met long before. She couldn't remember who it had been or even when or where, but it had to do with his features. They were far too smooth and regular to be called handsome. He was actually pretty.

"I'm pleased to meet you, Mr. Selfridge."

"And I'm pleased to meet you, Miss Beaunais."

His voice was soft, and the words came out in a rapid flow. His eyes met hers for an instant, and he moved gracefully as he bowed. He seemed shy, and Tangeree relaxed her defenses, feeling relieved. Randolph and Pejoe began laughing and talking again, and Dennis sat back down on the sofa where Phoebe sat as Tangeree stepped to a chair.

"Miss Beaunais's family are good friends with a very dear friend of ours in the West," Phoebe said, glancing from Tangeree to Dennis.

"Yes, Pejoe mentioned that Miss Beaunais was in the East to go to college," Dennis murmured quietly, smiling politely.

"Actually, she's studying medicine," Phoebe said. "She's going to be a doctor, aren't you, Miss Beaunais?"

Dennis blinked in surprise as Tangeree nodded, and he looked at her again. "A doctor?" he said in astonishment. "That's fascinating."

It seemed to come out almost of its own accord, reflecting awe and admiration. And it also seemed to embarrass him slightly that he had blurted it out. Tangeree tried to think of something to say to relieve his confusion, and Phoebe filled the gap of silence.

"I understand your mother is a Willoughby, Dennis."

"Yes, that's correct, from the Brookline Willoughbys."

"We might have some connection between our families, then. My brother's wife Genevieve is a Richards, and I believe her mother's name was Hermione Willoughby."

"Yes, it appears there is some connection, Mrs. Randolph. My mother has a cousin named Hermione, and I believe she married a Richards . . . ."

They continued talking quietly, and Randolph and his son laughed uproariously about something. When the visit by Dennis had first been mentioned at the breakfast table, Claire had shown some interest in the matter. Her interest had disappeared, and she was smiling absently and listening to her father and brother as they talked.

The housekeeper came to the door, and the group crossed the entry hall to the dining room. Dennis and Tangeree were seated facing Claire and her brother, and Dennis continued talking with Phoebe most of the time. Randolph made several comments to Dennis, indirectly inquiring about what he would like to do or what he enjoyed, and Dennis expressed a desire to see Independence Hall, the art museum, the Franklin Institute, and other points of cultural and historical interest.

Dennis was weary from the journey and went to his room when dinner was finished, and Tangeree went to her room. It puzzled her that Dennis and Pejoe were friends, because they had little in common. Pejoe was as garrulously friendly and open-hearted as his father and liked everyone, but it appeared that someone as quiet and reserved as Dennis would choose someone more like himself for a friend. But Dennis had seemed content enough, and had smiled as he

listened to the boisterous laughter and conversation
between Pejoe and his father. Tangeree was relieved
that Dennis was the kind of person he was, and she
didn't have to be on constant guard against someone
who was staying in the house.

Dennis was at the table at breakfast the next morning. Pejoe was still in bed, as was his practice during
the summer. The Randolphs talked about the possibility of having a party later in the week, and Dennis
expressed polite enthusiasm. Tangeree observed that
Dennis ate little, as was to be expected in view of his
slender build, and she felt an impulse to encourage
him to eat more. He looked very neat and clean in a
bright, informal shirt, dark trousers, and with his black
hair parted and combed back. When Tangeree left
the house to go to the train station, she saw Dennis
walking through the gardens behind the house with
a book from the library under his arm.

Tangeree had been prepared to work seven days
each week during the summer, but Palmer had insisted that she work only five and spend two days
reading and resting. There was a party on Thursday
that stretched toward the weekend when friends of
Pejoe's remained at the house, and they were joined
by friends of Claire's on Friday. The house seemed to
be swarming with people at the buffet breakfast on
Saturday morning, and Tangeree took a book and a
medical journal and walked through the gardens behind the house.

The private nook she had found the summer before
was an old stone gazebo in a willow thicket behind
the gardens. It had apparently belonged to some other
house that had been on the grounds previously, because the style was different from that of the Randolph
house and it was very old, crumbling and overgrown

with wisteria. Tangeree went around the box hedge at the rear of the gardens, then along the dim, overgrown path to the gazebo. As the path opened out, she saw a flash of bright color and stopped. Dennis was sitting on the thick mat of grass in front of an old stone bench and leaning back against it, reading.

He blinked in surprise as he looked at her and climbed to his feet, then he smiled in understanding. "You've been sitting out here, haven't you? I noticed that there was a path, but I didn't think that Pejoe or Claire would come here." His voice faded and his smile became apologetic as he closed his book and stepped toward the path. "I didn't mean to intrude, Miss Beaunais. I'll go elsewhere."

Tangeree suddenly became aware that she had been frowning, and she felt contrite. "No, please don't, Mr. Selfridge. After all, this isn't my property."

"I'm not sure whose it is," he chuckled. "It's a lovely place, isn't it? But it isn't the sort of place that the Randolphs would enjoy. So for my part, I'll grant you title to it."

Tangeree hesitated, then smiled and shrugged. "Well, there's no reason on earth why we can't both sit here, is there? I was going to do some reading."

Dennis nodded, turning back toward the bench. "Then I'll promise to show my gratitude for your companionship by not disturbing you."

He sat down on the grass in front of the bench again, opening his book. Tangeree usually sat on the bench, but it would be awkward to sit on it while he sat on the grass in front of it. She sat down on the grass, glancing at his book. It was a volume of Byron. She put her book aside and opened the journal, took her cigarettes and matches from her pocket and lit one. Feeling his eyes on her, she looked at him.

"Would you like a cigarette?"

"No, thank you, I don't . . . well, yes, please. I believe I would like one."

She handed him the cigarettes and matches, smiling. "Does it shock you that I smoke?"

He lit a cigarette and shook his head as he puffed on it, handing the cigarettes and matches back. "Thank you. And it doesn't shock me in the least, Miss Beaunais. You're a woman who actually does things, so you should do as you wish."

"What do you mean?"

"I mean you actually do things and accomplish things, as opposed to people who are fleas on the hide of mankind. As opposed to parasites, as it were."

His voice rang with sincerity. There was an implied criticism of the Randolphs, his family, and all like them, and the implication that she was superior in many ways to all of them. Immediate objection rose in her mind, because she liked the Randolphs, and she was their guest. At the same time, she felt confused and deeply flattered, and at a loss for words. But no words were necessary, because he looked down at his book and turned a page as he puffed on his cigarette, leaving her in privacy. And she suddenly realized that she had been talking with him without any of the strain she usually felt when talking with men. She puffed on her cigarette and looked at her journal, thinking. Before, she had always assumed that she was deficient in some way because of the awkwardness she felt when talking with men. But it appeared that she simply hadn't met a man she could talk to.

She became involved in an article in the journal, then she finished it and glanced at Dennis as he turned a page. His brows were drawn, and he rubbed his temples with the tips of his fingers as he looked down at his book. "Do you have a headache?"

He looked at her and smiled wryly, nodding. "I get them at times. I'm afraid to take laudanum, because I understand it's habit-forming. And salicylic acid upsets my stomach at times."

"Yes, laudanum is dangerous to use regularly, and salicylic acid does cause stomach upset. Are you interested in medicine?"

"I have a layman's interest in it."

Tangeree nodded and looked at her journal, then glanced back at him as he rubbed his temples again. Massage on the back of the neck was far more effective than either laudanum or salicylic acid for many headaches. She was alone in an isolated place with him, but she felt a complete lack of threat from him. And he was in pain. "Would you like me to massage the back of your neck? I believe that'll help it."

"Would you, please? It's very troublesome, and I didn't sleep very well last night because of it."

Tangeree put her journal aside and moved toward him, and she cupped her hand around the back of his neck, gently massaging the muscles and tendons. There was none of the tension in his neck that usually went with a headache, but his eyes closed and the line of his lips indicated relief from pain.

It was different from other times of helping those in pain, because the separation of self and healer didn't occur. She was acutely aware that he was a man, and that she was in an isolated place with him. He leaned toward her, his shoulder brushing her breast, but there was still a feeling of absolute lack of threat. And it was pleasant touching him, feeling his hair and skin under her fingers. He smelled fresh, and he looked neat and clean, like a little boy who had just been scrubbed by his mother.

His breathing deepened as he relaxed completely, leaning against her, and he looked like he was going to sleep. And he gave the impression of being smaller than he was because he looked almost vulnerable, with his eyes closed and his long lashes resting on his cheeks. The remote similarity between him and someone she had met before gnawed at the back of her mind, and she couldn't place it. His hair had fallen forward as his head drooped, and she pushed it into place as she sat back.

"Did that help it?"

He smiled, sitting up, and picked up her hand and kissed it quickly. "It feels wonderful," he said, picking up his book as he released her hand, and he climbed to his feet. "I'm very grateful for the relief from the headache, and I'm also grateful to you for sharing this place with me. Would you do it again some time?"

She almost said that she would be there during the afternoon. Then she thought again, and silently smiled and nodded. He tucked his book under his arm and walked away with a boyishly jaunty step, whistling cheerfully, and looked back and waved before he disappeared from sight among the willows.

Tangeree lit another cigarette, and began reading an article in the journal. She had difficulty concentrating on it.

21

SOME OF THE PEOPLE at the house had gone riding, and others were still there for the buffet lunch when Tangeree returned. Part of those who had gone riding returned while Tangeree was having lunch, and an overweight lout in garishly bright clothes hovered around her. Pejoe talked to Dennis on the other side of the room, persuading him to go somewhere, and they disappeared into the crowd. When Tangeree returned to the old stone gazebo, Dennis wasn't there. She waited, thumbing through her book and trying to concentrate on it, and he didn't come.

Two or three of the guests remained overnight at the house again on Saturday night, and more arrived after church the next morning to go for a ride. There were refreshments in the dining room and parlor and people milling about, and Tangeree lost sight of Dennis in the crowd. He didn't reappear, and Tangeree got her book from her room and walked through the gardens to the old gazebo, approaching it with bated breath. Then her heart pounded furiously as she saw Dennis sitting in front of the bench with a book.

The book was about the West, and like many it was written by someone who had apparently never been

there, a patchwork of information gleaned from sec-
ondhand sources and filled with errors and impossible
tales. They talked about it, laughing over the fanciful
stories, and they talked about the West. Dennis became serious and thoughtful.

"I'd really like to do something," he said wistfully.
"I'd like to build and make things happen, rather than
just live and then die. And I believe the West is the
place where I could really do things."

"Yes, there are all sorts of opportunities there,
Dennis."

"But I won't be my own man until I graduate, because I made a commitment to my family to go to
Harvard. I still have another year to go, but I suppose
that isn't too long. You have another year remaining
here, don't you? And I suppose you'll return to the
West."

"Oh, yes, I couldn't imagine living anywhere else."

"I can't imagine your living anywhere else," he said,
smiling contemplatively. "Women can vote in Nevada,
can't they? That's the kind of place a woman like you
should be. Even your name sounds like you should be
there, Tangeree. I suppose there are a lot of attorneys
in Virginia City, aren't there? My law degree might
not get me a job as a clerk in a place like that."

"I'm not sure how many are there. I've heard about
lawsuits between mining companies and things like
that, though, so there's probably a lot of work there
for attorneys."

"I believe the big advantage in being an attorney
there would probably be in the opportunities it would
open in other things. And that's what would interest
me most."

They continued talking, and he talked about the

railroads, bridges, tunnels, and other things that had
been built. Then he talked about the things that would
be needed as the West became more settled, the giant
undertakings that would pit men's machines, determination, and ingenuity against the land and the
forces of nature. And he talked about what he would
like to do. As he talked, her viewpoint of him changed.
Rather than sedentary, he seemed more of a dreamer
and a visionary, but one who could do what he en-
visioned.

Conversation was a pastime Tangeree had never
particularly enjoyed. She had always enjoyed talking
with her mother, discussing medicines and illnesses
and reminiscing about the past, and she had enjoyed
listening to others as they told of interesting things
they had seen and done. But idle conversation had
always bored her. Talking with Dennis amounted to
idle conversation, but at the same time it was different and it was exquisitely enjoyable. And, as the hours
fled, it ended much too quickly.

Dennis needed to go into the city for something the
next morning, and he went with her on the train. It
was a keen pleasure to stand with him on the platform
at the station before getting on the train. He looked
magnificent in his stylish hammerclaw coat, full cravat,
and striped trousers, with a cane tucked under his
arm and his tall hat tilted forward at an angle.

The other people on the platform knew who he was
and knew her, and knew they were only going in the
same direction at the same time rather than going
somewhere together. But it had the feeling of going
somewhere with him, and he escorted her courteously,
touching her arm to guide her and assisting her up
steps. They chatted with the others, and he was youth-

fully gallant toward the older women, sober and respectful toward the older men, and attentive to her when she spoke.

More than anything else, he radiated enjoyment of her companionship. They chatted and laughed during the train ride into the city, and he looked at things she pointed out and commented that she appeared to know more about Philadelphia than the Randolphs. When they reached the station in the city, he escorted her through the crowd and outside, and started to steer her toward the carriages for hire on the street in front.

"No, I use the horse cars, Dennis," she said, pointing to the side street. "And if you have the impression that I'm from a wealthy family, you're mistaken. I have a benefactor who is paying for my education, and I have pretty clothes and other things because he's generous. But I won't waste his money on—"

"You don't have to tell me, Tangeree," he chuckled lightly. "I knew when I first met you that you've had to reach for things. And I'm sure there have been times when it's been hard, but you wouldn't be the same woman you are if you'd been coddled. By the same token, I know you've had difficulties in studying medicine because you're a woman. But you'll be a better doctor as the result of having overcome those difficulties."

The same thought had occurred to her, but she hadn't defined it as concisely and succinctly in her mind. And while in a way it wasn't precisely a compliment, in another way it was an extreme compliment. She searched for a reply, then realized that none was necessary as he took her arm and walked toward the corner with her, the tip of his cane tapping the sidewalk. They turned the corner and walked through the people milling along the sidewalk by the horse cars, and Dennis glanced around and sighed, suddenly in a more subdued mood.

"I truly wish we'd met under different circumstances, Tangeree. I'd give half my life if we had."

"What do you mean?"

Dennis guided her out of the people moving back and forth along the sidewalk, and he leaned on his cane and looked down at the sidewalk as they stood by the side of the building, the people eddying around them. "I'd like to ask you to go to the theater and other places, but I'm restrained from doing so because it would put the Randolphs in the position of appearing as match-makers. They wouldn't want my family to have that impression, and as their guest I can't put them in that position. I know that sounds vain, because it assumes that you might consent to go with me, but I'll risk that in order to be honest."

It didn't sound vain, because vanity wasn't one of his characteristics. But it was irritating, because it clearly placed her far outside the pale of prestigious families that arranged marriages according to pedigree. And it suggested the horror with which his family might regard her as a potential daughter-in-law. "Well, we shall have to bear up under our misfortune, Mr. Selfridge," she said tartly.

"I know I've made you angry," he said quietly, nodding and looking down at the tip of his cane as he scratched at the sidewalk with it, then he lifted his eyes and looked into hers. "But I'd do it a thousand times in order to be honest with you, Tangeree. And to make myself clear to you. I'll be my own man in a year, and it's important to me that you understand my intentions."

Her aggravation melted as she saw the hurt in his

eyes, and as his words stirred a dancing joy in her mind. She looked away, brushing back a wisp of hair on her face. "Well, it doesn't make any difference, Dennis."

"It makes a difference to me, Tangeree. I can't think of anything that makes as much difference."

"In any event, I'm not very fond of the theater and things of that sort." She thought for a moment, then shrugged. "As far as going somewhere is concerned, that place along the river where you saw all the old mansions is very nice for a walk. People from the city go there on weekends, but no one who would know either of us. And the Randolphs needn't know."

His moody expression changed to a beaming, conspiratorial smile, and he nodded happily. "We could walk there from the house. It isn't far, is it?"

Tangeree felt her cheeks flushing and her smile escaping control and becoming too wide as she shook her head. "No, it isn't far."

"On Saturday afternoon, then?"

"Yes, very well."

He took off his hat and leaned quickly under the brim of her hat and kissed her, then he moved away, smiling back at her. The people on the sidewalk had thinned out and some of the horse cars were moving away, but dozens of people had seen. It shocked and embarrassed her momentarily, then a warm glow of happiness enveloped her as she stepped across the sidewalk to the horse car.

The men on the front seat of the horse car had been watching, and they chuckled as one of them lifted his hat and stood in the aisle to give her his seat. Two women in the seat across the aisle looked at Tangeree and chortled meaningfully as she gave the driver the fare and sat down. The driver snapped the traces and the car moved forward, passing Dennis as he walked along the sidewalk. He lifted his hat and waved it, and Tangeree waved. The women giggled, people chuckled and commented, and someone in the rear of the horse car whistled. Tangeree waved until Dennis was out of sight, then she sat back in her seat, her cheeks burning and ecstatic joy suffusing her.

At dinner that evening, Tangeree withdrew behind a wall of dissimulation to maintain outward composure as she conversed politely, but it was difficult because everything Dennis said seemed to be pregnant with undertones of meaning. On Tuesday and Wednesday there were hunts, and Pejoe and Randolph talked Dennis into going. The hunting parties always had dinner at the club in the village, and the house was quiet and lonely. On Thursday she left the infirmary for an hour and used nine dollars of her money from assistant's fees to buy herself a bright cotton dress for Saturday, wanting to spend her own money for it rather than buy it from the money Woodruff provided for her clothes. The family was at home for dinner that evening, and Tangeree's anticipation mounted higher as she exchanged glances with Dennis and thought about the weekend.

The heat of the summer started to settle, but it lifted again on Saturday, a bright, sparkling day of fresh breezes, with snowy clouds drifting slowly across a rich blue sky, and shimmering greenery. There were numerous footpaths and roads that wound through the rolling countryside south of the village and toward the groves and meadows where the estates had been. Dennis told her to meet him on a footpath a mile from the house. Tangeree saw him as she walked around a curve in the path, and he ran to her. She threw herself into his arms, melting against him as he held her tight-

ly and his lips covered hers, and the day fulfilled the
anticipation that had built up through the week.

They became lost among the roads and footpaths,
laughing and uncaring, then finally found the place
where the estates had been. Courting couples walked
with linked hands, families sat around checked table-
cloths in the shade of trees and ate their picnic
lunches from baskets, and clusters of giggling girls
exchanged sidelong glances with clusters of strutting
boys. Vendors sold ice cream, popcorn, and cream
soda, long barges mounded with coal drifted down
the river, and old men and women sat on the riverbank
and fished with long cane poles. Tangeree and Dennis
sat in the shade and ate ice cream, they walked along
the river, and they talked. Then they walked back
toward Germantown.

The next day was even more enjoyable, a greater
familiarity with him erasing all awkwardness. His
embraces were more passionate when they stopped to
kiss, his fingers digging into her back as he held her
and his breath short as his lips caressed hers, and his
hands rested on her breasts. As their embraces progressed toward greater intimacy, she realized that she
had lost the wrenching terror of sex that had been
seared into her mind years before. It had been sidestepped the way her former tension and clumsiness
in conversation with men had been evaded. In its
place there was a growing willingness that was tem-
pered by fear that he would know what had happened
to her years before, a fear that prepared her to stop
him and refuse if he went too far. But he reached a
point, then he stopped. It was mildly irritating, because she wanted the reassurance of being the one to
set limits, and because he stopped sooner than she
would have stopped him.

The hot, muggy weather of full summer came on Monday. It brought two cholera patients to the infirmary, possibly the first ones of a trickle that would continue through the summer, or possibly the headwater of a flood if the pestilence struck in epidemic force. She assisted Palmer in removing an ovarian tumor from a woman who had become bloated with the swollen growth, an eighteen-pound mass of fluid and tissue, and they labored over the woman in a choking cloud of carbolic acid to cleanse the abdominal cavity before they sutured the incision. The woman was from a wealthy family and Tangeree received another substantial assistant's fee, but the woman's temperature began climbing nine hours after the surgery. The penalty for venturing into the forbidden territory of the abdomen was paid again as the infection raged through the woman's body, and she died three days after the surgery.

On Friday a patient with perityphlitis was brought in, a young boy. Palmer was busy over a patient with a gashed leg that was developing pockets of suppuration. The doctors huddled around the bunk, watching as he probed and daubed with carbolic acid solution. He glanced at the boy and nodded Tangeree toward the surgical room, his expression reflecting his attitude that it was a waste of time, and he dismissed the boy from his mind as he returned to the man on the bunk.

Williamson pumped the handle on the atomizer, and Tangeree made an incision below the boy's navel, a cut just long enough to admit a cannula hose, its size symbolic of her reluctance to invade the abdomen. She hooked a cannula hose to a suction pump, then slid it into the incision and began working the pump to drain the inflammation. The end of the hose hanging in the can under the table coughed and spat the dark, slimy discharge, and a foul stench rose from it that over-powered even the biting smell of the carbolic acid.

Tangeree felt a sense of futility, of helplessness. The smallest drop of the putrid discharge was deadly in the tender tissues of the hot, moist abdomen, and it was impossible to reach under the convolutions of the peritoneum and into all the folds and crevasses of the intestines with the end of the hose. But she went through the procedure that Palmer had taught her because it was all that could be done, moving the hose around and estimating the position of the tip from the length she pushed through the incision. When discharge stopped coming from the hose, she clamped swabs soaked in carbolic acid solution in long forceps and eased them through the incision to daub around inside the abdominal cavity, then she sutured the incision.

The boy died. The terror of working with the young and the old was that they seemed to be able to decide to leave, and then do it. The boy simply stopped breathing. And it was hours too soon, with hours of life left and each moment precious. She slapped the pale, slack cheeks and tried to breathe life back into the boy as Williamson stood and looked at her in perplexity, but there was no response. The boy was dead. His glazed eyes stared sightlessly up at her as she put his head back down on the table. She walked back along the corridor to the room where Palmer was working over the patient, pulling off her cap and straightening her hair.

"He died, Doctor Palmer."

Palmer glanced up at her and nodded as he looked back down at the patient's leg. "Get it cleaned up in there, and let the orderlies know. Are the parents here?"

"I believe they're in the almoner's office."

"Go tell them, and the almoner can find out what they want to do."

"Yes, sir."

She walked back along the corridor and told Williamson to clean the surgical room and have the orderlies remove the body, then walked down the stairs to the almoner's office. As she approached the doorway to the office, she suddenly realized that the boy had been her patient. And he had died. She had seen death many times and in its many forms, but she had stood behind her mother or Palmer at the reckoning for responsibility. Palmer hadn't sent her on an errand with information. He had ordered her to discharge her responsibility. She lifted her chin and swallowed as she walked toward the doorway, clenching the sides of her skirt tightly.

The resemblance between the boy and his mother was pronounced. It was so distinct that it identified the couple among the dozen or so other people on the benches in the crowded, stuffy offices, even though the woman's face was lined with premature age from labor and hardship. The man with her was a laborer, in grimy clothes. His lank hair was pressed down from wearing the cap that rested on his knee, and the stubble on his face was streaked with gray. The almoner was shuffling through papers on his desk in the corner of the room, and he looked up at Tangeree. Tangeree marched across the office toward the couple. The woman looked up at her, smiling fearfully and hopefully.

"How's our little Tommy doing? Is he going to be all right?"

"I'm very sorry to have to tell you that your son has died."

The woman uttered a piercing shriek and threw herself at the man, and he put his arms around her. The almoner moved toward them to comfort and calm the woman. The man stared up at Tangeree with blazing hatred in his eyes. Others in the room looked at Tangeree, their eyes hostile with their anxiety as they waited. The almoner bent over the woman, murmuring to her and patting her shoulder, and he glanced at Tangeree and nodded. The eyes followed her as she turned and walked toward the door, her chin high, her hands clutching the sides of her skirt, and her teeth clamped together to keep her chin from quivering.

Palmer looked at her, and nodded toward the laboratory. She went into the laboratory and stood by a window, looking at the refuse and barrels of soiled bedclothes in the alley behind the building. It was late afternoon, the sun inclining toward the west and the sweltering air in the laboratory heavy with the odors of the chemicals and the stench of the infirmary. Time dragged by, and Palmer walked along the corridor with the doctors. They left and Williamson left, and Tangeree turned away from the window as Palmer came into the laboratory.

"I'm sorry, Doctor Palmer. That's the first time when I was actually the one who . . . let a patient die. . . ."

"He was dying when he came in here, Tangeree. And it'll happen again. A doctor who doesn't care when a patient dies is a doctor who won't work to save one, and you work harder than most. And you'll suffer more than most. It won't get any easier, but you'll learn how to deal with it. Go on home."

The day had been long and he was weary, his face sweaty and lined with fatigue above his mustache and beard. There was understanding in his eyes, but little sympathy or comfort. Tangeree nodded as she took the key to the closet out of her pocket and walked toward it, and Palmer went back out. She changed clothes and walked down the stairs, putting on her hat. When she reached the bottom of the stairs, she heard the woman still weeping in the almoner's office.

The main topic of conversation at dinner was the flower festival and the preparations for it, a wrenching contrast. Tangeree masked her turmoil of emotions behind a polite smile, and she listened and chatted. Dennis had become sensitive to her moods, and there was concern in his eyes as he looked at her. The resemblance between him and someone she had met before helped take her mind off the death of the boy at the infirmary as she tried, unsuccessfully, to isolate the memory. After dinner, she waited for the hours to pass and the next day to arrive.

Tangeree was at the rendezvous first, pacing back and forth and carrying her wide straw hat by the brim as she waited. Dennis came into sight around the curve in the path, running toward her, and she raced to him. She threw herself into his arms, abandoning herself to his kisses and seeking refuge, and he crushed her to him as he kissed her passionately. Then he held her tightly and they began talking, and he led her through the brush by the path and into a grassy glade. They sat down, and he listened with a musing frown, nodding.

"Yes, of course I understand, Tangeree. I'm sure it must be very frustrating that you can't do more, can't save everyone. And after you've done all you can, you want to share sorrow with relatives, not face blame from them."

There was understanding, sympathy, and comfort in his voice and his expression, and he defined her feelings far more accurately than she had in the rushing flow of words. She sighed and nodded, looking down at the grass and plucking at it. "There are so many things for which there just isn't a cure, Dennis. And as you say, it's very frustrating."

"And people aren't immortal. People are also what they are, and dealing with them in any situation can be as frustrating as dealing with disease. When people feel pain, they seek an outlet. Very often that outlet is anger at anyone they can blame for their pain."

Tangeree listened as he continued talking. He seemed very knowledgeable about people. He also seemed very wise and mature for such a young man with a youthful, boyish face, able to define her feelings so explicitly and explained them to her. He moved closer and took her in his arms as he talked soothingly, and he began kissing her.

Their kisses became more passionate and unrestrained, and a heady glow of pleasure suffused her, becoming more intense as they lay back on the grass and held each other. They reached the point at which they had stopped before, and passed it swiftly. His hands tugged at her buttons, and the throbbing glow within her made her delay, not wanting to stop him. She held him and clung to him, his heart pounding against hers. His hands moved over her, caressing and touching, and starting a tingling fire that raced through her.

The fear that he would know what had happened to her before still remained, a dark shadow in the back of her mind. His hands and the knowledge of his need for her made a raging, yearning need rise within her, and she wanted escape and refuge from the day before. She still delayed in stopping him, caught in a seething cauldron of conflicting impulses.

The moment of decision approached as the cool air touched her skin and his labored breathing warmed her face, then his naked skin brushed hers. The moment came and passed, and there was no longer volition to choose as he gently pressed into her. And the fear that he would know what had happened to her also passed as his trembling voice whispered his love against her lips and his body moved on hers, pressing deeper. Release from the fear brought a surging, triumphant joy, and she responded to him eagerly, thrusting at him.

He was more modest than her, tinging her love for him with affectionate, playful humor. She had a piquant sense of power over him through her beauty as she dressed leisurely, wanting him to see her and admire her in her love for him. They walked on along the paths and the roads to the place where the estates had been, and they mingled with the others. Their secret knowledge of each other seemed to make each touch of their hands and contact between their eyes more meaningful, a rich, warm bond between them. Barriers between them were completely relaxed, and she invited him with her smile and eyes to tell her of his need for her. When he did, they returned along the roads and paths to their place, and she let him watch her as she undressed.

They returned to the glade the following day, and the following weekend. Then it rained, and they went to the old gazebo on the next Saturday. The willows and the portion of roof remaining over the old gazebo afforded little protection, and Tangeree was torn with indecision when Dennis suggested coming to her room at night. She knew the Randolphs would react with outrage if they even suspected. Then she realized that Dennis had made a wise suggestion. Their disappearance at the same time on each Saturday and Sunday would have inevitably caused comment, and Dennis was very cautious in making his way to her room and back to his late at night. The other danger in the situation, that of pregnancy, was easily dealt with. Since childhood she had heard her mother talking to women whose husbands were trying to turn them into broodmares, explaining the cycle of fertility that Cherokee women had known for centuries, and the spoonful of vinegar, aloes, and perse to be taken when the three crucial days of the lunar month couldn't be avoided.

An ecstatically joyous new world opened up around Tangeree, and she longed to share it with someone. But the only one she could tell was her mother, and she couldn't write her about it because she felt even more guilty than before for coming between her mother and Dawson. And even as the gloriously bright and fresh new world was expanding around her, it was threatened by the remorseless passage of time. The weeks fled past, and she was reluctant to think of what would come after he left, not wanting to think about when he would be gone. Then the time came closer, forcing her to think about it and broach the subject with him.

Dennis didn't want her to write to him if he couldn't reply, and the household staff saw all her mail when it arrived. The separation without contact for the endless months until the following summer seemed too much to bear, and Tangeree thought of other ways they could contact each other. Then a partial solution presented itself when Pejoe mentioned the possibility of coming home at Christmas. He had spent the last Christmas with relatives in Massachusetts, and there was an indication that he hadn't particularly enjoyed it. It was discussed at the table over breafast one morning, and Dennis casually mentioned that he might be at loose ends the following Christmas. The Randolphs promptly invited him to return for another visit on Christmas, and he thanked them for the invitation as he exchanged a glance with Tangeree.

The last night was torture. They clung to each other until the last possible safe moment for him to leave. Then Tangeree stood at the window and watched a gray, rainy dawn break, the trees on the lawn swaying in the wind and the rainwater dripping from the eaves and splattering against the window. A stir in the house turned into a bustle, a carriage came around the house from the stable for the luggage, and Tangeree went into the bedroom and dressed. Pejoe rose late. Breakfast and the farewells were hurried. The most difficult part for Tangeree was the formal, friendly farewell with Dennis when she wanted to throw herself into his arms. Randolph went with them to the station, and Tangeree stood on the porch with Phoebe and Claire and waved as the carriages moved along the drive.

The term at Arundel began the following week, and the amount of time that Tangeree went without thinking of Dennis gradually lengthened from a few minutes to an hour or two when she was busy. Palmer took another trainee, a man named Roberts. Tangeree continued routinely assisting Palmer in his private practice with patients who preferred or didn't object to being treated by a woman. He left her in charge of his service at the infirmary when he was absent and gave her other responsibilities.

The hot weather ended without an epidemic of cholera, typhus, or typhoid developing in the city, and there was a long, beautiful autumn. The trees changed to rich, warm tones of orange, gold, and brown, the pastures turned to dusty buff, corn stood in shocks in the field along the rainroad tracks, and there was a tangy scent of woodsmoke in the air on the frosty mornings. Cold weather came with a rush and the fields were suddenly covered with snow one morning, and the winter sicknesses began.

Palmer tentatively explored Tangeree's reaction to remaining in Philadelphia and joining his practice after she graduated, and she was invited to apply for a teaching post at the Women's Medical College. Both offers were flattering and gratifying and she mentioned them in a letter to her mother, but she and Dennis had talked about Virginia City and it was her home. When she thought to check a calendar, she found that the halfway point between the time when Dennis had left and when he would return at Christmas had passed.

The days seemed to pass slowly when she counted them, but the weeks passed rapidly. The Randolphs made tentative plans for a Christmas party for Pejoe and Dennis, and talked about other things that Pejoe and Dennis might enjoy doing over the holidays. Thanksgiving Day passed and December arrived, a festive atmosphere began developing in the city and among the people on the platform at the train station each morning, and merchants in the city began decorating their windows.

The first indication of trouble was in a letter from Pejoe only a few days before Christmas, informing his family that Dennis wouldn't be visiting over Christmas. It was a crushing, devastating disappointment for Tangeree, and she was able to hide her feelings only because the Randolphs were also disappointed and less observant. Then a letter of explanation from Pejoe arrived two days later, and it was a shocking blow. A girl had named Dennis as the father of her unborn child, and he was in serious difficulty because of the possibility of lawsuit and because of the likelihood of a more physical form of retribution by the girl's brothers.

When it was first brought up at the breakfast table, Tangeree refused to believe it. Dennis was from a wealthy family, which made him a target for such accusations. But Pejoe's letter went into detail, because the scandal was a current topic of gossip and there were many details in circulation. One detail gave Tangeree food for thought. The girl's family was in the boatbuilding trade, well-known builders of yachts. She said Dennis had talked to her about his lifelong ambition to design, build, and sail yachts, and Pejoe commented amused on Dennis's inability to ride on a ferry without leaving his last meal aboard it.

And there were other things, too many things that fit too neatly. Tangeree realized that Dennis had developed what he did into an art. As she suffered an agony of remorse and self-disgust, she remembered that Dennis had remotely reminded her of someone. Suddenly she remembered who it was. The physical resemblance wasn't pronounced, but it was there. And there was a strong resemblance in other ways. Dennis resembled a man in Virginia City named Lassiter.

Pejoe related the entire story again as the family sat in the parlor on the night he arrived. Randolph clicked his tongue and shook his head, Claire listened avidly, and Tangeree controlled her features. Phoebe was torn between curiosity and her concern for the propriety of the subject as a topic of conversation between mixed sexes.

"I really don't think this is the time and place to

discuss this any further, Pejoe," Phoebe finally said reluctantly. "And in any event, it appears that the girl is a very common sort."

"That's not what they say," Pejoe replied, shrugging. "I don't know, because I've never seen her. But they say that butter wouldn't melt in her mouth."

"Well, common or not, I say she's foolish," Claire commented, and she looked at Tangeree and lifted her eyebrows.

"Yes, I agree," Tangeree said, nodding. "She's a fool."

22

THE CEREMONY was in the lobby of the old hotel building, and it was brief. It was less impressive than the ceremony had been in San Francisco, with the large audience in the hushed atmosphere of the assembly hall, the organ music, and the caps and gowns, but the dean made a comment that was very impressive. One hundred and sixteen had enrolled three years before, and twenty-eight were graduating.

Palmer left while Tangeree was talking to some of the other staff, and she went to the infirmary to say goodbye to him. He was looking at the stump of a patient's amputated arm, five other doctors hovering around him, and he glanced up at Tangeree.

"Have you changed your mind?"

"No, I'm going to Virginia City, Doctor Palmer."

"Well, I don't have time to talk to you, then," he replied in a jokingly brusque tone, then he laughed and held out his hand. "Goodbye, and good luck."

"Thank you, and thank you for everything."

"You earned it. Come on back if you change your mind."

"I will. Goodbye, Doctor Palmer."

"Goodbye, Doctor Beaunais."

Tangeree exchanged nods with the other doctors. Then she walked out of the room and back along the corridor. As she started to go down the stairs, she stepped back to make room for the almoner as he trotted up the stairs, two men following him and carrying a third who was unconscious, blood streaming down his face and onto his shirt from a deep head wound. One of Palmer's trainees ran out of the laboratory and went to get him, the almoner and the other men rushed along the corridor toward the surgical room, and Tangeree went down the stairs.

Frazier had asked her to come to the pathology laboratory, and she returned to the other building and went up the stairs. He was alone in the laboratory, standing with his hands folded behind his back and looking out a window as he teetered up and down on his toes. Tangeree closed the door quietly, and he turned and looked at her with his mocking half-smile.

"Ah, here is our graduate," he chuckled dryly. "One that we at Arundel arm with a diploma and inflict upon an unsuspecting world. Are you ready to set forth on your mission of reducing the population, Doctor Beaunais?"

"Hopefully it won't be that," Tangeree laughed. "We don't have enough people in the West as it is."

"That is a matter of opinion," Frazier replied, stepping to a cabinet and opening it. "In my opinion, people are much like horse manure in that they're less offensive when thinly scattered. Here—I have a present for you."

It was a microscope slide. Tangeree took it and held it up to the light of a window. "What is it?"

"A section of a piece of vegetable matter I removed from the veriform appendix of a cadaver and which a botanist at the university assured me was an apple seed."

Tangeree lifted her eyebrows, looking at him and back at the slide. "That's very interesting, Doctor Frazier. It would begin to appear that at least some people might have an opening between the caecum and the veriform appendix that would allow a foreign body to enter and start an inflammation, wouldn't it?"

"I prefer to avoid such wide-ranging conclusions without evidence of a similar scope," Frazier replied dryly. "My more limited analysis ranges around whether or not the botanist might have got what I sent him mixed up with some apple seeds he had lying about." He turned back to the cabinet and took a large wooden case from the shelf. "So you won't strain your eyes in trying to look at the slide, you may take this along for the purpose of viewing it."

The case contained a Hollander microscope, an instrument that cost hundreds of dollars. Tangeree gasped in surprise, then shook her head. "No, I couldn't take that Hollander from you, Doctor Frazier."

"I have two, and it could be that you will have time to continue your studies in between repairing the rabble in the West. There is progress being made in bacteriology, and you'll need a good instrument if you're to take advantage of it. You're more likely to take advantage of it than most, so take the microscope."

Tangeree hesitated, then smiled and nodded as she put the slide in one of the slots in the case and closed it. "Very well, and I'm very grateful, Doctor Frazier. I had intended to buy a microscope, but I certainly wouldn't have been able to afford a Hollander. How did you come to find the apple seed?"

"I've had a passing interest in abdominal inflamma-

tions for some years. My only child, a daughter, died
from perityphlitis some years ago. She would have
been about your age now."

As he spoke, his smile wavered, then returned. Tangeree started to make a comment of condolence, then
didn't, realizing that was not what he wanted. The
small man looked very lonely in his solitary detach-
ment from others, his bitter, sarcastic half-smile a
wall between himself and others. And there was a
pathos about him, in his grim, cheerless life. But somehow she had made contact with him and he hadn't
been unkind to her. She put out her hand.

"Thank you very much for the microscope, Doctor
Frazier. And for everything else."

Frazier silently shook her hand, then folded his
hands behind his back and returned to the window as
Tangeree picked up the heavy microscope case and
left.

There were papers to sign at the bank to close out
the account, and Tangeree took out the money she had
earned in assistant's fees. It amounted to over eight
hundred dollars, most of which was gone after she
went to a medical supply firm on Market Street. She
bought a carbolic acid atomizer, a case of scalpels,
sets of forceps, retractors, and other surgical instruments, an assortment of eyeglass lenses and parts for
frames, and an ophthalmoscope, laryngoscope, and a
stethoscope in the new metal design with flared ends.
Pharmaceutical firms in Philadelphia had pioneered in
preparing medicines in standard dosages, compressing
powders into pills and mixing liquids in dilutions that
were ready to administer to patients. The firm stocked
a wide range of medicines in standard dosages, in contrast to the bulk stocks of most firms, and she selected
a supply of common medicines and gave the clerk

the microscope to have it packed and shipped to Virginia City with the other things.

Germantown was where she had met Dennis Selfridge, but it was also where she had been extended unstinting hospitality by the Randolphs, and where she had known many moments of happiness and contentment. It was where she had spent three years of her life, watching the seasons come and go, passing the ancient beam and plaster buildings in the village, and seeing the crops in the fields as they sprouted, matured, and were harvested. It was a place she had made a part of herself, and there was an aching, poignant sense of leavetaking when everything was ready the next morning.

Phoebe Randolph had tears in her eyes, Claire sniffled and daubed at her eyes and nose with her handkerchief, and Randolph went with Tangeree in the carriage to see that her trunk got on the train. He nodded to a few people on the platform, made awkward, stilted conversation with Tangeree, and cleared his throat frequently and looked away. When the people began boarding the train, he patted her shoulder, leaned down to kiss her cheek, and dropped two double eagles into her pocket and strode away. He was standing by the side of the platform as the window by Tangeree's seat passed it, and he waved.

The train snorted and puffed into the station in the city, squealed and hissed to a stop, and habit pulled at Tangeree, urging her to follow the others to the entrance. A porter trundled the trunk on a cart to the baggage counter, and Tangeree went to the ticket counter. The tickets were a thick sheaf, and the bespectacled, balding old man went through them twice and explained them, looking at her worriedly over the top of his spectacles to see if she understood.

There was an hour's wait, then the train pulled into the other side of the station. Tangeree crossed the sets of tracks through the station on a sooty, elevated walk, and the conductor took her portmanteau, assisted her up the steps, and carried the portmanteau into the car to put it in the baggage rack over an empty seat. Others boarded the train as the engineer hissed softly, and brakemen trotted back and forth along the train and shouted to each other. A porter pushed a large cart loaded with luggage along the platform. The end of Tangeree's trunk was visible in the suitcases and boxes stacked on it.

The door on the baggage car opened with a distant rumble under the other noises, then rumbled and slammed closed. The whistle on the engine hooted, the car moved, then it jerked as the engine snorted rapidly. The car jerked more gently as the engine began puffing, and a man with a suitcase ran along the side of the train and leaped onto the step on a car. The sonorous echoes of the puffing of the engine faded as it pulled out of the station, then daylight brightened in the car as it moved out of the station.

A small girl in a bonnet stared wide-eyed at Tangeree over the back of the seat in front of her. A family with five children was across the aisle, and a boy among them sounded like he had croup. Four drummers in bright coats and straw hats dozed tiredly in their seats in the front of the car, the baggage rack above them filled with their sample cases. The rear of buildings and alleys passed the window, giving glimpses of streets with people, carriages, and other vehicles moving along them as the train picked up speed. Dingy washing hung on drooping lines between the rear windows of tenements, factories sprawled, and a slaughterhouse passed, cattle, swine, and sheep standing woodenly in the trampled, muddy pens, waiting. Then there were fields, streams, and wooded hills.

The train stopped at a small town, there were joyful reunions and tearful farewells on the platform as people got off and on, and the train went on. The novelty of setting out on the journey passed, and the seat became hard and uncomfortable. At noon the conductor passed through the car, calling out that the dining car was open. Some families had brought food and rustled papers as they unwrapped sandwiches. Tangeree went to the dining car and returned to her seat after the meal. Then she dozed, half-awakening at times and looking drowsily as the train stopped again, clattered across a bridge, or puffed on a hill. The train climbed mountains and wound around hairpin turns during late afternoon, and Tangeree went to the dining car and returned to her seat again.

Lights passed nearby and in the distance as darkness fell, and the train stopped at tiny stations lighted with oil lanterns and larger ones with gas lights. Tangeree awakened late at night as the train swayed and jolted heavily, going through a wide yard of tracks. The buildings on the outskirts of Pittsburgh passed. The ruddy glow of steel hearths brightened one side of the sky, and the air was thick with acrid fumes and smoke. There was a two-hour wait for another train in a waiting room where the atmosphere of late night hung heavy, babies crying, children whining, and people sprawling on seats. Then the train puffed into the station, and Tangeree pulled herself to her feet and picked up her portmanteau.

The faces in the car changed, bright and alert when they came into the car, and weary when they left a day or two later. There was a delay of several hours in a small town in Ohio named Dayton because a bridge had washed out, then another delay in Indiana because the tracks were up. After St. Louis, the East was left behind. The women were less inclined to wear hats unless they wanted protection from the sun, the clothes were more functional and less stylish, and the spaces were more open.

Kansas City had grown explosively since she had last seen it. Stock yards spread for miles around it, and the rail yard was filled with long lines of stock cars. After the train crossed the river, there were small towns and farms for a time, then the vast, empty prairie stretched out to the horizon on both sides. Two groups of noisy cowboys were in other cars in the train. They shot pistols and rifles at the passing telegraph poles, and the conductor rushed back and forth, angry and harassed. The train stopped at a place consisting of three houses and acres of stock pens, the northern terminus of a cattle trail, and the cowboys got off. Other cowboys were camped by the pens and had a large group of horses, waiting for those on the train, and they greeted each other with a bosterous uproar of whoops and pistols firing.

The towns were tiny and spaced far apart. The watering station on the open prairie between them consisted of a large water tank with a swinging boom under it, a windmill to drive a pump in a well, and a house for a caretaker and his family. Some had drawn other people and Indians, and a few were becoming small settlements, with trees, gardens, and a trading post. The train stopped at each one to fill its tank, feeling strangely silent and motionless as the prairie wind whistled around it.

At Denver the tracks went north to join those of the Union Pacific, and Tangeree glimpsed a section of the

Overland Trail. It was a deep gouge in the ground that cut almost all the way through a low mound, and at first she didn't recognize what it was because it was overgrown with sage and tumbleweeds. Then she overheard two men in the seat in front of her talking, one pointing it out to the other and telling him what it was. It brought back memories of when she had been a girl on the wagon train, the wagons toiling slowly along and taking days to travel the distance the train covered in hours.

The train went through South Pass with two engines, one pulling and the other pushing. The engines belched smoke and labored on the steep upgrades, and brakes squealed on the downgrades. The tracks curved around mountains on ledges overlooking deep gorges, crossed canyons on trestle bridges built of elaborate frameworks of timbers, and went through dark tunnels. Snow-capped peaks rose on all sides, and disappeared behind as the train reached the western slopes of the Rocky Mountains and passed from Wyoming Territory into Utah Territory. One of the engines was left behind at Ogden, and the train crossed the salty marshes and stretches of bare alkali north of Great Salt Lake.

There was a long delay at Tecoma because of a wreck on the tracks west of the town, and Tangeree went to a hotel for the night. She bathed and washed the grime from the days of traveling out of her hair, put on clean clothes from her portmanteau the next morning, and returned to the train station. As the train left the station it picked up speed, then slowed to a crawl and swayed from side to side as it went along a stretch of temporary tracks. The other tracks passed, a long section warped out of shape and an end of one track curled up, and the heavy crossties and gravel bedding scooped up. Men were working feverishly, and an engine and several battered cars were on their side in a shallow arroyo between the two sets of tracks. The train rocked heavily as it pulled back onto the permanent tracks, and began picking up speed.

The parched, sandy hills of Nevada passed as the wheels bumped and rumbled and the whistle shrilled. The breeze between the open windows in the car carried the dusty smell of the hills and the odor of smoke from the engine. The train stopped at towns, some no more than abandoned stagecoach stations with hollow shells of buildings and tumbleweeds were piled high against the crumbling, weathered rails of their corrals. Tangeree went to the dining car for lunch, then returned to her seat. The air passing through the car became torrid as the heat of the day settled, then the sun set and it cooled rapidly. The conductor closed the windows in the car and lit the small oil lamps by the doors on each end, and the lamps brightened as the light failed and darkness fell. Tangeree dozed off, and woke when the train stopped again. The weak yellow light from a window in the station illuminated part of the sign. It was Wadsworth.

When the train pulled away from the station, Tangeree rose and took down her portmanteau. Sleeping people were sprawled in their seats, their feet in the aisle, and she walked slowly along the aisle in the dim light from the lamps at the end of the car, balancing herself against the motion of the train and stepping around feet. She went into the tiny lavatory at the end of the car, lit the candle on the shelf, and ran water into the small basin. The water rocked in the basin from the movement of the train, and the flame on the candle fluttered in a draft coming in around the win-

dow. Tangeree washed her face, and leaned close to
the discolored mirror to see herself in the feeble light
of the candle as she tucked the loose wisps of hair. She
put her hat back on and pinned it, took her diploma
from the bottom of the portmanteau and put it on top,
then blew out the candle and returned to her seat.

The chill of the desert night filled the car, and
people slumped in the seats with their arms wrapped
around themselves as they slept. The eastern sky lightened, and the stars began dimming. Gray daylight
touched the hills and came through the sooty windows
of the car, gradually brightening, and details of the
terrain outside became visible. The conductor came
through the car and extinguished the oil lamps by the
door, and went into the next car. People in the car
stirred sleepily. The morning star gleamed brightly,
then it faded as the sun rose in tones of red that spread
across the hills. The train began picking up speed for
a dramatic arrival, and the wheels beat against the
rails. The conductor came back through the car,
shouting.

"Reno! Reno!"

People stretched, yawned, and began rising from
their seat. Tangeree rose to take down her portmanteau, the conductor touched his cap as he paused to
lift it down for her, and he walked on into the next
car, shouting. The car rocked as the train raced along
the tracks, and the whistle screamed. Buildings were
visible ahead as the train went around a long, gentle
curve, then they passed out of sight again as the tracks
straightened. The whistle whooped with a rising and
falling note, brakes squealed under the car, and people
moving about in the aisle held onto seats as the train
slowed. The bell on the engine tolled, the whistle
shrieked, and steam roared as the train braked jerkily

to a stop. Most of the people moved toward the front
door of the car. Tangeree picked up her portmanteau
and went to the rear door. A brakeman touched his
cap and reached for her portmanteau, handing it back
to her as she stepped down to the platform.

They were standing a few yards away, looking at
the larger group of people coming out of the cars in
front. Her mother lifted herself on her toes to see over
people, and her face was in profile. An expectant smile
wreathed her beautiful, olive features, and her small,
delicate hands were clutched together in front of her.
Her long, black hair hung down her back. The wings
of white at her temples had spread, and she was
wearing an unadorned dark dress that fit her slender
figure neatly. The white in her hair looked out of
place, because there was an enduring youth about her,
a combination of the lack of lines in her smooth face
and the alert way she stood and held her head.

Abigail Dowd had gained so much weight she was
almost unrecognizable, and the bright gingham she
was wearing made her look even larger. Bobby Bownay was a gangling boy, looking stiff and uncomfortable in brown, baggy wool trousers, a blue wool coat
that was too short for him, and a shirt and tie. His
hair was trimmed down to the skin in a straight line
above his ears, and his hat was pulled down tightly on
his head, the brim precisely parallel with the ground.

Abigail looked at Tangeree as she walked toward
them, curiosity but no recognition on her face. She
looked beyond Tangeree, then turned her head and
looked back in the other direction. Tangeree's mother
glanced around and saw her, then rushed to her with
a muffled exclamation of delight. She threw her arms
around Tangeree, clutching her tightly, and Tangeree
bent over her mother and kissed her.

"Ma, you look beautiful, and you look about twenty years old."

Her mother silently shrugged the comment off, on the point of bursting into tears of happiness, as she looked up at Tangeree with a beaming, ecstatic smile. She reached up and touched Tangeree's cheek in a light caress with the tips of her fingers, her large, liquid eyes moving over Tangeree's face. Abigail plucked at Bobby Bownay's shoulder and walked toward them, looking at Tangeree in astonishment.

"Laws, Tangeree, is that you? Here I was looking right at you, and I wouldn't have knowed you in a million years. I figured you might be some mine owner's daughter or some theater actress, but I didn't figure you was one of us. Now I can see it's you, but laws how you've changed!"

"It's been a long time since we've seen each other, Abby," Tangeree replied, turning to her. She put her arms around the woman and bent down to kiss her cheek. "You're looking well, Abby."

"Oh, your ma's keeping me fit except for the fact that I need two chairs to set down. And that's my own fault, because she's told me a thousand times that I'm rooting out myself a grave with my teeth. Bobby Bownay's growed a good bit since you've seen him, ain't he? Do your manners, Bobby Bownay."

"I'm pleased to meet you, ma'm," the boy muttered, extending his hand stiffly.

"We've met before, but I'm sure you don't remember it," Tangeree laughed, bending over and taking his hand. "And you've turned into a very handsome young lad, Bobby Bownay."

The boy flushed furiously as he stepped back. Abigail chuckled and patted his shoulder affectionately, looking at Tangeree's mother. "Here I was looking right at her, and I didn't know her. Ain't she growed? And she was a pretty girl, but she's turned into the prettiest woman I ever seen. Ain't she going to set this town on its ear?"

Tangeree's mother smiled and nodded. She put her hand on Tangeree's arm and squeezed it gently, looking up at her. "Let me see it, Tangi," she said quietly.

Tangeree opened her portmanteau and handed the diploma to her mother. Her mother gingerly plucked at the knot in the ribbon and untied it, then carefully unrolled the diploma and held it by the edges as she read it. People moved back and forth around them, the train whistle tooted, and the train pulled away, the bell clanging and the engine puffing.

The people on the platform thinned out, and the activity and the noise faded. They were alone on the platform, the boy looking around restlessly and scratching, Abigail craning her neck and looking at the diploma in awe and illiterate lack of comprehension, and Tangeree's mother slowly reading it and looking at the signatures and seal on it. She swallowed and blinked, a tear overflowing and running down her cheek, and she carefully rolled up the diploma and tied the ribbon back on it.

"I'll hold it until we get home, Tangi. I have a frame for it."

Tangeree smiled and nodded, picking up her portmanteau and putting her arm around her mother's shoulders. They walked along the platform, her mother carrying the diploma, and Abigail and Bobby Bownay following them.

PART FIVE

THE FRONTIER HEALERS

23

CHRISTOPHER WOODRUFF had in a large measure filled the gap left when the memories of her father had faded, and not only because of the heroic stature he had achieved in her mind through financing her education. He was easy to admire, a large and distinguished man with a powerful, authoritative presence, and still a kind, gentle, and courteous man.

The man at the door seemed in many respects a copy of him. He was smoothly shaven in place of Woodruff's full mustache and bristling muttonchop whiskers, his hair was trimmed short, and his eyes were a darker shade of blue. His face was tanned instead of flushed and ruddy like Woodruff's, and there were no lines and splotches of age. But the resemblance was remarkable. The strong lines of the nose, mouth, and chin were the same, and he had the same aura of authority about him. He was a strikingly handsome man, tall and muscular. And he was about four or five years older than she.

Tangeree had been expecting the housekeeper to open the door, and she was taken aback. The man's eyes held hers as she tried to recover her composure. She dropped her eyes to his chin, clearing her throat.

"I'm Doctor Beaunais. I understand Mr. Woodruff has returned, and I wish to speak with him if he is unengaged."

The silence stretched out. The man hadn't been listening, and he looked down at her, his eyes moving over her face. Their eyes met again, and the atmosphere between them crackled with tension, a mutual attraction between them at some fundamental level that bypassed conventional means of communication. Tangeree felt a strong, surging response to him swelling within her, and it brought with it the warning of the penalty in agony she had paid when she had been deceived by Dennis Selfridge. She set her mouth in a firm line and controlled herself as she dropped her eyes again.

"I beg your pardon, Doctor Beaunais," the man said apologetically, stepping back and holding the door open. "Yes, my father's in, and he's been hoping that you would stop by. I'm James Woodruff, and I'm pleased to meet you."

He had been at college and then absent attending to family business when she had returned to Virginia City from San Francisco. In retrospect the things she had heard about him seemed to be understatement. She nodded as she stepped inside. "I'm pleased to meet you, Mr. Woodruff."

"And I beg your pardon for being rude, but you aren't at all as I expected you to be."

In addition to matching her feelings about him, the compliment was one of the most extreme kind, an implicit compliment in a statement of fact. It invited a joking reply, but Tangeree smiled politely and nodded, looking straight ahead. He closed the door, then he hesitated and she could feel his confusion. Like his father, he didn't appear to be a man who often experienced awkward moments. He started to invite her into the parlor, lifting his hand to motion toward it, and the housekeeper came into sight around the curve in the stairway, trotting rapidly down the stairs.

"I'm sorry, Mister James, but I was helping Milly with that fresh linen."

"That's quite all right, Mrs. Jackson," he replied. "Doctor Beaunais has come to see my father, and I'll step up and let him know she's here if you'll show her into the parlor."

"Yes, I'll be glad to. How are you today, Doctor Beaunais?"

"I'm very well, Mrs. Jackson. How are you?"

"Oh, I'm in my usual muddle, but I'll live. Just come right this way, if you would."

The housekeeper's presence relieved the tension. James walked toward the stairs as Tangeree followed the housekeeper into the parlor. On the edge of her vision, she could see that James was still looking at her as he started up the stairs and she went through the doorway, but the gratification over his reaction to her was smothered by the dark warnings of painful experience.

The parlor was unchanged from years before, more functional than decorative and a reflection of the personality of Woodruff and of his daughter Christina. As Tangeree sat down, the housekeeper moved pillows on a sofa and adjusted the drapes, talking about the family's return the day before from their trip to Europe, the places they had been, and the things they had brought back with them.

Woodruff's booming voice came through the doorway as he walked down the stairs with James, and he stepped into the doorway, smiling expectantly. His hair, whiskers, and mustache were completely white and the lines in his face were deeper, but he was much like he had been before: large, flushed, and healthy-looking. Tangeree smiled affectionately as she walked toward him, and he chortled with delight as he embraced her and bent over to kiss her.

"Well, well, here's our doctor. Let me get a look at you." His eyebrows lifted and he glanced at the housekeeper and looked back at Tangeree. "Good Lord! I see what you meant, Hattie."

"Yes, sir, I told you," the housekeeper chuckled. "I told you she's a really pretty lady now."

"And you were absolutely right," Woodruff said, beaming down at Tangeree. "You've finally met James, haven't you, Tangi? And Christina is around here somewhere—Christina?"

"Here I am, Dad," Christina said as she came through the doorway. She had grown into a willowy, attractive young woman, and she smiled radiantly and and put out her arms as she walked toward Tangeree. "Tangeree, it's so good to see you again."

"And it's good to see you again, Christina," Tangeree replied as they embraced. "My, haven't you grown up?"

"Haven't we both?" Christina laughed. "She's absolutely beautiful, isn't she, Dad?"

"Indeed she is," Woodruff said. "Here, let's sit down so we can talk. Could we have some coffee, Hattie? You sit here where I can see you, Tangi. I want to know everything you've done!"

The housekeeper went out as they sat down, Woodruff and Christina on the sofa facing Tangeree, and James in a chair at one side. Tangeree told them briefly about the medical college, the Randolphs, and Philadelphia, acutely aware of when James looked at her, politely looked away, and looked at her again. The housekeeper returned with a coffee service and passed cups around. Woodruff stirred his and took a sip, nodding in satisfaction.

"The Randolphs are a little stuffy, like a lot of people there, but I liked them and I thought you'd be happy there."

"They couldn't have been more hospitable to me, Mr. Woodruff. And it was like leaving family the morning I left, for them and for me."

"Well, I'm more than pleased that everything worked out so well for you, Tangi. You've been back about four months now, haven't you?"

"Yes, I returned just in time for the worst part of the summer," she laughed. "You were lucky you were in Europe, because it was a hot one."

Christina grunted ruefully and shook her head. "It wasn't cool there, or on the ship. Incidentally, we saw an article in the newspaper in San Francisco about something you'd done. What was that, Dad?"

"Yes, that's right," Woodruff said, looking at Tangeree with a pleased smile. "It was right on the front page, Tangi, something to do with surgery on a girl's throat."

"That would be the girl from Bodie who had diptheria," Tangeree replied, nodding. "She was about to smother, and I opened her trachea so she could breathe. Unfortunately, the word of mouth around here has it that I simply slit her throat, so all my patients with any sort of respiratory problem watch me closely to see what I have in my hands."

They all laughed heartily, and Tangeree smiled as she put her coffee cup on the table by her chair and stood. "I know you have things to do after your absence, and I must be on my way."

"Yes, I suppose I'd better get down to the mine," Woodruff said, climbing to his feet and looking at James. "You go on down and see Martin about that business he wrote us about, then meet me at the mine."

"I'll go with you, Dad," Christina said, bouncing up. "I'll go get ready."

Woodruff hesitated, then nodded. "All right, but you wear a dress, Christina."

Christina had started to bristle defiantly as he hesitated, and she nodded in satisfaction, turning toward the door and looking over her shoulder at Tangeree as she walked toward it. "He's still trying to change me and marry me off before I take the mine away from him and James, but I won't change and I won't leave."

Tangeree laughed, and Woodruff chuckled fondly as Christina went out. James smiled at Christina, and looked at Tangeree as he put his coffee cup down and walked toward the door.

"It was very pleasant meeting you, and I hope to see you again very soon, Doctor Beaunais."

"Thank you, Mr. Woodruff. It was very pleasant talking with you."

James left, and Woodruff looked down at Tangeree with a contemplative smile as they walked slowly toward the door. "It took almost seven years, Tangi, and I know they were hard years for you. Was it worth it?"

"More than worth it, Mr. Woodruff, and it wasn't all that hard. In fact, I enjoyed most of it. And I'm going to pay you back, you know. It might take me a while to—"

"No," he said, shaking his head firmly. "I don't want to hear anything about that, Tangi. You see, the

way things stand now I can take a litttle credit for
the way you are. And I'm not going to let you take
that away from me."

His tone and expression were affectionate, but
adamant. Tangeree smiled up at him, standing on
tiptoe to kiss him, then walked toward the door.
"Good morning, Mr. Woodruff."

"Good morning, my dear."

Her gig was parked on the street in front of the
house, the horse tied to one of the tethering posts
by the gate. She saw James at the corner of the stable
behind the house as she went out the gate. She tried
to act as though she hadn't seen him, but some in-
voluntary impulse made her glance at him from the
corners of her eyes as she untied the tether and
walked along the side of the horse to the gig. He was
watching and saw her look, and he waved. Tangeree
waved, then felt aggravated at herself because she
had glanced at him and because she was clumsy in
climbing into the gig. She gathered up the traces and
clucked to the horse, turning it onto the street.

The horse pulled the small two-wheel gig effortlessly at a smart trot as she drove through the streets
toward the house, passing drays, wagons, and carriages. The scene was familiar from years before,
because Virginia City hadn't changed. The mine
tailings were larger, a few more houses had been
added and there were a few more shacks in the rocky
arroyos around the town, and some buildings had
been razed and replaced by larger ones. There were
other alterations, but none of that brought change.
Virginia City was unlike other places in that it was
a spirit and atmosphere, rather than streets of buildings.

It was still busy during the day, uproariously noisy

with revelry at night, and stirring even during the
hushed, early hours of the morning, as miners with
their lunch pails and lamps went to work and the
elevators in the superstructures over the mineshafts
groaned as they lowered miners thousands of feet
into the earth then raised stubby, heavy cars filled
with ore to trundle to the mill. The blistering sun
still baked Mount Davidson, the icy cold of winter
gripped it, and the Washoe zephyr scoured it. Most
of all, the constant pounding of the mill stamps continued, the heartbeat of Virginia City.

The house had a fresh coat of paint, and the trees
that had been nourished with the afterbirths of dozens
of babies had grown large, shading the house, part
of the garden, and the barn. A woman and a man and
woman were on the porch. The women spoke and the
man lifted his hat as Tangeree passed the porch and
drove toward the rear of the house. She smiled and
nodded to them. Most people had been reluctant to
trust her at first, but there had been several initial
successes that had started word spreading.

A cholera epidemic had struck Pioche, a small
mining town thirty miles away, and she and Leggett
had gone there and shared the credit for stopping the
spread of the disease. One of her patients had been a
man with a lacerated arm that would have been an
automatic amputation for most doctors, but the miracle of Lister's techniques had saved the man's arm.
An old couple named Jessup had been coming weekly
for years to get a bottle of tonic that was half whiskey
and half infusion of burdock and ginseng. The old
man was crippled and the old woman had to help him
along, and she had been going blind with cataracts.
The expression on the old woman's face when Tangeree had unwrapped the bandages three days after

surgically removing the cataracts had been a rich
reward. The old woman had spread the story all
over town. And there had been a few other successes
of a dramatic nature. But most people still trusted her
mother more.

Bobby Bownay came out of the house to unharness
the horse and take it to the barn, and Abigail was
singing cheerfully as she waddled around in the
kitchen and prepared lunch. Tangeree went to her
room, took off her hat and changed into a dark muslin
dress, then walked through the house to the examination room. A small boy with sores on his mouth was
sitting on the examination table, and Tangeree's
mother was mixing alum root salve on the table at the
side of the room. She looked over her shoulder as
Tangeree came in.

"How are the Woodruffs, Tangi?"

"They're healthy and in good spirits, Ma. I tried to
talk to Mr. Woodruff on that matter we discussed,
but he wouldn't listen to me."

"I told you he wouldn't," her mother replied, then
her smile widened, her eyes twinkling. "Did you see
young Woodruff?"

Tangeree shrugged and nodded, looking away. "I
saw him. He looks a lot like his father, doesn't he?"

"Like his father did forty years ago, I'd say. The
Gibsons out there have been waiting for you. Mr.
Gibson would like to see about getting some spectacles. You can go ahead and bring him in now, if
you want to, because I'm about through."

Tangeree nodded and went out to the porch to
call the man in. His wife came in with him, and
Tangeree led them to the chairs in the corner of the
examination room as she talked to the man. His
distance vision was satisfactory, but he was having

increasing difficulty in seeing to read. The woman was illiterate, and they chuckled as they talked about how the man's impaired vision was interfering with their nightly entertainment of his reading the newspaper aloud to her. Tangeree took her ophthalmoscope from a cabinet, moved Gibson's chair around to the light from the window, and examined his eyes. There was no evidence of disease or abnormality in his eyes. She gave him a newspaper to look at, put a wooden frame on his eyes, and dropped test lenses into the slots in the frame to find a set that corrected his vision.

Her mother finished mixing the salve and called in the boy's mother from the porch to give it to her, then went to the kitchen for lunch. It was a relatively quiet day, as most had been since Tangeree had returned from Philadelphia and assumed part of the heavy burden of work her mother had been doing. There were occasional nights when there was little time for sleep, but by working together at times and independently of each other at other times, the long stretches of days without sleep of past years had been eliminated.

And their different approaches to treatment of the ill and injured were compatible. There was a sharp contrast between the two, because herbalist medicine was based on an accumulation of empirical knowledge, and conventional medicine was based on a systematic, organized investigation into the theory of disease and the physiological functions of the body. Conventional medicine was broader in scope, and her mother had never and would never attempt amputation or any other of the other wide range of surgical procedures that Tangeree regarded as routine. Conventional medicine was also more aggressive in its approach to the treatment of diseases, with chemicals that often triggered side effects or were mildly injurious to the body in their onslaught against the disease, while herbalist medicines were in general of a nature that assisted the body's defensive and recuperative powers. But in most instances there was no conflict between the two, and they could often be used in conjunction with each other.

There was more of a conflict between Tangeree's and her mother's approach to being paid. Her mother continued to let people pay what they wished, but Tangeree had seen too many instances when people who could have paid in full had given five cents or nothing, at times when she and her mother had been in dire need.

She took the frame off the man's eyes and measured his head for the frame and earpiece size, then returned to the cabinet and took out the boxes of lenses and parts.

"The spectacles will cost three dollars and fifty cents, Mr. Gibson."

The man and woman winced, looking at each other, and the man shook his head doubtfully. "I didn't think they was going to cost that much."

"I know that's a lot, but the parts cost me a lot. Do you have a regular job?"

"Yes, I work at the Virginia Consolidated. Does that make a difference?"

"It would if you didn't have a job, because I don't charge anything when someone needs something and they don't have any money."

"Well, I ain't looking for somebody to just give me something, but I didn't think they was going to be that much. Don't you have any cheaper ones?"

"No, they're all the same price. If you wish, you

could pay fifty cents a week for the next eight weeks. That might be easier for you."

Gibson brightened, looking at his wife. She frowned in concentration as she counted on her fingers, then shook her head. "Fifty cents a week for eight weeks is four dollars, not three dollars and fifty cents."

"The extra fifty cents is because I'll have to wait two months for the money."

They looked at each other again, and the woman smiled and shrugged. Gibson looked at Tangeree, smiling and nodding. "We'll do that, then."

Tangeree nodded, taking the lenses and parts out of the boxes. She assembled the spectacles, put them on the man and adjusted the earpieces, and handed him the newspaper. He beamed happily as he looked at the newspaper through the spectacles, then took them off and carefully folded them and put them in his pocket as he and his wife left. Tangeree put the boxes of lenses and parts back in the cabinet, and went to the kitchen for lunch.

After lunch, patients came at intervals during the afternoon. One was a small girl with thrush, the membranes of her mouth and throat covered with the white lesions characteristic of the disease. The iodine treatment of conventional medicine was a quick, positive specific for thrush, but it frequently caused nausea and other side effects, and the girl wasn't in generally good health. The black snakeroot infusion took much longer for a complete cure with its more gentle action, but there were no apparent side effects. Tangeree and her mother discussed it, and decided on the black snakeroot infusion.

A woman brought a boy who had broken out with boils. A home remedy poltice had been used, and some of the boils had spread into areas of infection.

There was a danger of septicemia developing during the time it would take sanicle root infusion to act against the infection, and while the powerful, caustic carbolic acid solution always caused some sloughing of flesh, it stopped infection immediately. Tangeree lanced the boils and drained them, and applied dressings of gauze soaked in carbolic acid solution as the boy squirmed and whimpered from the sting of the acid.

The woman left with the boy, and a man arrived, wanting a tooth extracted. Tangeree had found her mother's procedure for tooth extraction to be far superior to the brutal wrenching out of teeth practiced by most conventional doctors, and she mixed the olive oil and morphine paste, put out the dental instruments, and assisted her mother.

Footsteps crossed the porch again during late afternoon, and Tangeree looked up as her mother went into the waiting room and chuckled dryly. "Don't tell me you're feeling bad."

"No, I'd like to see a doctor, but it isn't because I'm ill."

It was James Woodruff's voice. Tangeree's mother stepped back into the examination room, beckoning him. "Come on in, then, James."

Tangeree's dress was rumpled and her hair was untidy. She tugged at her dress frantically and started to lift her hands to her hair. Then she dropped them and nodded to him as he stepped into the doorway. "Good afternoon, Mr. Woodruff."

"Good afternoon, Doctor Beaunais. I come to see if you would be interested in seeing Faye Templeton and her theater troupe at the Bella Union this evening. I realize this is very short notice, but I found out only this afternoon that this is the last day of Miss Templeton's engagement here."

"I'm very grateful for the invitation, Mr. Woodruff, but I'll be busy this evening. I have some reading I must do."

Her inner conflict between wanting to go with him and wanting to avoid him was reflected in her tone, and it came out more flat and blunt than she had intended. There was a momentary silence; then her mother spoke.

"Tangi has a lot of reading to do, because she gets medical journals, things from pharmaceutical companies, and just about every new book that has to do with medicine. Did you enjoy your trip to Europe?"

James smiled and nodded, turning to her. "Yes, I'm happy to be back, but it was enjoyable. We went to England, Germany, and France."

"Yes, that's what I heard. It sounds like quite a tour. I'd enjoy hearing about it, so you'll have to have dinner with us soon and tell us about it. If you're going to see Faye Templeton tonight, you could come tomorrow night or another night this week."

He hesitated, glancing between Tangeree and her mother, and smiled and shrugged. "I didn't necessarily want to see Faye Templeton. But I wouldn't want to intrude."

"Oh, you wouldn't be intruding, James. Take your horse on around the house and get Bobby Bownay to take care of it for you. We'll be through here in a few minutes and dinner should be ready before long."

He glanced between Tangeree and her mother again. "Well, if you're absolutely sure I won't be intruding . . . ."

"I'm positive," her mother chuckled. "Go give your

horse to Bobby Bownay, and we'll be in there in a few minutes."

James smiled and nodded as he went back through the door. Tangeree looked at her mother, her lips pursed in pique. Her mother looked at her and shrugged innocently, her features neutral and her eyes dancing with humor. Tangeree sighed as she walked to her room to comb her hair.

Dinner was enjoyable. Surprise had been a large factor in the tension that had been between Tangeree and James during the morning. James had his father's aplomb and fit into the group at the table, and the atmosphere was relaxed and friendly. And he was entertaining. He talked about the places he and his father and sister had visited on their trip, and about other trips they had made. He was also well-informed, he had heard of Palmer, and he knew more than most laymen about recent advances in medicine. Tangeree searched for any similarity between him and Dennis Selfridge, and there was none. James was courteous, amiable, and attentive, but he wasn't ingratiating and didn't hesitate to disagree, and he seemed honest and straightforward. He seemed a little too perfect. Tangeree enjoyed the conversation and the dinner, but the warnings whispered in the back of her mind.

After he left, Tangeree and her mother helped Abigail wash the dishes and clean the kitchen. Abigail and Bobby Bownay went to their rooms, and Tangeree sat at the table again and lit a cigarette. Her mother took her pipe from the cabinet, filled it and went to the stove to light it, then sat down at the table.

"That young Woodruff has his eye on you, or I'll miss my guess, Tangi."

"He'll find someone else to eye," Tangeree replied, shrugging. "I'm not the only woman in the West."

"Oh, I know that," her mother chuckled. "And so does he. There was some talk about him and a girl in San Francisco a year or two ago. But the way it looks to me, any time she spent in collecting things for a hope chest was time wasted."

"And any time he spends eyeing me is time wasted," Tangeree replied. puffing on her cigarette. "I didn't tell you, Ma, because I was ashamed of myself and I still am, but I was fooled by a man in Philadelphia. And that taught me a lesson."

Her mother lifted her eyebrows in surprise. "You were? Well, I didn't think any man would be able to get close enough to you to fool you, Tangi."

"It isn't funny, Ma. It really hurt me."

, "I know it isn't funny, and I'm not joking, honey. But there are worst things than being fooled by a man. And the shape you were in for the longest time after what happened to us on the way up the Mississippi was worse."

Tangeree puffed on her cigarette, and shook her head and shrugged as she exhaled. "I don't know, Ma. Perhaps you're right."

"I know I am, honey. A frame of mind like that blocks you off from too much of life. And as far as having to do with men is concerned, there's nothing in the world that says you have to get married. At the same time, if you meet a man you love and who loves you, you're better off married."

Tangeree shrugged noncommittally. They were silent for a moment, then Tangeree looked at her mother musingly. "I cheated you out of that, didn't I, Ma?"

Her mother looked at her, then looked away and shook her head. "No, you've never cheated me out of anything, Tangi."

"I think I did, Ma. I've thought about that night a lot, and I know if I'd been a little more—"

"Tangi, I've thought a lot about that night, too. And what I've thought about most is the way I beat you that night. I'm more ashamed of that than anything I've ever done, and I don't like to think about it."

"You didn't beat me, Ma. You slapped me, but I think—"

"I beat you, Tangi. I *beat* you, and I don't like to think about it."

Tangeree sighed and nodded, reaching over to pat her mother's hand, and she rose and walked to the stove. She opened the stove and tossed the cigarette into it, thinking about whether to tell her mother what she had found out about Dawson. She decided not to. She closed the stove and returned to the table, and bent over her mother and kissed her. "Good night, Ma."

"Good night, Tangi."

24

THE WHEELS on the gig whirred and the horse's hoofs raised puffs of dust as he turned onto Fourth Avenue with a light, eager step, knowing that he was on his way home to a bucket of grain and his quiet, cool stall in the barn. Fourth Avenue was a busy street of saloons, offices, and stores, with the marshal's office across a wide corner from a large saddlery at the intersection with Empire Street. It was a street that was normally crowded, and one Tangeree avoided when there was a convenient choice of another route. But it was the most direct route home, the horse knew the town as well as she did, and she let him have his head, sitting back in the gig and relaxing as she held the slack traces loosely.

The street was unusually quiet. The meaning of the hush and the movements among the crowd of men in front of the Roaring Gimlet Saloon didn't register in Tangeree's mind at first. The night had been long and the childbirth had dragged slowly along for hours, past dawn and then down into the day, bringing hot, dry eyes, a numb daze of fatigue, and detached impatience toward the loud, bright-faced, and energetic people who had slept through the

435

night and who bustled noisily about and asked questions.

The meaning of other things didn't register as she approached the saloon, the restless movements and tossing heads among the horses at the hitching rail, two men pounding along the boardwalk toward the marshal's office, and a surging rush of men toward an alley and the corners of buildings. The baby had been the woman's first and she had been scarcely more than a girl. It had first been necessary to coax her out of her terror and explain away the myths and half-truths that had been told her by cruel and thoughtless women. But she had borne her labor well. Her tired face and the grateful face of her young husband had been wreathed in smiles as they looked at their strong healthy daughter. The night had been long but well-spent, and at home there would be an early lunch, a chat with her mother and a cigarette, and hours of sleep.

Then the meaning of the scene on the boardwalk registered in her mind. Two men faced a single man fifty feet away, coats pulled back from holsters and hands poised above pistols. The two were heavily armed, both with double holsters. The single man was tall, in a long black coat, and with black trousers tucked into high boots. His face was hidden in the shadow of his hatbrim, and his long handlebar mustaches drooped below the dark shadow. His single holster hung low on his right side, well down his thigh. He was as motionless as a statue, the fingers of his right hand curved to grasp as it hovered over the pistol. Tangeree snatched for the whip to lash the horse into a run.

Hands darted downward, pistols thundered with a shattering clap of sound that reverberated between the fronts of buildings, and smoke blossomed. The horse slowed, veering to one side then the other in fright. Pistols continued firing, the horses at the hitching rail kicked and reared as they whinnied in terror, and Tangeree slashed the whip down across the horse's back as a bullet from a wild shot struck the street in front of the horse, throwing a geyser of dirt up in his face. The horse reared, pawing at the air with his forefeet, and the gig tilted sharply backward with the horse towering over it, almost falling back on it. Tangeree pulled back on the traces to drag the horse's head down, and swung the whip around to sting the horse's stomach and make him settle. The horse plunged, kicked, and turned toward the boardwalk.

The gig bounced and jerked from the horse's rear hoofs pounding the front of it, and Tangeree sawed on the traces and shouted at the horse, trying to control him. The horse twisted from one side to the other, a haze of gunpowder smoke rose from the boardwalk. Billowing clouds came from the pistols as the men continued firing. One of the two men was down, resting on an elbow and firing a single pistol. The other was staggering backwards and firing both pistols from the hip in a wild fusillade. Splinters flew from the boardwalk and the front of the building, and glass crumbled from windows and fell to the boardwalk. The tall man faced the hail of bullets with glacial calm, holding his pistol at arm's length as he aimed and slowly fired.

The horse reared and almost pitched back again, the gig teetering as the horse loomed over it, and Tangeree put her weight back against the traces as she slashed the horse across the stomach with the whip. The horse settled and bucked, lifting the light gig by the shafts and slamming it back down. Suddenly it was all over, gunpowder smoke drifting up from the boardwalk and all three men down, and men running out of the alley, from behind the corners of buildings, and pouring out of the Roaring Gimlet. Men started running across the street, and one ran to the horse's head and seized the bridle. His face was vaguely familiar, as many were in Virginia City, and Tangeree scrambled out of the gig and took the horse's head.

"Thank you very much. For a moment I thought I was going to have him on my lap."

"He's a lively one, ain't he, Doc?" the man laughed excitedly, then nodded toward the boardwalk. "That was the Dexter brothers, and they both got it right in the gizzard."

Tangeree took the bridle and patted the horse's head, talking to him and calming him, the man ran on, shouting to someone across the street that it had been the Dexter brothers. It was a well-known name; they were rumored to be the ones who had been robbing express coaches carrying bullion from Virginia City, Gold Hill, and other mining towns to the railroad station at Reno. Nothing had been proven and the peace officers had been helpless. The Dexters had remained at large, and the express companies were contemplating extreme means of closing the gap between the law and justice.

It didn't seem totally unlikely that had happened. The marshal was under strong pressure from law-abiding elements in town to suppress gunplay, and he did, with severely harsh methods. But he and his deputies had been conspicuously absent in the moments before the shooting had begun, even though his office was only a few yards down the street. He

came into sight along the boardwalk as Tangeree
stood in the street and calmed her horse, a tall, stern-
faced man with thick mustaches and a wide-brim hat,
with a star gleaming on his vest as his coat swung
open. Three of his deputies followed him as he
pushed his way through the people, and one of the
deputies looked at Tangeree and pulled at the marshal's arm, pointing at her. The marshal looked at
her over the other people's heads and shouted, beckoning. Tangeree led her horse to the end of the hitching rail in front of the saloon, tied it, and took the
case off the floorboard of the gig.

One of the deputies pushed through the people
toward her, shouldering them aside. "Get the hell
out of the way! Make room for the doc to get in here!"

"What do you need a doc for?" someone laughed.
"They're dead, ain't they?"

"They got to be pronounced dead, ain't they?" the
deputy shouted back angrily. "Now move out of the
way and make room! Come on, right this way, Doc."

Tangeree followed the deputy through the crowd-
ing, jostling mass of laughing, excited men as he
shoved and shouldered them. The marshal and the
other two deputies stood over the two men on the
boardwalk in a small circle surrounded by the smiling,
agitated faces. The marshal touched the brim of his
hat, shouting over the uproar.

"Take a look at them, Doc, and see what you think!
Jake, get down there and keep them people away
from the other'un until we get done here!"

One of the deputies pushed into the crowd, forcing
his way along the boardwalk, and Tangeree knelt
by one of the men. He was on his side, and she carefully turned him onto his back. The mouth sagged
open, the tongue hanging out one side. A bullet had

gone through the stomach and out the side, under
the ribcage. Part of the small intestine had been pulled
through the hole where the bullet had exited by the
suction created by the bullet, and it was a flabby,
bloody mass in the side of the shirt. Another bullet
had gone through the chest, left of center and through
or near the heart. The sightless eyes stared upward,
and there was no pulse. Tangeree closed the eyes with
a thumb and forefinger, picked up the hat and put it
over the face.

"All right, the doc has pronounced that one dead!"
the marshal shouted. "Now get the hell back and give
us some room! You'll get your look at them, if you'll
just get back so we can do what has to be done!"

The other man was in the process of dying. It was
futile to try to do anything, because two holes in the
chest spouted gouts of blood and foamed with leakage from a lung, and there was a gargling rattle of
blood flooding into the breathing passages as the
chest moved in shallow, gasping pants. He was conscious, his eyes moving to her face as she knelt by him.
And when life couldn't be saved and awareness was
present, easing the passage into eternity was a vital,
inescapable duty, an inviolate dictum that had been
repeatedly stressed through her childhood by her
mother. Tangeree leaned low over his face and
touched it, looking into his eyes.

Many things they wanted to say, things that varied
from a confession of a trivial wrong done years before
or a message for a relative to a description of a place
they had once lived or a favorite food. And others only
wanted someone near. The shuffling and stamping of
feet on the boardwalk and the loud laughter and
conversation made it impossible to hear anything,
but his lips didn't move. And it was difficult to look

into his eyes with compassion and provide companionship, because the face was selfish and cruel. It was similar to faces that had looked down at her years before on a narrow dirt road by the Mississippi, and it was similar to the face behind Dennis Selfridge's mask. But it was her duty, and she did it. Then he was finished, and she closed the eyes with a thumb and forefinger and put the hat over the face.

"The doc has pronounced both of them dead!" the marshal shouted. "The doc has pronounced the Dexter brothers dead! Slim, pick out four men here and pissant them down and put them on the boardwalk in front of the office where everybody can get their look! All right, get out of the way and let us through! Get the hell out of the way!"

Part of the crowd went with the men carrying the two bodies, and others streamed out into the street and moved further along the boardwalk to join the thinner crowd around the third man. The marshal elbowed and shouldered his way through the people, his boots grinding glass that had shattered from windows. Tangeree followed him and knelt by the man. She put the case down and felt for the pulse, glancing over him. The pulse was firm and strong, but he was wounded in several places.

There was a bloody hole in the left thigh of the trousers. She leaned over the man and ripped the hole open. The wound was superficial, a graze along the outside of the thigh. There was blood on the right side of the shirt and a hole in the shirt, and she tore the shirt open. It was a longer, deeper graze, but it hadn't penetrated to bone. The left side of the shirt was soaked and clinging to his chest with blood around a hole, and she tore the hole open. It was serious, a hole in the shoulder on the edge of the chest cavity.

The bullet had missed the lung, but blood welled from the hole. She wormed her hand under his shoulder and felt for blood, but found none. The bullet was still in him.

"It's a bad'un, ain't it?"

Tangeree almost jumped as he spoke quietly. His skin was pale under the dark tan from his eyebrows down and gray on his lined, untanned forehead, but his dark, wary eyes were alert. He was about forty, well over six feet and with a rangy, wiry build, and he looked healthy. More importantly, the thin, grim lips under the black handlebar mustache and the hard, lined face reflected an unquenchable will to live. And there was a suggestion of dry humor in the line of the thin lips and the narrow, watchful eyes as he looked up at her. Tangeree silently nodded, pulling the case closer and opening it. The marshal knelt on the other side of the man and looked at Tangeree.

"What do you think, Doc?"

"He's seriously wounded, Marshal. I'll have to take him to the house."

The marshal grunted and nodded, and looked up at one of the deputies. "Go get a wagon to haul him to her house, Hank." He sat back on his heels and pushed his hat back with his thumb, looking down at the man. "What happened here, mister?"

"They called me a liar."

"Well, we don't go for shoot-outs on the street here, mister."

"And I don't go for somebody calling me a liar."

"It was the Dexters who started it, Marshal," a bystander said. "I heard it all, and this man here was talking to them real peaceable until they commenced hollering, and cussing, and carrying on. And it was fair, because they throwed down first. Me and Cal here seen it all and heard it all."

The marshal looked up at him, nodding. "All right, you and Cal go on down to the office so's I can get a statement from you." He looked back down at the man. "What's your name, mister?"

"Frank Bodine."

The noise faded, and there was an instant of silence. Then a murmur of excited conversation spread through the crowd and several men ran along the boardwalk, shouting and telling people the name. Tangeree hesitated as she folded gauze, looking down at the man, then put the gauze over the bullet hole in the man's shoulder. He was a well-known gunfighter whose name had been associated with the James brothers and Younger brothers. The Dexters had worn bright, nickle-plated revolvers with pearl handles in gunbelts studded with silver conchas. The man's pistol was in a dark, well-oiled holster, and it was businesslike and deadly-looking, blue steel and plain smooth wood on the handle. There was a long row of notches in the wood.

The name didn't surprise the marshal. He looked down at Bodine and nodded. "Did the Dexter brothers ask your name before they come out here with you?"

"No, they didn't bother to," Bodine replied, the ghost of humor in his eyes and the line of his lips again.

"I expect they didn't," the marshal chuckled. "They might have found somewheres else to go if they had. Well, like I said, we don't go for shoot-outs on the street here. Now them witnesses say that you didn't start it and it was a fair fight, so I ain't got no reason to hold you. But as soon as you can set your horse, I'd like for you to be on your way, Mr. Bodine."

Bodine's lips tightened as Tangeree moved his shoulder, pulling a bandage under him to tie the gauze down. "That suits me, Marshal."

"All right, we understand each other," the marshal said standing. "And here comes the wagon. Is he about ready, Doc?"

"Yes, he's ready," Tangeree said, closing the case and picking it up as she rose. "Tell them not to move his left arm any more than necessary."

"I'll sure do that, Doc. And I'm much obliged for your help."

Tangeree nodded, and the men parted in front of her as she walked along the boardwalk. A wagon pulled to the edge of the boardwalk, and the men on the boardwalk moved out of the way as the deputy and the driver climped down. Tangeree returned to her gig, put the case in it and untied the horse, then climbed in and gathered up the traces. There was a surging movement in the crowd on the boardwalk as the men carried Bodine to the wagon. Tangeree clucked to her horse, turning it away from the hitching rail, and the wagon followed her gig along the street.

The horse fought the bit and trotted, the wagon fell behind as it moved slowly along the streets, and it disappeared behind as Tangeree turned onto the street to the house. There was no one on the front porch. Bobby Bownay came out of the back door as Tangeree drove along the side of the house. He took the horse's head, and Tangeree picked up the case and climbed out of the gig. Her mother and Abigail were sitting at the kitchen table. Her mother smiled and pushed an envelope across the table.

"Here's another one, Tangi."

Tangeree picked up the envelope. Three weeks before, James Woodruff had gone to California on family business. And Tangeree had experienced wistful twinges of regret that she hadn't accepted any of his invitations to dinner and the theater, remembering what her mother had said about a woman in San Francisco. Then his letters had started arriving, at least two each week. She put the letter down and walked toward the doorway. "I'll read it later, Ma. There's a man with a gunshot wound on the way here."

Her mother sighed heavily as she rose and followed Tangeree through the house. "They've been at it again down there?"

Tangeree nodded as they walked into the examination room. "Yes, Frank Bodine killed the Dexter brothers, and he has a bullet in his shoulder."

"Bodine? And the Dexter brothers? Well, from what I've heard, we might have looked for something like that. What do you want me to do, Tangi?"

"You can get the chloroform and inhaler ready, because I'll have to anesthetize him. That bullet's in there deep, and it's going to be hard to get out."

Her mother took the inhaler from a cabinet and went to another cabinet for the chloroform, and Tangeree poured diluted carbolic acid into a basin, selected her surgical instruments, and put them in the basin. The jangle of harness and rumble of wheels became audible as the wagon approached along the street. It turned off in front of the house and stopped, and the deputy and the driver clumped up the steps and shuffled in, carrying Bodine. They put him on the table and stepped back from it, puffing heavily. The deputy took off his hat and wiped the sweat off his face with his sleeve, looking down at Bodine.

"Where's your horse and your tack, Bodine?"

Bodine looked up at the ceiling, his lined face

drawn and his lips thin with pain. He licked his lips and swallowed dryly, his eyes moving to the deputy. "My horse is in the stable on Auburn, and he's took care of. My tack's in my room in the Washoe Hotel."

"All right, I'll have it gathered up and brought to you. It looks like you'll need some more britches and a shirt."

"I'm much obliged."

"No, we're obliged to you," the deputy chuckled, turning toward the door. "You done us a good favor today. Good luck, Bodine."

Bodine grunted and nodded as the two men went out. Tangeree lifted the front of the shirt and coat, and looked at the wound on his chest. The gauze was soaked, and the wound was still bleeding freely. She walked around him and looked at the other wounds. The one on his thigh had already stopped bleeding, and there was but a trickle coming from the one on his ribcage. She nodded to her mother, and they lifted him into a sitting position and took off his coat and shirt. There were numerous scars from bullet and knife wounds on his hard, bony chest and wiry shoulders. They lowered him back to the table, and Tangeree started to unbuckle the heavy gunbelt around his waist. His right hand clamped down on the buckle, and his narrow, watchful eyes looked up at her.

"That ain't in the way."

"Very well," Tangeree replied, stepping back from the table and rolling up her sleeves. "I'll have to give you chloroform to get that bullet out."

He shook his head. "I don't sleep until I get to a sleeping place. And this ain't a sleeping place."

"Then you'll at least have to have some laudanum.

I can't have you moving while I'm probing for that bullet."

"I ain't going to move. Give me something to gnaw on."

Tangeree hesitated, then continued rolling up her sleeves and nodded to her mother. Her mother took the chest of dental instruments down, opened a drawer and took out a hardwood block, and put it between Bodine's front teeth. Bodine clamped it tightly between his teeth, looking at Tangeree from the corner of his eyes. Tangeree rinsed her hands in carbolic acid solution, then pulled the gauze off the wound on his chest and daubed around it with a swab dampened in carbolic acid solution. Blood continued welling from the wound, spreading across his chest and trickling down the side of his chest. Tangeree tossed the swab into the refuse container on the floor, then turned to the basin and selected a probe.

The mutilated tissues the bullet had torn through had swelled and closed together, and there was a spongy resistance around the tip of the long, thin probe. Bodine gripped the sides of the table. His teeth made a soft sound against the hardwood block as they tightened on it, and the muscles in his shoulder and chest became rigid under Tangeree's hands. She eased the probe deeper, feeling for the path of least resistance. The tip of the probe went two inches, then three. Then it would go no farther, and the loss of blood was becoming dangerously rapid from the tention in Bodine's muscles. She pulled the probe back out, dropped it into the basin, and selected a probe with a porcelain tip. The porcelain was more sensitive, transmitting the feel of what it found up the shaft to her fingers. She closed her eyes, concentrating on the feel of the probe. It went deeper and deeper, finding the path of the bullet through the torn flesh.

Then the tip of the probe grated against something solid. She opened her eyes and looked at Bodine's face. Tendons were standing out on his neck, and his features were rigid as his teeth pressed into the hardwood block. His dark, wary eyes were fixed on her. She scraped gently with the tip of the probe. He didn't react. It was bullet, not bone.

"Pass me the basin, Ma."

Her mother held it out to her. She held the tip of the probe on the bullet and reached into the basin for a slotted extractor, a long, slender, forceps-like instrument. She fitted the slot over the end of the probe, then held the probe steady as she slid the extractor down into the wound, using the probe for a guide. It scraped against the shaft of the probe, sliding down it, and Bodine's chest and shoulder quivered under her hand. Then the extractor bottomed, and she pulled the probe out, handed it to her mother, and cautiously opened the sides of the extractor.

The jaws of the extractor closed firmly on the bullet as she groped downward and closed the sides of the instrument. Then it resisted as she started to pull it out. The bullet was embedded in flesh, and shreds of flesh had been caught between the jaws of the extractor along with the bullet. She pulled harder. A sound came from Bodine's throat, and his shoulder and chest trembled under her hands, his breath coming in gasps. The bullet moved, and blood ran down the side of the extractor as it glided from the wound. The jaws emerged, thick drops of blood falling from the bullet clenched between them. Sweat beaded Bodine's ashen face, and he sighed deeply and relaxed

as Tangeree's mother took the hardwood block from
between his teeth.

Tangeree dampened gauze pads in carbolic acid
solution and pressed them down on the wound, looking down at him. "I know that was painful, but that
bullet was deep."

"I've hurt worser for less. You're a pretty good doc."

Tangeree smiled, taking a bandage roll as her
mother handed it to her. She wound it tightly around
his shoulder and chest, compressing the gauze pads
against the wound. She sponged the other wounds
with carbolic acid solution and bandaged them, then
checked the bandage on his chest for blood. The
bleeding had almost stopped, a single small spot of
blood showing through the bandage.

Bodine gripped the side of the table and slid his
legs off it as they lifted him to a sitting position. His
face was pale and his lips were a thin, tight line. He
leaned heavily on Tangeree as she and her mother
helped him off the table and through the house to a
bedroom, his boots dragging on the floor and his spurs
clattering. They put him on the bed, pulled his boots
off him and covered him, and he nudged the cover
aside and pulled his pistol out of the holster as they
left the room.

A man from the marshal's office had brought Bodine's things from the Washoe Hotel, and left them
with Abigail. There was a pair of saddlebags, a pack,
a double-barrel shotgun and a Winchester. Tangeree
gathered them up and took them to Bodine's room.
He had pulled himself up to a sitting position against
the head of the bed, with the coverlet around his
shoulders. His watchful eyes were on the door as she
opened it, and the barrel of the pistol peeked through
the opening in the front of the coverlet. It disap-

peared, the hammer on the pistol making a soft sound as he let it down. Tangeree carried the things into the room, put them on the floor by the bed, and leaned the shotgun and rifle against the wall.

"You can lie down. No one will bother you."

"This ain't a sleeping place."

Tangeree looked down at him. His face was stony, the line of the lips under the handlebar mustache thin and cruel, and his eyes hard and penetrating. It was the face of a killer, but he was also her patient. "I'll sit outside with the shotgun, then. You need rest."

He blinked, then his lips twitched with amusement. Then he shook his head. "I'm obliged and I'd trust you more than most, but it ain't in my nature to trust nobody. And I'm resting."

Tangeree nodded, turning toward the door. She went out and closed the door behind her, and returned to the kitchen. Lunch was almost ready. Tangeree drank a cup of coffee as she waited for Abigail to prepare a tray for Bodine. Fatigue and lack of sleep made her feel leaden and lifeless, and the thought of the possibility of infection in Bodine's wounds nagged at her. There was only a slight possibility of infection in the minor wounds, because she had cleansed them thoroughly with carbolic acid solution, and it wouldn't be dangerous if it did occur. But the instruments had gone deep into his chest, in the vicinity of major blood vessels, his heart, and his lungs, and even the slightest infection there would be deadly.

Abigail finished preparing a tray with soup, cornbread, and buttermilk on it, and Tangeree took it to Bodine's room. He wolfed the food down, chewing rapidly, becoming motionless as his eyes moved to-

ward the door and he listened to some sound in the
house, then chewing again. His demeanor was that
of a wounded carnivore that had sheltered to heal
before venturing out to kill again. And his taste in
food was that of a carnivore. He looked at the soup
and shook his head.

"I'm more used to eating meat than I am to drinking
the water that meat has been boiled in."

"You need light food. Beyond that, this is my home
rather than a hotel or restaurant, and you'll eat what
you get."

His eyes were steely as he looked at her, then he
chuckled and nodded as he began eating again. Color
was returning to his face and he looked more alert,
as though his wiry constitution was beginning to as-
sert itself and start the process of regaining strength.
But it was hours before his body temperature would
signal that the seeds of infection had been sewn in
his chest. He finished eating and pulled the coverlet
around his shoulders again, reaching for his pistol,
and Tangeree put the dishes on the tray and carried
it out of the room.

While Tangeree was having lunch, her mother came
into the kitchen and told her that a woman who
wanted spectacles was waiting. Tangeree finished
lunch and went to see to the woman. Then other
patients arrived, and she fought off her drowsiness and
fatigue as the afternoon wore on. Sunset came and Abigail hummed as she moved around the kitchen, and
Tangeree took a tray to Bodine. Then dinner was
ready and darkness fell, and it was only a few hours
before Bodine's temperature would reflect if infection
was developing. The others went to bed, and Tangeree sat in the kitchen and smoked, watching the
clock.

At eleven the twelve hours were up, and she went to the examination room for her thermometer and went to Bodine's room. He looked like he had been dozing, still sitting against the head of the bed with the coverlet around his shoulders, but his eyes were open and on her as she opened the door. She put the lamp on the table, put the end of the thermometer in his mouth and waited. Then she took it out and held it to the light of the lamp, rolling it in her fingers to find the line in the glass that indicated normal temperature. The end of the column of mercury rested precisely on the line.

"It appears that you won't have any inflammation. When that wound heals, you'll be all right."

"I'm glad to hear that. Do you take this much trouble with everybody you doctor?"

"I always do everything I can. And I worry a lot about inflammation. It kills more people than injuries do."

"Well, when I go to get shot again, I'll come back here to Virginia City to do it. The doctoring here is a lot better than in most places."

Tangeree smiled tiredly as she picked up the lamp, went out and pulled the door closed behind her. She took the thermometer back to the examination room and yawned wearily as she washed it and put it away. Then she walked back through the house to her room. She undressed and blew out the lamp, and immediately fell asleep when she relaxed in bed.

Then her mind struggled back out of sleep in response to an imperative signal that had been instilled in her in early childhood—her mother calling her name. She sat up, reaching for her clothes on the chair by the bed. "What is it, Ma?"

"Sam Leggett's here, honey. There's an epidemic

up at Sproule, a bad one. He wants to know if you'll
go up there with him."

It took her a moment to assimilate what her mother
had said as she blinked and looked at her mother in
the light of the lamp she was holding. Then she
yawned and nodded. "I'll be there in a minute, Ma."

Her mother closed the door and went back through
the house. Tangeree could hear the faint sound of
her talking with Leggett as she dressed. She walked
through the house to the kitchen, yawning and pushing back her hair. Leggett was sitting at the table
and drinking coffee, and her mother was standing
on the other side of the table and talking to him. He
looked up at Tangeree as she stepped into the kitchen.

"A fellow rode in from Sproule about an hour ago
and told me that half the town up there is dying.
That fancy degree you have didn't seem to get in
your way too much when we was over at Pioche a
few weeks ago, so I wondered if you wanted to go
along. You ain't doing nothing but sitting around
here, are you?"

Tangeree yawned, looking at the clock. It was a
little after two, and she had slept about three hours.
She nodded as she went to the cabinet for a coffee
cup. "All right, I'll go along with you."

"Your ma was just telling me about you getting
that slug out of Bodine. She said you didn't have to
cut him."

"No, I got it out with a Bradshaw extractor."

"That's that big long tweezer thing with a hole in
the middle, ain't it? I've been aiming to get me one of
them. He's lucky you had it handy."

Tangeree nodded as she went to the stove and
filled the cup from the pot. "Yes, that bullet was
deep, and it would have cut his chances down a lot

to have to incise. Ma, I checked him a while ago, and he's—" She broke off and frowned, looking at her mother. Her mother was standing with her shoulders bent forward slightly, as though she were in pain, and she was holding the right side of her stomach. "What's wrong, Ma?"

Her mother smiled and shook her head, then she dropped her hand and stood erect. "Nothing, Tangi. I just jumped out of bed too fast when Sam knocked on the door, and I have a little stitch. What were you going to say, honey?"

"I checked his temperature a while ago and it doesn't look like he's going to develop any inflammation. You can let him go whenever he looks all right to you, and the charge for his treatment and keep will be fifteen dollars. Are you sure you're all right, Ma?"

"Yes, I'm all right, Tangi," her mother chuckled, walking toward the door. "I'll get Bobby Bownay up to harness your horse."

Tangeree nodded, taking a drink of coffee, and looked back at Leggett. "What kind of epidemic is it up at Sproule?"

"It's stomach dropsy."

Tangeree looked away and silently sighed. She rubbed the back of her neck and yawned wearily. Leggett was a highly skilled doctor, but his terms and diagnoses didn't come from the medical lexicon. Anything except an injury or gunshot wound was usually described by him as dropsy of the heart, spleen, lungs, kidneys, or some other organ. "What did the man say the symptoms are?"

"Weakness, fever, coughing, and they're puking and pooting theirselves to death."

Tangeree took another drink of coffee, thinking.

Considering the season and the fact that Sproule was high in the mountains and much colder than Virginia City, it sounded like an early onset of vernal catarrh. It was normally a disease of winter that came in epidemic waves, and it was highly contagious, difficult to treat, and occasionally fatal. There was no specific for it, but the standard pharmacopoeia recommended treatment with jalap and calomel. She put her cup on the table and turned toward the door. "I'll get my things together, then, and I believe I'll take plenty of jalap and calomel."

Leggett grunted and nodded, and he took a gulp of coffee and sucked his teeth noisily. "I brung plenty myself. That's what I always use for stomach dropsy."

25

SPROULE was forty miles southwest of Virginia City and high in the Sierra Nevada. About half of its two hundred residents were incapacitated with vernal catarrh, and a large proportion of the remainder were either recovering from the illness or in the early stages of infection. The tiny town was a bleak, dismal cluster of unpainted wooden buildings and shacks around the superstructure of the single mine that was its reason for existence, and Tangeree and Leggett converted the saloon into a temporary infirmary and conscripted as nurses the two women who worked there and were euphemistically called dancing girls.

The mine was a marginal operation, producing a thin trickle of paydirt mixed with low grade ore that was hauled by dray to the mill at Genoa. The superintendent had been one of the first to become ill and had died, and the mine had closed down. The owners of boarding houses, cafes, and stores had extended credit to all the miners, but the distant and impersonal firms that supplied the businesses in Sproule had refused them credit. The cycle of financial collapse had quickly run its course, and the town was prostrate and on the verge of dying.

Neighboring towns had sent food and other essentials to avert famine, but the general malaise that gripped the town was as severe as the disease, and almost as debilitating. The cars of ore no longer came up on the elevator, the drays no longer came to haul the ore to the mill, and the town was deathly quiet and still. Men who should have begun recovering from the illness lingered in its grip, listless and purposeless. Those who should have been able to shrug it off succumbed, and the markers in the tiny graveyard at the edge of town multiplied.

The owner of the mine arrived from California with wagons filled with food, liquor, and other necessities, and with a skeleton crew from another of his mines. The man was over sixty, blind in one eye, and had a wooden leg, but he was a leathery, indestructible veteran of the gold fields of California, Australia, and South Africa. He took the place of the superintendent until another one could arrive, and there were enough able-bodied men in the town to supplement the skeleton crew and man two shifts on the main stope in the mine. The steam engine by the superstructure broke the silence in the town with its hissing and chugging, and the gears on the elevator cable drums squealed and clashed. The miners went down into the pit, and the loaded cars began coming up.

Life breathed back through the town. Harness jangled and heavy wheels rumbled as long lines of mules pulled drays up the road into town, ore roared through loading chutes and into the drays, and the men on the two thin crews sang and laughed as they went to work and left. The feeble, feverish men on the lines of blankets in the saloon began recovering their strength. The seriously ill started recuperating, and others struggled to their feet and left. They

trudged to the boarding house for clean clothes, their
lanterns, and to get their lunch pails filled, and they
lined up at the office to sign onto a shift. The two thin
crews became full crews, crews manned other stopes
in the mine, and the town bustled. Tangeree and
Leggett moved into a back room of the saloon with
the last of their patients when wagonloads of liquor
arrived to restock the shelves in the saloon, then left
when the last patients were out of danger.

James Woodruff had returned to Virginia City and
left for the East during Tangeree's absence at Sproule.
The Woodruffs had begun a process of liquidating
holdings in the East and investing heavily in land and
commercial interests in California, and James was con-
ducting the negotiations. He left a letter for Tangeree
explaining his absence, and he wrote several times
while he was in various cities in the East for short
periods. Then he was in Boston for several weeks, and
Tangeree exchanged letters with him.

His letters were always interesting, written in a
large, masculine hand and phrased concisely and
clearly. His letters were suggestive of him. He described places he went and related amusing ancedotes
about people he met, and he clearly devoted a flattering amount of time and effort to each letter. In tone
and content they were letters to a friend, not straying
beyond the limits that Tangeree had established between them, but there were occasional subtle hints of
something deeper.

Tangeree was torn with conflict when she read his
letters and thought about him. She wished longingly
that their relationship could be kept uncomplicated
and maintained as a friendship, because she found him
entertaining and she liked him. But she also felt a
strong tug of deeper emotions toward him. She care-

fully kept her letters in a friendly vein, with no hint or promise of anything else. And she scoured his letters for references to women he met or for glaring omissions of references, because many of his meetings with people were partially of a social nature.

And she tried to keep from thinking about the inevitability of the time when she would have to decide whether or not to make a commitment. At first James had tried to court her. Then he had cautiously tried to discuss her feelings and reservations when she avoided him. She had evaded conversation on the subject, and he had allowed their relationship to assume the form of a friendship as they grew to know each other better. He was patient, but Tangeree knew that the time would come when she would have to decide. And one of the things she had learned from Dennis Selfridge was the immense penalty in pain that could be exacted when a commitment of self was made. James Woodruff had nothing in common with Dennis Selfridge, but he was human. Commitment was a risk, and fate could be capricious and cruel. And being disappointed in James would be even more painful than being deceived by Dennis Selfridge.

A further complication was her deep friendship with Christina Woodruff and her father, which Tangeree didn't want to jeopardize through a misunderstanding with James or through being unfair to him. It seemed likely that Christina and her father at least suspected the situation, being close to it. The three were also a closely knit family, and it wasn't unlikely that James had made some mention of how he felt. But Tangeree saw them frequently as the weeks passed and autumn came, visiting with them and occasionally having dinner with them, and they gave no outward indication of knowing about it.

Autumn brought a settled routine of work that was in many ways reminiscent to Tangeree of her previous time in Virginia City. The Cargills still visited occasionally when they brought their drays of produce to Virginia City, and they left bags of potatoes, onions, peas, beans, and other things. Two of the sons had gone to Southern California and the other two were married, one to a surprisingly shy and dainty slip of a woman. The Elders had been frequent visitors during Tangeree's absence in San Francisco and Philadelphia, and her mother had delivered two more children for them. Their youngest son had a croup the doctors in California couldn't cure, and they came for the first time since Tangeree's return. Yvonne Elder was a pretty, charming girl approaching eight years of age, and at first Tangeree was startled to see how large the girl was. Then when she thought about it, in many ways it seemed much longer than eight years since she had held the tiny, lifeless form in her hands and had been driven by some compulsion to breathe life into it.

James returned for a week in October, and he brought Tangeree a small jewelry chest that was a perfect gift, just enough and not too much. And she hid her feelings upon seeing him again by looking at it and admiring it. He had dinner at Tangeree's house the next evening, and on the following evening Tangeree went to the theater and to Holland's Hotel for dinner with him, his father, and Christina.

The invitation came from the family as a whole as much as from James. They were all in the carriage when it came to the house, and the evening was enough like a family gathering that Tangeree lost the feeling of walking a thin line between her fears and impulses when near James. The evening was enjoyable, a comedy at the theater and lively, interesting conversation over the late dinner at the hotel.

The family invited Tangeree to their home for dinner the next evening, James came for her in the carriage, and the evening was as enjoyable as the previous one. Tangeree had a feeling of belonging to the family group, and she could be near James without the romantic implications of being alone with him. Dinner was delicious. During it James and his father joked and laughed about the foibles of some of their business associates James had seen while in the East. They sat in the parlor after dinner and talked, and Christina showed Tangeree the stereoscope slides that James had brought back with him. The only sour note was a mention of James's departure within a few days to return to the East. He and his father briefly discussed some of the things he would be doing, and it appeared that he was going to be gone until spring.

It was late when James took Tangeree home, the bright October moon shining down on quiet, dark houses along the streets on the edge of town. During the drive his conversation was in the same light, amusing vein as before. Then they reached her house and he became more serious as he helped her out of the carriage and walked up the steps with her.

"Have I left the impression that I had a very enjoyable time on the trip?" he asked. "Perhaps it sounds childish, but I had some very lonely moments as well."

Tangeree looked up at him in the moonlight as they stood on the porch, and she shook her head. "No, that doesn't sound at all childish, James, and I'm sure you did. It was pleasant on balance, though, wasn't it?"

"Not as pleasant as trips once were for me. I used to enjoy trips very much, but things have changed for me, Tangeree." He started to say more, then he hesitated and dismissed the subject with a shrug. "I enjoyed this evening and last evening far more than I did the trip."

"And I enjoyed them very much as well. I can't think of when I've enjoyed myself more."

"I'm very pleased you did. And I'd like to think that we could have many more evenings such as those." He again started to say more as his voice took on a more meaningful note, then he changed his mind, smiled down at her, and looked away.

They stood in silence for a moment, a relaxed, comfortable lack of conversation, and Tangeree pulled up the collar of her coat and pushed her hands into her pockets. The horses in front of the carriage moved restively, their breath faint plumes of condensation in the cold night air, and James glanced at them and looked back down at Tangeree.

"Could I persuade you to go with me to the Mazoa Restaurant tomorrow evening? Or elsewhere, if you wish. I promise I'll do my best to be as entertaining as the entire family."

Tangeree smiled in response to the note of humor in his voice, but hesitated. It was only a step beyond what she had done the previous two evenings, but it seemed a large step.

"I'll be leaving Monday, Tangeree, and I'll probably be gone until late spring. And I'd like to see you as much as possible before I go."

Suddenly it didn't seem such a large step, and Tangeree nodded. "Very well, James. And thank you for the invitation."

He smiled happily as he looked down at her in the moonlight, and he moved toward her. For a moment she thought he was going to kiss her, and she both shrank from him and waited to see if he would. Then he touched her arm and turned toward the steps.

"Good night, Tangeree."

"Good night, James."

A lamp was on the table inside the door, the wick turned low. Tangeree closed the door behind her and leaned against it, listening to the carriage move away from the house. The situation seemed to be closing in around her, forcing her more rapidly toward the point at which she would have to make a decision. She sighed heavily as she turned up the wick on the lamp. Then she picked up the lamp and walked toward her bedroom.

A shrill, penetrating sound awakened her a few hours later. She sat up in the darkness, listening. It was the steam whistle at the mill. It hooted at shift changes, a signal to families that husbands and fathers would be home shortly, and to boarding houses to begin dishing up steaming pots of food and put them on the trestle tables. But now it was screaming frantically, a banshee wail that shattered the early morning stillness and even drowned the pounding of the mill stamps. Disaster had struck in one of the mines.

It wasn't uncommon for one of the Woodruffs to be in their mine at odd hours, summoned there by the shift superintendent when something unusual happened. And if there were an accident or fire in the mine, both James and his father would be there, far underground and in peril.

Tangeree's mother was moving around in her room, and Tangeree climbed out of bed and crossed the room to the door.

"Ma, are you going down there?"

"They always send for me if they need me, Tangi, but it's a good idea to be ready to go."

Tangeree walked back across the cold floor to the bed and lit the lamp on the table. She began dressing, her breath making a mist in front of her face as she shivered in the biting chill of the frigid night air. Abigail got out of bed and dressed, the noises she made in her room muffled by the blanket of sound from the steam whistle. The yellow light of lamps shone through the crack under Tangeree's door as her mother and Abigail passed it, talking worriedly. Tangeree finished dressing and tied back her hair, picked up the lamp and went through the house to the front rooms.

Her mother was taking bottles of infusions from a cabinet in the examination room, and she glanced over her shoulder at Tangeree. "I put a lamp on the porch in case they send someone who doesn't know us."

"All right, Ma. I think I'll go on down there if they don't send someone pretty soon. I'd like to make sure that the Woodruffs are all right."

"I know, honey, but I think they'll send for us. From the way that whistle is carrying on, it must be something serious."

Tangeree nodded as she put the lamp on the table, and she went to a cabinet and began taking out her surgical instruments. She could remember several minor accidents in the mines before she had left for college, and her mother had told her about serious accidents that had occurred while she had been gone. The potential for accidents was a frequent topic of conversation among the Woodruffs, because the mines in Virginia City were far more dangerous than mines in other places.

The veins of ore in most silver mines in the world were from two to three feet wide, but in the Virginia

City mines they were up to thirty feet wide. Timbering in other silver mines only had to support the roof of a low tunnel, but for Virginia City mines it had been necessary to devise a unique method of square-set timbering. Open-sided boxes of heavy timbers had been constructed to take the place of the earth that was removed, and to support the sides and roof of large rooms. Then rooms had become stacked upon rooms in places where veins branched and extended vertically, and rooms had widened into vaults where veins were horizontal. Entire slopes of the Sierra Nevada had been denuded of trees to provide thousands of tons of timbers, and the mines had turned into vast underground buildings as they reached deeper, dozens of levels that consisted of labyrinths of rooms.

Fire was a constant danger, because it could quickly turn into a conflagration that would race through the levels and trap the miners away from the vicinity of the elevator shaft. Underground reservoirs of water seeped into the mines constantly and could burst and inundate all the levels below them if the excavating came too near them. There was a constant shifting and settling of the ground as a result of the deep excavations, and timbers in sections occasionally collapsed.

Any one of these calamities or a combination could have occurred. Tangeree put her surgical instruments and bandage rolls into a case and diluted carbolic acid in a large jug as her mother gathered up her things. The sound of the whistle died away, and Abigail brought in cups of coffee. Then Tangeree heard a sound on the street outside, and ran out to the porch. A wagon was coming along the street toward the house.

"Is that the Beaunais house?" a man shouted.

"Yes, that's right. What mine is it?"

"It's the Blackjack. Part of a level fell through on them."

Tangeree sagged with relief. Her mother was standing behind her, and she glanced up and smiled faintly as they went back into the house. The man pulled the wagon up beside the porch and came in to help them carry out their cases and put them in the wagon, and Abigail brought their coats. They put on their coats and climbed into the wagon, and the man clucked to the team and turned the wagon back toward the street.

The owners and workers of all the mines closed ranks to help when disaster struck. Windows in most of the houses were lighted, and a general stir of activity in the town turned into a seething bustle and blaze of light in the early morning darkness as the wagon turned onto the street in front of the gigantic hulk of the superstructure over the mine. Miners stood in large, quiet clusters with their lanterns lighted, waiting to see if they were needed, and the curious milled around and talked. Women stood with their children around them, some weeping anxiously and others waiting in grim, tight-lipped silence, their eyes hollow with foreboding and fixed on the main entrance of the building.

The pump wagons of the volunteer fire department were parked by the entrance, and half a dozen men were spaced across the entrance to keep people out. Leggett was standing behind them, looking rumpled and sleepy and wearing his nightshirt instead of a shirt. He pushed between two of the men and beckoned one of them with a jerk of his head. Tangeree and her mother climbed out of the wagon, and the men helped them carry their cases inside.

The distant sides of the vast building were lost in darkness, bulky, grimy machinery stood in the shadows, and the elevator platform in the center of the building was brightly lighted. The huge cable reels suspended over the platform were almost empty, and the thick cables stretching down from them and into the pit brought the dank smell and feel of the depths of the mine into the building. Steam engines and ventilation equipment that forced air down into the mine made a drumming roar, men scurried about, and large rubber water hoses stretched across the floor to the elevator platform. Several men were standing on the platform and quietly talking, mine owners and superintendents, and Tangeree glimpsed James and his father among them, towering over most of the other men.

Although Cummings was still in Virginia City and there was another doctor in town, neither of them could be found, and Leggett grumbled about it as he led the way across the wide central room to a smaller room at one side. It was a storage room, and boxes, barrels, and parts of machinery had been pulled out of it and stacked outside. Lanterns hung around the walls, and boards had been placed across large boxes to make rough tables. Blankets, bedsheets to make bandages, and slats for splints were stacked on one side of the tables, and bloody rags had been thrown into a pile in a corner.

"I've already fixed up a few and sent them home," Leggett said, nodding toward the rags. "Mostly banged-up heads, and one broke arm. They said there was a bunch more down there and some of them bad off, so I thought I'd better send for you all."

"When are they going to get them up here?" Tangeree asked. "They could be bleeding to death."

"They can't get to most of them until they clear away some timbers, and they want to get everybody else out of there first in case more of it falls in when they commence clearing. They've most of them out now, and it shouldn't be long."

Tangeree nodded, carrying her cases toward one of the tables, and her mother took hers to another one. A different sound came from the machinery outside, and Tangeree stepped back to the door as she unbuttoned her coat and took it off. The cable reels over the elevator platform were turning ponderously, and the elevator was coming up. She hung her coat on a nail in the wall, and stepped back to the door as the elevator reached the platform.

The large cage was filled with miners, but there were no injured among them. They streamed down the platform steps and toward the door, and a woman shouted and waved in tearful relief from the door as the men at the door held her back. One of the miners ran toward her, waving and shouting, his lantern and lunch pail swinging and clattering together. Other women and children appeared at the door, waving and shouting, and the miners rushed toward them. Tangeree started to walk back toward the table, then stopped. James was crossing the wide floor toward her.

"Do you have everything you need, or is there something I can get or do for you?" he asked as he approached.

"No, we have everything we need. Is it very bad down there?"

"Only a small part of one level collapsed, but it was over a stope where they were working and there were several men in that one place. And there was a small fire, but they got it put out before it spread."

Tangeree nodded, then spoke again as he started to turn to walk back to the elevator platform. "You're not going down there are you, James?"

"Well, yes, if I'm needed. I'm an engineer, and there might be something I can do to help."

"There are a lot of other engineers here. You stay out of that mine, James."

The question and comment had been impulsive, and she had said them without thinking. She felt a flush spreading up her face, her cheeks tingling. A wide, pleased smile spread across his face as he turned and walked back toward the elevator platform. Tangeree stepped back to the table, rolling up her sleeves, and opened the cases.

26

THE ELEVATOR came up again, bringing the last of the
men who were being evacuated and a few injured
men. Most of them were only bruised and shaken,
frightened and trying to hide it behind laughter and
conversation, several had minor cuts and scrapes, and
one had a gashed head. There was a wait of another
few minutes, then several seriously injured came up,
with broken bones and deep lacerations. Miners carried them from the elevator and put them on blankets
on the floor in the room, and they moved them onto
and back off the crude tables as Tangeree, her mother,
and Leggett worked over them.

The scene was nightmarish. A dozen groaning men
lay on blankets on the floor, their faces smeared and
their clothes caked with the soil that had tumbled in
on them, their bodies crushed by the timbers that had
fallen. Four mangled bodies were brought to be pronounced dead, and Tangeree worked rapidly to save
those who had lain too long under timbers and bled.
Her mother called her to look at a man with a deep
indentation in the top of his skull, and she took out
her button trephines and bored his skull to elevate the
depression. Then he died as she was lifting it. She

went back to her table and bound a man's crushed ribs, and cut the hair away from a gash on another man's head and sutured it.

A hand pulled at her skirt as she started across the room to get a set of slats to splint a broken leg, and she looked down. A young man lay on a blanket and looked up at her, his face pale and twisted with pain under the dirt on it. "Don't let them cut off my arm, ma'm. Don't let them cut off my arm!"

Tangeree knelt and looked at his right arm. It was a compound fracture of the forearm, and the jagged end of the ulna had ripped through the flesh. Dirt and splinters were in the wound, and a rag had been tied around the bicep to stop the hemorrhage, which had also stopped the flow of blood to the forearm. Amputation was necessary. She looked down at the pale face, hesitated, then looked at her mother.

"Ma, will you take that broken leg there?"

"Yes, I'm about through here, Tangi."

Tangeree looked up at the miners standing by the wall and motioned. "Take him off that table and put him over there, and put this man in his place."

The men crossed the room and moved the man off her mother's table as she finished, put the man with the broken leg on it, and lifted the man with the broken arm onto Tangeree's table. She looked at the arm again, then took the chloroform inhaler out of the case.

"I'm going to have to put you to sleep to work on it. I'll do my best to save it."

"You ain't going to put me to sleep and then just cut it off, are you?"

"I might have to take it off, but I'm going to do my best to save it. What's your name?"

"Jake Robinson."

"All right, Jake, breathe deeply when I put this over your mouth and nose."

He nodded, looking up at her apprehensively as she put the inhaler on his face, and breathed deeply. His eyes closed. She waited a moment and thumbed one of his eyelids back, then she began working on the arm.

The break reduced smoothly, and it didn't appear that the flow of blood to the forearm had been completely stopped. She moved one of the lanterns closer and sponged dirt out of the wound with a rag soaked in diluted carbolic acid, then loosened the rag around the bicep. Blood welled up in the wound, but it was on the outside of the arm and away from most of the major blood vessels. The arm was open to the bone along most of the forearm, calling for more delicate suturing than she could do under the primitive conditions in the room. She sponged out the wound again, then began binding the forearm tightly to a splint to hold the wound closed with pressure.

Her mother and Leggett finished working on the others as she was working over Robinson, and the mine superintendent came in. He talked with her mother and Leggett, and her mother came to her table.

"Tangi, he says that all of them except that one with the amputated leg and the one with the injured chest have families to look after them. They live in a boarding house, and I told him we'd take them home to look after them."

"I want to take this one as well. I have a lot more work to do on him."

Her mother nodded and walked back to the two men, and talked to them again. Tangeree finished binding the arm and took the rag off the man's bicep, watching the bandage on the forearm. The flow of blood had been reduced to a trickle, and it took over a minute for the first sign of blood to appear on the outside of the bandage. She picked up a sheet and began tearing it into strips to tie the arm to the man's body to stabilize it.

A wagon crossed the wide floor to the room. The miners carried the three men to it, then put Tangeree's and Yvonne's cases in it. Tangeree climbed into the wagon with her mother, and she leaned back against the sideboard wearily and waved to Leggett as the wagon moved toward the door. Other wagons were coming through the wide doors and crossing the floor to the elevator, and men were unloading heavy timbers from them and piling them onto the elevator. Several men were still standing on the elevator platform, but Tangeree didn't see James or his father among them.

Almost all the crowd outside had left, and the atmosphere was normal when the wagon got away from the street in front of the superstructure—that of Virginia City on any early morning. Dawn was beginning to break, smoke was rising from chimneys and people were moving about, and the mill stamps pounded.

Tangeree saw a small form hurrying along the street far behind the wagon, a small young woman carrying a baby. She disappeared from sight when the wagon turned onto another street, then came into sight behind the wagon again, running a few steps, walking a few steps, and gradually catching up with the wagon. Tangeree looked at Robinson and at the woman following the wagon, and told the driver to stop. He pulled back on the traces and stopped the team, and the woman caught up with the wagon, puffing breathlessly. She was young, no more than seventeen or eighteen, and the baby was tiny.

"They said you have my husband Jake," she said worriedly. "Is that right?"

Tangeree nodded, leaning over the side of the wagon. "Let me have the baby, and climb on up. What's your name?"

"Charlene. Is he going to be all right?"

"He's very seriously injured, Charlene, but I'm doing my best."

The woman nodded, climbing into the wagon and looking at Robinson anxiously as she sat down by him. The baby whimpered, and she took it back from Tangeree and rocked it absently in her arms, looking down at Robinson. The driver clucked and snapped the traces, and the wagon moved on along the street.

The driver and a miner who had come along carried the men into the house, putting the amputee and the man with the crushed chest on bunks in a spare bedroom and Robinson on the table in the examination room. Charlene hovered around Robinson, her face pale and drawn and her eyes filled with tears. Tangeree let her spend a few minutes with him while she went to the kitchen and drank a cup of coffee, then she sent her to the kitchen and called Bobby Bownay to help her set up the carbolic acid atomizer in the examination room. Robinson was starting to revive, and Tangeree anesthetized him again and began unwrapping the arm as Bobby Bownay pumped the handle on the atomizer and it filled the room with its spray.

In the bright daylight coming through the window, she saw splinters and fragments of dirt she had missed before, and she carefully cleaned them out of the wound. The deep separation of the muscle tissue would complicate and prolong the healing process. She went to a cabinet and took out a bottle of catgut.

It was a recent development, a ligature and suture material made of the dried intestines of sheep, and one which was absorbed by the body during the healing process. She hadn't used it before, preferring the linen and silk because they could be sterilized in carbolic acid, but the bottles were supposed to have been sealed under sterile conditions. And the advertisement for catgut had referred to an article in a medical journal that attributed many infections to leaving linen and silk ligatures in wounds. She took out a set of needles and dropped them in a basin of diluted carbolic acid, then opened the bottle.

It was late morning when she finished suturing the muscles and wound, setting the arm, and encasing the wound in a putty of carbolic acid, linseed oil, and whiting. The leg amputee was stirring and in pain, and the man with the crushed chest was semiconscious, in pain, and having difficulty breathing. Tangeree drugged them with laudanum, then slept for a few hours. When she woke, the man with his chest crushed was having even more difficulty in breathing and it appeared that fragments of his ribs had penetrated his lung, and the amputee's stump was oozing blood. She drugged both of them again, and replaced the bandages on the amputee's stump, tying them tighter. Late that evening, her mother told her that James had been by, and she remembered that she had agreed to go to dinner with him.

Charlene stayed in the room with Robinson, and went to her home the next morning for some of her clothes and things for the baby. All three of the injured men were feverish, and the man with the crushed chest was unconscious. Charlene sat in the room with Robinson and wiped his face with cool cloths, and helped with the other men. The man with the crushed chest had progressively more difficulty in breathing during the day, coughing weakly and bringing up tiny clots of blood. He lapsed into coma late at night, and died early the following morning. Tangeree sent Bobby Bownay to the mine with a message to the superintendent, and he sent two men and a wagon for the body.

The first indications of suppuration began developing in Robinson's arm and the amputee's stump. Tangeree opened the dressings and searched for the pockets of infection, the fiery red spots that were swollen and that would develop pockets of pus, and she cleaned them, disinfected them, and replaced the dressings. A day passed, and there were more places to cleanse and disinfect. It was an opportunity to learn, because there had been an article in a medical journal about the relationship between the level of infection in the body and the number of white blood corpuscles in the bloodstream. She took blood samples and made slides as the infection progressively invaded the wounds, and studied them under her microscope.

Tangeree was bent over her microscope examining a slide when her mother came and told her that James wanted to speak with her on the porch. Her first thought was that she was wearing an old dress and her hair was untidy. Then she remembered that he was leaving. She walked toward the front door, tugging at her dress and tucking wisps of hair into place.

She stepped out onto the porch. He was standing at the edge of the steps and looking along the street, and he turned and smiled. She smiled apologetically, lifting and dropping her hands in a helpless gesture. "I'm sorry, James."

"I understand, Tangeree," he replied, shaking his head. "And there's no reason to apologize. I know what you've been doing, and I wouldn't have bothered you but for the fact that I'm leaving this afternoon and I wanted to say goodbye."

"It wasn't any bother, James, and I would have felt awful if you hadn't come by."

He smiled and nodded, looking at her. She folded her hands, looking at him. They were silent for a moment, then he nodded again and turned to the steps. "Goodbye, Tangeree. I'll see you in a few months."

Tangeree started to tell him goodbye and tell him that she would look forward to his return. Instead, she blurted out what she was thinking. "Have I been unfair, James?"

His smile faded as he turned back, and he looked at her. Then he shook his head. "No, you haven't been unfair, Tangeree. I've been somewhat unsettled myself with these things I'm taking care of just now, and it'll be spring before they're put to rest. You apparently need time to think about things and you prefer to think about them alone instead of discussing them, and I certainly couldn't deny you that. So I don't think you've been unfair."

"Very well, James."

He smiled again, turning back to the steps and walking down them. "Goodbye, Tangeree."

"Goodbye, James, and Godspeed."

He climbed into the carriage, and looked out the window and waved as it moved away from the house and along the street. Tangeree waved, then turned and went back into the house when the carriage disappeared from sight along the road. She returned to the microscope, looked at the slide in it, and took it out and looked in the box of slides by the microscope for the slide of the blood sample from Robinson the day before. Then she hesitated, thinking about what

James had said. In a way, it had sounded as though he had given her until spring to decide. She thought about it, then found the slide in the box, put it in the microscope, and looked at it.

The number of white blood corpuscles in the bloodstream was an accurate indicator of the level of infection. It peaked and fell rapidly in the samples taken from the amputee as his stump began healing. Robinson's wound was more complicated and far more prone to infection, but he was younger and stronger than the other man and his overall recovery was more rapid. A week after his temperature subsided, he was moving about the house with his arm in a sling, coming to the table for his meals, and sitting on the porch with his wife.

The amputee gained enough strength to begin using his crutch, and the loss of his leg didn't seem to affect him emotionally, as it did many. He moved around the house for two days on his crutch, cheerful and smiling as he learned to use it, then he gathered up the bundle of belongings that had been brought from the boarding house and stumped off down the street with the bundle on his back. The last signs of infection disappeared from Robinson's arm, and it healed rapidly. There was a massive scar on his forearm where skin had sloughed away, and there had been some loss of muscle tissue, but the arm was strong and fully mobile.

The mine sent a check in payment for all the medical services that had been provided, and Tangeree received a large amount of publicity over Robinson's arm. *The Territorial Enterprise* had a long article about it, which included a statement from Leggett praising Tangeree's skill and competence, and it was picked up by a newspaper in San Francisco. Tangeree's mother, the Woodruffs, and others commented about it for a time, then the comments stopped and Tangeree forgot about it. Then in early December, a wagon brought a man from Reno who had been injured at the railroad station. The local doctor in Reno had been gone, the station master at the train station had remembered reading the article, and he had sent two of his men with the injured man.

The man had been a passenger on a train and had fallen from the step of a car while it was moving. His arm was severely lacerated. The people at the train station had wrapped the arm in dirty rags for bandages and tied a tight rag around his bicep, almost completely cutting off the flow of blood, and two major arteries had been severed. Tangeree pulled the ends of the arteries together and put a couple of tiny catgut sutures through them, sutured the muscles and the wounds, and bound the arm tightly. The arteries still leaked for a time, and infection began invading the multitude of deep wounds in the man's arm. The arm became dangerously infected and Tangeree wavered on the point of amputating it, then she began overcoming the infection.

The station master had sent a note with the man, advising her to write to the company headquarters in San Francisco for payment, and she wrote and itemized a list of charges totaling eighteen dollars for the treatments, medicines, and keep for the man while he had been at the house. A week after she wrote the letter, a man came to the house, identified himself as an attorney for the company, and gave her a check for fifty dollars. Tangeree looked at the check, shaking her head.

"I believe there's been some mistake," she said. "I asked for only eighteen dollars."

"No, no, there's no mistake," the man chuckled

expansively. "You see, it could have cost far more than fifty dollars in the compensation we paid the individual if he had lost his arm as a result of the accident. And from what I'm told, it's little short of a miracle that he didn't lose his arm."

"It was close. The rags they wrapped that arm in must have been ones they used to clean out trains, and the inflammation became so bad I almost had to amputate it."

"I'm sure it's because of your superb ability that you didn't have to, Doctor Beaunais. The reason I came to see you personally was to ask if you would care to attend patients in this area for the company. We make arrangements with doctors along our routes to do this, and we haven't really been satisfied with our arrangements in Reno. It would only amount to an occasional patient, unless there is a major mishap. And we hope that won't occur, of course."

"Yes, I wouldn't mind, but this is several miles from Reno."

"Our arrangements in Reno have been so unsatisfactory that we would be more than glad to deal with the distance," he replied, opening his briefcase and digging in it. He took out three sheets of paper covered with small lines of printing. "In event that you agreed to be our physician for this area, I brought along a copy of our standard contract."

Tangeree glanced at the pages, began reading, then shook her head. "This makes a medical text seem like a first-grade reader."

"Basically, what it says is that you won't engage in discussions with those who might be litigants against the company, or with attorneys representing them. If you are placed under subpoena to testify on a matter, then you must, of course. Other than that, you will discuss patients placed under your care by the company only with representatives of the company."

"It takes a lot of room to say that, doesn't it?" Tangeree commented, glancing over the pages again.

"Well, there are the various contingencies within that general situation that must be addressed."

"Apparently. I believe I'll show this to an attorney before I sign it."

"By all means," the man chuckled, taking a card from his pocket and handing it to her. "And if it's satisfactory, please have it notarized and mail it to this address. It's been a pleasure talking with you, Doctor Beaunais, and I'll look forward to hearing from you."

"It's been a pleasure talking with you, and thank you very much for the check."

The man left, and Tangeree put the contract and business card away. She took the contract with her when she went into town, and showed it to an attorney whose wife she had treated. He read it over carefully and told her substantially what the company attorney had said, and she signed it, had it notarized, and mailed it to the address on the card.

The days passed and the matter faded out of the forefront of her thoughts, then in the third week in January a wagon arrived with an aged employee of the railroad who had suffered a stroke while shoveling snow off the tracks in the Sierra Nevada. There was nothing she could do for him except care for him until she was sure his condition had stabilized, then she sent a telegram to the company headquarters. A wagon came from the station at Reno and took the old man away the next day, she sent an itemized list of charges to the company headquarters, and a check arrived in the mail.

A woman dropped a baby on its head in the station at Reno, and a carriage brought the woman and baby to Tangeree. The baby was only superficially injured, and Tangeree sent Bobby Bownay to stop the driver while he was changing horses at the livery stable. The carriage returned to the house when the horses were changed, and took the woman and baby back to Reno. Other patients from the station at Reno arrived at intervals of a few days to a week, most of them with minor injuries, and a carriage arrived late one night to take Tangeree to Reno and attend a woman who had gone into labor in the train station. She delivered the baby in a small room off the waiting room during the early hours of the morning, and the carriage returned her to Virginia City.

The following week, Abigail saw the carriage from Reno stop at the livery stable while she was returning to the house from milking the cow, and she came into the examination room and told Tangeree. Tangeree went out on the porch to look, and the driver was running up the street toward the house as the men at the livery stable changed the two teams. The driver saw her on the porch, and he slid to a stop, cupped his hands around his mouth, and shouted.

"Get your stuff ready, Doc! There's been a wreck east of Cedar Flats!"

Tangeree nodded and waved, and he sprinted back toward the livery stable as she went into the house. Her mother was in the examination room, and Tangeree nodded as she lifted her eyebrows interrogatively. "It's the carriage from Reno, and the driver said there's been a wreck east of Cedar Flats."

Her mother frowned and shook her head. "That sounds bad, doesn't it? You'd better be prepared for just about anything, Tangi."

"Yes, it appears so. If you'll put the inhaler, some chloroform, and some laudanum into a case for me, I'll get the other things."

Her mother nodded, opening a cabinet and taking the inhaler and bottles of chloroform from a shelf, and Tangeree put bandages, bottles of diluted carbolic acid, and her surgical instruments into cases. They carried the cases out to the porch, and Tangeree went back in to get a coat and hat from her room. The carriage was approaching rapidly along the street as she came back out, the horses galloping, and the driver leaned back on the traces and turned the horses in off the road. The horses slid to a stop in front of the house, and the driver leaped down from the seat and grinned at Tangeree as he reached for two of the cases.

"They're bringing the Sierra Cannonball over from Hangtown with the crane to lift the cars and engine, Doc."

Tangeree looked at him quizzically as she put one of the cases into the carriage. "What's the Sierra Cannonball?"

"It's a new engine they got, and it's the fastest thing on steel!" he chortled excitedly, pushing the other cases into the carriage. "With nothing but a flat truck with a crane on it behind her, it ain't going to take you long to get through Cedar Flats. Jump in, Doc. We got to hurry, or we might not get to Reno in time for you to catch her."

Tangeree climbed into the carriage and closed the door, and the driver scrambled onto the seat, gathering up the traces and whistling shrilly at the horses. The horses swung toward the street. Tangeree held the strap by the door as the carriage swerved sharply and lurched onto the street, then she leaned forward and looked out the window, waving to her mother and Abigail. Then Tangeree sat back in the seat, pushed the cases into a line against the other seat with her foot, and gripped the strap again as the carriage approached the turn onto the road out of town. One wheel stopped turning and dragged in the dirt as the driver stood on the brake lever and leaned back on the traces, and the carriage slowed. Then it leaned sharply to the right side, and it bounced and swayed onto the road as the driver whistled to the horses and the whip cracked.

The cases slid back and forth on the floorboard as the carriage raced along the narrow road that wound down Mount Davidson, the driver slowing for the sharp curves and cracking the whip as the carriage slid around them. The road straightened out on a gentle downgrade into Carson City, the people and buildings passed, then there was a long straight stretch into Reno. The horses pounded along the road at a steady canter, and the carriage bobbed on its springs, the wheels jarring over bumps and slamming through ruts. The groves of trees on the farmsteads in the rich Carson Valley were touched with a haze of green, the first buds of spring beginning to show, and the bright spring sunshine gleamed on the snowy heights of the massive Sierra Nevada, looming over the valley to the west. Small old settlements passed at long intervals, gradually changing to newer ones that melted into the scattered outskirts of Reno.

A seething, excited crowd had gathered at the train station, a large number of men and a few women, many boys and all of them stepping gingerly in the first days of having shed winter shoes, and numerous dogs racing about and barking. They were at the side

of the station and in the street at one side of it, the
station master adamantly strict about forbidding loiterers on the station platform, and the edge of the crowd
parted as the driver turned the horses into the alley
behind the station. The driver took two of the cases,
and Tangeree carried the other one and followed him
through the back door and through the musty luggage
and freight storage room to the station master's office.

The office was small, littered, and stuffy, and filled
with the clatter of the telegrapher's machine. The
telegrapher smiled and nodded absently to Tangeree
listening to the machine, and the station master turned
away from the window at the front of the office. He
was a tall, rigidly erect man with a bushy white
mustache, his blue uniform impeccably neat and his
cap set at a straight angle. He smiled, touching the
peak of his cap.

"Good morning, Doctor Beaunais. Well, you made
good time, Manny."

"I done the best I could without killing the horses,"
the driver replied. "Where's she at now?"

"She came through Quartz Canyon about five minutes ago," the station master said, taking his watch
from his vest pocket and glancing at it. "I'll give her
another eight minutes to Clear Creek."

"Quartz Canyon?" the driver gasped in surprise,
walking toward the door. "I didn't get the doc here
a minute too soon, did I? I'll watch for her from out
here."

The station master nodded as he went out, and
looked back at Tangeree. "We've got word that the
wreck ain't too bad, Doctor Beaunais. There's sixteen
people who was banged up some, but it's all scrapes
and cuts. No broke bones, and nobody hurt real bad."

"I'm relieved to hear that," Tangeree replied. "I was afraid it was going to be much worse. How did you find out about it?"

"There's a telegrapher on the train, and he climbed a pole by the tracks and hooked into the wires. They sent out a tent and blankets from Cedar Flats, and everything's took care of until you get there. There was a doctor on the train, a cripple of some kind the telegrapher said, but we have to have a company doctor look at them, of course."

His voice faded as the telegrapher moved in his chair, listening intently to the hammering of the machine. A smile slowly spread across the telegrapher's face as he listened, and he put his hand on his key, rapped out an acknowledgment, and chuckled as he looked at the station master. "She just tore through Clear Creek. And old Jake Wiggins said she sucked Clear Creek about a mile farther to the east as she went through."

The station master lifted his eyebrows in surprise as he took out his watch and glanced at it again. "She's really running a head of steam, ain't she? Well, we'd better get you out on the platform, Doctor Beaunais, she's going to be here just directly. Here, I'll take a couple of them bags."

"Manny said that a new engine was taking the crane out to the wreck," Tangeree said as they picked up the cases and walked toward the door. "I suppose that's why all the people are here, isn't it?"

The station master nodded morosely and looked from one side of the station to the other as they walked out onto the platform. "Yes, they're tromping down all the flower beds I had the men dig up just last week, and I guess it'll all have to be done over. She's a new engine that's supposed to be able to haul a train across the Sierra by herself, and they've named her the Sierra Cannonball. They've had her in the yards at Hangtown, fitting her out and steaming her up, and I guess she was the first thing they could lay their hands on to get the crane out to the wreck."

"I'd just as soon they had sent a different one," Tangeree said, smiling wryly. "I wouldn't want to be in a wreck myself between here and Cedar Flats."

"No, you ain't going to be," the station master chuckled as he put the cases down and glanced at his watch again. "Old Penrod Casker is the driver, and Penrod will get you there and back. Well, we ought to be able to hear her blowing for the crossing at Muldoon Bridge just about any minute now!"

The tracks west of the station stretched in a straight line for a distance of several hundred yards, curved out of sight behind thick groves of trees, and reappeared as thin threads of gleaming steel on their bed of crossties and gravel as they went up a wooded slope and disappeared from sight over the top of the rise. The noisy hubbub of excited laughter and conversation from the crowd carried along the boardwalk, and the distant wail of a train whistle was faintly audible over the sound of the crowd as the station master listened and nodded, a hand cupped behind an ear. The whistle rose to a shrill note, men in the crowd shouted for silence and the noise of the crowd subsided to a murmur, and the sound of the whistle was clearly audible. The crowd surged and moved, edging toward the tracks, and the station master walked along the platform and shouted, waving the people back.

The locomotive came into sight, popping over the top of the rise and racing down it. The sound of the whistle was a clear, ringing note in the air, with an undertone of the wheels beating against the rails and the rumble of the laboring steam engine. It was huge, a long blur of gleaming wheels and churning pistons under it, and a massive cowcatcher extending over the tracks ahead of it. The thick column of black smoke billowing from the stack was touched with a thin finger of white from the steam whistle, and it eddied around the single car behind the engine. A large crane was on the car, and tiny figures of men crouched around the crane.

It approached at blinding speed, dropping down the slope, disappearing behind the trees, and abruptly reappearing at the end of the straight stretch. The bell began tolling and the whistle took on a rising and falling note as the engine bore down on the station, rocking from side to side on the tracks. For a long, dragging second, it looked as though the engine were going to pass the station without slowing. Then everything but the cowcatcher disappeared in a cloud of steam. Distance had distorted the scale of size, and it was much larger than it had first appeared, the cowcatcher enormous as it shot along the track with the billowing cloud of steam around it. And the full impact of the sound came in a sudden, earshattering clap. The bell clanged, the whistle shrieked, and the thunder of venting steam blended with the agonized screech of steel dragging against steel as the huge engine came into the station, the cloud of steam enveloping the front of the station, the end of the street, and the crowd of people.

The frenzied whooping and whistling of the crowd became audible as the roar of steam diminished and the steam began dissipating, and the driver stepped out of the door and began climbing down. The driver was on a scale comparable with his engine, over six feet tall and with a barrel chest and bulging stomach, but he was remarkably light and agile for his size as he climbed down to the platform. A red handkerchief was knotted around his neck and his cap was at a jaunty angle, and he fit his role as one of those who had filled the vacuum left by the passing of the stage coach drivers, with an appreciation for drama and how it lightened the dreary monotony of the isolated towns of the West.

"Penrod, if you roll up all the rails getting there, how are you going to get back?" the station master laughed.

The huge man hopped down from the last step, his cheeks bulging with tobacco juice. He spat a thick stream over the edge of the platform and onto the gravel by the tracks, and grinned as he turned, wiping his mouth with the back of his hand. "I'll run her up the creekbeds, George. Is this lady my passenger?"

"She sure is. This is Doctor Beaunais."

"Penrod Casker, ma'am," the man said, lifting his cap. "And I expect you'd better ride in the engine, because the wind would blow that pretty hat away on the flat truck."

Tangeree nodded uncertainly, looking up at the engine. "Yes, well, I suppose that would be better."

"Oh, you'll be just fine in the engine," the station master said confidently, picking up two of the cases. "We'll just get you loaded up here. How's your sand, Penrod?"

"I need some," Casker said. "I used most of it climbing the hill, and I could stand to have my water topped off."

"All right, we'll get you fixed up," the station master

replied, stepping to the side of the engine and lifting the cases toward the door. "Shorty, grab these bags and help the doctor up!"

The fireman stepped to the door, a tall, angular man in clothes caked with coal dust, his eyes white circles in the thick coal dust on his face. He wiped his hands quickly on a rag and took the cases. Casker handed the other one up, and he and the station master walked along the side of the engine and looked at it as men from the station bustled around it. Tangeree lifted the front of her skirt and began climbing up to the doorway, stepping gingerly on the staggered ledges, and the fireman scrubbed one hand with the rag and grinned as he reached down to help her up the long step at the top.

"Thank you very much," Tangeree said as she stepped up into the engine. "That's quite a climb, isn't it?"

"It sure is, ma'am," the man replied, touching the peak of his cap and nodding. "I'm Shorty Higbee, and I guess you're the lady doctor that everybody's talking about."

"I don't know about that, but I am Doctor Beaunais," Tangeree laughed. "I'm pleased to meet you, Mr. Higbee."

"I'm mighty pleased to meet you, ma'am. We'd better put you right over here in this other corner, because Penrod sprays the whole county when he spits his tobacco juice."

Tangeree picked up one of the cases and followed Higbee as he carried the other two to the left side of the wide cab. The driver's seat was by a window in front of the door on the door on the right side, and the front of the cab was a maze of gauges, dials, and pipes, with the wide, thick door of the firebox in the center and near the steel floor. A narrow door in the rear wall of the cab opened into the coal bunker, coal spilling through on the floor in front of it. Higbee put the two cases in the corner behind the door on the left side, touched the peak of his cap again, and picked up a shovel and scraped at the coal, pushing it into a neat pile. Tangeree put the three cases in a row in the corner, and sat down on them.

There were metallic rattles and clanks outside the engine as the men from the station scurried around it, then Casker climbed back up, hopping lightly into the cab from the last step and looking over his shoulder at the station master. "You sure I've got a clear track, George?"

"The tracks's all yours, Penrod," the station master replied. "The short run's on the siding at Cedar Flats, waiting for you to go through. When do you think you'll be there?"

Casker munched his tobacco musingly as he stepped to his seat and turned two valves. Steam spurted somewhere in the bowels of the engine, and there was a ringing sound of pressure building. He slid onto his seat and leaned on his elbow in the window, looking down at the station master. "Forty-five minutes."

"Forty-five minutes?" the station master laughed. "You'll have them drive wheels wore down to a nubbin, Penrod. But I'll let them know."

Casker nodded and glanced over his shoulder at Higbee. Higbee reached for a rope near the ceiling of the cab, and the bell tolled as he pulled it. Casker pumped a chain dangling from the ceiling by his chair, the whistle whooped shrilly, and he pushed a lever. An explosive, rapid snorting came from the engine, and it jerked and rattled as the drive wheels spun on the rails. Casker adjusted the lever, the engine snorted and the wheels spun again, then the engine began chuffing deeply as the wheels gained traction. The engine moved forward ponderously, rapidly picking up speed. The people at the side of the station were momentarily visible through the doorway on the other side of the cab, a seething movement of excited faces and waving arms, and their cheers were faintly audible over the scream of the whistle, the clanging of the bell, and the deep puffing of the engine.

The last buildings of Reno and the tiny, scattered settlements near it passed behind. The engine continued picking up speed as he went around long, gentle curves in the tracks, and Tangeree leaned to one side then the other on the cases. Then the cases began sliding under her on a tighter curve as she struggled to plant her feet on the steel floor, and Higbee stepped toward her and pointed wordlessly to a handhold, a steel bar on the side wall. She clutched the bar and pulled the cases closer to it, looking out. The puffing of the engine became a steady, drumming roar, the sagebrush by the tracks was a blur below the door, and the hills flowed past.

Casker leaned out of the window with his eyes narrowed against the blast of the wind and his collar fluttering, his hand on the lever. He pulled the whistle chain and the whistle screamed, and tiny settlements by the tracks flashed past, people and a few buildings visible for an instant through the doorway. There was a long straight stretch, and he moved the throttle farther forward. The engine thundered along the tracks, the hills on both sides becoming blurred, and Higbee moved closer to Casker and shouted something in an exhilarated voice. Casker nodded, spitting a spray of tobacco juice, and he leaned back in the window and looked at a gauge. He pointed to it, and

Higbee picked up his shovel and levered the door of
the firebox open with it. Flames licked out of the
glowing cauldron as Higbee shoveled coal into it.

The settlements flicked past at intervals, Tangeree
leaned to one side and the other as she gripped the
handhold, and her stomach lurched as the engine shot
across high spots in the tracks. There was a long up-
grade and the engine gradually lost speed, the hammering rhythm of the puffing slowing and details of
terrain by the tracks becoming less blurred. Then the
engine reached the top of the incline and started
down the other side. Casker's hand rested on the
lever, pushed all the way forward. The engine picked
up speed, roaring along the track, whipping around
a curve and speeding along a straight stretch, and
snapping around another curve.

Then the engine screamed along the tracks, the
terrain on both sides fading together into mottled
shades of brown and a heavy vibration in the engine
making the guages and dials blur. Whiffs of the thick,
black smoke boiling from the stack swept through the
cab, and Higbee looked apprehensively, his eyes darting around the cab and between the doors. Casker's
eyes were slitted against the wind as he sat with his
hand on the lever, the lever still all the way forward.
The engine reached the downgrade and slowly lost
speed along the level track, and Casker spat, leaned
back into the cab, and looked at Higbee. Higbee
quickly grinned and nodded, shouting something, and
Casker nodded and looked back out.

Cedar Flats came into sight far ahead, a darker
brown against the sandy hills, and it turned into buildings scattered on each side of the track. Higbee pulled
the rope to toll the bell, and the whistle shrieked as
Casker held the chain down. There was a glimpse of

people clustered by the track, waving and leaping up and down, and the roar of the engine took on a deeper note as it blended with its echo bouncing off the front of buildings. Then the town was past, the engine climbed a grade, and the tumbled cars and engine of the wrecked train came into sight as the engine went around a slow curve in the tracks.

The tracks straightened again, and Higbee pulled the bell rope as he held one side of the door to the coal bunker and braced himself. Casker looked out, his heavy chin moving as he munched his tobacco, and he pumped the whistle chain. He suddenly leaned back in, jerked the throttle back, slammed another lever down, and spun a valve as he held the whistle chain down. Steam exploded under the engine and boiled into the cab, the whistle screamed, and steel grated against steel as the engine slid along the rails, slowing rapidly. Tangeree clutched the handhold tightly, leaning forward on the cases.

The engine shuddered to a stop and the steam began dissipating, and the crew from the wrecked train and several passengers swarmed around it. Casker climbed out, laughing and exchanging comments with men below the door on the right side, and Higbee leaned out the door in front of Tangeree and grinned down at several men as he joked and talked with them. Then he glanced at Tangeree as she straightened her coat and skirt and picked up one of her cases, and he picked up the others and held them down to a man.

"Here, Jasper, help the doc over to the tent with her bags."

A man in a brakeman's uniform took the cases, nodding and smiling up at Tangeree. Another man took her case, hands reached up to assist her as she climbed down, and she took the case back and followed the brakeman. Men were working on the twisted tracks a few yards farther along, and the engine and cars were on their side by the tracks. A path had been worn through the sagebrush between the tracks and an open-sided tent a few yards away, and the brakeman looked over his shoulder at the engine as they walked along the path.

"I expect that was sure some ride getting here, wasn't it?"

Tangeree lifted her eyebrows and nodded. "Yes, it was certainly different from any other ride I've had on a train."

"They said they'd be here in forty-five minutes, but I made it at fifty-two. What did you make it?"

"I didn't look at my watch. I understand one of the passengers were seriously injured."

"No, there's just a few cuts and scrapes, ma'am. There was a doctor on the train, a one-armed fellow, and he's been looking after them. I don't think you're going to have much to do."

Tangeree nodded, looking at the wrecked train. "What caused your train to wreck?"

"The roadbed washed out right by that gulley down there, and the rail give way as we come across it."

"It's certainly fortunate that no one was seriously injured. From the way those cars are thrown about, it seems a miracle."

"Oh, I've seen worser and nobody with a scratch," the man replied as they approached the tent. "But I've also seen people get their neck broke because of a rough coupling, so it don't make no sense." He put the cases down under the edge of the tent and turned away. "Well, there's your people to tend to, and there's the fellow over there in the corner who's been looking after them."

"Very well. Thank you very much for your help."

"You're more than welcome, ma'am."

Tangeree put the case down by the other two and stepped into the tent as the man walked back along the path. It was dim inside the tent after the bright sunlight, but no one appeared seriously injured at first glance around the blankets under the tent. There were a few white splotches of bandages, but most of the people were sitting up on the blankets and talking.

A gentle breeze swept through the open sides of the tent and rippled the canvas overhead as Tangeree stepped farther into tent, blinking to adjust her eyes to the soft light. The large man in the corner of the tent rose from where he was kneeling by a blanket. He walked toward her, a silhouette against the bright sunshine on the sandy ground on the other side of the tent. Then he stopped, looking at her, and Tangeree wondered if there were going to be professional jealousy or acid remarks about a female doctor. She lifted her chin and steeled herself to deal with either or both. He walked forward again, holding out his left hand.

"I'm Dawson."

His tone was quiet but not unfriendly, and Tangeree smiled as she avoided the empty, folded sleeve on his right side with her eyes and took his left hand with her right. "Beaunais. It appears as though you have everything well in hand, Doctor Dawson, and that I—"

The name registered, and her voice faded. Her eyes were adjusting to the dim light, and memories of him on the riverboat on the Mississippi came back in a rush as she looked up at him. He had changed. His hair and mustache were white, and his face was lined by the passage of years and by pain. But somehow he looked much the same.

"How is Yvonne?"

"She's very well."

He nodded, and they were silent again for a moment, looking at each other. Then he smiled. "I'm very pleased to see that you've fulfilled your ambition. There are few things that could please me more."

"And I'm very pleased to see you again," she replied quietly. "Very pleased indeed. How are you?"

Her question was clearly more than a polite interrogative, and he looked away and thought about it. Then he shrugged and smiled wryly as he looked back down at her. "Well, I'm here. Or most of me, in any event. Shall we look at the patients, Doctor Beaunais?"

There was no bitterness in his tone when he referred to his empty sleeve. Tangeree smiled, relieved, and nodded as they turned toward the blankets.

All the injuries were minor, and the bandages were remarkably neat to have been put on with one hand. A man thought he had suffered a heart attack as a result of the accident, and Tangeree listened to his heart and assured him he hadn't. A woman asked if the accident would complicate her liver dropsy. The replies to a couple of questions confirmed Tangeree's suspicion that the woman was from Virginia City and a patient of Leggett's, and Tangeree assured her that her condition wouldn't be complicated. A few had headaches and bruises that were painful, and Tangeree dispensed laudanum and salicylic acid.

They walked back to the cases, and Tangeree put the bottles back in the case and closed it. "Where have you been practicing, Doctor Dawson?"

"I haven't. I've been teaching for a few years now."

"Well, that's something for which there is a great need. Too many colleges are staffed by doctors who've never even seen a woman in labor or who haven't—"

"No, not medical college. I've been teaching in a grammar school."

Tangeree glanced up at him and looked away. His coat was clean but a little shabby, and his collar was worn. He was a proud man, and there was an agonizing pathos in the fact that his handicap or the emotional effects from it had reduced him from medical practice to teaching in a grammar school. She looked back up at him. "I do trust you're on your way to Virginia City."

He nodded, then smiled. "Do you remember writing to Clarence Ryan and asking about me while you were in medical college?"

"Yes, I do. I was trying to get in touch with you to . . . well, I thought perhaps you and Ma had lost contact with each other."

"I happened to see Clarence not so long ago, and he told me you'd written. Then I wrote to Arundel and found that Palmer was there. We exchanged a letter or two. He speaks very highly of you, by the way. So the upshot of it all was that I decided to come on out here. I didn't have much to leave behind."

Men were working on the tracks in front of the large engine, and it snorted and puffed as it cautiously moved forward to get the crane into position to reach the engine and cars by the track. Tangeree looked at it, thinking about what he had said, and looked back up at him. "Did you know all the time that Ma was here?"

"Yes, I knew."

"It would have been good if you could have come here a long time ago, then."

"Yes, it might have been better for everyone involved, but . . ." He pursed his lips musingly as his voice faded, then sighed and shrugged. "Well, it took me a long time to learn to shave with my left hand."

Tangeree looked up at him and looked away, nodding in understanding.

27

IT TOOK TANGEREE a few days to become accustomed
to hearing people call her mother by a different name,
but it was an adjustment she made gladly. Her mother
was radiantly happy, and Tangeree found a deep
satisfaction in the fact that an action of hers had at
least contributed to the cause of her mother's happiness.

Dawson fit into the household group smoothly, and
eliminated one cause for friction that had been creeping toward a crisis level. Abigail had been too lenient
with Bobby Bownay, and the boy had become in-
creasingly wilful and spoiled. Tangeree's mother had
been reluctant to thrash the boy because of her relationship with Abigail, and there had been ill feelings on the occasions when Tangeree had become
impatient with him and slapped him soundly. But
after the first icy glare from Dawson, Bobby Bownay
changed. Within a matter of days, Dawson became
the boy's mentor, and the boy became Dawson's constant companion and right arm.

Three weeks after the wedding, Dawson and Yvonne
left for Mississippi, so that Dawson could terminate

his affairs there and Yvonne could see the scenes of her childhood for a last time. It was after they left that Tangeree realized that they would return well after James was due back. And she was still undecided about how her situation with him would be resolved.

There was little time to contemplate the problem, because Tangeree had a crushing amount of work. All of her mother's patients came to see her, and she had a substantial number of regular patients herself. The railroad continued to send a few people, and they were responsible for more coming to see her. A brochure published by them listed their doctors in various areas along their route, and some travelers and others came through seeing her name in the brochure. Some of the wealthier people in Virginia City who had been seeking their medical advice and assistance in San Francisco began calling on Tangeree. A banker in San Francisco had a daughter whose arm was injured in a carriage accident, and in an ultimate testimony to Tangeree's growing reputation, he rushed the girl to Virginia City to have Tangeree treat her.

Tangeree's complete preoccupation with patients abruptly ceased when she received a telegraph message from Dawson saying that he and her mother would be returning in five days. It was brief, it gave no reason for the abrupt termination of their trip, and it was deeply disturbing. Abigail tried to cover her own apprehension with light, humorous talk, commenting on troubles between newlyweds. It irritated Tangeree, but she endured it as the days dragged by, recognizing it for what it was.

On the morning of their return, Tangeree hired a carriage in Virginia City and was at the train station in Reno well before daylight. She sat in the station master's office, forced to make conversation with the telegrapher. Dawn came and the sun rose, then the station master arrived and Tangeree was forced to make conversation with him. Finally she heard the train whistle in the distance.

When Tangeree saw her mother, chilling fear gripped her. She was walking with slow, cautious steps as Dawson held her arm, avoiding other people so they wouldn't bump into her. Her shoulders were pulled forward, and there was a pallor of pain on her smooth, beautiful face. Tangeree forced a smile and walked through the people toward them.

Her mother's face beamed with pleasure and relief as their eyes met, and Tangeree had a sickening, chilling suspicion that her mother had been afraid they wouldn't see each other again. Yvonne smiled up at Tangeree, involuntarily taking a step back to avoid a firm embrace. Tangeree put her arms around her mother gently and kissed her.

"Now what are you doing back here, Ma? Are you afraid I'll take all your patients away from you?"

"Oh, Tangi, Charles turned into a fussy ninny on me. I have a damned bellyache, and he wouldn't hear anything but that we had to come back."

Then they looked into each other's eyes. And they saw through each other's dissimulation. Both supremely skilled, one taught by the other, they could conceal nothing from each other. The pain was severe and Tangeree knew that her mother was frightened, and her mother knew that she knew. Her mother's smile faded. Tangeree stopped forcing her smile and looked up at Dawson. His face was haggard with worry and fatigue from the the trip, and he silently nodded in greeting. Tangeree nodded and put her arm around her mother's shoulders.

"I have a carriage around at the side of the station."

"I'll have to see to the luggage," Dawson said.

"No, I'll get the people here to see to it," Tangeree replied, and pointed. "Let's go around this side, because the steps are lower."

They walked around the station and Tangeree and Dawson helped her mother into the carriage, then Dawson got in the carriage and Tangeree went into the station. She talked to the station manager, who called two porters to find the luggage and carry it to the carriage. Tangeree looked up at the driver as the porters left and he climbed up to his seat.

"I want to go at a slow walk, every foot of the way."

The driver nodded, gathering up the traces. Tangeree climbed into the carriage and sat down facing her mother and Dawson. Her mother was leaning back in a corner of the seat, holding Dawson's hand, and she looked out the window as the carriage moved slowly away from the station.

"Why are we going so slow, Tangi? I have a belly-ache, but I'm not made out of eggs. I want to get home."

"You'll get there, Ma," Tangeree replied, tugging on the leather window slides and letting the windows down. "We'll have a nice, slow drive, and you can enjoy the fresh air. And you'd better enjoy it while it's here, because it's starting to get hot during the day now."

"You've forgotten what heat is, Tangi," her mother sighed. "Or I had, at least. I almost cooked in Mississippi." She looked out the window again, a faint, reminiscent smile on her face. "I saw old Granny Stokes in Tupelo, Tangi. That woman must be over a hundred years old, and she's as spry and pert as you are. She gave me a little piece of crochet to give you.

I have it in the luggage, along with some other little things I got for you."

"It sounds like you got plenty done, even though you weren't there very long, Ma. Did you enjoy it?"

Her mother's smile faded. She pursed her lips, thinking, then shook her head. "No, I didn't. When people want to go back somewhere, Tangi, they're always thinking about and looking for a time, not a place. And people can't go back in time."

Tangeree took her cigarettes out of her reticule and lit one as she nodded, listening to her mother. It didn't sound like her mother. It was too plaintive and hopeless, and it didn't reflect her mother's unquenchable optimism and will.

And it continued. Tangeree smoked cigarettes and tossed the stubs out the window, and her mother conversed desultorily in a thin, weak voice. Dawson sat in silence with a funereal expression, holding Yvonne's hand, and the miles dragged past as the carriage crept along the road.

Abigail and Bobby Bownay came out of the house as the carriage approached. Tangeree stood by the carriage and waited for the driver to unload the luggage as her mother walked cautiously up the steps, with Dawson and Abigail helping her. The driver put the last of the luggage on the porch, Tangeree paid him and gave him an extra dollar for driving slowly, then she went in as Dawson and Bobby Bownay began carrying in the luggage. She put away her coat and hat, went to the examination room for her case, and went to her mother's bedroom.

There was fever and severe pain in the lower right abdomen, and there had been frequent nausea, some vomiting, and constipation during the past few days. The symptoms were indicative of several illnesses.

But as in many other instances, an intuitive feeling penetrated the confusion, and Tangeree knew what it was.

She went to the examination room for a microscope slide and a sterile needle, and she went back to the bedroom for a drop of blood from a finger, returned to the examination room, and prepared the slide. Then she put the slide in the microscope. The white blood corpuscle ratio was high, but not extremely high. It was a concentrated, localized infection. And her diagnosis was confirmed. She stood by the window and wept in anguish and in helpless frustration.

Her mother was propped up in bed on pillows when Tangeree returned to the bedroom. Dawson sat by the bed and held her hand, and Abigail stood by the door and talked with them about Mississippi. Tangeree crossed the room to the window, lighting a cigarette. There was a knock at the front door, and she looked over her shoulder at Abigail.

"Go tell them I'm not seeing anyone today, Abby. If it's serious, they can go see Doctor Leggett."

"Tangi!" her mother protested. "We've never turned anybody who's sick away from our door."

"You're ill now, and that's all I'm going to think about. Go ahead, Abby."

Abigail glanced between Tangeree and her mother with a worried frown, then nodded and went out. Tangeree took a deep puff on her cigarette and exhaled, looking out the window. Dawson cleared his throat and stirred in his chair.

"Well, what do you think it is, Tangeree?"

Tangeree looked out at the trees behind the house and at the garden patch where she and her mother had dug years before, the snu shining down brightly, gleaming on the leaves, and making dark shadows in

the furrows. Her mouth was dry, and tears burned in
her eyes again. She blinked them away, taking a puff
on her cigarette. The silence behind her stretched out
and became tense, and she could feel their eyes on
her. She took another puff on her cigarette and turned.

"It's the first stage of perityphlitic abscess."

Dawson recoiled, his face paling as he looked at her
in consternation, then he shook his head violently.
"No!" he barked. "No, it couldn't possibly be that! And
how could you tell a first stage? There's no way to
tell! There's no swelling, and there's no—"

"Hush, hush, Charles," Tangeree's mother interrupted, patting his hand. "There's no point in shouting."

"But I'm not going to listen to that, Yvonne," he
said, turning to her. "It could be ileus, or it could be
. . . a lot of things! But I'm not going to listen to anything about perityphlitic abscess! Don't you understand, Yvonne? That means there's no hope!"

His voice broke, and he turned his face to the wall.
He drew in a deep, shuddering breath, his shoulders
trembling as he controlled himself. Tangeree's mother
patted his hand again, then looked at her.

"Are you sure, Tangi?"

Tangeree swallowed, and she took a puff on her
cigarette and exhaled, silently nodding. Her mother's
lips tightened and she sighed, then she tried to smile.
It brought burning tears to Tangeree's eyes again,
and she looked away.

Abigail's slow, heavy footsteps approached, and she
stepped into the doorway. "They said they understand, and they hope that you get better right
away. . . ." She blinked, her face paling as she glanced
around the room. "What's wrong?"

"Go see about lunch, please, Abby," Yvonne said

quietly. "We're just discussing things and working things out."

Abigail nodded, her eyes apprehensive as they moved around the room again, then she walked slowly along the hall. Tangeree took a puff on her cigarette, looking back at her mother. Her mother looked up at the ceiling, and Dawson cleared his throat and reached for her hand. Tangeree turned back to the window, opened it, and threw the cigarette out.

A compulsive need to do something seethed within her, as it had many times before, but it had a more frantic intensity than ever before. A logical, straightforward procedure to treat the disease had occurred to her long before, but it was untried and gravely dangerous. And it was based on theory rather than direct knowledge of the nature of the disease. She had thought about it idly at times, wondering if she would have the courage to use the procedure if she were ever faced with the conviction that it was an absolute necessity.

She turned aback around, looking at Dawson and her mother. "There might be a way to deal with it."

Dawson's head snapped around, hope and then doubt on his face. "A way to deal with perityphlitic abscess?"

"At this stage, yes. A lot of people think that the origin of the abscess is the veriform appendix. Palmer does, and I've read articles in journals by any number of others who do. And I do, too. That being the case, there might be a way to deal with it."

"The veriform appendix?" Dawson said, frowning in perplexity. "But the name means—"

"Then call it appendicitis," Tangeree said, shrugging. "It amounts to the same thing, because general peritonitis is the result, regardless of where the inflamation begins. I happen to believe it begins in the veriform appendix, and a lot of other people do."

"Then how would you treat it?" Dawson asked.

"By incising the abdomen and taking out the veriform appendix while the inflammation is still localized in it. It serves no known purpose, and the body should be able to functinon quite well without it."

Dawson stiffened, his eyes opening wide, and he shook his head. "Incise the abdomen? But that's so dangerous that it amounts to the same thing as. . . ." His voice faded and he pursed his lips, thinking about it. Then he looked at her mother.

Her mother nodded. "Tangi, if that's what you think you should do, then I want you to do it."

"No, no, Ma," Tangeree replied firmly, shaking her head. "We're three people who know medicine, and we'll all decide what to do."

"No, I want you to decide, Tangi. You've known about this kind of condition for a long time, haven't you? I can remember your talking about it when you were just a girl."

"Yes, but at the time I had only a vague idea of what it was, and felt that a cathartic shouldn't be administered. But I'm not going to decide this by myself, Ma. There's too much risk involved."

"Tangi, there's a risk in everything," her mother sighed. "And if you don't risk anything, you'll never have anything. Sometimes you take a chance and lose, but you'll never win unless you take a chance. You have an instinct for sickness, Tangi, and you've had it since you were a child. Now you have the education to go with that instinct. I trust your judgment far more than I do my own, and I want you to decide. And I'll agree with you, whatever you decide. How do you feel, Charles?"

Dawson looked at her, and nodded as he looked at Tangeree. "Your mother's right. You know much more about medicine than I do, and I believe you should decide. And I'll agree with whatever you decide."

Tangeree turned back to the window and lit a cigarette, and she smoked it as she pondered. She examined her feelings, wondering if the frantic need to do something to help could be misdirecting her, or if personal conceit about her theory of the infection might be committing her mother to death. And all of her intuitive feelings and everything she knew about the disease still pointed in the same direction. She tossed the cigarette out the window, closed it, and turned away from it.

"I'll incise and remove the veriform appendix."

Dawson drew in a deep breath and nodded, releasing her mother's hand and standing. "What can I do?"

"I'll need about five gallons of carbolic acid from town, and I'd like you to assist during the incision."

He nodded again, bent over her mother and kissed her, then walked toward the door. Tangeree walked toward the door and hesitated, looking at her mother. Her mother smiled warmly. Tangeree forced a smile as she went out.

Dawson took Bobby Bownay with him in the gig to get the carbolic acid, and Tangeree got Abigail to help her take everything from the shelves, cabinets, and tables in the examination room and carry it to a spare bedroom. And she thought about ways to build a barrier of carbolic acid between the incision and bacteria that could cause infection.

She looked through the childbirth pallets for a new one for her mother to lie on, and she put it in the washpot with all the carbolic acid she had, stirring it to soak it. Her mother would need something to wear during the surgery, and she found a new childbirth shift, cut it open across the stomach, and put it in the washpot. Then she thought about the cap she had worn while assisting Palmer, and the stray hairs it might have kept from falling in a wound. She found a cloth to wrap her hair and one to keep her breath off the incision, and she put them in the washpot.

When the pallet, shift, and cloths had soaked thoroughly, she wrung them and hung them up to dry. Then she sat at the kitchen table and sharpened her scalpels in the painstaking process she had learned from Palmer: whetstone, then leather, and then oiled silk. Other people came to the front door to see her or her mother about their illnesses or ill children, and Abigail sent them away. Then word began spreading, and people came to express concern and sympathy.

The gig returned from town, and Tangeree helped Dawson and Bobby Bownay carry in the bottles of acid. Abigail had lunch ready and Tangeree had a queasy nervousness in her stomach rather than an appetite, but she hadn't eaten breakfast and she knew she had to eat. She sat at the table and forced down the food, and Abigail took soup to her mother. Dawson went into the bedroom for a few minutes, then returned to the kitchen and sat looking at his plate, picking at the food on it.

Leggett heard about Yvonne's illness from some of the patients who went to see him, and he came to the house. He went into the bedroom and spent a few minutes with Yvonne. Then he came to the kitchen for Tangeree and she walked through the house and out onto the front porch with him. He was deeply troubled by her mother's illness, and noncommittal about her diagnosis and what she planned to do.

"I don't know anything else to do, Sam," Tangeree

said. "I do know she's going to have perityphlitic abscess within a few days, and I'm not going to sit and wait for it to happen."

Leggett looked at her, then sighed morosely and shook his head as he looked away. "Well, I don't know, Tangeree. The one thing I do know is that if you think that's what you ought to do, then you ought to do it. I wouldn't say that about many, but I'll say it about you. Are you sure there's nothing I can do?"

"No, I can't think of anything, Sam."

He nodded, walking down the steps. "I'd better get on back down there, because they're piling up on each other in my office. I didn't realize how many people you and Yvonne were taking care of until I started getting some of them. When are you going to know how she is?"

"Tomorrow."

"I'll be back tomorrow, then," he said, untying his horse and stepping into the saddle. He gathered the reins, and turned the horse toward the road. "Good luck, Tangeree."

Tangeree nodded and waved, and went back inside. Dawson was carrying the bottles of carbolic acid into the examination room, and Tangeree went into the kitchen for buckets of water.

She had sponged down the examination room with diluted carbolic acid several times, but now she wanted it soaked. They diluted pails of the acid and threw it on the walls and floor, and they scrubbed with brushes. The dust blown into the house by the Washoe zephyr came from between the boards and made dark streaks, and they threw more acid and scrubbed until all the dust was gone. Hours passed, the air in the examination room became searing with the penetrating fumes, and Tangeree continued scrubbing as Dawson wielded a brush furiously with his single arm.

When the room was clean, Tangeree brought in all of her surgical instruments from the bedroom and sterilized them carefully, then placed them on sterilized trays with cloths damp with carbolic acid over them. Dawson helped her, his eyes red from the fumes of the carbolic acid, his features drawn in a frown of concentration, and his fingers quick and dextrous. People who had heard and had come to find out more knocked on the front door, and Abigail walked back and forth between the door and the kitchen. Tangeree and Dawson finished with the instruments, and she began preparing the sutures, ligatures, swabs, and basins.

Dawson went to the window and looked out at the sky. "Will you have enough time to do it before dark?"

"Yes, I'm almost through here, and there'll be time. And Ma's been lying in there and listening, so I'm sure she'd like to get it over with. You could get her into the shift now."

He nodded and left. Tangeree finished filling a basin with swabs, covered it with a cloth, then went into the bedroom and carried in the atomizer. She assembled it on the tripod and placed it just inside the door, then called Abigail and showed her how to operate the lever. Dawson returned from the bedroom, and went for the childbirth pallet and cloths. Tangeree put the pallet on the table, checked the chloroform inhaler, and checked all the instruments again as Dawson and Abigail stood by the door and waited. Then she picked up the cloth for her hair and began wrapping it around her head, looking at Dawson and Abigail.

"Abby, send Bobby Bownay out to sit on the porch

in case any more people come. And you can bring Ma in now."

They went out, Abigail calling Bobby Bownay from the kitchen. He went outside and closed the front door. A moment later, Tangeree's mother came in, Dawson and Abigail holding her arms as she moved with slow, shuffling steps. She smiled at Tangeree warmly, and Tangeree nodded, wrapping the cloth around her face. Dawson and Abigail helped her onto the table, and Dawson picked up the inhaler and stepped back to the table. She turned her head and looked at Tangeree.

"I love you, Tangi."

"I love you, Ma."

She looked up at Dawson and smiled. He leaned down and kissed her, then gently put the inhaler over her nose and mouth. Tangeree rolled up her sleeves, and scrubbed her hands and arms in a basin of diluted carbolic acid. She turned away from the basin, lifting her hands and shaking them to dry them. Dawson thumbed back one of her mother's eyelids, then he stepped around the table and opened the front of the shift, baring her mother's lower stomach. He took a swab from the basin, wiped the carbolic acid on the lower right side of her stomach, and stepped to one side. Tangeree moved closer, looking at Abigail as she stood by the atomizer, her face pale and her hands trembling visibly.

"Abby, you look at the floor, ceiling, or wall. Whatever you do, don't look at what I'm doing, because I don't want you to faint. And you can go ahead and start."

Abigail cleared her throat and nodded nervously, then turned her back and began pumping the lever. The atomizer coughed and spluttered, then began spraying a mist. The mist spread, approaching the table, then swirled around it. Tangeree looked at the table behind her, flicked the cloth off a tray of instruments with the tips of her fingers, and picked up a scalpel with a curved one-inch blade.

"Swab."

Dawson lifted a swab from the basin with forceps, and she took it and compressed the capillary bleeding. The keen blade moved on, stroking and painting the red streak of skin parting, the skin almost seeming to part ahead of the blade. And it pulled her down toward it until she was hovering over the incision in the position that made her back ache agonizingly during a long surgical procedure—the position that had made some visiting doctors at Arundel chuckle, but Palmer had understood the intense, undivided concentration, both hands involved and the scalpel an extra finger. Blood spurted as she struck a larger vein.

"Catgut ligature."

He took it out of the jar with a tiny forceps and handed it to her. The scalpel slid into her right palm, clamped there by the two smaller fingers. Her right forefinger and thumb dug out the end of the spurting vein and clenched it, and her left fingers whipped the loop and knot, the movements coordinated with the ease of long practice. Then the blade moved on.

The surgical field became blurred with blood, and she swabbed and threw the squares of cloth on the floor. Blood spread up her fingers and to her wrists as she ligatured another large vessel and moved on. There was more capillary bleeding, and she compressed it. The field became blurred again, and the floor around her feet became littered with bloody swabs as she wiped and moved on.

Then the incision was long enough, the skin open and the glistening white sheath of the aponeurosis laid bare. She picked up a scalpel with a tiny blade, and slit through the membrane down the entire length of the incision with one straight stroke. The muscles of the abdominal wall were exposed, and she reached for a scalpel with a straight one-inch blade.

The scalpel sliced through the rich, tougher tissue of the muscles, and there were more and larger veins. She paused, whipped ligatures, and cut on across the incision. The peritoneum, the thin membrane that enclosed the abdominal cavity, showed in the depths below as the incision lengthened. Then the muscles were parted all the way across.

"Retractor."

Dawson picked it up with forceps and handed it to her. She placed the blades in the mouth of the incision and applied steady pressure, spreading the incision open. And it was huge. Not a modest and discreet slit to allow access for a cannula hose to suck out putrefaction, but a gaping cavern that would admit a hand into the forbidden territory of the abdomen.

The peritoneum was a shining blanket, concealing what lay under it. The thin walls of the intestines would open from the slightest touch of the tip of a scalpel, flooding the cavity with their contents and with death. She took the scalpel with the tiny tip again, estimated the location of the caecum, and nicked the peritoneum. It opened over the large roll of the caecum.

Leaning close to the incision and inserting her left hand, she put the tip of a finger in the opening of the peritoneum, lifted, and stroked with the scalpel. The taut, shiny tissue separated in a curved arc as she cut toward the great bend where the veriform appendix

dangled. The light was dim in the cavity. Bulging
forms and shapes were barely visible, vital organs and
vessels that would explode in a spray of blood if they
were touched by the scalpel.

A lack of total certainty in the back of her mind
kept trying to turn into shrinking fear. The knowledge
of whose life it was that lay under the tip of the scalpel and her gory hands was a gnawing agony. Pru-
dence clamored in her mind, turning her to flee, to
retreat, suture, and pray. The slice through the delicate web lengthened.

Then she saw it. Lurking in the veil of its mesentery,
the fan-shaped shield of membrane that enfolded and
supported the veriform appendix, it was more than a
tiny, dangling extension of the caecum. From the size
of a small finger, it had expanded into a fat, sausage-
like growth. And even in the dim light, it was almost
iridescent with the putrefaction it contained, its taut
skin a greenish-yellow. It was an ugly, grotesque, and
bloated thing, ready to explode.

The mesentery was engorged by the organ. It was
laced with blood vessels that supplied the organ, and
it appeared inflamed to a degree by its proximity to
the abscess. And it concealed the lower wall of the
caecum where it became one with the veriform appendix. It was the final barrier, and a dangerous one.

"Small forceps."

Dawson handed her the instrument, and she gently
pushed at the fan of the mesentery, separating it and
making a path to the base of the veriform appendix.
One route led into a thick mass of blood vessels, and
she tried another way. Then she could clearly see the
joining between the caecum and the veriform appendix. She coaxed the opening wider, making room to
get a hand in. Then she blindly put the forceps on the

table behind her, not taking her eyes off the point where she would place the ligature.

"Catgut ligature."

Her face was inches above the incision as she leaned low over the table, her eyes riveted to the base of the veriform appendix. The coiled ligature moved into her field of vision as Dawson held it under her eyes, his hand trembling. She took the ligature and eased her right hand into the incision with one end of it. The veriform appendix appeared so close to the point of rupture that she was afrad to touch it and move it, almost afraid to approach it.

She cringed at the thought of the biting stricture of the ligature closing in on the fragile tissue at the base of the fat, pulsing organ. The ligature slid smoothly around it, guided by a finger, snug at the joint between the caecum and veriform appendix. She whipped the knot and then pulled it, tension building as she waited to see a spurt of putrefaction.

A tiny waist formed at the base of the organ as the knot tightened. It became smaller and smaller, then the knot tightened firmly. And there was no rupture. She whipped another knot and pulled it down, then a third. Then she lowered the scalpel into the incision, trimmed the ends of the ligature away from the knot, and dropped them on the floor.

Then she eased her left hand into the incision, bending her wrist and guiding the tips of her fingers under the veriform appendix. Her fingers touched it and wriggled under it. Then it nestled in her palm. She slid her thumb and forefinger up to the base, pinched it tightly a hair's breadth away from the tight clamp of the ligature, and lowered the scalpel. The blade nicked through it, and it was separated.

"Basin."

Dawson reached for an empty basin on the table and held it out. Tangeree wormed her left hand back out, pinching the severed base of the organ to keep it from spilling, and straightened up as she put it in the basin. The putrefaction gushed from it as it plopped into the basin, the foul stench overpowering the reek of carbolic acid. Dawson's face was pale and drawn as he looked in the basin, then at her. She turned and rinsed her left hand in a basin of diluted carbolic acid, then leaned low over the incision again.

"Swab."

He handed her a swab, and she pushed it down into the empty mesentery, daubing. The swab had dark brown stains on it when she pulled it back out, matter that had come from the tiny remnant of the base of the organ, a puckered lip drawn up tight by the ligature. She threw the swab down, held out her hand for another one, and daubed again. There was only a faint smear of the brown, and some blood that had either been on her fingers or had come from a tiny vessel in the mesentery that had ruptured during her groping. The ligature was holding, and there was no leakage. She straightened up, took the retractor out of the incision, and put it on the table behind her.

"Sutures."

Dawson picked up a small forceps, reached into the basin, and took out the needles with the sutures dangling from them, handing them to her one at a time. Tangeree pushed the needles through the edges of the incision, drew them together, and whipped the knots, making the smooth, straight line of neat, closely-spaced sutures that had always brought a grunt and nod of approval from Palmer. She reached for scissors and trimmed off the ends of the sutures, then soaked a cloth in diluted carbolic acid and placed it over the incision.

Then crushing fatigue descended over her. Her knees trembled, her arms felt lifeless, and a numb lethargy gripped her. She stumbled away from the table and toward the window, pulling the cloths from her face and hair and dropping them, and she leaned against the window, putting her cheek against the cool glass. The atomizer stopped hissing as Dawson spoke to Abigail, and he moved around the table, removing the chloroform inhaler, listening to the breathing, feeling the pulse. Abigail went out, leaving the door open, and the carbolic spray hanging in the room settled and dissipated. She returned with the coffeepot and cups, and Dawson brought a cup of coffee and put it on the edge of the table near the window.

"You were right, and you did the only thing that could have been done. It was her only chance."

Tangeree nodded, looking out the window. Dawson returned to the table and looked again, checking the breathing and pulse, and he and Abigail talked quietly. Tangeree picked up the cup and took a sip of coffee, saw her hand, still gory with her mother's blood. And she wondered if she had planted the seeds of death in her mother's body with that hand, if bacteria under a fingernail or in a crease of a finger where the carbolic acid hadn't penetrated had been left behind and had already begun its deadly process. She had recently read in a journal of a hospital that had developed a procedure for excising ovarian tumor, and the techniques had been perfected until the mortality rate from bleeding, shock, and other surgical trauma was less than one in ten. But the mortality rate from infection was over eighty percent.

Tangeree drank the coffee and summoned her strength. They carried Yvonne through the house to the bedroom, with her gripping one end of the child-birth pallet, Abigail carrying the other end, and Dawson bent over and supporting the center with his arm. As they put her on the bed and covered her, Tangeree bent over her mother. Her features were in calm, serenely relaxed lines, the pallor of pain was gone, her breathing was deep and regular, and her pulse was firm and strong. Tangeree stepped away from the bed and walked toward the door, and Dawson pulled a chair to the side of the bed and sat down.

She washed, cleaned the instruments and put the examination room back in order, then went out on the porch. It was almost sunset. Bobby Bownay was sitting on the edge of the porch, meek and apprehensive from the events of the day. Tangeree sent him inside and sat down at the top of the steps. A haze of smoke hung over Virginia City from evening fires, and the mill stamps made a drumming background of noise. A woman and a couple, regular patients of her mother's, came to ask about her mother. They talked for a few minutes, then left.

Abigail moved around in the house, lighting lamps and preparing dinner. Bobby Bownay came out and asked Tangeree if she wanted dinner, and she shook her head. Darkness fell and the moon rose, its pale, blanched light spreading and brightening. The street became quiet, windows in the houses along it glowing with yellow lamplight, and the road at the end of the street became quiet. Over the thumping of the mill stamps, there was a distant whisper of the music and revelry in the saloons and gambling parlors as the town assumed its evening character.

A horse cantered along the street. Tangeree slowly

sat up as it approached, and she looked at the tall, wide-shouldered man on the horse. The horse slowed, turning toward the house. It was James Woodruff. He reined up and got out of the saddle, taking off his hat as he walked toward her.

"Tangeree, I understand your mother is ill."

Numbing fatigue gripped her, and her mind was filled with dark foreboding over her mother. Still, happiness rose within her as she looked at him and listened to his voice. Then she looked away, nodding. "Yes, she's very ill, James."

"What's wrong with her, Tangeree?"

Tangeree sat back, explaining the condition, what she had done, and the dangers. He sat down on the steps by her and listened, frowning worriedly. She finished and he was silent for a moment as he looked away into the moonlight, thinking about it. Then he nodded and spoke.

"Well, it's obvious that you did the only thing you could have, and it's also obvious that there are few who could have done as much. We'll just have to wait and pray that infection doesn't develop."

"I did everything I know to prevent it," she sighed, shrugging. "But there's so much that we still don't know. . . ." She shrugged again, and looked up at him. "Did you finish sooner than you anticipated? In your last letter you said it might be another month or so before you'd return."

"Yes. I might have achieved better results if I'd remained longer, but I wanted to get back. I arrived on the late train and I intended to come and see you in the morning, but the housekeeper said she'd heard that your mother was ill." He hesitated, then spoke again. "My father and Christina are in San Francisco and I was going to join them and return with them later in the week, but I think now that it would be better if I remained here."

"No, I wouldn't want to interfere in your plans, James."

"There is nothing and no one as important to me as you, Tangeree. My first concern is to be of what help I can to you."

The moonlight shone on his face and in his eyes as he looked down at her and spoke, his voice soft with concern and sympathy, and with love. Tangeree looked away, pushing her hair back from her face. She wanted him to stay, to be near in the event calamity struck. But asking him to stay would be a tacit commitment. She hesitated, fearing the risk of commitment.

Then she thought about what her mother had said about risk, about the necessity for risk if any gain were to be achieved. To gain happiness, it was necessary to risk pain. And she loved him. She looked back up at him.

"Please stay, James. Come and see me tomorrow, if you would."

His eyes searched her face as he detected a change in her tone. Then his eyes were bright with joy. He put his hand on hers and bent over and kissed her, a warm, gentle pressure of his lips, then he rose and walked toward his horse. "I'll be back in the morning, Tangeree. Good night!"

"Good night, James."

The saddle squeaked as he got back on his horse and turned toward the street. The horse cantered along the street, the patter of its hoofbeats becoming lost in the other noises of the night as it neared the end of the street. Tangeree lit a cigarette, the match flaring brightly in the darkness. Under the gnawing anxiety and dark cloud of depression in her mind, she felt a warm contentment that a decision had been made, a promise of joyous happiness. She smoked the cigarette, then she rose and went into the house.

The house was quiet. The wick in the lamp on the kitchen table was turned low, and the corners of the room were in darkness. Abigail sat at the table with her head pillowed on her arms, asleep. Tangeree walked quietly through the house to her mother's bedroom. The door was ajar, and she stepped inside. Her mother appeared to have undergone a transition from the unconsciousness of chloroform into deep sleep, the sleep that pain had been denying her for days. Dawson, holding her hand, had dozed off in the chair. The soft yellow light from the lamp on the table by the bed highlighted the planes of his face and made dark shadows in the lines and hollows. He was frowning worriedly in his sleep. Tangaree went back out of the room and into her room for her coat, and she returned to the porch. She sat down at the top of the steps and lit a cigarette.

For a time she relived her experiences with her mother, triumphs they had achieved together, and death watches they had stood together. Then fatigue overcame her racing thoughts, and she dozed. The moon was setting when she woke, and the stars were a brilliant, sparkling blanket above. The nighttime chill of early spring had settled, and she pulled her coat closer. She was drowsy, her thoughts languid and sluggish, and she dozed again. The moon had set and the darkness was complete when she woke again, and she felt more rested. She lit a cigarette and smoked it, then she went into the house and looked at the clock in the kitchen. An hour remained before it

would be time to check her mother's temperature to
see if her body was reacting to infection.

Abigail was still at the table. She stirred and rose,
yawning and scratching her head. She built up the fire
in the stove to make coffee, talking sleepily, and Tangeree talked with her to keep her mind and eyes off
the clock. They had a cup of coffee, then Abigail took
the pail and went to milk the cow. The first light of
dawn was beginning to touch the eastern horizon.
Tangeree went out to the chopping block and split a
few billets of wood with the axe, leaving the back
door open for the light of the kitchen lamp to fall
across the chopping block. Abigail returned from the
barn, and Tangeree carried in the wood and glanced
at the clock. Ten minutes remained.

She walked through the house to the examination
room. It was dark, and reeked strongly of the carbolic
acid. She found her case and felt through it for the
thermometer, then put it in her pocket and walked to
the window. The light was slowly spreading across
the sky, the stars becoming dim in the east. When
more than ten minutes had passed, she left the examination room and walked through the house to her
mother's bedroom.

Her mother's eyes were closed, and Dawson was
awake, his face sagging and lined in the light of the
lamp. He looked up at Tangeree as she walked toward
the bed. "She woke up a while ago," he said in the
soft voice of the sickroom. "She was thirsty, and I gave
her a drink."

Tangeree nodded, standing by the bed and looking
down at her mother. Her mother was sleeping shallowly, her eyelids trembling. Taking the temperature
would be a matter of touching her mother's shoulder

to arouse her, and then putting the thermometer in her mouth. Her fingers touched the thermometer in her pocket as she hesitated, wanting to know and not wanting to know. Her mother's eyes opened. She blinked, then smiled faintly.

"Hello, Tangi," she whispered weakly.

"Hello, Ma."

"Charles said you did everything just right. He said no one else could have done it, or would have known what to do."

"I got it out all right, Ma. If there's no inflammation, you'll be all right."

"How long has it been?"

"Just about twelve hours."

"Well, let's check my temperature, Tangi."

Tangeree swallowed, fingering the thermometer in her pocket. Her mother smiled up at her. Tangeree took it out, took the cap from the end of the wooden case, and slid the thermometer out into her hand. Her mother opened her lips, and Tangeree leaned over and put the end of the thermometer under her mother's tongue. Dawson reached out and took her mother's hand, and Tangeree turned and walked away from the bed.

The window was bright against the dark wall, dawn breaking in the east. Tangeree walked to the window and leaned her forehead against the cool pane. She looked out at the gray light turning brighter and at the haze of smoke rising from the town, and she counted in her mind. Then she turned and walked back to the bed.

She took the thermometer out of her mother's mouth and lifted it so the light of the lamp gleamed on the glass barrel of the thermometer, and Tangeree rolled it in her fingers, searching for the scratch that indicated normal temperature. Then she found it. The column of mercury came precisely to the mark.

Her eyes burned and a tight constriction formed in the back of her throat from the overwhelming surge of relief and triumph that flowed through her. She fumbled the thermometer into her pocket, clearing her throat and swallowing, and turned back toward the window.

Her mother gasped softly in relief. Dawson uttered a choked sound, and he began weeping quietly. Tangeree walked back to the window and looked out, wiping her eyes, then she opened the window.

The cool, fresh air of early morning and the early morning sounds of Virginia City flooded into the room, dispelling the oppressive sickroom atmosphere. Roosters crowed, dogs barked, and a cow lowed. The mill stamps pounded, the steel shoes lifting and dropping on the steel faceplates with their drumming roar. The sun was rising over the eastern horizon into the clear blue sky. It was a beautiful morning, the beginning of a beautiful day.

THE RANCHERS

Wyoming in the 1800s was the heartland of the booming cattle ranches, whose owners were made rich overnight by the growth of the railroads, which could take their perishable beef from coast to coast.

Charles Goodpasture, the hard-edged, handsome ruler of the biggest cattle kingdom in Wyoming, hungered for the land—and body—of Leslie Kendrake, the high-born English beauty whose only hope was in a mysterious man named Parker, whose distant past held a dark secret that seemed to haunt him even now—here in this lawless land where the greed of few promised the destruction of many.

THE HOMESTEADERS

Nebraska territory in the late 1800s was a harsh, rugged land where survival depended on how well a man could handle a gun, how long he could work without dropping, and often how fast he—or she—could run when the enemy was at his heels. To this God-forsaken land came hundreds of drifting souls, seeking a place to make their homes and fulfill their dreams of prosperity and freedom.

Among these pioneers was Joseph Barrow, a dedicated and determined man, and his beautiful step-sister, Jessie, whose blazing spirit ignited in him passions that he had never known before. Together they faced the most awesome challenge of their young lives, as they set up as homesteaders in the wild country where women were almost unheard of—and a kindly gesture from a neighbor even rarer.